MW00780060

GALAPHILE

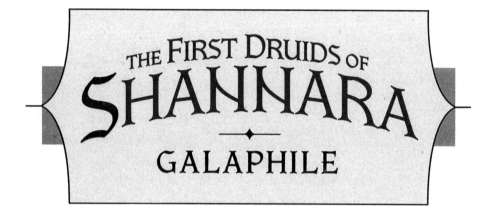

THE FIRST DRUIDS OF

SHANNARA

GALAPHILE

TERRY BROOKS

NEW YORK

Copyright © 2025 by Terry Brooks

Penguin Random House values and supports copyright. Copyright fuels creativity, encourages diverse voices, promotes free speech, and creates a vibrant culture. Thank you for buying an authorized edition of this book and for complying with copyright laws by not reproducing, scanning, or distributing any part of it in any form without permission. You are supporting writers and allowing Penguin Random House to continue to publish books for every reader. Please note that no part of this book may be used or reproduced in any manner for the purpose of training artificial intelligence technologies or systems.

All rights reserved.

Published in the United States by Del Rey,
an imprint of Random House, a division of
Penguin Random House LLC, New York.

DEL REY and the CIRCLE colophon are registered
trademarks of Penguin Random House LLC.

Map by Jared Blando copyright © 2024 by Terry Brooks

Hardback ISBN 978-0-593-12980-7
Ebook ISBN 978-0-593-12981-4

Printed in the United States of America on acid-free paper

randomhousebooks.com

2 4 6 8 9 7 5 3 1

First Edition

Book design by Elizabeth A. D. Eno

For All Those True Believers Who Just Keep Asking

Northland

Tiderace

Kshu

Taupo
Rough

Bone Hollow

The Stage

Stridegate

Razor Mts.

The
Lazareen

Valley
of the Fortrers

Anatcherae

Skull Mt.

Malg
Swamp

Rampling
Steep

Knife Edge Mts.

River Lethe

Jannisson
Pass

Upper
Anar

Aseach

Teller
Ridge

Olden
Moor

Heaven's
Well

Paranor

Rabb

River

Maelmord

Graymark

Starns's
Camp

Wolfsktaag
Mts.

Chard
Rush

Darklin

Graymend

Hall of Kings

R
a
b
b

P
l
a
i
n
s

Sterlock

Dun
Fee Aran

Valley
of Shale

gon's Teeth

Hadeshorn

Pass of Jade

Recker
Line

H
e
a
v
e
n
s
h
o
r
n

E
a
s
t
l
a
n
d

ennon
ass

Mountains
of Runne

Pass of Noose

Anar Forest

sis

Cillidellan

Rainbow
Lake

Silver River

Culhaven

The
Wedge

Capaal

Mist
Marsh

Battlemound Lowlands

Lower
Anar

Ravenshorn
Mts.

Leah

L
o
w
l
a
n
d
s
o
f
C
l
e
t
e

Prekkendorran
Heights

Plateau

Blande

GALAPHILE

The tall man walked out of the dust and grime of the wind-blown flatlands toward the village that sat huddled by the only river within twenty miles. He was cloaked and hooded against the weather, although the day itself was hot and desolate—as if whatever life was out there in the near desert had long since burned away. The clouds and dust devils whipped past him, blowing in an easterly direction toward the Highlands of Leah. Dry today, dry tomorrow. The weather had been that way for better than two full moons, and the likelihood of any sort of change was low.

The boy who stood on the roadside in front of the general store watched the man approach with no small amount of wonder. The stranger carried himself with purpose and radiated a certainty that suggested he was here intentionally. But what in the name of sanity would bring anyone to this shades-forsaken piece of discarded civilization? Friends and relatives? No, not a man such as this. Something else drew him. Something dark.

The boy glanced down the roadway behind him toward the few buildings that lined the street and formed almost the whole of the village of Parrish Rahn: the general store, leatherworks, iron forge, weapons and tools works, and medical clinic. That was all there was, save for Jark's Stables, which sat on the right at the far end, stuck in and behind the forge. A few small cottages nestled together at the town's edge, and farther on, farms and ranches held distant, dust-scoured dwellings and barns. Not a place anyone would bother to seek out without a good reason.

So what was it that had drawn this stranger?

He was tall but bent, too, in the way of one whose life had dealt him more than a few disappointments and hardships. Yet he moved with ease and calm.

The boy straightened as the man continued to approach. A tray of household goods and yard tools hung from a strap about his neck—an invitation to buy something from inside the shop. This was his current means of employment, but he didn't think the man who approached was a buyer. Usually, he could tell, but not always. In any case, a sale was a sale.

The man stepped right up to him. "Morning, son."

The boy bristled. With his parents seven years dead, no one had the right to call him son anymore. Still, he smiled and nodded and said, "In need of any tools? Got all kinds inside the shop. Maybe something you could use?"

The man pulled back his cowl to reveal a bearded face roughened by age, weather, and life. A huge scar ran down his left cheek from forehead to jaw, and his long black hair had turned white where the injury extended across his scalp. It was a look that would have intimidated many, but not this boy. He had seen worse in the short course of his life. No, it was not the injury or the worn look that troubled him. It was the man's eyes. One eye looked left; the other looked right. The boy didn't understand how the man could even see.

The man saw his regard and gave him a quick smile. "The left one's fake. Lost it in the fight that won me this." He pointed at the scar across his brow. "Only the other one works as it should." A pause. "You got any writing quills inside your store? And ink?"

The boy stared. "You can *write*?"

Right away, he wished he had kept his mouth shut. But out here, almost no one could write besides him. They hadn't learned, didn't care, and had no need to communicate with anyone at a distance.

"I mean," he added, "not that many can around here."

The tall man laughed. "I can read, too. How about you?"

The boy straightened. "Read *and* write. Mama taught me before she died. After that, I just kept practicing on my own. If I don't understand something, I ask about it. But no one else reads or writes much."

"No, I don't suppose they do. Don't need to do either this far out from everything." He paused. "But you do, and that says something."

The boy shrugged. "There's just me and some of the couriers that come through that can write."

"You seem a bright lad," the man offered. "You said your mother's gone. My sympathies. You live with your father, then?"

"He died same time as my ma. Sage fever—the one that spots you, then chokes you."

"Hmmm. No parents, yet you seem comfortable enough. With a job and all. Do you know your way around here?"

"Of course. Not much to it, after all. What can I show you? Give me a coin and I'll be your guide, if you want one."

The scarred man reached into his pocket and pulled something out, then held it in the palm of his hand for the boy to examine. It was a gold piece, and the boy felt his mouth go dry. That coin was worth a lot. More than he would see in two weeks of work at the store.

"I'm looking for someone," the man said. "Maybe you can help me find him in exchange for this coin. He's called Ratcher."

The boy nodded slowly. "I know him well enough to keep my distance."

"Oh, so he's a dangerous man, is he?"

"Dangerous enough. He's killed two other men since he arrived last year. Barehanded. Saw him kill the one myself. Down by the stables. Fellow picked a fight with Ratcher, called him some bad names, flashed a knife at him. Didn't matter. He never had a chance. Ratcher was twice his size and much quicker." He eyed the gold coin and saw it vanishing if he continued. Still, there were things more important than coin. Honesty, for one. His mother had taught him that. He shrugged. "I'll take you to him if you insist, but you should think twice about it."

"Thought it through before now, and that's enough thinking for me. Take me to him and the coin is yours. What happens after that is my problem. Fair enough?"

The boy shrugged. "Wait here. I got to ask for time off before I can leave."

He ducked into the supply goods store and found old Wrent behind the counter as usual. He asked permission and was summarily excused with a warning about loss of pay if he was gone for more than ten minutes. He set his tray aside and was out the door in a flash.

"Ready when you are," he said.

The stranger nodded. "Well and good. Show me the way."

They walked deeper into Parrish Rahn, following the sole street, which was mostly empty at this time of day. The boy was used to it, comfortable with the village's desolation. The stranger was harder to read. He looked around as they walked, scanning everything. Comfortable but clearly of a cautious bent. The boy wondered again what it was that had brought him to this place in search of Ratcher.

"You're Elven," the man observed, glancing over. "Full-blooded, I suspect. Yet you live here in the Southland?"

The boy nodded. "I lived in the farmlands east of the Rhenn until my parents died, then I caught a ride with a train hauling Westland grains and ended up here. I didn't want to stay in the Westland anymore. I had no relatives, and I didn't mean much to anyone." A shrug. "I needed to be somewhere else, so I went east. I ran out of means when I got here, so I decided to stay."

Though, in truth, it was less a decision than a lack of choice. He had no desire to end up in a home for unwanted children, but he was not saying that. He was also not admitting that it was too sad to stay where his parents had died. That was the other part.

"I noticed the ears and the slant of your eyes. Those narrow features. Elf blood is hard to hide—not that you should try. It's a heritage to be proud of. I've had more than a few Elven friends. I was in the Westland about a year back, though mostly I spend my time in the Midlands."

The boy nodded. "Travel a lot, then?"

"All the time. Guess you don't get to?"

"Naw, I just stay here. Got to make enough to live on. No one helps an orphan these days. Not out here. It's been hard times for all. The clans and the families all protect their own when they're not picking fights with one another." He shrugged again. "I tried the city life once. Lived up in Kern for several months a few years ago, but it was too rough. Too many bad people. So I came back. I like it better here."

The stranger nodded. "I noticed your hands. Strong, supple. You've got some skills?"

"Some. I'm a good tracker. I can hunt down anything; I work on it in my spare time. One day, I'll make my own way in the world. Maybe go back to the Westland and live with the Elves again, if they'll have me."

"Hmmm. Yes, you might be wise to do so, if you really are as able as you seem."

The heat was intense, but the tall man didn't seem to notice, his attention focused on his surroundings. The boy found himself looking over at his companion repeatedly, trying to unravel his mysteries. He thought of warning him about Ratcher again, but the other's determination suggested it wasn't a good idea. Best to just let things be and see what came of it. Hopefully nothing bad, but there was only so much you could do in this world to protect others.

They walked to the end of the business district, and the boy turned his companion toward the stables. The sign on the barn was clear enough: JARK'S STABLES. It was a decent-enough-looking establishment, with stalls, a hayloft, feed bins, and pastureland for grazing. A closer look, however, showed the loft mostly depleted of hay, the bins all but empty, and the pasture on its way to being grazed out. The barn door stood open, revealing the interior of the building.

"Over there," the boy said. "That one's Ratcher."

He pointed. Off in one corner, a man sat at a bench working on riding and hauling equipment. A range of worn gear was scattered about him, but his focus was on reattaching a stirrup that had broken loose from a saddle. He was a big man—not only in size but also in girth.

The boy did not voice his doubt, but it was there. Ratcher was at least twice the size of this stranger and much rougher-looking.

"Well, now, take a look at that one." The stranger shook his head in disbelief. "No wonder I'm supposed to think twice about approaching him. Bet no one's put him down since he was cradle-sized. Might be he could cause a problem, if he wants. We'll see."

The boy cringed. "Maybe you shouldn't . . ."

His companion glanced at him, handed over the gold coin, and nodded. "You don't have to stay longer if you don't want to. You can run
along. I'll catch up with you later."

*Or maybe you won't be catching up to anything once Ratcher is
done with you.* But the boy did not say these words aloud. Instead, he
shrugged. "Think I might stick around."

The scarred man gave him a look. "Worried about me?"

"A bit. You sure about this?"

The stranger smiled once more. "World's a devious place, and not
much is what it looks like."

He strode toward the stables and stopped at the entry. A gust of hot
wind blew in after him, cloaking him momentarily in dust.

"Ratcher?" the stranger called out.

The other man looked up, studied him for a moment, then looked
away again. "Go away."

"I need to speak with you."

"But I don't need to speak with you."

"Maybe you do. I've heard rumors about you. I could use someone
like you in my camp. It's a stable future—more stable than drifting from
town to town, eventually outstaying your welcome."

The big man scowled. "My welcome's just fine, thanks. Now off with
you. I have work to do."

Somewhere close by, a door slammed. The sound was so loud and
unexpected that it made the boy jump. He took a deep breath to steady
himself as a dog started barking. He saw Ratcher look up again, and this
time he did not look away.

The stranger moved closer. "Tell you what: I'll make a bargain with
you. We'll have a contest, you and me. A quick throw-down. First to fall
loses. You take me down and I move on. I take you down and you listen
to my proposal. What say you?"

Ratcher stared at him. "I don't know what you've been drinking, fellow, but you better get back to it. For the last time, go away!"

He turned back to his work once more, but the stranger just stood
there, watching him work, making no move to leave. The boy was uncertain how this was going to end, but he wasn't about to leave now—
even if it meant a dock in pay. He sensed he was pretty close to his

ten-minute limit, but this man's death ought to be witnessed by someone, so he stayed.

The minutes ticked by as he and the stranger waited. Finally, Ratcher glanced up again, and his annoyance was unmistakable. Without a word, he set down his work, got to his feet, and stalked over.

"You just don't listen, do you?" He spit out the words as if they were distasteful. "Fine. Let's have at it."

He lumbered right up to the stranger and seized hold of him as he might a scarecrow . . .

. . . only the stranger wasn't there. There wasn't anything there but a shadow with no substance. The stranger reappeared five feet away, watching the big man grope at empty air.

The boy's jaw dropped open in shock.

There was a moment when everything stopped; then Ratcher turned toward the scarred man, his face twisted in rage. "Sneaky, aren't you? Doesn't matter. That won't save you from what's coming."

With a shout, he launched himself at the stranger, but once again, he had him and then he didn't, the scarred man slipping through his grip as if made of butter. Ratcher twisted, turned, roared in fury this time, and came again.

The boy watched it all happen and couldn't begin to see how the stranger managed to escape. Each time, he appeared to be caught, and yet each time, he wasn't. It was as if he were made of nothing but shadows and light. Ratcher was big and strong and very quick for his size, yet it all counted for nothing. He attacked over and over, and every single time, the result was the same. All smoke and no substance.

Finally, choking on dust and gasping for air, the beleaguered man stopped in his tracks and stood facing his opponent. "How do you do that? Just disappear and look like you're still standing there?"

The stranger shrugged. "Magic. It's a skill, learned like any other. Also, you signal your moves before you make them, Ratcher. I can see what you are going to try to do and how you intend to do it. Easy enough to escape when you know what's coming. Do you want to talk now?"

Ratcher was huffing and sweating. "You ain't taken me down yet!"

The stranger gave him a look. "Do you really want me to do that on top of everything else? I will if you insist, but you won't like it. Why don't we just have our talk and be done with it?"

A wiser man would have taken this offer, the boy thought later. But Ratcher was all muscle and bone and stubborn pride, so he charged at the stranger once more. This time, the stranger didn't attempt to shift away but stood his ground as if it were nothing at all to face this monster.

Ratcher collided with the man, arms stretched out like an open vise waiting to close, and it was like he had run into a wall. Ratcher went down in a befuddled heap while the stranger remained standing, looking for all the world as if he hadn't felt a thing.

"Warned you," the stranger said.

Ratcher lay sprawled in the dust. "How . . . did you . . ." His voice broke, and he spit out blood. He shook his head. "All right, we'll talk."

The stranger walked over and held out his hand. Ratcher took it, and the stranger pulled him to his feet with ease. The two men stood there looking at each other.

"Still don't see how you did that," Ratcher said.

"I could teach you," the stranger answered, "if you have the skills, that is. Not everyone does. But even if not, I have need of a big bruiser like you, and I can pay handsomely. If fighting is what you like, I can promise you plenty of opportunities to practice your skills. And the training to improve them."

Ratcher frowned again. "I only fight those who bother me, because I look like a good target. I'd prefer to be left alone."

The stranger grinned. "Then I can offer you that in spades—a place of fellowship where you'll be trained as a warrior, but only be asked to fight in defense of yourself and your comrades. Come with me."

"Come with you where?"

The stranger pointed north. "Beyond the Rainbow Lake, at the back of those mountains they call the Dragon's Teeth. I have a camp with other men and women just like you—men and women who want as quiet and full a life as they can manage in these lawless times but are trained to defend what they've got."

Ratcher stared at him doubtfully. "Why me? You took me down easy enough. What sort of help would someone like me be?"

"Plenty. Not all of us have magic. Sometimes we need to hold our own with brawn and fists—which is where you come in. I'm offering you the chance to be part of a family here—one that looks out for all its members. Only one rule: You don't betray us. Ever."

He paused. "Care to give it a try?"

Later, as the boy walked away from Jark's Stables in the company of the stranger while Ratcher went to pack up what possessions he had, he found himself wondering what sort of place it was that the other had founded. He had called it a camp and spoken of training but had not said much more about what it was intended to accomplish. Except that it could be a family—and that was the word that had caught in the boy's mind particularly.

The life of a friendless Elven orphan in a Human world was not an easy one, and the boy had been looking for something better ever since he had left home and come here. But this was a harsh world with few opportunities, especially if you were young and poor. Having friends and family to aid you was necessary, and the boy had lost the latter and found few of the former. Having something approximating a family was an enticing prospect—even if it wasn't the family he'd been born into.

Being a boy of fourteen and bold enough by now to ask for answers he didn't have, he said, "What is it like, this camp of yours?"

"Like I told Ratcher, it is stability in a lawless world—the kind of family who look out for their own. It is also a training ground for the body and mind. Those who wish to learn more about themselves and their skills have an opportunity to do so—be it with weapons or magic."

"So can anyone join?"

The stranger grinned, clearly knowing what the boy was after. "I will admit it is an elite company, and I make all the choices myself. I choose selectively, lad, picking those I feel will best benefit our community as a whole. Ratcher was an obvious candidate. A doughty fighter, but un-disciplined and untrained. I will give him both discipline and training, and I know he will be a good addition to my band."

The boy walked a bit farther in silence, then said, "I wish I were big and strong enough to go with you."

"Like I said, it is not only brute strength I am after. You are something else—something potentially more important. You are smart and willing to learn—and maybe not just fighting but magic as well. Magic can run strong in those of Elven blood. Would you like to find out more? Would you like to discover if that propensity exists within you?"

The boy flushed with a mix of excitement and uncertainty. On the one hand, the prospect of possessing magic intrigued him. On the other, it was disturbing enough that it left him doubtful. He'd had little contact with magic and worried about the power it might wield over a user. If he had the ability to use magic, how would that change his life? His outlook? Would he be in control of his actions, or would the magic dictate his moves?

"I don't know," he admitted.

"You will." The stranger flashed his biggest smile yet. "You will learn because you must. Meeting up with you, youngster, is the sort of good fortune I am constantly searching for. You must learn the truth about yourself, and I am the man to teach you. If you like, you are welcome to join my little band. Are you interested?"

The boy could hardly believe what he was being offered. "Do you mean it?"

"I do."

The boy considered this glimpse he'd caught of a pathway that could change his life. "I think I am. I don't have anything better to do with my life. So yes, I want to find out."

"We leave today. Will that be a problem?"

The boy shrugged. "I don't have much to my name, and Wrent's already docked my pay for being out so long."

The tall man stuck out his hand, and the boy clasped it with his own.

"I'm Starns. What's your name, son?" the man asked, and the epithet did not rankle as much this time around.

The boy smiled. "I'm Galaphile. Galaphile Joss."

TWO

Galaphile's excitement remained high as Starns led him and Ratcher up-country, traveling through the Kennon Pass into the forestland beyond the skyscraping pinnacles of the Dragon's Teeth. Eventually they arrived in deep forest highlands that clogged the entire middle of a wilderness ringed by the massive wall of mountains.

As they traveled, Starns told Galaphile some of what would be required of him and how he would be expected to spend his time.

"It requires extensive practice and constant repetition to acquire an education. This is true of life—and of survival. The world into which you have been born is far more troubled than your time in Parrish Rahn—or even your months in Kern—might have suggested. And it will take both cunning and training to survive it."

As Starns explained, this was a world that grew out of the wreckage of wars fought thousands of years earlier. Galaphile knew a little of this from his mother and what books he had managed to scrounge, but it had all seemed so distant in Parrish Rahn. Now, however, Starns's descriptions brought it vividly home.

The Old World of Men and their civilization had perished during the Great Wars—a worldwide destruction brought about by weapons and greed and foolish decisions that put an end to thousands of years of Human evolution and culture. Humankind was practically destroyed in the process, and the world was forever changed. In the aftermath, new Races evolved from the remnants of the old—formed and shaped by the poisons that had been released across the globe. The new creatures took on—or were given—names from ancient mythologies and stories: Trolls, Dwarves, Gnomes, and the like. As well, the Elves—a species that had been alive and viable for longer than Humans—resurfaced to claim their place in the world.

But this new world was wild, untamed, and dangerous beyond belief. The Races fought one another savagely—and mostly in a lawless vacuum. Still, slowly, camps and villages formed, then towns and cities, but those took another thousand years to find any sort of permanent stability. And it was two thousand years following the Great Wars before more stable societies began to knit back together. Yet the lawlessness persisted.

Galaphile listened intently, fascinated by the details, remembering what little his parents had taught him of this world before their death. At that point—when he was still a member of the Elven community and mostly unconnected to the larger, wilder world—it had all seemed more like a terrible fairy tale or a story meant to frighten young children. Yet though they were safe in their Elven haven, the proximity of this more lawless world was never that far away.

Then Galaphile's parents had been taken from him, and his safe world had disappeared. That was when he had ventured into the Southland and settled in Parrish Rahn. He had always been intending to move on, but his age and lack of coins held him back. Now he was faced with a life of scant security, little order, and much struggle.

The Midlands, where Galaphile now lived, mostly consisted of small towns and communities filled with men and women struggling to simply stay alive. Life was hard and dangerous for everyone. Bands of thieves and raiders lived by what they could steal and scavenge, preying on folks who already struggled to make ends meet. And those left with nothing had no choice but to join these gangs or start their own, preying on others in turn.

Due to its remote location, Parrish Rahn had largely been protected, but it was still far from secure. Three times slavers had taken its citizens and burned its buildings; three times the community had been forced to rebuild. Galaphile had lost friends and neighbors to one fate or another—including his best friend, Abis, when he was only ten. After that, he remained mostly an outsider in the community—hence his reason to be looking for something safer and more protective.

Following Abis's death, he had briefly given city life a try, in Kern. But that was even worse. It was not unusual for entire cities to be overrun, looted, and burned to dust. It was not strange for their inhabitants to be either enslaved or slaughtered. It had happened in Wells Haven, a city of several thousand not twenty miles away, less than two years ago.

Yet as Starns explained it, survival was about attaining dominance over the threats that faced them—finding sufficient men and women, weapons and protective armor to stand up to anything short of an army that came against him and his. He was a survivalist, with skills and training and a natural flair for command, and he knew all the best ways to stay alive. He had started out with a handful of followers and built on that core until he had more than a hundred fighters and camp dwellers.

His life's mantra, as he called it, was always to be one step ahead of, and one sword blade or spear point stronger than, his enemies. Strike first and strike harder. Never leave anyone alive to come back at you. Never show mercy to those who sought you harm.

It was a harsh, brutal policy that ran contrary to most of what Galaphile had been taught by his parents, but it was a policy that life after their deaths had taught him to understand. And for Starns, brutality did not exclude fellowship. You could make friends. You could establish a sense of community.

Still, Starns was unusual in his dedication to military tactics and strict chains of command. Rival bands were often larger and more predatory, but they lacked his skills and insights into military life. Where he had developed this approach was something he never talked about. In truth, he never talked about any part of his early life. What mattered to him was the present. What mattered was keeping himself and his people alive and protected.

Galaphile knew he had survived this long by living in a place too poor and distant to attract much danger. Men like Ratcher were big

and strong enough to rely on their physicality to stay alive, but Galaphile was not. For him, Starns's lessons were all the more valuable. With
knowledge came experience. And with experience came skills and understanding.

With his Elven blood, he would never be like Ratcher—even though
he came to like the man and enjoy his company in camp. As Ratcher
had told Starns on that first day, he greatly preferred a life of peace to
a life of fighting. And brought to a place where he did not have to constantly prove himself or struggle for dominance, he was able to reveal a
side both kind and compassionate, for all his brutish appearance.

But unlike Ratcher, Galaphile was not a large, physically powerful
individual whose size was enough to impress others. He had to make
his way based on personality alone, which forced him from his shell. As
an Elf in the Human world, he had always felt very isolated, and—save
for Abis—had found it difficult to reach out and make friends. But here,
he had no choice. If he was to find his place in this camp, it would be
through fellowship.

To his astonishment, however, he found he enjoyed making connections, and he soon established himself as an equal and accepted
member of the community—though he still lacked a truly close friend.
But maybe that was because he was younger than most. Or because he
could never be as easy with killing as so many of his campmates were.
He would never want to take the lives of others—even if it proved necessary.

"We live in a world of kill or be killed," Starns declared. "A harsh
truth, but a truth nevertheless. And one you must understand if you
want to survive."

The camp that Galaphile would now make his home comprised well
over a hundred men, women, and children. It was situated in the south-
eastern corner of the valley that lay between the two great arms of the
Dragon's Teeth. This valley was mostly unoccupied but well situated for
finding food and water—and for providing a modicum of cover from
attacks. There were various camps and enclaves throughout this protected territory, but for the most part, they were farther north, east, or
west of the place Starns had chosen.

For the next eight months, Galaphile slavishly followed the lessons given by his self-appointed mentor. He worked and studied and trained, developing his fighting and tracking skills and building up both physical strength and mental acuity. He was encouraged to train with the older men and women of the camp, to challenge himself to match their abilities and gain an equal measure of their skills. It was hard going at times, but Galaphile was an orphan and a survivor more than he was anything else, and learning to survive was something he was used to. He was not a quitter, and he was used to being tested by those who were better than he was—especially since this enabled him to improve.

His dedication must have impressed his mentor, for while Starns never said too much about it, his steadily increasing expectations suggested that he required more because he was convinced Galaphile was capable of more.

Yet still he kept Galaphile within the confines of the camp and away from any sort of real danger. For now, it was enough that, while considerably younger than almost everyone else, he was still being trained on the same level. The men and women of the camp knew of Starns's special attachment to the boy and even kidded him about it. But no one ever suggested he was being unfairly favored. Galaphile was well liked and even admired for the grit he demonstrated and the obvious consistency of his improvements. An invitation to the camp alone wasn't enough to gain you fellowship; it was how you behaved while there that mattered. And hard work was respected.

So Galaphile worked hard, all the while wondering how long it would take before he was tested in the way the other camp members had been. One day, he would be sent out on a real expedition, where dangers existed, but not yet.

By the time he passed into his sixteenth year, Galaphile was no longer a boy. He was pushing six feet in height and only thirty pounds shy of two hundred in weight. He had grown tough and wary in a way he had not been when Starns had first discovered him. He was trained and fit and ready to take on anything.

At least in his own mind, he was—but he still had not been tested. He was two months into his sixteenth year when his moment finally arrived.

It was just another ordinary day, and Galaphile was training with weights in the camp's yard, stripped down to no more than shorts and shoes, when Starns appeared at the gates and summoned him over. "Get dressed. Intruders are approaching, and you're going out with a couple of others to see what they are after. You've been asking for a chance to prove yourself, so here it is."

He turned away before the boy could ask just where it was that he was going. Still, giddy with excitement, Galaphile rushed to his bunkhouse, dressed in his forest gear, painted his face, donned his skullcap, and rushed back out again. At last—an outing! It was what they called their forays; all the old hands used the word freely whenever they were going on a mission. Galaphile had asked repeatedly to be taken along and had been refused each time—until now.

He found Starns waiting at the central assembly point with Merek, Ostonoble, and Crunch. The first two were more established camp members with whom Galaphile had trained often. Crunch was a newer recruit, big and dangerous, whom Galaphile had thus far managed to avoid.

"Over here!" his mentor shouted. "Be quick!"

Galaphile was there in seconds, heated and anxious and flushed with excitement. "What's going on?"

"A scouting mission," Starns advised, looking from face to face. "Two dozen Gnomes and a handful of Dirt Trolls"—which were a lesser form of the larger Trolls, and not much liked—"have come down out of the north. They're up in the headlands of the Whisper Winds and backtracking down the banks of the Squirm. There are Procks among them—three, at least. I'm not sure what they are doing down here where they don't belong, so you're going to find out. Count their numbers, check their gear, take note of how they are outfitted. Catalog any oddities. One of you also needs to get close enough to listen in tonight, once they've camped, if you can manage it. Shadow them until then, but don't let them find you. Stay quiet. Stay hidden. Be smart. I'll see you back here by dawn."

He paused. "Merek is senior in age and experience, so he will lead. Do what he says. No arguments. Galaphile is junior, but don't make the mistake of thinking that he is any less capable. In fact, I'd recommend that he be the one who sneaks into the enemy camp, as he is younger and quicker. He has the necessary survival skills to do what I am asking. Also, it's time to learn something of his potential."

Then he turned away and was gone without a backward glance. Galaphile waited for the others to take up their packs, then did the same. He knew his hunting and tracking abilities were first-rate and was eager to test them out. He carried only regular hand weapons—short and long knives and a six-pack of throwing stars. The other three men bore swords, bows and arrows, maces, and more knives and stars. But they were older and more experienced, Galaphile thought. Fair enough.

There would be time for that later.

They set out with Merek in the lead and the others following. No one said anything as they departed.

Galaphile assumed a place at the back of the little group, already thinking about what he might find ahead. The Squirm was a river that flowed out of the southern stretches of the Dragon's Teeth and ran into the cup of the forestland in a northerly direction. The river got its name from the fact that it cut back and forth through gatherings of huge boulders and sheer cliff walls before ending in a small lake called the Scrunch, way up toward the northeastern end of the mountains. The Squirm lacked speed, direction, and depth, but it was tenacious—and even in the dry weather the Four Lands were facing currently, it was running full. Finding a starting point would be easy enough. Avoiding a chance meeting with the Gnomes and their companions would be trickier.

What Gnomes—and especially Procks—were doing in this part of the Four Lands was a mystery. It was not where they resided and not where they normally hunted or roamed. The area was well south and west of their homelands—a part of the country into which they seldom ventured, and certainly not with what might be a war party. The Gnomes were troublesome enough, but the Procks were especially dangerous. They were birdlike creatures of a sort that most closely re-sembled oversized vultures and were reputedly ferocious. Fortunately, they were fewer in number than other predators and reclusive in nature if not forced into submission. The Gnomes used them as hunters, and no ordinary outing would involve them.

Even more troublesome was the presence of Trolls, who under most conditions wanted nothing to do with Gnomes. As far as Trolls were concerned, Gnomes were simply a bothersome presence and an unpleasant fact of life. But perhaps there was a different relationship between Gnomes and Dirt Trolls.

Whatever the case, it was difficult for Galaphile to imagine that this group was here for any reason other than to cause trouble.

Still, he felt excited to have this opportunity to discover what drove them. He was trained to both track and infiltrate—and had been tested over and over—but this was his first chance to do either on an actual expedition. He would need to keep his wits about him. He would need to pay attention to the three men who accompanied him—all of whom had been on many expeditions of this sort before. As excited as he was and as ready as he felt, he would have to move carefully and act with caution. This was his moment to prove himself, and he could not afford to waste it.

The band of four walked on through the day, following the river, headed downstream toward an eventual encounter with the invaders. As a precaution, Merek sent Ostonoble ahead to scout for signs, with the understanding that he would return to advise the others as soon as he encountered anything. But their day passed without incident.

It was Ostonoble, still acting as advance scout, who eventually spied the group they were searching for as the sun was setting, and by then, the invaders had already set up camp and were hunkered in for the night. An odd choice, according to Merek. If they were raiders, why were they not using the night as cover for their nefarious deeds? Normally, raiders preferred to move in darkness. No one had an answer, though Galaphile summoned the courage to suggest that maybe they were waiting for another party to join theirs and were camped at a predetermined meeting point.

"Good thinking," Merek said, which was praise indeed.

They hid in the trees about five hundred yards or so back, wary of being discovered. There were no signs of the Gnomes or Trolls anywhere outside the camp, but the Procks circled overhead in regular spirals. To avoid attracting their attention, Merek chose a stretch of forest where the tree boughs were so thick and heavy that overhead searchers were unlikely to detect them.

Night descended.

Galaphile and his companions sat in silence, ate a cold meal, and drank from their water jugs. Then, on Merek's orders, Galaphile set out to see what he could learn of the intruders' intentions. This was going to be an important night for him.

The intruders' camp was rudimentary—not much more than a gathering of fires with a few Gnomes and Trolls on watch and the others seated close to the flames or asleep, though Galaphile noticed that the two groups stayed very much apart. Even the Procks had gone to roost. The night was deepening quickly, lit only by stars in a cloudless sky with a full moon to the east. The sounds of insects and night birds were audible as the boy slipped down to the river and crawled through the heavy brush that grew along both banks in a slow, steady advance.

Eventually, he worked his way close enough that he could make out some of what the Gnomes were saying. He had studied their language as a part of his training, so he could translate what he heard. Mostly, the talk was of home and family—and in some instances of hunts and adventures one or another of them had experienced. He did get the distinct impression, from the little that was said on the subject, that this band was scouting for new hunting territory and better sources of clean water, which the land surrounding Starns's camp could provide.

He sat quietly, his concentration on what was happening before him. He occupied a place within the brush that was almost entirely dark, having learned how to sit invisibly and listen during his months of training. What he was doing now was nothing new—save for the potential danger of being discovered.

As he sat, he thought about how his life had changed. Over the past few weeks, Starns had begun to talk about teaching him magic now that he had mastered many of the other skills. Some uses of magic, his commander had said, were acquired through practice; only a handful were a gift of birth. Others were the result of finding magical objects, and others still derived from submitting to dark forces and questionable rites that could damage the user. There were men and women out there, Starns said, who had sold themselves to such magic and would never be the same as a result.

Galaphile, however, wanted no part of any of it. He wanted an education and a cause, sure. He wanted to acquire skills. But brushing up against magic—or, even more concerning, directly engaging in it—was another matter. He still found himself distrusting what it might do to him, and so he wanted nothing to do with it.

At midnight, having learned that the group planned to remain in the area indefinitely—though for what purpose, he could not be sure, as no one ever said anything specific—Galaphile waited for the sentries to turn away or move elsewhere, then crawled out from his hiding place and slipped away. Before long, he was back with his three companions. After a short conference, Merek decided it was time to return to Starns.

By dawn, they were back at camp. Galaphile waited for Merek to present his report, then presented his own, relating in detail everything he had seen and heard. At the close, he added, "I wish one of them had said more specifically what they were after besides better hunting grounds and a source of clean water, but they clearly didn't have any immediate plans for moving on."

Starns nodded. "Then we'll wait a bit to see what they intend—and keep an eye on them using other trackers. Well done, all of you. Go wash up and find something to eat. You are excused from training for the rest of the day."

Galaphile departed with the other three, hungry and dirty from crawling around in the brush but happy with how things had gone on his first outing.

A few days later, he was sitting alone in the dining tent at midday, nursing a cold glass of ale while munching on fresh bread, when Merek wandered in and took a seat next to him. Galaphile pushed over the bread and poured the man a share of his ale, but a glance at Merek revealed that the man had a troubled, angry look. Something was wrong. For a moment, neither spoke. Then Galaphile asked, "Has there been another outing?"

Merek nodded but still didn't speak.

"Where to?" Galaphile prompted. "The Gnome camp again?"

Merek nodded, finally saying, "Starns decided the Gnomes seek to encroach on our territory and steal our food and water. He sent men out—me included—to put a stop to it. A dozen of us went back there early this morning, under Starns's command, all armed to the teeth and ready to fight. Starns led us back to the camp, where the same group were sleeping. Then he split us into two groups—one down along the river, one uphill in the trees—and told us we would attack the camp together. Ordered us to wipe them out. No quarter. No survivors left. Everyone dead."

"Everyone?"

"No exceptions, and no mercy. We couldn't be sure what they were doing there, so it seemed safer just to eliminate them. I couldn't believe it. I didn't like those people, didn't want them there, but still . . . just to kill them like that . . ."

Galaphile stared. "You killed them all?"

"Every single one. Most of them were still sleeping when it happened." He took a deep breath and exhaled. "He had us burn them all in a pit and cover them up. Said we were never to talk of it again."

He looked away and kept his gaze averted. A few moments later, he got up and walked off without looking back. Galaphile watched him go, then continued to sit where he was and think things through. It made him sick to his stomach. To just kill helpless people while they slept—for any reason—felt wrong. This wasn't something he had ever expected of Starns. It wasn't something he thought would ever happen. Killing during a battle: That, he understood. Killing raiders who were trying to steal your supplies also made sense. Killing others while they were asleep, just for something they might do? What was the point of that? He tried to imagine a reason for it and couldn't.

By the time he got up to go off to training, he was wondering how much of what he assumed he knew about Starns and the purpose of his camp was wrong.

THREE

Galaphile did not think of his new home as a raider camp in the beginning. What he believed was that he had attached himself to a committed and well-trained group of men and women fighting to make the land safe; that he was committed to stopping those who would see the world overrun by power-hungry madmen intent on bringing everyone else to heel. He believed Starns was a voice of reason with a passion for sanity and order. Not a force of chaos.

Because chaos there was—in plenty. The Elves, for the most part, stayed apart, just as they had before the Great Wars, isolated in the vast forests of the Westland within their protected cities and with their magical heritage. Trolls, as well, seemed to stick to the wild emptiness of the barren Northland, and the Dwarves mostly remained in their Eastland mountain communities. Most of them seemed satisfied to live apart from the other Races, tending to their own lives and avoiding contact with the madness and greed crowding in on them from all around.

Truthfully, it was the Humans and Gnomes who were the worst offenders.

Humans were warlike and constantly engaged in battles with one another, pitting one faction against the others, all in search of power and domination. The Gnomes, however, mostly seemed to just love chaos and disruption; their lives were spent living off the weakness and misfortune of others.

Yet, as Galaphile eventually came to realize, Starns wasn't much different from any of those he had come to abhor. Galaphile had thought otherwise at first—in large part because it allowed him to feel better about what he was doing for a man he greatly admired and wanted to believe in. As time rolled on, however, he began to see that none of it was true. Starns was carrying out missions that were mostly about consolidating power or protecting his own—and his definition of *his own* began and ended at the borders of his camp. If you were with Starns, you were his. If not, you were the enemy—and would be treated as such. As well, Starns's actions frequently cost lives or resulted in devastating injuries that left fighters on both sides broken in the same way his enemies did.

Worse, nothing ever really changed. The struggles wore on, band fighting band, while the overall state of the Four Lands remained in chaos. Sometimes Starns was a winner; other times he was a loser. His people rose and fell with him. But at the end of the days and weeks and months, when Galaphile looked back on all that had happened, he could not point to much of anything that was improved in the wider world because of anything he or anyone else in Starns's camp had done.

Save in one very personal way. Within weeks of Galaphile's first outing, Starns took him aside for a private discussion. He walked Galaphile to a secluded grove down by the training fields and sat him down for a talk.

"You've grown strong and skilled," he said. "Your talents and accomplishments are praised by everyone who knows you, and you have advanced well beyond where anyone thought you would. But I knew that you possessed the ability to do so from the first day. You were never the biggest or strongest or fastest, but you were always the most dedicated. Add to this your intelligence and it is not surprising that you have come so far. You have my heartiest congratulations on your achievements."

He paused as Galaphile blushed, never at ease with praise of this sort;

in his mind, there was always room for improvement. No matter what he accomplished, he was always striving to achieve more. Truthfully, he thought his mentor was overstating his success, but Starns brushed his shyness away with a wave of one hand.

"So now you are ready to learn something more. To take on a greater responsibility. Do you know what I am talking about?"

Galaphile did, and he faced the prospect with still-mixed feelings. "Magic," he said.

"Just so," Starns agreed. Starns was teaching several others in the use of magic, Galaphile knew, but he had never been invited to join their number—despite what Starns had promised him on the day he had joined the camp. He had been afraid his mentor thought him unworthy, but now he wondered if it was a bit more like learning to walk before you began to run. Perhaps some physical discipline was needed before undertaking any mental control.

"Almost every camp has possession of some form of magic," Starns continued. "It is the way of things now. Before, there was science to control the evolution of our world and the progress of our people. Now there is magic. So you must acquire and use it if you are to remain in control. You've seen what's out there. Gnomes and Trolls and all sorts of beings that weren't here in the Old World but are surely here now. These creatures have no love or consideration for us. They are self-centered and determined to dominate or eliminate us. That is not going to change. So if I don't have the use of magic, I place myself and my people at a disadvantage. I need all the tools available to me in order to make certain this camp survives. And so will you."

"Aren't we safe enough already?"

"Are any of us ever safe enough? Haven't you noticed the increasing number of intruders wandering into our forest refuge? Haven't you seen repeated attack by forces large enough to be called small armies? Is there any reason to think things are getting better instead of worse?"

Indeed, in his seemingly endless forays and explorations within a hundred miles of their camp, he had seen it all. For the most part, their enemies and would-be dominators had been kept at bay. But their struggle to keep their own people protected was constant and soul draining.

"Yet we are better trained and better equipped," Galaphile argued.

"We are smarter and more skilled. We have a leader who knows what he is doing. We have survived well enough until now. I don't see . . ."

"Which is exactly the problem, Galaphile. You haven't yet learned to *see* things the way you need to. This is not only about training you in the use of magic but also about training you to look ahead, to imagine and foresee the forces that might be coming to destroy you. What is true today might not be true tomorrow. Our struggle to survive is constant. We have to look beyond what we see now and imagine what we might see in the future. We cannot assume that things won't change, because the odds are good that they will."

"And is this what you tell all your magic students?"

Starns laughed at that. "No, but it is what I am telling you."

"Why me?"

"Because one day, you might find yourself in my shoes. Few of the others ever will."

Galaphile stared, then shook his head in rebuke. "I would never presume to replace you!"

Starns grinned. "Nor should you! I don't intend to be replaced for a good long time. But one day, I won't be here—and who better than you to take my place? You have the intelligence and determination to be the next leader. You have everything—save the one thing I just mentioned. You don't know the slightest bit of useful magic. If you don't rectify that, you will be risking the lives of not only yourself but also everyone around you."

"So you're saying I have to learn magic to survive?"

"You have to learn magic so that *all of us* will survive. You have to set an example. You have to be ready to use magic if the need arises—which I am certain it will. To do that, you have to start learning it now."

Galaphile sighed, less willing to embrace this supposed truth than his mentor would have wished, but aware of the other's intention that he do so. "And when do you want me to start?"

Starns nodded in satisfaction. "No time like the present."

The hours spent learning magic were longer and harder than his physical training had ever been. His mentor started him out learning control over the four main elements—air, earth, fire, and water. He taught him how to use one to impact the others, showing him combinations of arcane words and gestures that could achieve the desired results. They repeated their efforts until Galaphile could master all four. Fire could be used to burn air and summon spirits. Earth could be made so light that entire sections of ground—even those with trees—could be elevated. Air could be hardened sufficiently to knock apart stone walls. Water could be made to take the shape of living creatures and mimic their habits. All of this was achieved through spells—words and gestures combined.

Slowly, steadily, Galaphile learned to create artifacts and tools from nothing more than small bits of one or more of the four essential elements. He learned how to create visual impressions of himself that were virtually identical to his flesh-and-blood self.

Finally, he learned how to move as fluidly as his mentor himself—quick, sudden, and spontaneous, there one second and gone the next. Starns showed him how to make it appear as if he were in one place when he was actually in another, as his mentor had once done with Ratcher. How to create imaginary forms of mythical creatures. How to bind men's hands with nothing more than properly configured words; how to lock weapons sent to bring him down. And how to impart confusion or fear into the minds of would-be enemies.

Gradually, Galaphile learned all the formal spells and forms of conjuring already known to Starns, working with him for long hours and practicing until he had mastered every single one. Some of what Galaphile learned seemed pointless, and some techniques were so complex that he was never really convinced he could carry them off successfully should the need arise. Yet slowly but very surely, Galaphile became comfortable with the use of magic, gaining profound and dependable confidence in himself.

On Galaphile's eighteenth birthday, Starns surprised him by declaring that his lessons were over.

"You have used me up," the older man declared with a smile. "I have no more to teach you. If you wish to know more, you will have to continue your studies with a stronger master. Up in the northwest, above the territories of the Elves, there is a place known as Welkrin Run. To arrive there, you must go to the Valley of Rhenn and from there hike north along the Rill Song River until you are just this side of the Kens-rowe Mountains. There, in a stretch of deep woods, lives a man who knows much more than I do about the usage of magic. He knows of the old forms—the ones that were here in this world before we were. *The Elven magic.* The kind that I could never wield but that perhaps—with your Elven blood—you could learn to master. If you are ever ready to do so and wish to command a deeper, purer magic than you have at present, go to him and tell him I sent you. If you prove to be as talented with him as you have learned to be with me, it would be very much worth your while to accept his services."

"Who is this man?" Galaphile asked curiously.

"His name is Cogline, but not all know that. Just ask for the hermit who lives near Welkrin Run, and someone will guide you to him. He is a strange man but brilliant, too. You will see for yourself."

Galaphile nodded. "I am satisfied for now."

Starns smiled. "For now—but things change. I guarantee you that, one day, you will want to learn more, command more, master more. All magic users do. I was one of them, and I once studied under him. But in addition to lacking Elven blood, I lacked the willingness to devote myself to a life solely of study for however many years it took. Being part of the world felt more important. But then, I knew my strengths and limitations. You are the best student I have ever trained, and I think you are capable of more. Remember that."

Galaphile promised he would, but at the same time, he was certain that further education was unneeded.

FOUR

Two more years passed with few changes in Galaphile's life. His experience continued to grow and his life skills to improve, and he continued to practice the magic that Starns had taught him until he became nearly as adept as Starns at its usage—although clearly less experienced.

By now, he was a bit over six feet tall and two hundred pounds in weight, and his agility and swiftness were unmatched. Every time he sat down to a meal in the compound, he ate twice what anybody else did just to sustain himself—though this was swiftly causing problems. Food had grown scarce in the regions around the camp, and while Galaphile was teased repeatedly for being the cause, the reality was that the forest game still had to feed hundreds. Though Starns had kept the size and membership of his compound strictly limited, the game that used to be so plentiful in this part of the Four Lands had slowly been diminished over the years. And not just because of Starns's group. Several new camps had taken up residence nearby—one to the north and the others to the west. Starns tried driving them away, but his efforts failed. The encroachers simply melted away, then returned after things had quieted. And each time, the other camps grew steadily larger.

Galaphile was paying close attention to what this meant. More than once, he suggested to Starns that perhaps it was time to move on, as their present site had remained largely the same for more than a decade, and the camps forming in opposition to their own had been increasing at a steady rate. Camps of Gnomes, Procks, Trolls, and mixed-Race bands were always around and hunting them—and now and then, members of their camp were lost to such creatures.

As the years had passed, it indeed seemed that Starns's determination to establish a permanent camp was attracting more and more groups with similar notions. His success had spoken, and where he had succeeded, others soon followed—especially as the Dragon's Teeth provided a natural fortress against the intrusions of the larger world. By Galaphile's twentieth year—and his sixth with Starns—establishing such private camps had become the norm for citizens outside the major cities.

Life in a world without an established order, and where the population was growing quickly, was both difficult and merciless. The strong lived and thrived in packs, while the weak became isolated and perished. Private camps such as Starns had created seemed to spring up overnight, but few were self-sufficient, and most were predatory. Now there were twenty such camps within a hundred miles. Most were small and unthreatening, but two or three were a match for their own. With resources already stretched, Galaphile argued that Starns might be better off finding a stronger, more easily defensible site for his camp—perhaps farther west, closer to the homelands of the Elves and the protection of the Westland forests.

But Starns was dismissive. No other camp possessed the experience, training, and determination that his did. This was their turf, and there was no good reason for them to move on. Let the other camps move or continue to face the wrath of his band.

Galaphile was unhappy with his mentor's disregard for what he considered an obvious danger, but he knew better than to press the matter. Starns was the undisputed leader of this band, and going against him was cause for ejection. He was not angry with Galaphile for now, but he was also quick to brush the matter aside as a young man's concern.

And Galaphile soon had more pressing concerns anyway, when love came calling.

Before his twentieth year, Galaphile had never even kissed a girl—mostly because his training had absorbed so much of his time. Besides, he had grown up with most of the folks in the camp, and knew them too well to view them as anything but companions and friends.

Then he met Mayele.

He had gone down to Mirror Lake—a small and isolated body of water fed by underground springs—just to have a few hours of private contemplation. He was sitting there staring at the waters and wondering whether or not he should stay with Starns and his camp—something he thought about frequently these days. It was a hard choice between logic and loyalty. Then, suddenly, a young woman was sitting down beside him, blond hair long and flowing, her eyes a dazzling dark blue.

"You look like a lost child," she teased. "Like you wandered off and now don't know how to get back home. What are you thinking about?"

Her dazzling smile fixed on him with such brilliance that he thought he might have lost his voice. He tried to reply and couldn't, so he just shook his head.

"So first you lost yourself, and now you've lost your voice?" Her laugh was warm and comforting. "Happens that way, now and then." She held out her hand. "I'm Mayele. My family and I are newcomers; we found our way here through a friend. We came for the security and order that most places lack. I've noticed you around. I'm told that your name is Galaphile Joss."

He nodded and finally found his voice. "That's me."

"I want to thank you for something. Starns wasn't all that ready to admit us into the camp—three women with no men and no real skills—but he let us in anyway. He said you were the one who taught him to do things like that, because you can never tell what purpose others will serve. So that is how he measures things now."

Galaphile blushed, unaware of any of this. He had talked to Starns about being more open to those who wandered in, but he hadn't realized he'd had any impact on the other's stubborn way of thinking. "Glad I could be of help," he managed.

"I hear that Starns has been training you in magic. Is that true?"

He nodded.

"Is that what you want to be? A mage? A magician?"

He shrugged. "I just want to know how to do things that might help others. I want to learn as much as I can about how everything works—magic included."

She looked off into the distance. "Maybe you could have helped me when my father got the sickness and we couldn't make it go away. A little magic might have helped. I wish I had known you then."

"It probably wouldn't have helped," he confessed. "Healing's not one of my skills. More's the pity. I lost my own parents to disease when I was seven. I was on my own for a bit until Starns took me in at fourteen."

She gave him a look he couldn't read. "Then I guess that's something we have in common—losing a parent, I mean. Tell me something else about you."

He gave her a doubtful look. "Why?"

She shrugged. "Because you don't seem to have many friends, and I think I might like being one of them."

Bold, he thought. But he liked her and he wanted to be friends with her, too. It didn't take him long to recite what there was to know about himself. Then he asked about her.

"I came here with my mother and younger sister when a friend suggested it was safe," she said.

"Where did you come from?"

"A small village to the south. You wouldn't know it; no one ever does. With my father gone, we felt too exposed to stay there on our own. A friend who had moved here found out about my father and suggested we would be better off joining this camp. He had always admired our self-reliance and survival abilities, so he recommended us to Starns. After all, with my father gone, we had survived on our own for several years. But now my friend wants to partner with me, and I don't have the same feelings for him, which makes things horribly awkward."

"So, what, you chose one of the bigger guys in the camp to protect you from his affections?"

She laughed. "Maybe a bit? Is that terrible of me?"

Galaphile grinned. "I suppose it depends. What's expected of me in return?"

"Just someone to talk to over dinner? You mostly seem to eat alone."

It seemed a fair bargain to him, and he was amused when she shook hands on it in a businesslike manner. But still, he suspected he got more out of the bargain than she did. He wasn't exactly warning the other guy off, but having someone to talk to at dinner really was an unexpected pleasure.

Galaphile liked her right from the beginning.

He liked her a lot.

She was forthright and intuitive, and he quickly came to suspect she had sought him out for more than just his size. Even at the start, they talked easily and at length, and he felt more comfortable with her than he had felt with anyone since Abis or his parents.

He was never sure how much he told her on that first night at dinner, but it was considerable. He did remember afterward that he could not stop looking at her. Something about her was so appealing that he couldn't help himself. She was pretty, but it was more about the sound of her voice and the way she phrased her remarks and even the way she seemed to like teasing him.

As the days and then weeks passed, he found himself wanting to spend more and more time with her. The hours when they were together felt full of light and life, while those without her felt increasingly pale and dim.

Although it had never happened before, he realized quickly enough what was occurring. He was falling in love.

Loving someone as passionately as he loved Mayele was daunting. It demanded things of him that he had never considered, such as how to work another person into his independent existence. It wasn't that he didn't want this to happen; he did. It was just that it required him to consider someone else's wants and needs as deeply as his own. It required him to include her in his thoughts of the future and his plans for his life. Plans he still wasn't sure of himself, given how uncomfortable he was growing with Starns's rule. Mayele and her family had just found a new home with the camp. Could he make them relocate again so soon?

As it happened, however, Mayele took most of those decisions out of his hands. Astute, aware, and considerate, she realized his uncertainty well before he did, and she had already made up her mind that he was the man she wanted to spend her life with. If things had been different—if they had not been living in hard and dangerous times—their relationship might have worked out differently or played out over a longer period of time. But they were surrounded by predators from other camps, all of them scrambling for ever-more-limited resources. They were always one step away from a fight or a battle or a confrontation. Still, Galaphile quickly came to learn that she was the one he most wanted to turn to at these moments. The one he wanted to fight to protect; the one he wanted standing at his back in battle. The one who comforted him when he lost friends and comrades, and the one with whom he wanted to share his most intimate hopes and dreams.

Before long, both were looking forward to a day when he could take Mayele from the compound and start a new life in the Westland, where the threats and dangers were considerably fewer. His Elven blood would give them access denied to others, and her mother and younger sister could accompany them.

He had heard stories about what life was like in Elven country, and these, combined with his own early memories, told him how much safer it was to reside within Elven borders. Law and order still held sway there, with an operational government that looked after its citizens—unlike the chaos in the rest of the Four Lands.

But of course, this meant leaving Starns—the man who had taught him all he knew and to whom he still owed an immense debt. The more he put off that conversation, the harder he knew it would be.

Still, one way or another, it was time for him to leave.

He found that opportunity much more quickly than he had expected, but he found it in a way that changed his entire life.

He was out hunting on a gray, rain-swept day that many others would have avoided. But Galaphile knew more about the local game than most, and he understood that certain creatures actually preferred to seek out food in such weather, which could discourage bigger predators. So on this day, he had chosen to head south into the deep forests of the valley, off the high ground and down into the places populated by various rodents and burrowing animals, with an eye toward seeking out waterbirds as well.

For once, Mayele was not with him. She had gotten ill a few days ago;

it was no more than a bad cold, but she did not feel up to the journey. He was reluctant to leave her, but he remained one of the best hunters in the camp, and stores were running thin. Besides, he knew Starns would not be happy if he ranked spending time with his girlfriend over feeding the entire community. So he set out early that morning, the sun not yet risen and the day already a fogged-in, swampy morass of mist and rain.

The sun was just beginning to lighten the heavy clouds when he was an hour into his hunt, and the chill of morning still enveloped him—making him miss the warmth of Mayele beside him even more. He had already captured four rabbits and two birds, however, and was feeling lucky enough that he had decided to continue on. He was all the way to the southern wall of the Dragon's Teeth when midday approached, and by then he had so many kills that the weight of them was becoming a strain.

So he retraced his steps at a steady pace, intent on being home before dark. By the time the landscape became familiar, he was already thinking ahead to dinner and an evening with Mayele, hoping to find her much recovered.

It was the smell that stopped him first. There was burning in the air, the smell of soot carried on a slow wind—a wordless warning that something was on fire. He saw flakes of ash while he was still some distance off, then caught his first sightings of smoke.

They were coming from somewhere close to where the camp lay. Somewhere too close.

His breath caught in his throat.

Then he detected the unpleasant smell of burning flesh.

He threw down the carcasses and began to run, driven by the very worst of his fears. *Please, please, no!* he screamed inside. *Not that, please not that!*

He was frantic, terror rising up to roil within him. Such a thing could not have happened, he told himself. Starns was a warrior. His chosen people were warriors. There wasn't a force out there sizable enough to defeat him in his own camp. He must be mistaken. He must!

He broke through the trees, discarding all caution as he raced toward the camp and the clouds of billowing smoke. Whatever it took, however much it cost, he would see things set right! Nothing mattered to him but that. He would provide the strength and the skills and the courage that was needed . . .

He crested the rise to the flatlands on which the camp had been settled, and all the air went out of him.

Everything was in ruins.

Around him, the encampment burned and smoldered. He was facing a scene of total destruction, and seeing it almost brought him to his knees. It was only sheer rage and a need to be certain that kept him upright as he entered its confines.

Everywhere he looked, there were bodies lying still. Twisted and torn, mangled and bladed, put to death in every way imaginable. His eyes swept the wreckage for any signs of movement, any indications of life, yet found nothing but death.

"Shades!" he howled. "For the sake of everything you've taken from me, show me *some* mercy!"

But there was none to be had. There was no life anywhere.

He was weeping as he walked deeper into the camp. He glanced down at the dead—or rather at what remained of them. Blood and gore were everywhere.

There was Wisten, the strong-handed, well-ordered cook who had prepared so many grand meals. Over there was Crunch—a dozen Gnome hunters scattered about him, brought down by his blade. There was Etton Pale, the best swordsman he had ever seen, pinned to a tree by half a dozen spears.

And others, so many others, all now crossed over into the shadows.

The ones he could identify were bad, but worse were the ones hacked and mangled beyond recognition. Was that formless pile in the blue tunic really Kestral, he of the sharp eye and sharper wit? And what of Donsalin, the archer? His head lay off to one side, detached and battered. Could that be Panniss, almost cut to ribbons—she of the quick wit and sharp tongue, whom he had seen only last night telling stories by the firelight after dinner?

Still, he kept walking. He didn't know what else to do. Maybe there were some yet alive. Maybe only a few, but still . . . Maybe really only one or two . . . but . . .

Then he saw Starns, and his heart broke completely. Their trusted leader—the founder of their band, the mentor who had trained him in fighting, spy craft, and magic—was dead. And worse: defiled. They had cut off his hands and feet, then displayed them before him as he was hung by the neck, so he was forced to view the severed parts of his body as he died.

To make him view pieces of his ruined body as he slowly suffocated was cruel beyond words, but it also spoke of the disdain and hatred his enemies held for him. It was instantly clear that everything that had happened here had been meant as a form of retribution. Not a single soul was left alive. This was revenge in its most blatant form. This was an act of sheer, uncontrolled rage.

But as to who was responsible . . . well, the possibilities were sadly far too numerous. Starns's us-against-them policy had left him with far too many enemies over the years—yet another reason Galaphile had been thinking of leaving.

He stared at the remains of his mentor and those who had died closest to him a few moments longer—though for an instant, he was also reminded of the times Starns had done similar things to their Gnome enemies. Then he walked over and cut down what remained of Starns. The man's dead eyes were open and staring, and there was nothing left of him that spoke of the person he had been. Galaphile laid him out next to his hands and feet and left him as he was. There was no point in burying him, and no time to waste in grieving. The enemies were gone, but there was nothing to say they wouldn't be back. He couldn't afford to be found if that happened.

"I won't forget you," he whispered to Starns before he walked away. "I won't ever forget what you did for me."

Then he went looking for Mayele, knowing already what he would find. No one could have survived this massacre. But he had to be sure.

He found her quickly enough, sprawled out inside her tent, stabbed to death in her sickbed, next to her mother and younger sister. Galaphile knelt beside Mayele and took her in his arms one last time, holding her close, brokenly whispering what small eulogy he could before his tears consumed him.

Then, in spite of his resolve not to, he found a shovel, carried the three of them out of the camp, and buried them beneath the trees where they wouldn't be easily found and uncovered by predators. He even used heavy rocks to protect their remains. As he worked, he mourned Mayele, despairing over her pointless death. He would never recover from this, he told himself. He would never love anyone as deeply again.

When he had finished, the day was darkening quickly. He knew he had to leave, to travel far away and find a new life. The old one was lost. It was time to start over.

Thoughts of revenge were pointless. He had no way of identifying the perpetrators, and the possibilities were too numerous.

And would Mayele even want him to? He wasn't sure. She was a much gentler soul than he was. Also, what did this attack say about Starns's ambitions and efforts to secure his space in the world? He had ruthlessly killed others to keep his people safe, and now he had been ruthlessly killed in turn—just another casualty of a bigger, more vicious cycle.

No, Galaphile knew he had to leave and never come back.

Fortunately, this was something he knew how to do. He had done it before, after all—and had been planning to do it again. Just not for these reasons. And he had intended that Mayele would be beside him, but there was nothing he could do about any of it now. It was already in the past, and whatever future there was for him, it was waiting.

It was fully dark when he departed the devastation of his early life and began walking west.

FIVE

For the better part of the night and much of the following day, Galaphile walked with no particular destination in mind. Initially, his intention was simply to get away from both the physical wreckage and the emotional devastation he was leaving behind. He walked without thinking of anything beyond putting one foot in front of the other. He wasn't in shock, but he still felt numb, disconnected— until the memories of what he had witnessed rose up like barbs that stung and burned. He kept seeing the dead—all of them. He kept imagining what their last moments must have been like. He kept wondering what would have happened if he had stayed home with Mayele instead of going hunting. If he had remained in the camp, perhaps he might have been able to save her. Or perhaps he, too, would be as dead as his former companions.

That he had lost both his love and his mentor in such a terrible way, without any chance to say goodbye, was impossible to bear. The best he could manage was to promise himself that he would make good use of what Mayele and Starns had taught him and find a way to build on it. He would treasure the best of his memories and let the passage of time smooth over and dull the worst.

But he knew that he would remember it all, good and bad, forever.

After long hours of walking, wrestling with his grief and loss, he began to give some small thought to the future. He had a life to live, as miserable as it seemed at the moment. What was he going to do with himself? What could he do that would make a difference?

His feet bore him steadily west, toward the life he was supposed to have shared with Mayele. To the place he was supposed to have been able to tell Starns that he was going.

But it wasn't until night approached that the thrust of his plans began to change. Up until now, he had only thought of escaping to the Elven world. But embracing the Elven life meant more than just embracing a life of law and order. What most distinguished the Elves was their use of magic.

Starns had trained him in magic. Maybe the best way to uphold Starns's legacy—or at least what he wished had been Starns's legacy—was not to run from it, but to embrace it.

"I will do what Starns wanted me to do," he told the night. "I will learn to master magic the way he wanted me to. I will create a life of the sort that Starns wanted for me but did not live to see."

Besides, there was a good chance that those who destroyed the camp and killed Starns might one day come looking for him. Some among them might know of him and have taken note that he was not among the dead. So perhaps these extra skills would come in handy.

To some eyes, it might have seemed odd that he was taking on such a responsibility, considering that he had disapproved of much of what Starns had done as leader of their camp of rebels. Galaphile had never embraced the my-people-only philosophy his mentor had made his own. He had never approved of all the killing and bloodshed. If things had continued on as they had been, he would have left the camp on his own, and not because of the massacre. Yet now he was choosing to make what he was abandoning his personal goal in life?

Yes! Because I will do things differently. I won't just look out for my people but will try to make things better for all people, everywhere. So that no one else has to live through what I just experienced.

Bold, foolish promises that he had no reason to think he could ever fulfill. What could one man do to change a world—and a young man at that? He would need to become a master magician, and how likely was that? Right away, he felt foolish for even thinking such things. He flushed at the vanity he was exhibiting—at the wildness of the goals he was embracing.

Yet still . . . one step at a time was the way a journey was made, and perhaps it could be so here. He just needed a path, a direction, and a teacher. He needed Cogline—the man Starns had once told him to find when he was ready to study magic more seriously. But magic of the old Elven kind, of the Old World before the birth of Men. Magic that could accomplish anything and against which no other force could successfully stand.

Yes, that was what he needed to study. That was what he needed to make his own. Then maybe he could live up to his most outrageous claims and truly make the world a better place. A place where people didn't kill one another just for the rights over a patch of ground and what food it provided. A world where all Races could live in peace and harmony, sharing knowledge and resources.

Five days later—five days of numb and mindless grief—he had reached the foothills of the Dragon's Teeth. Tomorrow, he would begin his climb out into his new life. Above him arched a sky brilliant with stars. He lay on his back and watched them twinkling, finding in their fixed permanence a degree of comfort. The world might change, but the stars remained, cycling across the heavens in the same pattern from year to year, generation to generation, millennium to millennium. Once, they had shone down on a more peaceful world, so perhaps they might again.

At times, he drifted and dreamed, but his dreams were of dark things. Death and dying, doomed souls running and being cut down. So mostly, he tried to stay awake by watching the stars as they slowly turned across the sky. And all the while, he thought ahead to where he was going and what he would find. He imagined unlocking the secrets of new forms of magic—ones that would enable him to change the world so that it would serve its populace in a way it had not since before the Great Wars.

When the sky lightened and he knew he would sleep no more, he roused himself long enough to eat some small portion of the foodstuffs he had scrounged from the ravaged foundation camp. His journey lay before him: far away, across the broad expanse of the Streleheim to the west, where the dark shadows of the Elven Duln Forests loomed, and beyond that and north the peaks of the Kensrowe Mountains. That way he would find the Elven people and the heritage he had never really known. And that way he would find Cogline, the magician Starns had mentioned.

He set out again, ready to embrace whatever this new future held.

Over the next fortnight, he exited the Dragon's Teeth and walked the grasslands, keeping a close eye on the country around him, always on the lookout for predators or anything that seemed out of place, but he found nothing of either. Until one nightfall, when he once more encountered Gnome hunters.

The day was ending in a flurry of clouds that had gathered and merged in the twilight skies, and deep patches of fog were beginning to creep down from the Westland forests and out onto the grasslands. He was moving slightly north by then, toward where he believed the Valley of Rhenn lay, which would provide passage toward Arborlon. But the shifting ground fog and the increasing clouds overhead were making it difficult for him to be sure he was continuing in the right direction. A good thing, too, because he had just stopped moving, measuring his path ahead once more, when he heard the sounds of something approaching.

Out of reflex, he dropped down into the tall grasses and waited. The sounds of leather traces, muffled voices, and the huffing snorts of animals gave him a rough clue of the size of the party on its way, and it was not a small one. But he still could not see it clearly.

Then the clouds parted momentarily, allowing the last light of day to flood the Streleheim, and he got a good look at what was out there. Gnomes—more than a few—traveling with pack animals and a train of prisoners linked together by ropes about their necks, with their hands tied and their feet hobbled. The prisoners appeared to be Elves of varying ages, from youngsters to adults, and both men and women. There might have been as many as fifteen or twenty whom the Gnomes had captured and were marching east, back toward their own country.

Galaphile had time enough to count the number of captors, and there were fewer of these—ten or less, if he was counting right. They were a well-armed and hard-looking lot, and their prisoners were be-draggled and slumped as they trudged along. Whatever had happened to them had clearly not been pleasant. There was a hopeless look to their expressions, and a couple of the women and children were crying.

The train of Gnomes and their prisoners passed in front of him not twenty yards away, and he was careful not to move an inch as they did so. Then he slowly stood up to look after them. What to do? What was happening was not his business, and he had no good reason to try to disrupt it. He could turn away and continue on with his journey as if it had never happened.

But that wasn't what he was going to do. That wasn't who he was, and it wasn't what was right. In this world, too many others let such atroci-ties pass by as if they didn't matter, looking out only for themselves. For him, however, the choice was clear. You never turned your back on someone who needed help. It was a lesson he had learned early, from his parents, and had remained a part of his growing friction with Starns. His mentor had protected those who were his with an almost fanatical fervor, but Galaphile had always wanted to extend that protection to all the innocent and oppressed.

Well, now was his chance to put desires to action.

Galaphile started after the Gnomes and their line of prisoners, weap-ons drawn.

He wasn't sure what he was going to do, only that he had to do some-thing. Silent, swift, and virtually invisible in the mix of mist and twilight, he snaked through the tall grasses and caught up to the tail end of the line, then killed the two guards trailing it so stealthily and quietly that even the prisoners ahead of them did not notice. He then fell into line and began to cut the prisoners loose one by one, motioning for them to lie down flat in the grasses. It was not a difficult task. The sounds of the wagons and animals helped to mask his own, and not once did any of the Gnomes turn back or seem aware of what was happening.

He knew by now what he would have to do. If these prisoners were to stay free, he would have to kill or disable all of their captors. Or at least scare them so badly that they would flee on their own.

He worked his way through three more guards, all of them flanking the prisoners as they marched along. None of them were close together, so dispatching them from behind was simple enough. A few times, a prisoner or two noticed, but all of them simply stared in shock as he quickly freed them and then motioned them down. The prisoners ahead just kept walking, too tired or too dismayed to give any thought to what was happening behind them.

But as he was about six prisoners from the head of the caravan, a young woman turned, caught sight of him, and gasped. Ahead, the remaining Gnomes finally turned back and realized what was happening. Shouts and screams erupted, and weapons flashed into view. Any further chance of sneaking about was finished. The surviving Gnomes howled in rage and attacked.

But Galaphile had a trick or two up his sleeve, thanks to Starns. Summoning his magic, he used the same tactics that Starns had employed on Ratcher all those years ago, making it seem he was in one place when he was actually in another. Swiftly, he moved through the line, using throwing stars to take down another pair of baffled and frustrated Gnomes while still cutting the ties that bound the prisoners as he went. He worked silently and with the consistency of purpose and determination that he had mastered in his training.

Once, one of the Gnomes managed to catch hold of him and cried out to his fellows as he slashed at Galaphile with his knife. But Galaphile blocked the blows and threw the Gnome down so hard that it knocked him senseless. Then he vanished again.

As a final act, he conjured bolts of fire that he flung at the flanks and backsides of the hauling mules, startling them so that they bolted off into the wilds, braying and squalling, dragging the wagons and their contents behind them.

The Gnomes were reduced to three survivors, and enough was enough. They broke and fled their mysterious attacker, disappearing in the same general direction as their animals and wagons. Galaphile stood his ground to watch them go and did not turn away until they were all well out of sight.

Then he dispersed the magic and began working his way back down the line to help the bewildered prisoners to their feet, cutting away the remaining bonds fastened about their ankles and hands. Most said little beyond offering thanks, but a few begged him to escort them back home so they wouldn't get attacked on the way.

"We're from small villages beyond the Duln and outside the protection of the Rhenn," an older man advised him. "Some of us have been on our feet for three straight days. Some have lost friends and relatives to those killers. Some don't have any home left to go back to."

Others chimed in with similar stories and pleas, and Galaphile knew that the only reasonable solution was to escort them. After all, he was already traveling that way, and there was always a chance that the Gnomes might circle back. If he remained with the group, their chances were certainly better than if he left them to make their way on their own.

Dark had fallen by now, and the mists had grown thicker. "Can you walk a bit farther?" he asked them. "It would be best to be out of range if the Gnomes return."

All insisted that they could, though some looked more able than others. But there was no reason to continue to stand around—not out here, exposed on the open grasslands. So Galaphile matched them up two by two, pairing a strong walker with a weaker one, and they set out. They would travel as far as seemed sensible—or at least as long as they were able—and then stop to rest for the remainder of the night. They would take turns keeping watch, and in the morning, they would continue on.

They marched back the way they had come for about two hours. The old man who had first spoken to Galaphile was familiar enough with the landscape to lead them in the right direction. They traveled slowly, but there was no sign of any pursuit. They stayed away from the path on which they had been traveling, working their way steadily toward the Rhenn and the promise of Elven help. Galaphile himself was tired by now after many days of walking, and when he started to feel lightheaded, he called a halt. Leaving a couple of those he had freed to act as watchers, he lay down and promptly fell into a deep and thankfully dreamless sleep.

When he woke, someone was shaking him—an Elven boy of maybe ten or twelve. "Stranger? Stranger, wake up."

The boy jumped a foot when Galaphile jerked into a sitting position, knife in hand. "No, it's all right! There's no danger. It's daylight. The others just said I should wake you so we can go on."

Once more, they set out toward the Duln. By now, the trees were clearly visible in the background, and the cliffs that bordered the entrance into the Valley of Rhenn lay just ahead. Smiles and a visible relief spread through the group, and Galaphile felt himself smiling as well. Aiding these people had helped to dispel some of his grief.

The boy who had woken him was keeping close, talking as they walked, telling Galaphile all sorts of things about himself and his life. Galaphile listened politely . . . until he brought up the matter of magic.

"Can you do a lot of magic?" the boy asked. His name was Tamlink or Salmitt or something like that; Galaphile had already forgotten. "Like you did when you rescued us? Real magic, like the master magicians of the Westland? Like the Elven sorcerers?"

"I can do some," Galaphile answered. "Not a lot."

"I bet you can," the boy said, wide-eyed. "I haven't seen anyone who's nearly as good at it as you are. You could disappear and everything! Those Gnomes had no idea what to do."

"I'm still learning," Galaphile confessed.

"Is that why you were journeying here? To learn from the Elven masters?"

Galaphile sighed, wondering how much he should reveal. "Maybe," he conceded. "I am looking for a teacher."

"There are lots of teachers, but most aren't very good. They just do a few tricks and that's all. At least the ones I know. But Eldon knows one or two who are quite good. You should talk to him."

He pointed back and singled out the old man. "He's been alive a long time and has seen a lot of things. He knows the good ones from the bad ones. You should talk to him."

Galaphile nodded and promised he would, but that was a matter for later.

They passed into the shadows off the cliffs of the Rhenn, and within an hour they were met by Elves who were warding the valley against unwanted entrants. The Elves greeted them and were quickly advised about Galaphile's role in his charges' salvation. The warders were impressed and gracious—especially when they noted his Elven heritage. They formed an escort to take the whole ragged bunch on through the forests and into the Elven home city of Arborlon.

As the escort was forming up, the boy reappeared, practically dragging behind him the old man he had called Eldon.

"Here he is," the boy announced. He looked back at Eldon. "Tell him what you told me about magicians."

Eldon looked both embarrassed and flummoxed. "Boy is a handful, if I do say so. Told him this wasn't my business, but he made a point of saying how you helped us and how maybe I should help you in turn. So here I am."

Galaphile smiled in spite of himself. "Go on, then. Any help you have to offer is welcome."

"You want a teacher, correct?"

"I do. I was given to believe there was a man by the name of Cogline who lived in the Westland who was very skilled in the most complicated of the magical talents."

The boy clapped his hands and laughed aloud. "Oh, sure. We know him, don't we?"

The old man grunted. "Boy thinks he knows everything, but in this case he's right. Good thinking, Jillett. Cogline's the one you want to see, and we can tell you where to find him."

SIX

Unfortunately for Galaphile, intent on the next steps in his journey, their Elven escort had other ideas. They wanted Galaphile and his charges transported back to Arborlon for a celebration welcoming home the freed captives and honoring their rescuer. The King of the Elves, Galaphile was assured, would settle for nothing less. Too many members of the Elven nation had been taken of late by the Gnomes, and the Elves had endured enough. Some good news on the subject would be welcome.

But Galaphile wanted nothing to do with honors or celebrations. He had just lost more than a hundred friends and was far from in a celebratory mood. All he wanted was to continue on his quest.

So he declined the offer with apologies, claiming his journey was a matter of life and death, both for himself and others, that could brook no further delays. He thanked the Elves for their kindnesses and promised he would return when he had finished his own business to receive whatever sort of thanks their ruler deemed appropriate—even though he expected no rewards or recognition for having simply done the right thing and aided some strangers in need.

This mollified the escort, so Galaphile turned back to Eldon and Jillett. "What directions you can provide to find this Cogline would be welcome."

The old man nodded. "Go out through the valley to the plains, then turn north and follow the Drey forests to where they diminish and swing west. You'll see road signs for Emberen, but don't go there. Stick to the borders of the Drey until you reach the Rill Song River. Don't try to cross; instead, follow the river north into the woods at the foot of the Kensrowe Mountains. Eventually, you'll come across a tiny village called Welkrin Run. Once you find the village, just start asking after Cogline. He doesn't use that name everywhere, but he does so there."

"Ask for a short-sized, short-tempered hermit," Jillett added. "That's what he is, Eldon says, so that's what people will remember—even if they don't know the name."

"I was in Welkrin Run once, some years back," the old man added. "Never met Cogline, but I heard about him often enough. They talk about him, they do—those that know him. Someone will guide you to him. If that's what you want."

"It is." Galaphile clasped hands with both the old man and the boy. "Thank you. I won't forget this."

Then he released their hands and turned away, striding off toward the already darkening horizon, wanting to put as much distance underfoot as he could before nightfall.

"Be safe, stranger!" the boy called after him. The old man said something, too, but his words were lost in a burst of wind.

A short time later, Galaphile was back out in the Streleheim and hiking north along the eastern border of the Drey, thinking of what lay ahead. He found himself recollecting what Starns had told him of the man he was on his way to find. Cogline. A loner; a recluse. But a man with extraordinary skills and experience who could teach Galaphile things that perhaps no one else was able to. Having a chance to learn magic from him was the best opportunity that the young man could hope for, and he intended to make the most of it.

He walked through the night, pondering the possibilities that awaited him. He should have been tired, but the night was warm and windy, the skies were clear, and the smells of the grasslands felt like they were encouraging him to move. Or maybe that was his restlessness speaking. Memories of Mayele still haunted him—a grim reminder of the grief that tracked him relentlessly. If he stopped for too long, thoughts of all he had lost would begin to sneak in, so maybe it was best to keep moving forward, to keep looking ahead.

By morning, he was tired enough that he needed a few hours of sleep, so he moved over into the edges of the Drey, found a patch of grasses beneath an old oak tree, and settled in. His sleep was deep and undisturbed, and again he did not dream. It could have been risky sleeping so hard, yet no sense of urgency tweaked him with a warning. In the end, he woke at midday, and after eating some of the food with which the old man had supplied him, he set out anew.

Three days later, he reached the main roadway that led into Emberen and passed it by as instructed. From there, he walked until the forests bent to the west and then turned that way to follow along. At night, he stopped again and found a suitable place to rest.

On this night, however, he dreamed of Mayele yet again and the life they would have had together—with hearth and home and children and love. He was devastated when he woke from having seen Mayele alive once more, smiling and happy and very much a part of his life.

By the time he reached the shores of the Rill Song two days later, the flat, grim mood that had settled over him after the dream finally began to lift. On seeing the glimmer of the waters, he hastened his pace and found himself standing at the edge of a river that stretched at least several hundred yards wide.

Following the old man's advice, he turned north and followed the Rill Song for another four days, until it again began to wind its way into forest trees, with the bulk of the Kensrowe rising up behind. At some point amid all those massive trees, he would find the village of Welkrin Run.

Toward evening on the fourth day, he came upon the village just as Eldon had told him he would.

Welkrin Run was little more than a clearing in the middle of the forest. There was a small stable in need of repair, comprising a little holding pen and a barn so tiny it couldn't possibly house more than two or three mounts at once. The rest of the town consisted of a tavern, a clothing shop with its lights off and its interior dark, and a weapons mart that looked as dark and empty as the clothing shop.

Past this central business district were a series of small cottages and huts. A few lights flickered in the windows from behind shutters and curtains, but no people or animals were in sight.

No one was about on the solitary street, either. The street was not even a real street, for that matter, but more of a pathway. The only evidence of life came from behind the candlelit windows of the tavern. Galaphile took a quick look around to make sure he hadn't missed anything, then headed for the only open establishment.

He walked through the tavern doors and stopped. The room was virtually empty. An older woman was cleaning the tables, but judging from her lack of effort, she apparently considered it a worthless endeavor. A pair of men sat off in one corner, speaking in hushed voices, and the barkeep appeared every bit as ragged and worn as his establishment. Bearded like an old bear, one eye patched over, burly arms scarred, he slouched behind the counter, bent over staring at some papers as if they were unreadable. Once in a while, he would write something down. That he could write at all was a plus, but it seemed his sole redeeming feature.

Heads turned as Galaphile entered, then looked away. Apparently, this wasn't a place that regularly welcomed strangers. Still, Galaphile had grown up in a town much like this one, so he knew its ways. He walked over to the counter and faced the barkeep.

"We're closed," the man said without looking up.

Galaphile looked around. "Your customers seem to have drinks."

"They were here before I closed."

"I've come a long way."

"Not my problem. I didn't invite you."

"Maybe you can rent me a room for the night?"

"Don't got any rentals. Better move on."

Galaphile left it there a few moments, just staring at the man. The room had gone quiet. Eventually, the man raised his head. "Thought I told you . . ."

Galaphile locked eyes with him, then brought up his hand and made a small twisting motion. The barkeep kept talking, but no words came out of his mouth. He gasped inaudibly, then touched his throat. Galaphile gave him a few moments to try to work past the magic, then reversed it and leaned forward.

"You should be more careful," he told the barkeep, leaning close. "Customers don't like to be turned away like that. I've been traveling for close to a month, and I would like to think I'm welcome here. Am I?"

The barkeep nodded wordlessly, but there was anger in his eyes. "Trickster," he muttered.

"Magician," Galaphile corrected him. "And I think I would like something to cut the dryness in my throat. But if you're too busy to serve me, I'll just help myself."

Another motion and an empty glass lifted off the counter and stopped beneath a spigot inserted into a barrel, which then opened to fill the glass. One more motion stopped the spigot and carried the full glass through the air to Galaphile's hand. He held the glass in place for a moment before taking a long drink.

"There you are," he said, smiling. "Much better. Now I'll just sit down for a bit at one of your empty tables and maybe have another when I'm done. Don't worry, I'll pay you for what I take. But in the meantime, go about your business."

He walked over to an empty table and took a seat. Everyone was staring at him, but no one said a word. He let the silence linger, sipping his ale and examining his surroundings. He took his time draining his glass, then summoned the woman cleaning the tables. She wandered over to him with a sullen look, and he handed her the glass. "Another, please."

The woman glared at him but did as she was bid. She walked over behind the counter, refilled the glass, exchanged a few words with the barkeep—who was apparently still angry—then brought the glass back to him.

"He said you'd better pay him," she advised. "You can give me the coins if you want."

Galaphile nodded and produced what the ale should cost, with a little more for the woman. "Thank you," he said as she turned away. "But I thought taverns liked to serve their customers."

She turned back. "Not this one. This one has *him* for a barkeep, and I got the displeasure of having to live with him."

She walked away, and Galaphile sipped at his second glass. The barkeep was watching him but made no effort to approach. The two men at the other table stayed around for a few more minutes, then got up and left. No one else came in.

Time passed, but still Galaphile made no effort to leave. Later, when the woman came by again, he called her over. "Tell me something. Do you live here?"

She rolled her eyes. "Said we were together, didn't I? So yes, this is where I live. I work here nights, helping the old man out. You want another?"

"No. How much longer do you work?"

She glanced back at the bar. "Until he decides to go to bed. Then I lock the doors and call it a day. That's how it is."

"Can I talk to you after you've closed?"

"What for? I don't have anything you want."

"Maybe you do. How long have you lived here?"

The woman snorted through her nose. "All of my life, since I was a young girl. Marriage is a prison with no keys, let me tell you."

"You know the people and places around here well?"

"Pretty well." She sounded suspicious. "What do you want, stranger? You have something specific in mind, don't you?"

Galaphile nodded. "Do you know a man who calls himself Cogline?"

The woman straightened, a clear look of recognition in her eyes. But she shook her head. "Don't know what you're talking about!" she said loudly. Then, lowering her voice, she whispered, "You're just looking for trouble, aren't you?"

Galaphile shook his head. "I'm just trying to find this man. Can you help me?"

"Perhaps. Ask me that question again when I finish up here. I'll be done shortly. Meet me out back. Outside, so we can't be heard."

She stepped away. "Nice trick, filling the glass without touching it. Wish I could learn that one! Would really help with certain customers." Her laugh was low and deep. "Now get out of here so I can convince him to close up!"

Galaphile finished the last of his beer, then rose and left. He knew he was taking a chance by trusting this woman, but he also knew that finding any sort of help would be difficult. The look in her eyes when he mentioned Cogline told him she knew something, and her willingness to talk was encouraging.

He would take help wherever he could find it.

He made his way to the back of the building and stood in its shadows for what seemed an eternity. At one point, he almost decided to move on—except he had no useful place to move on to. So he waited some more.

Sure enough, after long minutes, she appeared through the back door and walked over to him. She was wearing a coat and scarf, and she walked with anxious glances over her shoulder as if expecting to be followed.

When she reached him, she shoved him farther back into the shadows and leaned in close. "I don't have a lot of time; he'll come looking if I stay too long. So listen close and don't waste my time. Cogline lives perhaps five miles from here, but you might want to think twice about visiting him. He's strange and short-tempered, and he keeps cats. And whatever you want of him, it'd better be important. He's not tolerant of strangers."

Much like the rest of the village, it seemed. "Will he talk to me once I find him?"

"If you give him something interesting to talk about, yes. If you waste his time, no. You'd better be sure about this before you do it."

Galaphile nodded. "I'm very sure."

"Then head down the road until you see the tree arches. Pass through them and into the woods beyond. Follow the pathway until you see his house. Stand at the gates and don't try to go inside. Wait on him. He will know you are there. Got it?"

He nodded. "Thank you. I owe you a favor."

She made a dismissive sound. "You owe me nothing. Tonight's entertainment with the floating glass, and the annoyance of my insignificant other, were enough for me." She paused, then shook her head. "Wish I could go with you, but that time's passed me by long back. Goodbye and good luck."

As he was about to turn away, she grabbed his arm. "Hey now, if you get the chance, come back and tell me about what happened. Because something always happens around Cogline. It will be worth the wait to hear about it." She grinned. "And maybe you can show me another trick or two. It's boring here."

She pushed away from him, smiling, then disappeared back into the building.

Galaphile waited until the lights all went out inside, then started north into the deep woods beyond the village.

SEVEN

Galaphile followed the narrow roadway out of Welkrin Run, passing by the few huts and cottages, all of which had gone dark. His thoughts drifted from one possibility to the next as he tried to imagine what exactly he was walking toward. He knew nothing about Cogline save that he was reclusive and deeply skilled with magic, but he wished he knew more. He wished he were better prepared. Still, he'd faced greater odds than this with less preparation, and he would find a way to make things work out in his favor.

The night was deep and silent, and the walk was more than a bit forbidding. There was an old poem from somewhere in the past that Galaphile suddenly remembered—one of those odd memories that surfaced now and again. He wasn't sure how much he actually recalled or how accurately, as the poem was a relic from all the way back before the Great Wars destroyed the Old World, and he had not thought of it in a long time.

He whispered to himself the words he remembered:

These are the woods, so dark and deep
And I must walk miles before I sleep,

While all around the invisibles creep.
So many secrets do they keep!
But I can never expect to know
What they themselves refuse to show.
For I must never willingly go
Where things of darkness choose to grow.

Something about the feel of the night, the smells and tastes of the wildwood, and the padding of his feet against the earth set a cadence to the words, and suddenly he found that he remembered it all quite well. As he conjured a light and moved on, he found himself repeating the same lines over and over, almost as if he could gain comfort by doing so.

He was so caught up in this exercise that he almost walked right past the arched trees he was supposed to be looking for. They stood to the right of the path, which was now little more than a lightly traveled trail. The trees were bent by the passage of time—but also by some art, Galaphile suspected. There was a certain majesty to the way their weathered trunks bent and their moss-laden branches drooped. All were massive and grand, speaking of ages come and gone. How old were these ancient sentinels? he wondered. How many centuries had come and gone in their lifetimes?

He paused to look at them a moment longer, then pushed his way through their curtained boughs toward the darker shadows that waited beyond. He gazed about as he walked, but other than the forest there wasn't much to be seen. No night birds or animals were moving, and he heard nothing save the sighing of the wind as it blew through the trees. Another trail snaked along ahead of him, winding past the largest trunks, skirting the thicker walls of ground cover, and avoiding places where the roots twisted and turned to make footing treacherous. He walked slowly, preferring to take his time, anxious lest he mistakenly bypass the place he was seeking.

The poem from ancient times, lyrics and music both, disappeared into the inhale and exhale of his breathing and the steady beating of his heart. He kept himself focused on everything around him, all his senses fine-tuned. He did not feel any sense of entrapment or danger. Curiously, it was more a deep sense of being taken into protective arms and cradled. Whatever waited within the shadows was not there to cause him harm.

He was not sure how long or how far he walked, but something told him that this was the right path for him to be taking.

After a time, he lost all sense of anything but a driving desire to continue. Then, finally, he came to an iron fence that rose twelve or fifteen feet into the darkness. The fence was constructed of sturdy iron poles inserted into the earth and bound by crossbars. Directly before him was a solitary gate chained and locked in place. He knew instinctively that the fence was impassable until the gate was opened. He walked up to it and peered into the darkness beyond.

As if his motion had triggered it, lights came on along a pathway that wound through thick, shaggy-boughed trees to a huge castle-like structure beyond, and he extinguished his own. Save for the guiding lights, the house and its surroundings were encased in darkness. There was no sign of life, but a dwelling of this size and scope must house someone or something. Someone or something that might well be asleep, given the late hour.

Then a snuffling sound issued from directly behind him, and he whirled about defensively—and immediately wished that he hadn't.

The woman's words at the tavern came back to him.

He keeps cats.

But not the sort he had expected, for he found himself face-to-face with the biggest cat he had ever seen—one roughly the size of a warhorse and far more terrifying. Its coat was a shaggy patchwork of black and gray, and its lips were drawn back to reveal sharp teeth almost as long as Galaphile's hand. As he stared at the cat, its massive, whiskered face bent down level to his own, its lantern-yellow eyes fixed on his, its tail swishing about slowly. Galaphile took a deep breath to steady himself but remained still. What else was he supposed to do? If the cat wanted to cause him harm—shades, even if it wanted him dead!—he had very few options. He might have considered using magic, but it was just as likely that any sound or gesture would anger the beast. Then he would be undone for certain.

Don't panic!

The seconds passed—or maybe it was minutes or even longer; he couldn't tell. He stood there facing the cat as it stood facing him, and its breath on his face was rank and meaty. Eventually, he grew so nause-ated that he had to turn away. Slowly, he reversed himself until he was staring back at the castle-like dwelling once more, wondering at the insanity of turning his back on such a beast. He took deep breaths for several minutes in an effort to steady himself, aware that the cat was still back there.

And then, suddenly, he sensed that it wasn't.

Once again, he turned slowly to look, and indeed the huge beast had disappeared as swiftly and silently as it had come. He peered into the trees, searching for some trace of it, but failed to find anything. He took several long, deep breaths, exhaled them slowly, and waited.

He keeps cats indeed. Well, the woman had tried to warn him. He thought the creature might be one of the rumored moor cats that were usually found in the eastern mountains, but how had Cogline tamed such a beast?

He turned back to the iron fence . . .

And found himself face-to-face with a short, skinny man who was standing on the other side, looking back at him.

"You're trespassing!" the man snapped.

For a moment, Galaphile simply stared. To say that the man was odd was an understatement. His body was painfully thin, almost skeletal. He had a scraggy beard and long, tangled hair, and he did not seem all that old, save that his hair was white.

"Are you Cogline?" Galaphile asked.

"Might be. Might not be." The scarecrow scowled. "Who wants to know?" A pause, then his face took on a decidedly confrontational look. "Who are *you*? Why don't we start with that?"

Galaphile shook his head. "I will only speak with Cogline. If you are him, please say so. Then I will answer your questions."

"Will you now, bold fellow? A trespasser announcing your condi-tions for conversation as you stand helpless on my doorstep?"

Galaphile smiled. "I am only being cautious. What I have to say—for that matter, what I came here to do—is Cogline's business alone. Are you him?"

The scarecrow's face squinched into a knot as he glared back at Galaphile. "Would you like to spend another few minutes with Sister to discover how she feels about such insolence? I would be happy to call her back!"

"You are referring to the moor cat?"

"Of course! I guess you're not as stupid as you look."

Galaphile took a deep breath. Whatever else happened, he did not want to encounter that cat again. "I have come a long way to find you. As you are living where I was told I would find Cogline, I have to assume that you are indeed him. I was told to find you by a man named Starns, who said you could teach me what I needed to know."

Cogline stared at him wordlessly. An instant later, he felt the warmth of Sister's breath on his neck and prepared to face his end. But then the scarecrow snapped his fingers and the warm stench of the cat's breath vanished once again. There was a thump behind Galaphile, and when he glanced around, he found the big cat sprawled out five feet away, relaxed but still keeping watch, those huge lantern eyes fixed on him.

"Never mind Sister." The scarecrow shook his head in disgust. "Too much pussycat, not enough moor cat. Genetic, I imagine, but she does serve a purpose. And she can sense things about people. The fact that she didn't attack speaks well of you."

Galaphile sighed out a breath. "Then can we talk now?"

"That depends. Starns sent you, you said? Does he still think to rule the world with a few acolytes and a spattering of magical spells?"

"Starns is dead," Galaphile replied. "Along with all of his followers and more than a handful of the Gnomes who attacked them. I was with him for six years. Since I was out of the camp at the time, I was the only one who survived. And with nowhere else to go, I did what he had once told me to do and came here to find you." He paused. "So *are* you Cogline?"

"I am. And I am sorry about Starns. He was a difficult man, but he had good intentions. I wish him peace and rest." He paused, then added, "Now tell me of yourself. What exactly brings you here besides a misguided desire to follow Starns's orders? And what am I supposed to teach you?"

So Galaphile told him of his time with Starns and of the magic he had learned from the man.

"The world, as it stands, is broken," he finished. "Just predators and prey. But I want to restore it to a place of order with peace for all the Races—as it was long ago. And magic is the tool I need. I must learn the more complex and powerful forms of magic, and I need to learn from the best, which Starns said was you. So here I am, and here is where I intend to stay. I will do whatever it takes to master whatever skills you agree to teach me. I will do whatever work you ask of me in return."

The older man snorted. "And what makes you think I might want to take on a pupil in my nonexistent school of magic?"

"What can I say to convince you to try?"

The scarecrow studied him silently, then said, "Show me what you can do. Just a few things. Pick ones you are comfortable with."

Galaphile thought a moment, then began. He worked his way through various forms of magic: conjuring images that appeared to be real; levitating small items such as sticks and stones.

"Enough!" Cogline interrupted him finally. "I admit you have skills, pathetic as they are, but most of it is trifling stuff that will get you killed almost instantly should you encounter anyone with real talent."

He paused. "But . . . there is some hope. That last trick—the one where you appeared to be in different places when you were really in none of them—showed some real promise. That is a difficult magic to master, and you seem to have done it."

"Starns taught me," Galaphile said, feeling again a stab of pain at his mentor's loss. "The first time we met, he used it on a man twice his size and fooled him completely."

"Yet it wasn't enough to keep him and his people from being slaughtered, was it?" Cogline said sourly. "What's your name, young man?"

"Galaphile."

"Well, listen to me, Galaphile. You are a long way from being an adept, and I have seen skills such as yours better employed by children. Oh, you'd make a decent enough apprentice, but a full-blown mage? I think not. It would take years to make something of you—and only if you were diligent and quick to learn. And I know little of your temperament." He paused. "Really, I think you should let this business go or find another teacher."

Galaphile shook his head. "I can't. I know what I must do with my life if everything I've lost is to have any meaning, and for it I need magic. Better magic, stronger magic."

"Because you want to change the world?" Cogline scoffed. "That's a big ambition for such a young man. What makes you think you can achieve it?"

Galaphile shrugged. "Perhaps I will not, but at least I mean to try. And that's better than most folks could say!"

"If you were a mage, what would you do with your skills? How would you use them to improve the world?"

For a moment, Galaphile thought Cogline was being sarcastic, but there was a serious expression in his eyes that seemed to beg the answer.

So, then. "I would disband all the infighting camps," Galaphile said, "and show them what a world could look like when they all work together, instead of in their own best interests. I want to build a legacy of magic users and magic teachers that will bring order to the chaos. I want to set an example of what a world could look like if we all pulled together and shared knowledge for the betterment of all. I want things to make sense again, and I want all the killing to end."

Cogline nodded, and Galaphile thought he saw a trace of approval in the man's eyes. "It is good to have a purpose," Cogline said, "even if it is unattainable. But I do question if you fully understand what you are getting yourself into, asking for this level of training. Anyone would."

He paused, giving Galaphile another long, steady look. "On the other hand, I can see that your sense of commitment is strong—almost as strong as your ideals. So yes, I'm intrigued. Experiments are a large part of mastering magic, and I think you might be a worthy experiment. You can test the strength of your resolve, and I can see if I can create a savior." He chuckled. "How does that sound?"

Galaphile laughed softly and rubbed at his arms. "A little scary. But I am ready for this experiment as well."

This time, Cogline actually smiled—though the expression was a bit feral and far from reassuring. "Then let me tell you what you will be facing if I let you through these gates. You will become my servant and my student both. I will drive you and use you and teach you until I am convinced you can succeed in fulfilling your aspirations. And the moment I think you will fail, I will dismiss you. I will give you two years to learn and another two to improve what you've learned—if I'm satisfied you are making sufficient progress. Fair enough?"

Galaphile nodded. "More than fair."

"And make no mistake. What you know about magic at this point is negligible, so believe me when I say this work will be the most difficult and demanding thing you have ever done. I will not go easy on you, because I cannot. There are creatures and beings that remain out there in the wake of the Great Wars—things that are far more powerful and dangerous than I am. If you intend to face them—and you will need to if your ambitions are as big as you claim—then you must be more determined and more capable than you ever dreamed of being. One day, you will have to face such a creature, and your skills will determine if you live or if you die. Do you understand me?"

"I do," Galaphile said—although, in fact, he wasn't sure.

Cogline huffed a laugh. "Well, I doubt that you do, but someday you will."

He gestured at the gate. The lock released on its own, and the gate swung open.

"Enter, young student," he said. "Your lessons are about to begin."

EIGHT

From that day forward, Galaphile lived and breathed Cogline's teachings. And Cogline had been right when he said this would be the most difficult and demanding thing he had ever done. At times, it was so challenging that he considered giving up entirely. At others, he despaired over his apparent inability to master the nuances of the more complex magics. There were accomplishments he could look back on and take pride in, sure, but there were twice as many failures. In the end, it was only his determination and stubbornness that kept him on course.

Their lessons began comparatively simply, with a tour of Cogline's domains—wing by wing, and room by room. And perhaps this alone should have served as a harbinger of things to come, because Galaphile was instantly overwhelmed and promptly forgot half of what he had been told to remember.

A few things he retained, however. He was never to leave the grounds without permission; otherwise, he could not be guaranteed safe passage. Those areas assigned to Galaphile as his quarters were his responsibility. The others were left for the old man who prepared meals and did occasional cleaning for Cogline.

The three of them were the sole residents of the vast compound save for the two giant moor cats—Sister, the huge monster he had already encountered, and Brother, who was smaller and sleeker and impossible to detect until he was right on top of you. Apparently, he had the ability to simply disappear at will.

The compound was also a maze of magical booby traps and alarms. One wrong step and Galaphile would pay with a shock strong enough to knock him off his feet, some object hurtling at his head, or some other unpleasant deterrent. He learned about many of these the hard way. Cogline assured him he would eventually remember each trap's location and how to undo it, but the process would take time.

Cogline also showed him around the borders of the fence that surrounded the compound.

"There are any number of things that live in this forest that I do not care to have running around inside the fence," Cogline advised him at one point as they walked the grounds, indicating a huge snake curled up just outside the fence. "Such as that. Big enough to swallow both of us up. Mostly, the safeguards I've installed will protect us while we're inside the fence, but much of what we do needs to happen outside. So bear that in mind."

As if there were the slightest chance that Galaphile would do anything else.

"And these," Cogline directed a bit later, pointing toward a gathering of drooping trees that sat just outside the fence perimeter, practically touching the railings. "Do you know what those are?"

Galaphile had a good guess at what they *weren't,* because by now he was aware that almost nothing around him was exactly what it seemed. "They look like willows, but I'm guessing they aren't."

"You would be right. Those are slenderlings—a carnivorous plant that uses its branches to ensnare and strangle its victims before consuming them. They are immensely strong and very aggressive. They would have no problem reaching over the fence to grab you."

Galaphile shuddered as he suddenly noticed the drained corpse of a deer being slowly enfolded into the trunk.

"You need to understand something," Cogline continued. "These sorts of creatures all evolved out of the chaos following the Great Wars.

You know their history, I presume? Of course you do. A cataclysmic upheaval, generated by Human folly and rash behavior, that changed everything. The world we had known for over two thousand years—one of learning and education—was wiped out completely, and the population of Humans almost eradicated. New species were generated out of what little remained of the old. Books and learning were lost, and education became solely about survival. But Humans are resilient creatures, and so the world was able to continue in a drastically modified form."

He paused. "What I have built here is a preserve of a sort—a collection of both what remains and what has evolved from the Old World—so that I may continue to learn and explore. I own and control fifteen square miles of land, all kept safe from the outside world and its madness. No one is allowed within my sanctuary who is not here by invitation. And that now includes you, for as long as I allow you to stay. To remain here, you must commit yourself to my commands and my teachings. Do you think you can do that?"

"I came to do that." Galaphile's response was firm. "What am I to do?"

"First, you are simply to listen. We are surrounded by enemies—some intentional, some unaware of the threat they pose to us. You must learn how to deal with these threats—how to meet and destabilize them, how to turn potential enemies into committed friends. But first you are to learn the uses of magic. How to recognize it, how to master it, how best to make use of it, and most of all how to know *when* best to make use of it. This will take perseverance. It will take patience and a willingness to sacrifice in every way you might think possible. It will require time."

A raised finger kept Galaphile silent. "It will be demanding work, but it will demonstrate if you are worth my time and trouble. Either you will go on or you will be dismissed. The choice will be solely mine. Am I understood?"

His young listener nodded.

"From what you have revealed of yourself, it is apparent that your intentions revolve around finding ways to better civilize and tame the baser instincts of your fellows—Human and otherwise. It is a tall order and, from my point of view, a seemingly impossible task. But I admire your convictions and your courage in undertaking it.

"To survive in this world as it presently stands, you will be required to master destructive powers equal to those of the very ones you seek to change for the better, just to survive their efforts to eliminate you. So as training, know that every time you leave these grounds, something will be waiting to feed on you. Some of them are creatures that evolved, and some are of my own making, but most are products of the war that nearly destroyed us all. It has taken me years to cultivate my surroundings in a way that allows for all of them to coexist. I chose this site for my home because it is well beyond normal communities and well away from the larger populations. It is considered by most to be a wilderness. Practically the only safe place to travel when you step outside my gates is on the roadway leading from here to Welkrin Run, and I have laid protections leading into the village. Step off that roadway, however, and you instantly become prey."

They walked on for a bit. "Do you see those dark patches of grass over there?" He indicated several masses of thick smudgy ground cover that looked lush and full despite being colored an almost vapid gray. "Those are sinkholes. You can't tell from looking at them, but if you step into one of those, you will be swallowed up so quickly, you won't even have time to call for help. There are a few types of mixtures you can wear on your shoes when you go out into the wilds that the plants can't tolerate. Carry those, and the sinkholes will let you pass. Come, there is much more for you to see."

And so it went, for the entire course of the first month. Every day, Cogline continued teaching him about the various dangers that lurked outside the fence. After that—as Galaphile grew more familiar with what was out there—came lessons in disarming or nullifying these threats, rather than simply recognizing and avoiding them.

Cogline also insisted that if Galaphile was to be a unifying force in the Four Lands, he would need to learn the languages of the various Races he would be helping to unite, so anytime he was not studying magic, he was immersing himself in the speech of Trolls and Dwarves and Gnomes, until some days he no longer knew which tongue he was speaking.

And so the first six months passed.

At times, he thought his education would forever revolve around languages and learning how to live safely in this region that Cogline himself had helped to make so dangerous. He wondered how the man had successfully come to recognize—and survive—so many deadly creatures. Surely, based solely on odds, one of them should have bested him by now. He likewise wondered how much of what he was encountering existed out in the larger world and why it seemed so concentrated here.

"Everything in my compound was harvested or caught for the purpose of bringing it here. This is my world, the place where I study all things natural and the ways they function. I teach here, as well, so this is my own private training ground for students such as yourself—although I do not teach as much as I did when I was younger. Still, what you learn has to do with survival and understanding all the new things that the cataclysm has created. The new world is full of new forms of life, and you must learn how to deal with all of them. Our best advantage as magicians will always lie in knowing more than our adversaries do. That said, while nature is wicked in very lethal ways, we humanoids—all shapes and kinds—are worse. So in addition, this is my effort at preserving a world that should not be destroyed."

Galaphile laughed in spite of himself. "Well, it seems plenty wicked enough from what I've seen. I expect I'll be lucky if something doesn't get me at some point."

Cogline clapped him on his shoulder. "Not lucky, my young friend. Prepared."

It went on this way for weeks and months, until Galaphile lost all track of time. But the more he learned, the more likely he was to survive the dangers he would eventually encounter—as repeatedly proved to be true once his practices became intensely real and increasingly dangerous.

His first test occurred nine months into his time with Cogline, when he was sent out into the field with no weapons or armor save for his wits and magic. Unarmed and unprotected, he was to cross a deep ravine in an unfamiliar part of the forest, and from there advance into a stretch of deep woods and rugged brush. He was to conduct a survey of every actual or potential danger he encountered and write down the name and location of each one on a sheet of paper that was overlaid with a topographical map. He was to use magic if he felt threatened or in any danger, and the choice of which magical defense to employ was at his discretion. He was to remain afield for an entire afternoon and return at dusk of the same day.

Though he would not go alone on his first time out.

Sister would accompany him. Just in case.

Galaphile was more than a little intimidated by this assignment. He had a working knowledge of possible dangers but no sure way of telling where they might be found or how many ways they might be able to hide themselves. Worse, he was under the supervision of the giant moor cat without any real knowledge of how to communicate with her. Still, he had little choice save to proceed.

He crossed the ravine using grappling hooks and ropes, as a descent into the darkness below was just asking for trouble. He rappelled over quickly enough, although not as smoothly and easily as the moor cat did. Sister simply made the twenty-foot leap from one side to the other lazily, as if jumping a puddle. Which only served to remind Galaphile of the intimidating size of his companion.

Once across the ravine, he began to navigate through the jungle, using the map to chart his way. At first, it was easy enough. He was able to identify the slenderlings and a passel of treacherous sinkholes. He found various mushrooms, grasses, and clumps of flint weed that were obviously poisonous and took careful notes on their location. He spied a nest of vipers and a hanging limb that served as a resting place for several three-eyed bats.

At one point about an hour into his journey, he encountered a bushy wasp nest—home base for a large number of furry wasps that were not overtly predatory but were highly protective of their Queen and her consorts. Their sting, he knew, was poisonous and could kill a Human. The nest sat directly across a small clearing that was warded on both sides by copious numbers of wormholes and snake pits. There was no way around them.

So, for the first time, Galaphile used magic to solve his dilemma, levitating himself over the obstacles to the far side of the nest and safely beyond the dangers that protected it.

By the time he landed, Sister was waiting for him, her bright, knowing eyes narrowed, though whether with congratulations or disapproval, he couldn't tell. And he found himself wondering just how she had made the crossing.

He supposed he would never know.

On he went, deeper into the jungle and farther away from the edge of the ravine.

He took note of a den of prensors—lethal hunters with huge claws and the wickedly sharp bills that gave them their name. He encountered krands, a form of long-legged insect so sensitive to air currents that they could sting you to death in seconds if you so much as breathed in their direction, forcing him to create a tunnel in the air so that any movements from his passage would be contained. Just to be safe, he also made himself invisible to their sight and slipped past with soundless steps.

His most humiliating moment came when he encountered a patch of bare earth sitting right in the middle of a ring of trees, broad and open and empty of life. He had never seen anything like this before, and it stopped him in his tracks. Was something buried there? Sister stopped behind him, showing no interest at all in the patch but gazing at Galaphile as if to see what he would do. Galaphile studied the dirt for a few minutes, detected nothing, and decided he would test it with the toe of his boot. He got to within a few inches of the path before Sister snatched him by the seat of his pants and hauled him backward. Then, while Galaphile stood there stunned, the moor cat picked up a fallen branch, carried it over, and used her huge jaws to fling it out onto the empty ground.

Instantly, the patch erupted. Dozens of sharp, narrow prongs exploded upward, penetrating the branch and tearing it to pieces. As the prongs withdrew, Galaphile realized they were roots that had snaked their way underground from one of the nearby trees or plants, in search of something to feed on. Which had almost been his leg. It wasn't his presence that would have alerted them; it was the weight of his passing.

He looked back at Sister, expressed his thanks, then made a few new notes for his records—writing: *Escaped by the seat of my pants*—before finding a new path and moving on.

Afternoon was lengthening, and night was coming on. He was nearing the end of his journey and needed to get back across the ravine while it was still light enough to see where he was going, so he increased his speed. Sister ambled along behind him, never in a hurry. But he supposed that when you were as big as she was and each step covered three times what one of Galaphile's did, staying close wasn't a problem. He was tired by now, and his concentration was less intense than it had been earlier.

He was no more than five hundred feet from the ravine and already thinking ahead to dinner and sleep when things got really strange. Directly ahead of him, a light flashed out of the shadows and began to grow larger. It stopped him where he was, and when he glanced back at Sister for reassurance, he found that she had stopped as well. The moor cat didn't look especially concerned, but Galaphile was uneasy nevertheless.

Then the light flashed so brightly that he was momentarily blinded and had to look away to allow his vision to clear. When it did, he found himself staring at a small, wizened figure dressed in dark robes with a hood that hid any features in shadows. Then the figure's head lifted slightly, and a bit of lingering daylight revealed his face clearly. The small fellow was no more than three feet tall; long white hair stuck out from beneath the hood in every direction, giving him the appearance of a disgruntled porcupine. He had a small, sharp beard capping his chin, a nose that resembled a potato, and a truly fearsome scowl.

"Halt right there!" the fellow commanded in a voice that seemed far deeper than his stature commanded. "State your business!"

Galaphile stared. Who in the world was this?

"State your *own* business!" he snapped back, suddenly irritated.

"Ah, ah, ah," scolded the little man. "I asked you first. You must answer me before I will answer you. Besides, I live here! This is my residence, not yours. Now state your business!"

Galaphile shrugged. There was nothing to be gained by prolonging this argument. "My name is Galaphile, and I am here at the request of Cogline, who owns the land inside the fence. I am in the process of doing a survey. Can you tell me about yourself?"

"I don't know that I should," the little man countered. "You should never give away information about yourself to strangers, and the fact that you have done so suggests you are poorly informed about the ways of the larger world. What if I were an enemy of some sort?"

"Well, what if you were? How does knowing my name and my business assist you?"

"I am asking the questions here! You are at best a visitor, come for reasons that are unclear to me. Or you are perhaps a trespasser. How am I to know if you have anything at all to do with Cogline?"

Galaphile almost smiled. "Because I have Cogline's cat with me?"

"What cat?" the man demanded sharply, and Galaphile turned. With a sinking feeling, he noticed that Sister was no longer behind him.

Turning back, he tried once more. "Then my word isn't enough?"

"Your word is of dubious value, given how blithely you are parading about these sacred grounds as if you owned them. Why should I let you go any farther?"

"What do you intend to do then? Keep me here all night? Make a prisoner of me? Wouldn't it be better to simply let me pass so that I can remove myself from your presence altogether? Otherwise, you trap us both for no good reason. I ask again, what is your name?"

"You know my name. You just don't want to admit it."

It was getting dark fast by now, and Galaphile did not want to be caught out here when he couldn't be sure of his way. And he wondered where the moor cat had gotten to.

"Sister!" he hissed into the darkness, hoping she would show herself. But she didn't.

He wheeled back to face the little man—who was no longer quite so little. All of a sudden, he had grown from three feet to six and had gained correspondingly in weight, making his fierce expression more intimidating than ever.

"Not so confident now, are you?" the big man demanded.

Galaphile held his ground, but it took more than a little courage. He knew nothing of this fellow. He barely knew anything of the land he was passing through—only what Cogline had told him. This person in front of him might be anyone or anything at all. Sister, his protector, was gone. How much danger was he actually in?

Too much—and he knew it.

"You should turn around and go back the way you came," the man announced. "You had no business coming here in the first place, and you certainly have no business going any farther! Turn back! Go on—

now!" His hands made a threatening motion. "Go back the way you came and don't ever come back here again without my permission."

Galaphile took a deep breath and exhaled slowly. *Calm yourself,* he thought. *Figure this out.*

"I wish you would tell me your name and your place in this forest. Can't we figure out some solution to this matter?"

The other man was now close to eight feet tall, grown suddenly huge, and he looked more intimidating than ever. Galaphile was without weapons or means of protection save magic, but what would work against this fellow? Sister was gone—or at least she appeared to be. But Galaphile knew his future with Cogline depended on passing this part of the test.

His opponent laughed softly. "Perhaps you already know the answer to your question," he whispered, his voice now soft and persuasive. "Perhaps you always did."

The words caught Galaphile by surprise. He puzzled over them, trying to get a sense of what this creature was attempting. For a second, neither spoke, each staring fixedly at the other.

"You should ask yourself this," the other continued, and Galaphile was shocked when he began to shrink back down to his original size. His face turned old and weathered again. "What are you doing out here? What is it that you think you will find?"

Galaphile thought it through. What sort of answer did the other expect? "Perhaps I don't know yet. Perhaps I am here to find out the answer," he replied. He hesitated. "Perhaps I am here to find out something about myself. Perhaps I already have and am now ready to cross that ravine and leave you to your peace."

"Nothing more? You want nothing more?"

Galaphile shook his head. "I don't think so."

The little man smiled. "Perhaps you are more astute than you look. Your words suggest you have learned something, after all."

Then, abruptly, as if there was nothing further that needed saying, he disappeared completely.

Galaphile stood where he was for what felt like endless minutes, but the little man did not reappear. Confused and more than a bit shaken, he set out once again, working his way toward the ravine, then casting his grappling hook and rope to gain a secure hold and rappelling back over to the other side. Within a handful of minutes, he had arrived at Cogline's mansion, where he found the man sitting in his favorite rocker on the covered porch, holding a pipe comfortably in one hand while the other scratched Sister's head.

Without a word, Galaphile produced his map and various discoveries and handed them over. Cogline took the papers without bothering to examine them and gave Galaphile a look. "Did everything go as you expected?"

Galaphile started to nod, then shrugged instead. "Mostly. At the end, though, there was this little man who stopped me and demanded to know what I was doing. Then he became a much bigger man. I gave him my name and purpose, but he would not tell me his. When I asked, he said that I already knew it. Then he disappeared."

"What did he say to you right before he vanished?"

Galaphile hesitated. Cogline's questions suggested that he already knew or at least suspected the answers. "He asked me if I knew what I was doing out here. And did I believe there was something I would find. I told him I was here to discover that."

Cogline paused, then nodded once more. "Perhaps he was asking you if you really knew what your purpose was in coming here. Essentially, asking you if you had discovered what it is you were seeking. And not just in the moment but also in the larger sense of simply being out here at all."

He paused again, letting Galaphile ponder. The young man nodded slowly, suddenly realizing the truth. "That was you, wasn't it? Asking me those questions?"

Cogline nodded. "And do you have the answers to give?"

"I don't know. I don't think so. Not yet. Not entirely."

Cogline studied him a moment. "It is wise of you to realize that. One day, you will. I ask you to remember to be open to the answer when it finally comes."

They sat together quietly after that, staring out at the night, each one lost in his separate thoughts, and neither of them said anything more.

NINE

At the end of two years, Galaphile's skills had improved immeasurably. He was actively studying at least four languages and navigating huge swaths of the forest successfully, so Cogline announced that he had decided to keep the young man on as his apprentice for a further two years. In fact, he even told Galaphile that he could genuinely see him achieving the status of mage. Not necessarily inside the two years but not so far down the road, either.

Granted, Galaphile's mentor was still difficult to work with and highly demanding, but Galaphile found the work both challenging and fulfilling, which he knew impressed his teacher. Cogline was not the sort to bestow praise, but he seemed genuinely pleased with Galaphile's commitment to his craft and ability to learn its more difficult aspects.

Galaphile was grateful for the chances he was being offered but at the same time wary of the demands that lay ahead. There were already many times when he simply couldn't do what was needed quickly enough. Speed and dexterity were crucial in handling magic, and sometimes his reflexes were not up to the task. As well, when confronted by any potential danger, he was expected to be able to identify it, determine the steps required to manage the situation, and execute them quickly. Most of what he encountered was new and confusing, but for Cogline, this was no excuse.

"Much of what you are likely to encounter in life, young Galaphile, will be new to you, and your thinking must be nimble and your actions quick. In every case, you must use your education, instincts, and reasoning to overcome your ignorance. All too often, you are going to be the only one available to address a problem, and creatures of dark magic are horrific and unforgiving. They will have no problem deciding to kill you as swiftly as look at you, so your resolve must be no less. In many ways, you must become as swift and sure as the most lethal predator."

Galaphile understood what he was being told and was willing to embrace the danger. He had known from the first that taking up magic was not a casual undertaking, and that by doing so, he would be constantly at risk both from his own ignorance and from those who saw him as a threat. Worse still, he understood that while he was embracing his craft willingly, many of the dark and dangerous creatures he would be facing had been born to this way of life. It was one thing to acquire knowledge of the ways of dark magic; it was another altogether to have grown up with it.

He had grown used to the forest beasts—but these were, Cogline assured him, the least of his problems. There were darker and more dangerous creatures out there, lurking in places even Cogline had not fully explored.

In contrast, mastering new languages was so straightforward and direct that it became almost a form of relaxation, and his fluency grew by leaps and bounds.

Two more years passed, and Galaphile became more and more confident in his abilities, as well as fluent in every language Cogline had determined that he must learn. At the end of four years, Cogline told him that his training had come to an end; the time had come for him to take his knowledge and skills out into the wider world.

"You have done well here, my boy," Cogline told him, "and you are now at the limits of what I can teach you. But you are certainly *not* at the limits of what you still can learn. Your isolation here has been necessary for your training, but it has left you severely ignorant of the ways of the wider world. So if you are serious about making the Four Lands a better place, then the time has come for you to put words into action."

Galaphile didn't need to be asked twice. He had been waiting for an opportunity like this but had been hesitant to press. "Where am I going?"

Cogline broke into a huge grin. "Well, I am glad to see you so eager to find out. As it happens, you're going back to where you came from, or relatively close. Northeast, to the city of Whip's End, which lies in the northern foothills below the high end of the Dragon's Teeth fronting the Streleheim Plains. It's a small city, but its people are probably the most independent bunch in the region. Many belong to rival gangs that I am sure will feel familiar, given the time you've spent with Starns. Mostly, the gangs fight with one another, but of late, one man has risen to immense power and is threatening the whole city—including a friend of mine. I want him stopped."

Galaphile nodded. "Is there magic at play?"

"Honestly, I am not sure exactly what's in play; that will be for you to determine. The man you are helping is Varisol. He's a Dwarf and a doughty warrior currently masquerading as an innkeeper. He might be small, but he is also brave, so trust him before any other. Do you think you can manage this?"

Galaphile nodded, confident that after four years with Cogline, he was more than ready to face whatever was waiting for him in Whip's End.

He slept restlessly that night, eager to be on the move—to be actively bettering the lives of innocent citizens of the Four Lands using all the lessons he had been taught. And his first task would likely be locating Whip's End from Cogline's admittedly rather sketchy directions. Moreover, he knew nothing at all about this fellow Varisol that he was supposed to be helping, from what Cogline had told him. He had been isolated in Cogline's compound for four years now, and no doubt the world beyond Cogline's fences had changed considerably. Galaphile knew his mentor kept abreast of goings-on in the Four Lands through magical devices he called Spanner Eyes, which he had designed, constructed, and installed himself—though Galaphile knew little more.

Cogline had never showed him how they worked or let him use the network.

When dawn arrived, Galaphile bade his mentor farewell, promising to be smart and careful and to heed everything Cogline had taught him. This was his first time away from the compound since his arrival, and there would be no Cogline, no friendly moor cats, and no familiar surroundings to back him up.

"Remember this," the older man told him as they parted. "Where you go and what you do is up to you. You must carry out the task I have given you, but afterward, let fate guide you and follow your instincts. Most of what I can teach you, I have. Now it is up to both of us to see how you use it."

And so Galaphile departed, bringing an oddly unsentimental end to the past four years of his life.

It took him a little under a month to reach the city of Whip's End. The weather was warm and calm throughout his journey, the skies clear and bright, and he saw almost no one on the journey save for a wagon train of perhaps a hundred members moving south of the swamp country toward the burgeoning city of Kern along the banks of the Mermidon River. When he paused to speak with the members of the caravan, he learned that many of those dissatisfied with life in the wilder, less civilized parts of the Four Lands were starting to congregate along rivers, where viable trade routes could be established, leading to better, more independent lives.

Galaphile thought about this after the wagon train had vanished from sight. He knew many people did seek improvement in their lives, and he was impressed by the lengths they would go to to make that happen. He also found himself thinking how he might go about quelling the lawlessness in the parts of the country that had already fallen under the sway of outlaws and ruffians. An army could be useful, but where would you find men and women willing to risk themselves in service to such a monumental effort at peacekeeping? How would you persuade them to do what was needed? How would you convince them that risking their lives was worth the effort?

As for locating the city of Whip's End, he did so mostly by chance.

Knowing he was searching for an area of high population density, he started looking for light along the horizon each night as he reached the far end of the Streleheim, and on the twenty-third day just after sunset, he was rewarded with lights flaring to life and burnishing the horizon against the backdrop of the Dragon's Teeth.

He walked the remainder of the way in the next day, and gradually the surrounding countryside became denser—first revealing a few camps, then cultivated areas of houses and fields. By midday, he had found a road, and soon he was walking along it in a growing flow of traffic, finally reaching the city proper in the company of dozens of other men and women as the sun set. Around him, crowds surged from doorway to doorway along streets that were clogged with taverns, gambling dens, pleasure houses, smoke shops, and food stalls.

After years with only Cogline and his solitary servant for company, it was disorienting to say the least. There was a wild, unhinged energy to the streets, and more than one fistfight and a few knife skirmishes broke out around him as he walked.

It was a diverse population, he noticed, with everything from Humans to Elves and Dwarves and even a few Trolls and Gnomes in residence. And despite Cogline's word about the troubles brewing in the city, this gave him some hope that the various Races *could* someday coexist in relative peace.

That is, if they ceased their drunken fighting.

He navigated the winding streets, reading the signs that hung from the eaves and posts, wondering how to find one man in all this chaos. Cogline had told him that Varisol owned a tavern called the Short Shot, but Whip's End was far bigger than the one-street town in which he had been raised and the tavern could have been anywhere. Once or twice, he was approached by those sensing a stranger and looking to take some advantage, but once they got a closer look at Galaphile, they quickly backed away. Over the years, he had grown lean and hard with muscle, and he carried himself with assurance that few cared to cross. Which helped protect him from those who might use him, but hindered him in another way, for many of those he tried to ask for directions just skittered away nervously.

By now, Galaphile had traversed half the city and still hadn't seen any sign of the tavern or found anyone who would talk to him that seemed to know of it. He could go on as he was, but that hardly seemed efficient. Eventually, he drew to a halt at an intersection that split in all directions toward dozens of bars and taverns. He paused, looking again for someone to consult.

Then he noticed a young girl, maybe thirteen years of age, standing off to one side, staring boldly across at him. She gave him a moment to stare back, then walked over with a confident smile that made her seem far older than her apparent years.

"You seem lost," she said. "Are you? Can I help you?"

Seeing her even closer, he wondered again how old she was. She was a tiny thing, but her features, her cocky smile, and the confident way she carried herself seemed far from childish. Her face was pretty in an Elven sort of way, framed by long reddish-blond hair. Her brilliantly coral eyes held a sparkling cynicism that made her seem older than her apparent years.

He smiled back, making a quick decision. "Do you know how to find a tavern called Short Shot? I've been told it's worth a visit."

"You have, have you?" She laughed. "By whom, I wonder. The Short Shot's a decent enough place, but it's hardly a tourist destination."

Galaphile found himself grinning back at her, amused by her blunt candor. "In truth, I'm looking for its owner: a man named Varisol. Do you know him?"

"I do." She surveyed him once more. "I can take you to him, but it will cost you a couple of coins."

Galaphile nodded his agreement, and with another laugh and toss of her head, she turned her back and walked away, calling, "Come on, then," over her shoulder.

After a moment's hesitation, he followed as she wove confidently through the crowd, her rose-gold hair a beacon. A few minutes later, she waved an arm and he saw the sign for the Short Shot ahead.

He reached into his pocket and pulled out three gold coins. Definitely more than the favor merited, but he wanted to do something to help her. For some reason, she reminded him of Mayele. He didn't know why. Physically and age-wise, they looked very different. They even walked differently. But there was . . . something.

"Take these coins and go back to wherever you came from. You're too young to be guiding strangers on the streets. Go anywhere you want, but don't stay here."

She abruptly broke out laughing. "Too young? Stranger, I think you just took a big step in the wrong direction."

"But I . . ." Galaphile suddenly found himself at a loss for words.

She took the coins, then smiled and patted his hand. "I'm going to try very hard to think the best of you in spite of your apparent lack of common sense. I'd do what I could to enlighten you, but it might take longer than I've got. Just wait out here and try not to wander off."

He thought to stop her, but she was too quick and vanished into the tavern in the wink of an eye. He watched her go, wishing he had handled what had just happened better. Even so, he waited where he was, undecided about whether she was gone for good or not.

When long minutes had passed and she hadn't returned, he became impatient enough that he simply walked up to the tavern doors and went inside. The large room was crowded and noisy and filled with clouds of smoke and the smell of alcohol. There were the usual tables scattered about, all occupied, and a standing-room-only bar. Someone was playing an old piano near the back of the room.

Feeling the unfamiliar press of bodies around him, Galaphile was reminded of how long it had been since he had been inside a place like this. In truth, he had not much missed it.

He moved to the bar and caught the eye of a server. The man walked over. "Something to drink?"

"No. I'm looking for the owner of this tavern: a man named Varisol. Is he here?"

The bartender—burly and fit—gave him a look. "Your lucky day. Or not, depending. There he is."

He nodded to the back of the room, where a Dwarf built something like a tree stump—with a craggy face, a bushy head, and a belt full of knives—was stalking toward him. The bartender chuckled to himself and moved away. Galaphile stood where he was until the Dwarf was standing in front of him. Though he barely came to Galaphile's chest, he nevertheless gave the appearance of being his equal. They stared at each other for a moment or two and then, to Galaphile's shock, the girl who had escorted him here emerged from behind Varisol. Her impish face bore a look of undisguised pleasure as she smiled up at him.

"What did you say to my daughter, stranger?" the Dwarf demanded. One gnarled fist rose up, curled tightly about the handle of a knife.

Daughter? For a second, Galaphile was speechless. Then he asked, "Are you Varisol?"

The man threatening him frowned. "I am."

"Fair enough," Galaphile declared. "My name is Galaphile Joss. Cogline sent me to find you, said you needed my help. I asked this young girl for directions, and she said it would cost me. She looked in need, so I gave her three gold coins. Now it seems she might have played me for a fool."

The girl was laughing. "Really, you should see your face!"

Varisol straightened and eased the girl out from behind him to where he could face her straight-on. "I warned you about this unbearable habit you've developed of interfering with my business—and defrauding strangers! Go to your room until I send for you. Now!"

Pouting, but managing a sly wink for Galaphile, she scurried off the way she had come and didn't glance back.

"She is . . . quite bold," Galaphile observed.

"Hmmmph," Varisol grunted. "Probably the lack of a mother's good influence. Now, let's sit and talk, you and me. Figure out why Cogline thought you could help."

TEN

Varisol led Galaphile away from the bar and back through the crowd to a doorway that opened into a small office containing an elderly desk with a chair behind and two in front, a few wall hangings of scenery, and a mostly empty bookcase. The Dwarf motioned for Galaphile to take one of the seats in front as he walked around the desk to the chair in back. Galaphile noticed, as Varisol seated himself, that the level of his chair had been adjusted so that he was positioned to face any visitors sitting across from him at the same height.

They had no sooner seated themselves than the door opened once more and one of the serving girls placed glassfuls of ale in front of them, then departed. The Dwarf picked up his glass and hoisted it in Galaphile's direction. "Your good health."

"And yours," Galaphile replied, lifting his own to clink against his host's. He glanced at the closed door. "That girl out there—she's your daughter?"

"Adopted, in case you were wondering. All two stone and a few ounces of trouble. A handful. She pretty much does what she pleases. She came around looking for work after her parents died and proved she could do it, so I took her in. Smart and plenty able, she is. But head-strong, too."

"Full of spirit?"

The Dwarf laughed, his voice deep and resonant. "Full of something anyway. Her name's Nirianne. Now tell me of Cogline. How is he these days? It's been almost six years since I saw him in person. Even as re-clusive as he is, he gets out and about every now and then. How do you come to know him? He usually wants nothing to do with anyone."

Galaphile launched into a shortened version of his history, conclud-ing with how he had spent almost the whole of the last four years learn-ing the fundamentals of advanced magic from Cogline.

"As my first act after my formal training ended," Galaphile finished, "he dispatched me here to stop a man who is changing the power bal-ance in the city and causing you problems."

The Dwarf snorted. "Typical, sending me aid without a word of notice. He is a man of few words, Cogline, but a good judge of char-acter and possessed of impressive capabilities despite that. If he's sent you, then he believes you up to the task. But you do look rather young. You've done this sort of thing before?"

Galaphile shook his head. "Practically, no. But as I said, a gang leader, Starns, took me in after my parents died, much as you did for Nirianne, so I have some experience with gang rivalries." Though it had been four years, he still felt a flash of pain every time he thought of Starns, Mayele, and all his adopted family lying dead within the camp. "He was my first real teacher—the one who got me started with magic. He was the one that sent me on to Cogline. They both thought me promising enough, I guess."

The Dwarf regarded him silently, and it was clear that he was taking Galaphile's measure. "I've heard of Starns, by the way. A determined and resourceful man. But he got caught up by his enemies and cut into pieces, they say."

"Yes. I was out of the camp when it happened." Again, Starns's trun-cated, hanged body rose up before him, followed by Mayele's limp corpse. He shuddered. "I got back too late to save him or any of the others, so I went to learn what I could from Cogline and stop that from happening to anyone else. Eventually, I hope to bring some peace and order to the Four Lands. There's not much of either left in this world, not this side of the Elven nation. And I want to do what I can to change that."

Varisol smiled. "That's a big undertaking, my friend."

Galaphile shrugged. "Perhaps. But maybe I'm making a start of things here in Whip's End. What can you tell me about whatever it is that's causing all the trouble? Is magic somehow involved?"

"Well, as to that . . . Let me tell you the story and you can judge for yourself."

Varisol took a long drink of ale and leaned back in his chair. "I lived in the deep Eastland for many years. I drifted over here when the city was still young and growing fast, working as hired muscle for a number of different outfits. Then I found this tavern and decided to buy it with the money I had saved up. I fixed it up, opened the doors, and started my business. By that point, I had a few friends and worked hard to make more. I've always liked people and saw the opportunity to be something other than a fighter for hire. I now own three taverns and a few other businesses, though this will always be my favorite.

"In truth, I thought I deserved the success that I had found. I worked hard and played fair. I didn't lie or cheat or steal. If someone was in trouble and needed help, I gave what help I could. If someone was wronged, I did my best to help see justice done. Do things the right way for others, and others will do things the right way for you—or at least that was my belief. It still is, to a degree, but the world has gotten meaner and harder of late.

"Still, even in a place as rough as this one, things worked the way I expected for a long time. Then Hydrach appeared. He was a gambler of sorts—a small man with large ambitions. He made a name for himself in various gambling and other shady circuits. He was annoying but not trouble at first."

The bitterness he felt was evident in his tone of voice.

"Then Hydrach showed up one day with this creature he called a Ruhle. This . . . this thing he found or made or conjured or whatever was a huge, silent, empty shell that followed him around like a dog. It was immensely strong, and he used it to silence those who challenged his judgments—because, unlike me, he *did* lie and cheat and steal. Many tried to kill this monster, but nothing worked. The Ruhle just smashed them like kindling. It protected Hydrach as if that was its personal mission in life.

"The complexion of the city changed after that. Hydrach began to take control of everything. I'm already in deep to him myself, and I'm not the only one. No one is safe from this man and his creature, and if things keep going the way they have been, he will own the whole city inside a year. I thought someone would put an end to either him or this monster he's found, but no one can find a way to do it. Even experienced assassins and trained killers have failed. No weapon can reach Hydrach; it's like he's had a wall built around him. And anyway, the Ruhle makes short work of anyone who tries. Come after it and it tears you to pieces. Even the biggest and strongest go down in seconds. Weapons don't seem able to even touch it. It comes and goes on Hydrach's command. When it's done its killing, it disappears."

"Do you think Hydrach is using some sort of magic to protect himself?"

Varisol grunted in affirmation. "I don't know what else it could be. And again, that monster is always with him, ready to dispatch anything that approaches. It is an uncanny sort of alliance."

"Or something like it," Galaphile mused. "When you say you are in deep with him, what do you mean?"

"I was one of the first Hydrach came after. He told me he was my new partner. From now on, fifty percent of the profits I was making in any of my businesses would be his. I told him no, of course. Foolishly. He brought the Ruhle into my taverns and left a handful of my workers dead. I began paying him what he wanted after that—I had to. Been doing so ever since."

Galaphile studied him a moment. "Does Nirianne know?"

"I don't think so. I hope not, anyway, or she might go after him herself. But no one seems to be able to stop him—unless Cogline is right about you."

Galaphile thought about it a moment, then picked up his glass of ale and drained it. "Where can I find Hydrach?"

"You won't have to," Varisol sneered. "He'll come to you. He'll be here tonight around midnight to collect his weekly *rent,* as he calls it."

"Then maybe I can have a bath and a meal first. Is that possible?"

Varisol looked at him askance. "Are you sure this is all you want? Nothing more?" He frowned. "Do you know something about this that might help us?"

Galaphile shrugged. "I might . . . but I have to see this man first. If I'm right, however, we might be able to take care of this problem right away."

Varisol took Galaphile to a room with a private bath and told him to make himself at home. Galaphile did so, happy to clean off the dust and grime of his long journey, then re-dressed in his least filthy outfit. When he was finished, he returned to the tavern's central room, ordered food and drink, and consumed his meal while mulling over what Varisol had told him. He thought he understood what method Hydrach was employing to make him so invincible, and while it was reasonably impressive, it was not quite as impervious as the man probably thought. Magic was a great tool if the user was the only one present, but when another adept arrived, the greater mage usually triumphed. Galaphile hoped that would be the case here, as he was almost certain *he* was the better mage. He also hoped—rather fervently—that he wasn't mistaken in what magics he thought were being employed. If he was, tonight could have a very different and rather unpleasant ending.

He stayed where he was for several hours as the clock ticked toward midnight and the tavern's closing time. Varisol came over once to talk to him, and Galaphile warned him away.

"I don't want Hydrach to know that there is any connection between us. So don't look at me—or do anything that indicates you know me—once he arrives. Just let me handle this by myself."

Varisol gave him a look, shrugged, and walked away.

Of Nirianne, there was no sign. Whether she was confined to her room or had chosen to absent herself on her own, Galaphile couldn't tell, but he was just as happy to have her gone. The last thing he needed was to worry about her interfering in his plans for Hydrach and maybe getting herself injured or killed. He thought several times of warning Varisol that it would be best if she stayed away, but he assumed the man had already done so and let the matter be.

Still, this would be Galaphile's first real test out in the world, where there were innocent bystanders to worry about and not just the threat itself. It would have been foolish for him to deny that he was nervous, but he worked hard at maintaining a calm demeanor. He felt ready for this confrontation; he felt sure he understood what he was up against. Still, this was the kind of situation where, if you were even a little bit wrong, you could end up more than a little bit dead.

He took heart from the fact that Cogline clearly believed him capable of handling whatever would be thrown at him tonight. His mentor wouldn't have sent him off like this, on his own, if he didn't. And now he would find out how thorough his education had been.

It was a little before midnight when Hydrach appeared. Sitting alone at his table in a room that was now nearly empty of customers, Galaphile looked up as the man entered and knew who he was instantly. Hydrach pushed through the doors as if he owned the place and walked over to Varisol, who was standing at the bar. He was wearing garish clothing that would make him stand out in any crowd, yet he showed no signs of discomfort or caution. Rather, his behavior suggested that he felt in complete command of the situation.

Hydrach called out his greetings with a clear indication that, while they were addressed to one man, they were intended to be heard by the entire establishment. "Varisol, my old friend, come share a drink with me!"

Without appearing to do so, Galaphile watched closely.

Hydrach clasped an arm about the Dwarf and gave him what was clearly an unwelcome hug. "Here we are, two businessmen working hard to make this little community a more wholesome and industrious place! Let's celebrate the successes of our joint venture."

Slipping away from the intrusive arm, Varisol signaled the barkeep for glasses of ale. As he did, Hydrach gave the room a quick visual sweep, taking in the few faces that remained as the closing hour neared, in a disinterested sort of way. But Galaphile knew better. This was a man who sized things up in advance to avoid being caught unprepared. Bending to his drink and feigning his own disinterest, Galaphile waited patiently for the right moment, noting that Hydrach was fingering a strange amulet secured on a chain about his neck.

He smiled faintly in response. His suspicions were confirmed.

Facing each other, Hydrach and Varisol spoke in lowered voices so as not to be overheard by anyone else in the room, but Galaphile had developed the ability to enhance his hearing, and so he heard it all.

"Time for my payment," Hydrach said—though less a request and more a demand. "Do you have my coins?"

"I do, but again there are fewer than there were last week. Business continues to be down. People are holding on to their earnings more tightly."

Hydrach shrugged. "You're not the only one to have told me this lately, which is why I have decided to change my terms. If profits are down, then you pay the same as you did at . . . say, the end of last month, regardless of your take. If profits are up, we're fifty–fifty again."

Varisol lost his temper. "You crook! You have no right to change your terms midstream."

Hydrach smirked. "Don't I? My companion might deem it otherwise. He doesn't like it when people speak badly of me. Makes him angry."

Again, Galaphile noted Hydrach fingering his amulet.

"If your companion decides to kill me," Varisol spat, "then you lose everything! If I am dead, there is no one left to pay you."

"Oh, if something happened to you, I would become owner by default. I mean, who do you think will challenge my claim? Your daughter, Varisol?"

Even from his short acquaintance with Nirianne, Galaphile knew that was exactly what would happen. Besides, he had heard and seen enough. Hydrach was every bit the scum that Varisol had painted him, and Galaphile knew his suspicions were correct—both about Hydrach's magic and about the nature of his companion.

With a surreptitious gesture, he quietly cast a glamour over his appearance, aging himself by about six decades—whitening his hair and wrinkling his face, shrinking his body until he looked small and unassuming. He rose from his table and walked up to the bar. "Gentlemen, gentlemen, please calm yourselves!"

His voice, too, was rendered a tad frailer and softer than normal. Both men stared at him.

"Stay out of this!" Varisol warned, clearly not recognizing him.

Hydrach said nothing, but surprise and caution appeared in his hard eyes. Yet again, his fingers stole up to stroke the amulet.

Galaphile smiled.

"I seek only to keep the peace in my favorite place of refuge," he said. "How can I help resolve this conflict between you? If it is money at stake, I will pay that myself."

Hydrach scowled. "This is none of your business, old man."

Galaphile reached inside his cloak and pulled out a handful of gold coins. "Would these do?"

The other man's eyes were fixed on the coins, calculating the odds of an additional payout. By now, Galaphile was sure he knew how the man's magic worked and held himself ready to engage with his own.

But maybe Galaphile's acting skills weren't as solid as he had hoped, or perhaps the extra payday came across as odd, because Hydrach suddenly seemed to grow suspicious. In a flash, he gripped the amulet with one hand and slashed at the air in front of Galaphile with the other. As if Hydrach had opened a rift in reality, the Ruhle exploded into being: a monster at least eight feet tall, muscular beyond anything Galaphile had ever encountered in Cogline's woods. It wasn't a Human or any other recognizable species. Its face was a smudged mismatch of features, and it began to survey the three men it stood among, seeking its victim.

Only Galaphile never gave it the chance. He was already in motion as the creature appeared, because he recognized the truth. Hydrach and his creature were not companions; they were master and servant. The creature was held in thrall by the magic emanating from the amulet.

Darting around the still-materializing Ruhle, he reached out, seized hold of the amulet, and snapped it loose from its chain with the aid of a few simple words of magic. The moment the chain parted, the magic it contained was his.

"Take your revenge," Galaphile told the creature, gesturing at Hydrach, and the monster turned on its former master instantly with hatred in its eyes. Both arms swept out, took hold of the suddenly helpless Hydrach, and drew him in. Hydrach screamed—but it was too late. The Ruhle's mighty arms encircled the mage and crushed him, pulping his fragile body to blood and bone in mere seconds, consigning him to the fate he had designated for so many others.

"Shades!" Varisol gasped, leaping backward from the sudden spray of blood and flesh.

The Ruhle stood where it was for a few moments more, staring down at the remains of its former master. Then it turned to Galaphile, its new master, with a grudging resentment, awaiting further orders.

Galaphile met its seething gaze. "Leave this place and never return. As recompense, I will destroy this amulet so you are never summoned again."

The creature nodded its amorphous head and vanished. Galaphile used his own magic to crush the amulet into powder.

In the resultant silence, Galaphile resumed his former appearance and glanced around. The tavern had emptied, the last customer fled into the night. Even the barkeep had gone missing. Galaphile walked over to Varisol and placed a steadying hand on his shoulder.

"His power over the spirit creature was centered in the amulet. That alone had always been enough to secure his command. As for himself, he was guarded against weapons and danger but not against the loss of his talisman. He made two critical mistakes. First, he forgot to protect himself against any countermagic—and particularly against anything seeking to take the amulet from him. And second, he forgot to ward himself against his own creation, taking his command over it for granted. Plus, he was arrogant enough to think an old man couldn't cause him any harm."

"Well, I'm glad you figured it out!" Varisol exclaimed in horror. "I don't ever want to see anything like that again!"

Galaphile smiled, squeezing his shoulder. "With any luck, you won't have to."

A back room door crashed open and Nirianne came charging into the taproom. "What's going on here? I heard a scream."

She rushed over to her father and Galaphile but almost slipped on what remained of Hydrach, catching her balance just in time to keep from going down. She drew up quickly, her face scrunching in disgust as she glanced down at the floor.

"Ick! What is all this gunk?"

Her father huffed out a strangled laugh and shook his head. "I think you should be the one to explain," he said with a look at his companion.

But for once, Galaphile was completely at a loss for words.

ELEVEN

L ater that night, in the aftermath of Hydrach's death and the Ruhle's banishment, Galaphile dreamed.

The dream was deep and complicated but felt real enough that he would wonder afterward how much of it was a dream and how much a vision. He was worn and tired and elated and excited all at once when he took to his bed, the events of the evening already feeling impossibly distant. He was unsure of his plans for the morrow, or where to travel next. Cogline had told him to let fate guide him and to follow his instincts, but he had no instincts for what came next.

The dream changed that, for he could not ignore the importance of what he was being shown—even in his sleep.

He walked through gardens of such brilliant colors and wondrous smells that it seemed he had passed into another life entirely. He wondered if perhaps he had crossed into another world or even walked in the future world that he would help create. He was at peace and at the same time besieged by a mix of wonder and anticipation. Was this real? Was this happening now, or was it yet to come? Was this some part of his future he was being shown so that he could prepare himself? All seemed possible, and yet he could not identify which was truth and which only fiction.

He traveled the gardens visually at first, his sight taking in one amazing setting after another. Then he began to walk. There was an undeniable magic that drew him ever deeper and farther along the path onto which he had somehow wandered. There was an abundance of life here. Birds of all sorts flitted past—many species he had never seen and all vibrant, be it with colors or feathers or song. Animals darted or slunk about him, all as varied as the birds and some as unfamiliar.

Time passed as he traveled, but he had no real sense of how much. He felt no urgency, no desire to move any faster than he was. Revelations were everywhere, and he drank it all in. He wanted to be here so badly that even in the process of witnessing all the many wonders, he found himself worrying about how dull and colorless the real world would feel once he was forced to return.

Come to me, Galaphile. Come to me.

The voice spoke unexpectedly and at the same time in the softest of tones. It did not frighten him; it only encouraged and somehow promised things that he could not begin to imagine.

As he followed the voice, the gardens melded into a forest of soft firs and whispering pines, and the world about him changed again. Now the garden blended seamlessly into the woods, flowers and trees coexisting in a way that he would never have found in his own world. He wondered at this but at the same time felt it welcoming and real. His steps and his pathway were clear and inviting, and not once did he question what was being done to him. He belonged in this world, he told himself. He had been brought here for a reason. Be it a vision, dream, or simply his imagination, he belonged.

You do belong, Galaphile, *the voice assured him.* **This world is the beginning of a new life, and the promise of a new future. Come to me.**

And he did so without question. He pushed ahead with determination and a greater sense of purpose. He could feel himself nearing a destination—not one he knew about or would even recognize, but one to which he was meant to go.

The profusion of colors and scents increased as the forest deepened and the world changed yet again. He noticed the visual changes first, the ways in which the colors intensified and altered from what he would have expected. The trees took on more varied and brighter hues of green, and there seemed to be new colors everywhere. The leaves became more spot-

ted and striped; their veins ran clearer and wider. Purples, pinks, and shades of blue mingled among the greens, and the overall look was both lush and vibrant.

Everything was larger and more fully developed in its growth and the richness of its look. Even the skies were unfamiliar in their beauty, the clouds more a pastel rainbow than mere white, their shapes fluffier and more fully realized. The sun was not in evidence, and yet the world was filled with light. He was somewhere besides the world he knew but at the same time not in a place that was totally unfamiliar to him. He simply couldn't trace the source of his knowledge.

Then the voice spoke to him one final time.

Come to me in the Gardens of Life. Come to me at the Silver River. The Past will bring you into the Future.

Then the world of his dreams and all it contained vanished, and he slept.

His sleep was long and deep, but when he woke it was still nighttime and stars were visible when he walked to the window. Thinking back on all he had dreamed, he felt a clear sense of relief. He did not think he needed to worry about his future any longer, or about what to do next. The dream had assured him in no uncertain terms that it would come to him—if he went to the Gardens of Life and the Silver River, wherever that was.

He returned to his bed and lay thinking about all he had been shown. Eventually, he drifted off to sleep once more, and when he woke the next time, the sun was rising, the skies were bright, and his new path lay before him. Clearly, there was something else waiting to happen, somewhere else he was meant to go, someone new who would help him find his way. Everything he had dreamed last night was a promise of things to come, though he also sensed it would challenge him in ways he had never dreamed, and that his success was not guaranteed. But simply knowing his next steps was sufficient for now.

Energized, he rose to face the new day, anxious to see what surprises it held.

He bathed and dressed in the clothes he had washed out last night, wondering again about the Silver River and the Gardens of Life.

Wherever and whatever they turned out to be.

He was still pondering this question when he walked out into the tavern proper and found it empty save for Nirianne.

"I'm glad you washed," Nirianne observed with an arched eyebrow. "You were rather covered over in blood the last time I saw you." She was sitting at a table at the front of the room, eating breakfast rolls and scrambled eggs and drinking some sort of gnarly-looking liquid. "Come sit with me," she invited.

He did so, looking enviously at the food and suspiciously at the drink. She rose abruptly, departed the room, and returned a few moments later with a similar plate and cup for him. "Here, this is your breakfast," she said. "Eat up. Later, you can tell me what in the world you have been doing to make you such a magnet for trouble."

Galaphile tucked into the food gratefully, though he still eyed the drink askance.

"Do you know how old I am?" Nirianne asked as he ate.

He would have guessed from her size and her youthful appearance that she was maybe twelve or thirteen, but he was not about to test *those* waters. Judiciously, he said, "You speak and act like someone who is clearly older than she looks. But you're obviously not yet twenty."

She gave him the arched eyebrow once more. "No, I am sixteen. It's an awful age. Too young to be an adult, and too old to be a child. I know my father loves me, but even he thinks I am just passing time until he finds me a mate or a partner. But I don't want that. Do you?"

He thought momentarily of Mayele, then quickly shook his head. "I don't." It was too painful the first time around; he would not risk that again.

"We're a good match, then, you and me, and I think we should begin our friendship anew. And in token of that . . ." She plonked three gold coins down beside him and grinned at his look of confusion. "Father's right; I should stop conning his customers. So, once you're done eating, would you like me to escort you through this miserable community of thieves and cutthroats and show you a few places of interest?"

Somehow, he noticed, despite all of her talking, she had also managed to efficiently tuck away her breakfast.

Truthfully, a tour wasn't a bad suggestion. Maybe she or someone they met would be able to tell him more about these Gardens of Life or the Silver River. And if not . . . her company was at least diverting. He found himself intrigued that anyone so young could be so forthcoming and astute. Maybe she wasn't just the flighty troublemaker everyone assumed her to be.

As he finished his breakfast, she told him that her father was sleeping soundly for the first time in weeks.

"Whatever that fellow you killed was into him for, he seems glad to be free of it. And by the way, don't forget your drink. I made it for you specially," she added with a sly twinkle.

Galaphile gazed down into the sludgy cup dubiously but was not about to let her challenge go unanswered. So he raised it to his lips and drank it down in a few big gulps, to her obvious amusement. And then he blinked, because the drink was really quite good—no matter how unpleasant its appearance.

"Well, that was . . . enjoyable," he said, after finishing it.

She laughed. "It sounds as if you forgot the word *surprisingly*," she countered with a toss of her hair.

"You might be right," he conceded. "Shall we go?"

Her smile was genuine. "Indeed."

They departed the tavern and set out on their walk. Nirianne led the way with an obvious assurance that told Galaphile she knew exactly where she was going. She walked him the length and breadth of the neighborhood, identifying every business or activity they passed. At this early hour, not much of anything was happening and most of the businesses were still closed. She took their measure anyway, offering a judgment on each person or place, revealing that her knowledge of her hometown was both extensive and full.

He was more shocked when he realized she knew every business that had been extorted by Hydrach and how much each was in for. All of Varisol's efforts to keep her ignorant seemed to have been in vain.

When he commented on this, she added, "I was trying to figure out what to do about Hydrach without getting myself killed in the process, but I hadn't worked out any solutions yet. It's a good thing you showed up when you did. Oh, and don't tell my father that I know. He's rather proud of how well he's kept it from me, and I'd hate to disappoint him."

Galaphile laughed and agreed and let her continue to lead him, not really doing much more than enjoying the new day and her company. She was going to be a formidable woman when she grew up, and he almost pitied the men who were sure to fall under her spell.

Once the various businesses started to open, Nirianne took him into what was billed on a self-aggrandizing sign as a HALL OF FAMOUS EVENTS but turned out to be a very small and not very interesting collection of local tidbits. That is, *not very interesting* until they encountered the caretaker—an elderly man who had lived in the community since childhood and was eager to share a seemingly endless collection of tales. He held Galaphile engrossed for more than an hour, then suggested they visit the cemetery. But once they were outside in the streets again, Nirianne proposed that they take in a gambling hall called the Round Table instead, which given her propensity for the unexpected should have come as no surprise.

"I doubt there is a thing in the community that you don't know," he observed archly. "Not that it's any of my business, but I'm surprised your father lets you run around so freely."

She laughed again. He was becoming accustomed to the sound—bright and carefree and knowing. "Oh, he doesn't. He's very strict with me. He's just busy with his tavern business—and, until you changed things, preoccupied with Hydrach—so he isn't aware of a lot of what I do. And what's the old saying? Better not to know than to find out the hard way."

Galaphile wasn't sure that was any kind of saying at all, but he shrugged and nodded anyway. With Nirianne, there wasn't much else to do.

They reached the Round Table, and Nirianne led him inside. Minders stood at the doorway but paid no attention to her beyond a friendly wave. They took a hard look at Galaphile, however, and asked him to relinquish his weapons if he wanted to go inside. He sighed and complied, suspecting Nirianne was far from unarmed herself.

The interior of the gaming hall consisted of three massive chambers filled with tables and players. There were games of all sorts to wager upon, not to mention food and drink. As they walked, any number of people hailed Nirianne, and she was quick to return their greetings with her own. She even introduced Galaphile to a few of her favorite dealers and players.

"That man over there?" she said, indicating an ordinary-looking man inspecting a hand of cards. "He's the only one at the table I recognize. The others must be strangers and likely don't know him. If they did, they would run for the hills. Astroll has a remarkable memory; there's never been a run of cards he couldn't master. It's how he makes his living."

She pointed next at a collection of men and women at a dartboard. "That thin, sort of aged-looking man—that's Winkler. Never loses. Or almost never. I've never seen it happen anyway. He's a machine."

They wandered on. "Hey, want to see an arm-wrestling contest? They hold those in the back. I've heard there's someone here now who can beat almost anyone. Let's go see!"

He followed her bobbing head wordlessly, not particularly excited about arm wrestling but content to let her lead. Everything she had showed him so far had been worth seeing. They entered the back room, and Nirianne led him along one wall toward the rear of the chamber, where half a dozen tables were open to contestants. You signed up for table one and waited your turn. If you won at that table, you moved on to the next. If you were the last one standing, you won the grand prize, which was one hundred gold coins.

There were signs of considerable excitement at the lead table, so Nirianne maneuvered them over. Two men were locked in combat, seated across from each other with elbows resting on the tabletop, hands joined, bodies rigid, and all their considerable strength being brought to bear as each man sought to force the other's hand down. These men were stripped to their waists, their bodies running with sweat, their muscles taut and straining from their efforts.

Galaphile gave them a glance, then gave the surrounding crowd a closer look as well. The intense interest and raucous encouragement of those gathered made him smile in spite of himself. That anyone would be so engaged in such a silly show of strength seemed odd.

"Look, the big man is overpowering the smaller one," Nirianne crowed.

She sounded impossibly excited by this, and Galaphile took a closer look to see what was happening. Sure enough, the bigger of the two was forcing his opponent to give way. The cheers and shouts of encouragement were wild and unrestrained—loud enough to make it seem as if the entire building were shaking on its foundation. Feet were stamping and hands clapping as the audience crowded as close as the guide ropes allowed. Both men's heads were bent low, almost resting against the tabletop as they struggled for domination, their focus entirely on the match. Galaphile waited for the smaller man to regroup and take back the advantage he was losing, but he seemed drained. It was odd, he thought suddenly, to think of either of these men as being the bigger or smaller. Both were enormous, their huge bodies ridged with muscle and damp with sweat.

But in the next instant, the man losing seemed to gather himself once more, pushing through his weariness and stopping the descent of his arm. The bigger man tried everything, but the smaller one held firm, his arm locked in place.

Then slowly, carefully, he began to push the other man's arm back the way it had come, back toward the center point and then farther on into his opponent's territory. His counterattack was relentless, and the other combatant couldn't seem to stop it.

Seconds later, the battle was over, the smaller man pinning the other's hand fast against the tabletop. Cheers went up from the crowd. Apparently, the winner of this bout had just won the championship pot.

The pair unlocked their hands, shook briefly, and rose. Someone threw them towels, and others passed over glasses of ale. After toweling off and taking a long swig of his beer, the winner turned to the observers and raised his arms victoriously, eyes scanning the crowd . . .

Until they came to rest on Galaphile and suddenly froze.

The shock that went through Galaphile was likewise potent. He knew this man—and had believed him dead for the last four years, lost in the massacre with Starns and the rest.

The man gave him a dark scowl, which instantly changed to a grin. "Galaphile Joss, as I live and breathe!"

It was Ratcher.

TWELVE

A fter the congratulatory crowd had dispersed, Ratcher led Galaphile to a small table in the main part of the building, and they sat. Nirianne, Galaphile noticed, had faded into the background, knowing enough to leave the two men by themselves to talk. Once they were finished, he would find her and finish out the day however she wished. But uncovering the mystery of Ratcher's fate was too intriguing to leave for later.

After food and drink had been provided, the two stared at each other in awkward silence for a moment.

"I thought you were dead," Galaphile said at last. He wondered at the same time why he wasn't—which immediately generated a few possibilities he didn't want to think about. Had Ratcher betrayed Starns?

"I thought the same about you," Ratcher growled, hunching his huge shoulders as if preparing for a fight. Though still grizzled and bulky, he looked worn as well. "I was certain of it."

"I thought you were still in the camp when it was destroyed."

"Funny, I thought the same about you. I'd been gone for a week; I was out east to survey some folks who said they wanted to join up. We

all had quite an unpleasant shock when we returned, so I ended up settling them here instead."

Galaphile grunted. "And I was off hunting down south, but just for
the morning. Everyone was dead when I returned. All of them. Even
Starns, and I thought nothing could kill him."

"And that girl you were so fond of, too? Mayele?"

He nodded. "Killed like the others. How did it happen? Do you know?"

The other man shrugged. "I don't know much about any of it. By
the time I got back, everyone looked to be several days' dead. I didn't
see your corpse, but I thought maybe they'd taken some prisoners with
them when they were finished."

The two exchanged brief glances, each still clearly remembering the
sight of the slaughter they had returned to find. He could tell by the horror in Ratcher's eyes that his tale was genuine. Whatever had happened
to Starns's camp, it had not been at Ratcher's hands.

Galaphile exhaled sharply, breaking the silence. "We were lucky.
Very lucky."

Suddenly, the big man seized his hand and held it fast. "Lucky don't
begin to describe it. *Blessed* might be more the truth." He clung hard for
a moment, then released Galaphile's hand. "I must say, it's good to see
you safe and well, youngster."

"You, too. So have you been in Whip's End the whole time?"

"Naw. Been here, there, and all abouts. Marking time to no good
purpose, looking for something to do. When I saw the notices about
the arm-wrestling matches, I decided I could use the money. I've always
been more brawn than brains anyway."

"I saw your last match. Looked like the man had you there for a
minute."

Ratcher laughed—a big booming bark. "The man was tougher than
I thought. He did come near to taking me indeed. Then I got angry at
the idea of losing, and that was that. So what have you been up to since
the camp fell?"

"More training—although in magic this time. You know that Starns
had been teaching me . . ."

Ratcher barked another laugh. "His best student ever, he said."

"Well, Starns told me to find a certain man if I wanted to learn
more—and it turns out I did. I studied with him for four years, then

when my training was over, he sent me here to deal with a man who was starting to cause problems for people in this city."

Ratcher cocked his head. "Let me guess. Hydrach?"

Galaphile nodded slowly, and Ratcher grinned.

"So that was you last night over at the Short Shot? Word's been spreading all over the city about that confrontation. Rumor has it you played a bit of a trick on the man, and his pet monster tore him apart—not that anyone's mourning him, mind you. Seems like he had half the city over a barrel. Well, you always were a clever lad, even as a squirt."

He laughed again, and Galaphile laughed with him. "Yep, look at us. Brains and brawn. So now that you've won all those coins, what will you do with yourself?"

Ratcher shrugged. "Go somewhere else. Find something else to do to make some more money. I don't have much of anything to do otherwise. Nowhere to go, no family or close friends." A broad grin. "Just a big open country for me to explore. I've seen a fair piece of it already, so why not see some more?"

Galaphile stared at him a moment, then suddenly remembered the words from his dream: *Come to me at the Silver River. Come to the Gardens of Life.* He took a chance. "Do you know anything about the Silver River? Anything about the country?"

The big man nodded. "I spent some time fishing and exploring there when I was younger, before Starns. Pretty land, and the Rainbow Lake is something else. Why? Are you thinking about going there?"

"It's more like I've been summoned. It's complicated. The problem is, I have no clear idea of how to get there. So maybe you could guide me? Maybe for some more of that fishing and exploring?"

Ratcher grinned. "Why not? Now that I've lined my pockets a bit, I've got nothing better to do until I need money again. And it would be good to spend time with an old friend. We can hike there in about three weeks." He shrugged. "We can leave whenever you want."

"Would tomorrow be too soon?" Galaphile asked, suddenly eager to get on with this next chapter.

"Tomorrow it is. I must say, I don't love the idea of hanging about here when everyone knows how much gold I have in my pockets, and this way I'll have a mage to protect me—and it!"

So it was agreed—and Galaphile even put a spell on Ratcher's winnings that would warn him if anyone tried to steal the coins in the interim.

They talked some more and then parted, agreeing to meet up at the Short Shot in the morning.

When Ratcher had departed, Nirianne materialized as if by magic—making him wonder how closely she had been observing, after all. Together, they continued on to the cemetery for a look at tombstones and vaults. He half listened to her tales about those who occupied them, but his mind was elsewhere, consumed by his expectations for the journey ahead—and some suspicions about his teacher. Cogline had urged him to follow his instincts. Had the mage already known of this summoning? Or even arranged it? Could he see into the future in some way, or was this merely a coincidence?

When Galaphile returned to the tavern and parted from Nirianne, he went to his room and packed his gear. Over dinner with Varisol and Nirianne, he told them he was leaving on the morrow.

"We'll miss you," Varisol said. "And I won't forget what I owe you. You are welcome here at any time, as my personal guest."

Galaphile thanked him; he would miss the crusty Dwarf as well.

"Where are you headed?" Nirianne asked.

He decided to keep the true destination to himself. "Off to the south, on a little vacation with my old friend."

"The arm wrestler you met earlier?"

"The same. We are old comrades. I thought he was dead, killed in an attack four years ago. Turns out he thought the same about me. Anyway, we decided to spend a bit more time together, do some hunting and fishing, maybe catch up on our lives. We set out in the morning."

He couldn't help noticing the way Nirianne seemed to go deep inside herself for the rest of the meal after that. Her usual chatter and eagerness faded as she retreated into her private thoughts and consumed her food with barely another word. She seemed disappointed in him somehow, but he couldn't determine why.

So maybe he was not entirely surprised when she knocked on his door later that evening.

Before he could say anything at all, she was through the doorway and standing before him, hands on hips, expression firm and determined, eyes fiery with resolve.

"Take me with you," she said.

Short and to the point. He met her gaze with no small measure of confusion and disbelief.

"I told you, it's a vacation with an old friend," he replied.

"No, it's not. You're looking for something called the Silver River— a place you've been summoned to."

That confirmed his suspicions about how closely she had been watching him. No wonder she knew everyone's business in town.

"I am strong and capable," she announced as he continued to stare at her. "I can manage well enough on my own here, but I want more to my life than just scuffing around in Whip's End. My father's content with remaining here and owning his tavern, and he wants me to be happy with the same, taking over the business from him eventually. But I want more than that. I am *destined* for more than that; I can feel it. Something that means more to me. Something that will help other people."

It was so much an echo of his own thoughts that he started. "Like what?"

"I don't know. But I know I can find it. And part of that means getting out of Whip's End."

"I don't think your father would approve."

"Possibly not. But he hasn't approved of a lot of things I've done. And if I had listened to him whenever he told me not to do something, I never would have learned anything. I'm not saying that everything I did turned out the way I expected or that I have no regrets. But if you want to grow up, you have to strike out on your own at some point. I've done that here as much as I can, and now I need to experience the wider world. So again, I'm asking you to take me with you."

"I don't think that's a good idea."

"Why? Do you think me too weak to keep up with you? Do you think me too young and foolish to handle it if something unexpected happens? Well, I'm not. I'm skilled and smart and ready. I want you to teach me the way you were taught. Not as a magician, maybe; more about how life works. About how to live. And like I said, you might need me."

Clearly, she would not be dissuaded, and he was already beginning to consider the possibility of doing what she asked. But there was one big issue at stake that she wasn't fully considering.

"What I am about to undertake," he said, "could be genuinely dangerous. I don't know this for sure, but the risk is there. I believe you think you are ready for this—and possibly you are—but I have to consider how it would impact your father if anything happened to you. He would be devastated, and he would hold me responsible. As he should if I failed to protect you from the dangers I suspect are waiting. You are sixteen years old—too young for this. It is bad enough that I am risking myself. I cannot risk you as well."

She scowled. "There is always risk from the unknown. But we both know how to take care of ourselves. You know your own skills, but you don't know mine. I have them; I am trained to defend and protect myself. And while my father might not like the idea of my going, he would understand the reasons for it. He would understand my decision."

"Your courage is beyond question, and maybe your skills would indeed see you through. But this is my quest, which makes me responsible for whatever happens. There is magic involved in what I do, Nirianne. I don't know the extent of the danger, but I do know who will be held responsible if anything bad happens. I can't find a way to justify it. I couldn't live with myself if I were to let something happen to you."

"And yet you risk your arm-wrestling friend."

"Ratcher is a grown man," he countered. "And one who is serving solely as a guide. When I reach my destination, rest assured that I will be going on alone."

She seemed to consider his words in the silence that followed, to work them through in her own mind. She nodded slowly. "I guess I see what you mean. You think me too young to make the decision for myself, and you don't care to make it for me. My father would see things the same way as you. This is not to say that I agree with such thinking; it seems to me I am old enough to make the decision for myself. But I can't force you to agree."

"No, you can't. Not this time."

"Then will you come back when it's done, this journey and whatever might happen on it?"

"That much I can promise. Once it is over and done with, I will come back and tell you all about it. I swear."

"Tell me this, then," she pushed on. "How old do I have to be before I can make the decision to come on my own?"

He smiled. She was persistent. "In truth, I would argue that the decision isn't yours to make in the first place. It's mine, just as the quest is mine. And if I don't think it is a good idea—which I do not—then there is nothing more to say about it."

She considered him a moment longer, then shrugged. "It was worth asking. I see your point; I just think you are wrong. But I'll say goodbye now. I hope you come back safe."

Then she stalked out of his room and was gone.

Galaphile slept uneasily that night, and not for as long as he would have liked. He found himself appreciating Nirianne's grit and determination, her desire for more than what Whip's End could offer. In truth, he admired her. But risking her life in whatever this next step might bring troubled him.

That said, Starns had taken him in at the age of fourteen. And what would his life have been like, stuck in Parrish Rahn, if Starns had refused to take him on the grounds that he was too young? Nirianne was already two years older than he had been when Starns had changed his life.

He sighed. No, he had made his decision, and he was not about to rethink it.

He washed and dressed and went out into a morning still young and dark and cool to find Ratcher already waiting. Rain clouds were building on the northern horizon, with a promise of a damp day ahead. In the moments before they took off, he paused to look back at the silent tavern. Nirianne was nowhere to be seen, and he thought that best. If she were there, she would likely try to change his mind once more, and he wasn't sure he would be able to hold firm.

Turning his back on the Short Shot, he and Ratcher set out, traversing the streets and alleyways of the city, traveling south until they were once more in the countryside, then continuing south around the western edge of the Dragon's Teeth. The sun, when it rose, lay dim behind the slowly gathering clouds that threatened rain.

By midmorning, it was pouring. Both men had donned rain gear, which gave them some protection but not nearly enough to keep them dry. The rain came quick and fast, strong with the scents of the countryside and with a biting wind. They bent their heads and plowed on, one foot after the other, talking now and then but mostly intent on battling the weather.

The morning dragged on, damp and windy and rough with scattered debris, and it wasn't until midday that the weather started to ease back into the tolerable range. They passed a cart or two on the road, and a handful of other walkers and one horseman, but each simply settled for a wave of greeting and passed on. It was the kind of day when conversation was not required.

By nightfall, the rain had eased, and they found a relatively dry overhang under which to spend the night.

The following morning dawned dry and comfortable with moderate temperatures beneath a partly clouded sky. They continued south around the Dragon's Teeth, heading for the Kennon Pass. This was new territory for Galaphile, so Ratcher chose their route. Fortunately, they were mostly alone on their journey, and whatever brigands or raiders traveled these lands chose to leave them be—likely due to Ratcher's size. Game was evident in abundance, and the big man used his bow and arrow to take down a wandering deer, providing them with dinner for the next few nights.

They talked a bit as they traveled, exchanging reminiscences about the camp and some of their adventures in the past two years, though Galaphile found himself at a bit of a disadvantage here. Not that he didn't have stories; they were just too outrageous to be believed.

Once or twice, Galaphile had a sense of something tracking them, but on looking back—and once even backtracking for several hundred yards—he found nothing. Still, he didn't like the sensation and continued to be watchful, although no apparent danger threatened.

As the day waned, they again made camp. But just after dinner, when the campfire had burned down, the sun had set, and the night creatures were starting to wake, a high-pitched, mournful howl rose out of the dark. It was so heart-wrenchingly terrible, so filled with the promise of death, that Galaphile and Ratcher both jumped to their feet, weapons drawn.

For endless moments, both stood alert, waiting for something to happen. But nothing emerged from the darkness.

"Shades and shadows, what *was* that?" Ratcher hissed.

Galaphile had no answer, and he wasn't sure he wanted to find out. Before he could answer Ratcher's question, however, the cry sounded anew—more terrible than before and decidedly closer—causing him to shudder all the way down to his toes.

"What sort of animal sounds like *that*?" Galaphile whispered back.

They stood where they were for a long time afterward, searching the darkness but finding nothing. The night was a black curtain, the sky clouded and wholly dark.

Then a rustle sounded from off to one side and both wheeled to face it. It seemed the whole world had gone silent in the wake of the howling.

A solitary form stepped out of the darkness, staring at them. "Chilling, aren't they? When wolverns howl, they freeze your blood right down to your toenails. You didn't know about them? Haven't heard of them before? Is this new country to you? Could you use some help? I possess a few skills that might be useful, and I don't eat much. You might be better off—safer, even—if you were to take me along."

The two men stared in disbelief. Nirianne stood before them, cradling a shell in her hands. A slight twinkle poked through her earnestness as she offered them a big smile.

"Wolverns?" Ratcher questioned.

A shrug. "It's what I call them. My choice of a name. After all, I made them up."

She sat down before what remained of the fire and set the shell aside. "Got any food left? I ran out this morning."

"You invented . . ." Galaphile stuttered. "Wait, that was you? You made that howling sound?"

She nodded. "I figured out how to do it a few years ago. You need a shell like this one and some practice, then you can do it, too. Scares any other predators away quite well. See?" She lifted the shell and put it to her lips.

"That's fine; you don't need to do it again!" Ratcher cried.

Nirianne set the shell back down, looking disappointed. "So, food? I'll need to be strong and fit if I'm to keep up with you tomorrow. Who knows what else might be lurking out here?"

Galaphile started to say what could have been any number of things in reply, then chose to say nothing. Whatever he uttered, the result was almost certainly going to be the same. Like it or not, Nirianne seemed determined to stay.

THIRTEEN

Despite or perhaps because of Nirianne's "wolverns," they spent an uneventful night. Morning arrived in a blaze of shimmering sunlight, the skies a clear and brilliant azure. You couldn't always rely on mornings to deliver what they seemed to promise, but on a day like this, Galaphile was willing to hope.

After a light breakfast, the trio set off again. They were a curious bunch, Galaphile thought, any way you cared to examine it. A wizard, some hired muscle . . . and a girl who, though sixteen, still looked closer to twelve.

Ratcher was clearly dubious about adding Nirianne to their company, but Galaphile was all too aware that there was little he could do. Nirianne had taken matters into her own hands, and there was clearly no shaking her now. Still, Ratcher went silent and stayed that way for almost the rest of the day—which the girl took as an indication that she should carry the conversation. So she did—at length. She talked about anything and everything, and while she did know quite a bit about the world for a girl of her age who had never traveled, Galaphile was certain that much of what she claimed was invented.

Nevertheless, there was something calming in her cheerful demeanor, which demanded little and gave much.

As the days rolled on, they traversed the Kennon Pass and from there headed east along the shores of the Mermidon River. And somewhat over two weeks after they had first set out, they reached the place where the Mermidon diverged, the northern channel continuing east into Dwarf country while the lower branch wound southward to empty into Rainbow Lake.

Both rivers flowed wide and full at this junction, making an easy crossing unlikely, but Ratcher knew of a more reliable ford farther east, where a ferry ran across the Mermidon, so east they continued. Another two days saw them across the river, and four days later, they had reached the shores of Rainbow Lake, and the wonders of the skies that perpetually showered its vast waters with brilliant bands of watery colors.

They continued to follow the shoreline of the lake east and then south, crossing the waters of the Silver River four days later. From there, it was only half-a-day's walk to their destination, Ratcher advised.

But Galaphile was somewhat dismayed by Ratcher's announcement that they were going to have to pass through at least portions of the Mist Marsh to find what they were looking for. The prospect gave even Nirianne pause. Both had heard the stories of what happened to those who went into the marsh unprepared.

"People disappear in those swamps all the time," Galaphile said as they approached the place where they would enter.

"Exactly! They just go in and never come out," Nirianne added. "Poof! Gone as if they never existed."

"That won't happen while I'm around," Ratcher said. "I grew up near here. I know my way around. I've traveled these places more than once over the years. Never seen anything like this Gardens of Life you're looking for myself, but rumor has it there is a path to it through the marsh. If it's there, I'll find it. You can put your trust in me."

Galaphile and Nirianne exchanged a doubtful look but followed him in anyway. The day was nice, the weather good, and the swamps not particularly frightening to look at. Besides, Ratcher assured them, they probably only needed to skirt a portion of the morass. They'd be in and out in a few hours. Before sunset, they would be clear. Hardly enough to even worry about.

He actually said those exact words, which caused the other two to exchange a second, more doubtful look.

Nonetheless—as Galaphile had told Nirianne earlier—he knew the time had come to continue on this road alone. He tried to convince his companions to turn back, but in this Ratcher proved as stubborn as Nirianne, and to Galaphile's dismay, they both insisted on accompanying him into the marsh. So all he could do was what he had to in a place this dangerous—watching every step, keeping a wary eye on their surroundings, and staying as unobtrusive as possible.

While the swamps looked benign at the outset, they quickly grew much worse. The scraggly trees and creeping vines closed about them, locking a canopy so densely above their heads that they could barely see the sky, and the reek of the stagnant water and rotting vegetation began to clog their nostrils.

As the hours passed and the evening approached, the sounds of hunting birds began to rise out of the constant hum and buzz of the insects. Shadows filled the clear spaces above the branches, and the flap and whoosh of fliers was everywhere at once. From some distance off, they heard the screams of moor cats and the cries of lesser predators. Sometimes, chunks of brush burst apart as other creatures—most the prey that the hunters sought—raced for safety.

The sun began to sink more quickly, the skies thickened with clouds, and the entire swamp was soon enveloped by trailers of mist. There was an eerie look to their surroundings now—more unstable, more surreal. It felt as if the whole landscape were constantly shifting; what was there one minute was gone the next, vanished as completely as if it had never existed. None of the three talked; they simply made their way as best they could with Ratcher leading, Nirianne following, and Galaphile bringing up the rear.

The latter thought more than once about summoning magic that might help light their way through the thickening fog, but that light might attract predators as well. Best, likely, to stay hidden.

He trudged along at the tail end of the trio, doing his best to make sense of what he saw or sensed around him, working hard at keeping himself calm and focused. But there were increasingly large numbers of shadows moving all around him—sometimes so close, it seemed he could reach out and touch them—though none came from anything he could identify. However, Ratcher seemed unconcerned, and Galaphile tried to persuade himself that if his companion wasn't worried, then he shouldn't be, either.

They were a good six hours into their march when the rains began, so heavy that the droplets felt like sleet. The three had to walk with their heads bent and their hands raised to shield their faces. At first, Galaphile thought to suggest they stop and seek shelter. But there was nowhere that offered a respite, and the less time he spent in this morass, the better. He kept pushing on, intent on keeping up with the other two.

It wasn't enough, however.

One minute he was walking along with half an eye on Nirianne, and the next he found himself walking alone. He stopped where he was and looked about, then hurried back to find a side trail he assumed the other two must have taken. He walked a hundred yards along it, but there was nothing. No Ratcher, no Nirianne, and no signs of their passage.

He retraced his footsteps with a growing sense of desperation, certain his companions would have missed him by now and returned to find him. Back on the main trail, he continued forward and still found no trace of them. He called out in desperation, but the mists seemed to eat up his cries, and there were no answering hails. And though he kept walking, there was no sign of Ratcher or Nirianne.

They were gone.

And he had no idea where they were.

He tried calling out once more, but all that came back was the sound of the rain falling through the heavy canopy in the otherwise silent, quickly descending night. Perhaps if he just sat there waiting, they would appear. Would they pick up his trail and follow it? Ratcher was a seasoned tracker and hunter. Surely, he would find the right path.

But Galaphile, too, had trained as a tracker, and he had seen no trace of their passage.

He sat himself down beneath a thick enough patch of overhang that he was fairly well protected from the downpour and looked gloomily around him. By now it was completely dark, the marshy ground sodden and the air heavy with curtains of steadily falling rain. He sat there so long, he lost all track of time.

Once or twice, he tried calling out again, but his hopes that his efforts would succeed were steadily lessening. Eventually, the endless silence made him so despondent that he simply huddled there, watching for any signs of movement. There were a few, and some of them were made by creatures much bigger than himself, so he was careful to remain still and hidden. Twice, he fell asleep briefly but shook himself awake.

Where were they? Had something bad happened to them? Were they injured or even dead? If so, he would never forgive himself.

Still, whatever the case, something was clearly wrong.

The third time he fell asleep, he did not wake up again for a very long time.

Nirianne was unsure when Galaphile disappeared. He was following her closely, so there was no reason to think he would disappear as suddenly as he did—or at least, as suddenly as it appeared he did. One second he was there, and the next he was gone. She called to Ratcher at once, and together they shouted out Galaphile's name.

Then, having no other choice, they backtracked to see if they could determine where they had lost him. The fact that there had been no warning cries or sounds of any sort suggested that he hadn't come to any gory end. But the suddenness of his disappearance was disturbing, and they discussed possibilities endlessly as they searched first one way and then another for the better part of two hours. Ratcher was a tracker and a hunter, but the sodden ground quickly absorbed any tracks, and he found no trace of Galaphile.

The Mist Marsh was known for swallowing up wayward and inexperienced travelers, but Galaphile was neither. That there was no sign of him at all—and no sign of his passing—was troubling.

And more troubling was how much it bothered her. She had known him only for a few weeks, but still she felt this odd connection between them that transcended the difference in their ages. Something made her feel that losing him now would be a tragedy. That, if she lost him, she might lose a good chance at making something better of her life.

It was nonsense, one part of her warned. But it was real, too. Still, trying to reason it through at this point was senseless. For now, all she could do was search. He could not simply disappear, and he was too skilled to be taken unawares.

No, she would find him. She had to.

But night passed into morning, and they searched without finding a single trace of him. Nirianne suggested pushing ahead into the Highlands country to see if they could find Galaphile there, but Ratcher convinced her there were trackers in the villages below them who knew the marsh better than they did and they should go that way to seek help.

"We need their experience," he insisted. "They will find him."

"I hope you're right," she said quietly.

"I am. I know Galaphile well. I spent four years with him in Starns's camp. He was a boy when we met, and even then he showed me something of what he was made of. He overcame all sorts of dangers and threats over those years. He is skilled and smart, and he always finds a way. Know what? He's probably out looking for us right now!"

She laughed in spite of herself, then shrugged. "All right. Let's find some help and try again. But I know what you mean. Galaphile is a bit of a surprise, so perhaps he'll surprise us again this time."

Which he would—though the surprise would be long in coming and nothing of what they expected.

FOURTEEN

Galaphile Joss woke slowly and with more than a little difficulty to find himself in what appeared to be a foreign land.

He was no longer in the Mist Marsh amid ruined stretches of swamps and mire. He was no longer anywhere he recognized. The night and cold and smells of dying plants were gone, and he woke to such an amazingly bright, fresh morning that he was certain he was still dreaming. It was only with some difficulty that he was able to acknowledge that he was somewhere entirely different from where he had fallen asleep the night before.

First and foremost, there was sunshine everywhere—bright, warm, and enveloping in the way of the best days of summer. It was not summer, he knew; it was too early in the year. Yet here he was, right in the midst of this most lovely of summer days, surrounded by flowers and grasses, by fully leafed trees.

Dazzling colors greeted him in every direction he looked—soft pastels and deep warm rainbows all perfectly mixed and matched. The place was alive with a wondrous mix of sounds and smells, and of growth so well tended that there did not seem to be a flower out of place. How he had gotten to this place he could not imagine, but he found himself smiling.

There were birds everywhere, all of them at work—building nests and foraging for food, feeding their young and swooping about. All appeared at peace here. On the ground, small animals went about their business, and off in the trees he caught glimpses of deer and elk, but also of wolves and foxes. For now, though, predators and prey alike seemed nothing more than disinterested companions in a world that both found welcoming and safe.

Galaphile stared about him in wonder for a long time before rising. Somehow, he had stumbled into a world that resembled the paradise children were told would one day belong to them. Was he dead? He seemed to remember that a paradise of this sort was the destiny of the dead, if the dead were made to rise and . . .

Then, suddenly, he remembered the dream.

Just like that, in the space of an instant, he knew.

He was inside the Gardens of Life! This was the place to which he had been summoned.

The recognition brought tears to his eyes, and everything else fell away in the wash of emotion that enveloped him. He had found what he'd come looking for. Nirianne and Ratcher were gone—lost in the storm and the night—yet he had found his way here.

He began to walk, astonished to discover the birds and animals showed no regard for him. Not a single one bolted or shied away—though he did not try to approach them or suggest he meant in any way to interfere with them.

Walk to me, a voice whispered.

It was so sudden that he was startled in spite of himself—though a part of him had also been anticipating the voice.

A light appeared ahead of him, soft and vaguely pulsing, a guide to lead him on. He followed at once, eager to learn more, to discover why he had been summoned.

Through the gardens he walked, and though he had had no breakfast, this alone seemed to refresh him. He walked without tiring, gazing at the wonders around him. He might have chosen to question why he was being given this great gift; he might have asked himself why he was here and not someone else. But it honestly did not occur to him to do more than simply follow the light and—with a patience he had not known he possessed—wait for the answers he knew were coming.

The walk continued, time passed, and his expectations grew. At one point, the light slowed and waited for him to catch up, then enfolded him in such brightness that he was momentarily blinded. When his vision returned, he found himself cleaned and groomed, dressed in a white robe with a scarlet waist sash and a sheathed knife of such beauty that he was afraid to even think of touching it.

Where was he being led?

Why was he here?

What was expected of him?

Because there wasn't even a scintilla of doubt in his mind that *something* certainly was.

Ahead of him, the light began to grow brighter, increasing to such a startling brilliance that he was forced to shield his eyes. Thus he missed crucial seconds of the transformation that took place as the light increased in size and changed in shape, revealing the figure of a man standing before him. The man was ancient, white-haired and bearded, leaning on a staff. He was well over seven feet tall, his copious robes sufficient to lend his narrow frame some needed bulk.

Welcome, Galaphile. His voice was low and deep—a whisper that rattled in his throat. *You stand in the Gardens of Life, my home and my haven. I am the King of the Silver River, protector of all life in the Four Lands.*

Galaphile extended a half bow but kept his silence. He felt the old man's eyes assessing him.

Would you be the one who strives to bring a sense of peace and order to the Four Lands, young one?

The question caught him by surprise, but Galaphile nodded at once. It was exactly what he wanted—exactly what he had promised himself he would seek following the death of Starns, Mayele, and all the others.

How much will you give of yourself to see your goal realized? How much will you sacrifice?

He did not need to think about it. "Everything."

A bold claim to make. You do not yet know what that means. You cannot. You have not yet discovered what you will be required to give up if you do as you say. Even if you should live long enough to realize your dream, you cannot know. Think of what you have already surrendered. How much more of the same will you be willing to part with?

Galaphile thought of the loss of Mayele and Starns. Could he endure the likes of that again? But if he had to, he knew he would. The goal was bigger than one man.

So, "I have made a vow," he said. "To myself and to those I have already lost. I swore that I would find a way to change things so that none should suffer such losses again. I vowed I would find a way to make their deaths count for something. Somehow, I must find a way to extinguish the madness that consumes the Four Lands so that the fighting comes to an end."

But how is that possible? The battles among the different factions and Races have been going on for decades. What can one man do that will make a difference? What can you do to stop it?

In truth, he didn't know. But he believed there was a way to be found if he looked hard enough.

He stood before the old man and shook his head slowly. "I don't know yet. But I will find a way or die trying."

The self-described King of the Silver River nodded. *You will find it more quickly if I show it to you. Walk with me.*

He turned away and began to advance into a forest thick with massive trees. Galaphile moved after him, determined to find the answers he sought.

The odd pair—ancient god and young magician—passed into the forest and . . .

In seconds, he was asleep once more . . .

. . . but awake again in what felt to be an instant.

Now he stood in a new place—entirely different from the ones he had left behind. He stood on a battlefield with carnage all around him—far more than what he had seen in Starns's camp. Here death stretched on for miles, raw and brutal. Men and women of all Races—even children—lay motionless in a sea of destruction. The stench was ungodly, and the air was filled with the sounds of flies and carrion birds as they picked over the remains.

Should you do what you intend—and fail—this will be the cost, the King of the Silver River intoned. *Failure will destroy you and all those who stand with you. This is the price failure will exact, and you will bear it. Are you still determined?*

Galaphile did not want to believe such a cost could be his to bear. He did not even want to credit that what he was being shown could ever come to pass. Yet he knew it was true. This was what he would be choosing to risk, and there were no guarantees that he would be able to avert it.

Yet he heard himself say, "I will find a way to prevent this. I will not let it come to this."

The old man's smile was chilling. *So many have said this before—many who have failed to find a way or to keep their promises. Do you truly think you are the exception to the rule?*

Galaphile nodded. "I have to believe it. What purpose is there to my life if I do not at least try? How can anything change if no one takes a risk?"

The King of the Silver River smiled. *Just so. Walk with me.*

Once again, he turned and moved away, out across the battlefield, deeper into the endless killing fields. Yet slowly, as they progressed, the carnage began to fade until all of it was gone and darkness again descended . . .

Galaphile slept once more, then abruptly was wide awake again . . .

This time, he stood outside the walls of a massive fortress—a collection of towers and walls and parapets and ramparts so vast that it boggled his mind. He had never dreamed that such a place even existed. Yet from the look of it, this fortress was a work in progress, not yet complete.

He stood with several others, all unknown to him, yet it was clear they looked to him for guidance. One of them—a woman of considerable presence and strength—stood closest, and he realized that he knew her, even though he could not remember her name. The others were a mismatched bunch, but still all looking to him. All but one. Behind the others stood a woman with skin so white she appeared to be made of chalk, looking away into the distance toward something he could not see.

She was different.

The others were followers, believers.

She was something else.

Though what, he could not say.

This is your future, then. This is the road you will travel, and the place it will take you, and the future you will build with your own hands and the hands of those who believe in you. These are important people who will help you on your journey and see you to its end. Look for them. Find them, bond with them, trust in them, and they will see you to your goal. This much is given to me to show to you.

A long pause followed as the King of the Silver River appeared to consider what he would say next, his bearded face solemn, his gaze unreadable.

But remember that all this may be lost to you at the end. All those who help you may be gone. The cost of such an endeavor is great, and the strength it will require is mighty. There will be little peace for you, little rest. Do you accept this?

Galaphile stared at the King doubtfully. Did he? But he knew he must. "I accept it," he managed.

Now one thing more.

The old man gestured anew and once more turned away. Galaphile moved to follow him and fell back into darkness instantly . . .

The sleep lasted longer this time—he felt as much as it was happening—but he did not fight against it. He was being offered valuable glimpses into his future, and each scene was showing him something of vital importance. He must let the King of the Silver River reveal everything that was needed . . .

He woke anew . . . aware that something important was happening.

Though how he knew, he could not say. His surroundings were benign. The sun shone down on fields and hills, and on a small cluster of trees that shadowed a solitary figure. A man—though his features were indistinguishable and his face was turned away. There was nothing strange about him, nothing that should cause concern, yet Galaphile instantly felt a deep sense of unease. There was something hidden away deep inside that both repelled him and begged him to draw closer, just to determine its nature.

It was hard to say what gave rise to this feeling, but Galaphile could not ignore it. He wanted to move toward this man—close enough to see his face more clearly and perhaps determine what about him was so disturbing. But when he tried to move, he found he could not.

A closer look is forbidden, whispered the King of the Silver River. *Some things must wait until their time. But the man you've glimpsed is the one who will haunt you the most in the years ahead. Watch out for him most of all. Avoid him for as long as you can if you would secure peace for the Four Lands. In this life, it will be hard.*

Galaphile frowned. Who was this man? Why was he such a threat? He looked tame enough.

"Why can't you show him to me?" he demanded.

Some things are forbidden. A future of significance is never to be revealed in such a way that it can be changed before it arrives. You must rely on your instincts and your awareness, young Galaphile. You must trust in yourself to tell you what matters and what does not. What to do and what not to do. You must live out your life without ever knowing for certain where it is taking you.

"So how will I be able to avoid this man if I do not know who he is? How will I be able to recognize him?"

The King of the Silver River was silent for a long time, as if considering whether to speak at all. Galaphile waited with a growing uneasiness, knowing this supposed enemy would be formidable.

It will happen as it must.

Another long silence followed as Galaphile searched for something more to say, something more to ask, but found himself at a loss for words. Instead, he glanced back toward the mysterious stranger . . .

And slept again.

When he woke, he found himself back in the Gardens of Life, still in the company of the King of the Silver River, still puzzling over all that he had been shown. He stood looking at the old man while a strong sense of loss pressed in around him. How should he begin the task he was committed to undertake? Where should he start, and what should he do first?

When you leave me, the King of the Silver River told him, *you must go to the site of the fortress you will build to house your followers. Your future starts there. You must go alone to discover what is needed, then you must do what your conscience and your instincts tell you. This will be a long journey, so you must be patient. Trust in your instincts to guide you.*

"But my companions on this journey . . ."

Will be waiting back where you first found them. Find them there again after you have accomplished your first task. The route of your life is settled, Galaphile. Now you must follow the path you have chosen to its end. Though understand that, due to your time with me, you are no longer exactly who you were. Contact with my realm changes a person. You will be a much greater warrior than you were before. You will be a much more capable magician. And you will become better still with time should your needs require it and your instincts not betray you. Choices will reveal themselves as you travel, so look for what needs to be done. It will not always be what you think, so be open to the possibilities. Be confident. But be intelligent, first and foremost.

Galaphile's mind spun with shock. How changed was he from his time in the Silver King's domain? So many questions to ask, along with an entire raft of questions he had not even thought of yet—questions that waited down the road. And yet he knew his time was growing short.

"When will I see you again?" he asked.

When it is time.

"But if I need you . . . ?"

You will have yourself and your friends, Galaphile.

"But if that is not enough . . . ?"

One ancient hand rose in warning. *It will have to be.*

Galaphile nodded, knowing this was all the help he would get. The King of the Silver River was already beginning to fade away.

One thing more.

Galaphile reached out to the King impulsively, but his hand passed right through as if the ancient man were nothing more than mist.

Time has passed, the other continued. *And things are no longer as they were. Be wary. Trust in the lions when they come. They will be there to ward you.*

And then he was gone, and Galaphile was asleep once more . . .

FIFTEEN

In the village of Tranksen, some hundred miles east of the city of Whip's End, lived a boy. Tranksen was smaller and decidedly less prosperous than Whip's End, and most of its citizenry lived a hand-to-mouth existence, scraping by as best they could. This boy was from a family of five. There had been several more, but they had died younger than he was, which was ten years old.

His family was poor, and his life was difficult. He had no friends and little education, and what learning he had acquired had come through his mother. He was the youngest child, and most of the others, save his sister Quaz, had left home. Quaz and his mother kept the house running—as much as they could with so little to hand—but this effort left them with scant time for much of anything else, including him. Still, he told himself that he was happier alone, content with exploring things that puzzled him. He was interested in the unknown and took great pleasure in discovering how things worked.

He was frequently on the wrong end of beatings—from other boys mostly, but some adults, as well, and his father in particular. He learned how to fight back, but he was often smaller than his aggressors and thus less able to defend himself successfully. As a result, he spent a considerable amount of his youth being sullen and resentful. But eventually, he learned ways to get even with his persecutors—some of them quite vicious, and occasionally even terminal. But he was clever about it, too, so that none of his victims were ever linked to him. He kept a low profile, and none thought him smart or resourceful enough to be behind the bad things that were happening.

His personal interests were few and particular. He was interested in magic, even though he knew little about it, because magic was power. And he had so little power that the idea of being able to acquire it was intriguing. He had heard tales and read stories, listened to the talk of others, but no one really knew much about magic, so most of what he had acquired that was useful had come from unusual sources. Once, he had encountered a traveling carnival and made friends with a surly oldster who claimed to have magic. Indeed, he could perform more than a few amazing feats, but before long the boy realized these were more sleights of hand than actual magic—though studying them still proved valuable.

But the most important thing, he found, was reading. His mother and sister had given him a rudimentary understanding of letters, and from there, he studied. Reading opened doors to understanding and made him increasingly eager to find ways to widen his limited knowledge.

His father left when he was twelve. Where he went, no one knew, but the boy was glad to see him gone. The beatings lessened considerably, and the peacefulness of life improved with only his mother and sister to contend with. Until his mother married again and the new man of the house proved to be even less pleasant than his father. Quaz had turned sixteen, found a mate for herself, and moved out, leaving him alone with his mother and her new husband. So he realized it was time for him to go as well.

He said farewell to no one, not even Quaz. He packed a bag with food, clothing, a blanket, and an extra pair of boots and set out. He took passage with a wagon train filled with merchandise intended for towns along the way, paying for his passage with labor, and so began traveling north into the plains.

For several years he jumped from wagon train to wagon train, exploring the world while trying to ferret out the secrets of magic. During his travels, he encountered several other magicians—and a few genuine ones this time—and learned more of what he was searching for. There were places where artifacts of great power might be found, where stores of enormous treasures were hidden away. There were also a handful of enormously powerful mages, it was said, who could be convinced to teach you. But such took years of learning, and he wanted power faster than that.

The boy became a young man, and still his search for power continued. He formed no relationships with others—men or women—save those, of necessity, that forwarded his agenda. He sought no family of his own, coveted no land or home, and desired nothing of love or lasting connection.

His own mother had taught him the futility of that.

But always, he kept looking, kept searching, for any information that might gain him the power he wanted. He learned of a magician named Cogline, far up in the western reaches of the Kensrowe Mountains, who was rumored to take students should they prove dedicated enough. But that seemed both too distant and too involved. Plus, he did not think this Cogline would approve of his reasons for seeking power in the first place.

Then he heard rumors of a group of Gnomes in the northern Charnals who were guarding something of value—though no one seemed to know exactly what—and he knew he had finally found his target.

This was real. This was what he had been waiting for all these years. So, without further ado, he set out.

His quest was long and at times exceedingly difficult, even given his young age and prime physical condition. Even to get to the mountains, he was forced to travel through a country populated mostly by war-like Gnomes—not to mention four-legged creatures that were better left alone. But once he arrived at the mountains themselves, things got exponentially worse.

The Charnals were a vast range, and the Gnomes and their treasure could be anywhere within it. So he engaged in months of fruitless searching. Moreover, water was scarce, and though he knew how to forage for food and hunt for game, there was little of either to be found on the high, rocky slopes.

But just as he was about to abandon the quest entirely, he stumbled upon a hidden valley containing a structure that might have been a temple or a fortress—for it possessed aspects of both. And there were creatures down there the likes of which he had never encountered. Gnomes, by the look of them . . . but something more as well. Clergy, of a sort. They were hard-faced and determined as they moved about their sanctuary, clearly armored beneath their robes.

The young man found himself grinning. There was something kept hidden within this complex, that much was certain; there was a treasure of some sort to be found.

But what? Would it be the source of power he desired, or something else entirely? Maybe something he could later trade for power, at the very least?

For the next few days, he did little more than observe the compound, learning its rhythms, the cycle of its acolyte-guards, its entrances and exits. But even as he observed the fortress, he had the quiet awareness of . . . something, observing him back. It was only a faint sense of unease at first, like the feeling that someone was watching you when your back was turned. But gradually it grew more insistent, nudging at his awareness as if seeking to gain his attention.

Intrigued, he found himself spending more and more of each day hidden from sight and with eyes closed, in an almost meditative state, reaching out for . . . whatever it was in turn.

Soon, he could almost hear it, like whispers from another room, indistinct but seductive. Whatever this presence was, it wanted him. It knew him. It called to him.

Images came first. Something, trapped in a room. It needed him to come for it; it wanted him to free it. Whatever it might be.

But there *was* power here; he sensed it. A deep well of power, dark and greedy, that longed to be let forth into the light. That sought . . . a partner? A mate? Someone that would let it unfurl in all its vast glory, not molder in the dark, alone, confined, caged . . .

It wasn't exactly sentient, he felt, this thing that the Gnomes watched over. It didn't communicate in words; more in impressions. It had no emotions save for a pulsing need. But the longer he opened himself to its call, the more he understood.

Freeing it would change his life. Would make him the most powerful man in all of the Four Lands.

And that, he desired more than anything.

Still, he had no idea what this thing would turn out to be. He only knew that he needed to steal it away. He would do anything to gain the power it promised.

After a week of observing, he made his move in the dark of night. The building below sat silently waiting, and there was no evidence of life. There would be guards, but he knew their rhythms by now, and so knew how to avoid them.

He ghosted down the slopes, off to one side of the building he needed to enter, slipping effortlessly through the guards' patrols. A side door leading into what he suspected were the kitchens was his goal. He picked the lock—a skill he had learned during his travels—and eased inside.

A deeper darkness greeted him. He stood where he was, waiting for his eyes to adjust, then started forward.

He sensed a mounting urgency in whatever it was that called to him—not exactly eagerness, but more a kind of loudness that grew as the distance between them decreased.

With that alone as his guide, he snuck through various corridors that angled and twisted and even twice turned back on themselves, hoping not to encounter any interior patrols. But his luck must have held, because he encountered no one as he was led down into cellars buried deep underground. He followed corridors lined with locked, windowless doors, though he did not bother testing them, as his senses told him that what he sought was not held within. The cellar air was stale and smelling of dead things, but he focused firmly on why he was there and centered his thoughts on the thing that called to him.

Soon, he arrived at a huge iron door that sat directly at the end of a corridor, and he knew the thing he sought was inside. The door had locks to match its size, but these, too, yielded to his picks. He was surprised there weren't more magical wards in place, or alarms that went off when he cautiously pushed open the door, but . . . perhaps whatever magic was at play here was somehow aiding him?

The room behind the door was large and filled with old books, manuscripts, and ancient artifacts that the young man found unrecognizable. But the pull of the magic was almost magnetic now and swiftly led him to a large wooden box bound with metal at the corners and across its top.

Curious, he lifted the lid—which also did not seem to be bound with either lock or magic—and peered inside. What lurked within was a huge, ancient volume that looked as old as time itself, its cover scarred

and discolored, its binding still intact but showing considerable wear, and its pages stained on their edges with time or hard use.

It was also clearly the source of the power that had drawn him to it.

He reached out a hand, almost tentatively, and touched it to the surface of the book—then gasped. It was as if a bolt of lightning had run through him and out again—or something had unlocked in his mind.

In its wake came just silence and quiet and perhaps an odd sort of contentment, like a small, furry creature nestling against him. The book was no longer loud in his mind, no longer external, but maybe sort of . . . part of him?

He lifted it clear of its container in wonder, surprised by its extensive weight. For just a second, he thought he felt it shift ever so slightly in his hands. But when he looked more closely, it appeared as inert as ever. On its cover in large, boldfaced Gnomish script, embossed in a time long past and likely forgotten, was a solitary word:

ILDATCH

The name meant nothing to him, although a flicker of an indistinct memory suggested that he might have encountered it somewhere, once upon a time, in his studies.

Undeterred, he clutched the book close, cradling it like the treasure he believed it to be, and slipped from the room into the hallway without, then back through the hallways and out of the building and off into the night.

No one saw him come, and no one saw him go.

The book made sure of it.

From there, he fled back into the lower Northland, putting as much distance between himself and the place from which he had stolen the ancient tome as he could manage. He never sensed any pursuit, but he felt threatened nevertheless. It might have been his fear of losing his precious find—a thing of magic to which he had no right. It might have been the weight of the utter and complete attachment he had developed for the book. There was an undeniable lure about it that transcended anything he had ever experienced, and he knew instinctively that there were those who would not hesitate to kill him to obtain possession.

So for the next few days, he fled, walking both day and night, stopping only when he was tired enough that rest was required. Even then, he slept fitfully and still half conscious, watching over his find.

He did not know what the name of the book meant. All he knew was that he had gotten his hands on something special. Though it had grown far less intrusive, he could still feel the magic it contained, pulsing in a way that suggested it was very much present and waiting to be summoned. His skills were still few, but his understanding of how magic worked was sufficient to tell him it would take time to master what this book contained. It would require study and learning. But he was certain he could do it. All he needed was time and privacy.

So he needed to find someplace isolated where he could begin his studies. Somewhere no one would disturb him, but that still would provide him with food and shelter. He needed to keep others away from him, and himself away from others, while he worked.

He found just what he was looking for perhaps a hundred miles north of Tranksen—an isolated farm in the middle of nowhere, rundown but not yet gone to seed. He was in country he knew, close enough to his birthplace for him to feel comfortable but far enough removed to feel safe.

A few animals still lingered, though the crops had long since failed. There was a stream nearby for water, and a nearby forest for game if and when the remaining animals were gone. The farmhouse itself was in good shape—and empty save for the body of an old man who had died in his sleep a while back. So he hauled the body into the woods and buried it, scrounged some food for the animals, and began his studies.

He spent a year studying everything that the Ildatch had to teach him, and he found himself changed by it in turn. Much of his life before the book became indistinct and hazy, then faded from his memory completely. But the past wasn't what mattered. Only the future was worth thinking about.

His future, with the book. The book that, at times, seemed almost an extension of himself as he internalized its lessons.

He even forgot his name, but it didn't matter. No one saw him save the book, so there was no reason to remember it.

The book was all that mattered.

SIXTEEN

At the end of his second year, the new owner of the Ildatch abandoned his stolen farmstead home and drifted farther north, toward the mountains and mires and hellish stretches of dead land that fronted the Troll countries, to find a new place to carry on his studies. His command of magic had strengthened considerably, meaning that his needs had changed as well. He no longer needed to study the book now so much as to test out its lessons, and for that he required more privacy, larger spaces. So he had decided to build his own place of residence—a protective fortress into which no one could intrude.

He found the spot he was seeking beyond both a sordid stretch of the Lethe River and the Knife Edge Mountains. Here, in the midst of a wide-open plain completely devoid of life, he came upon a range of smaller mountains centered on a cliff that, from the right angle, looked almost like a Human skull. There were indications of eyeholes and fleshless nostril passages, the hollowed indentations of sunken cheeks, a rounded head, and, lower down where the cliff face rested against the ground, a suggestion of jaws and teeth. He found this immensely appealing. With only a little honing and shaping, he could intensify the look and create a truly intimidating fortress.

But he could not do this alone. For the sort of building he was envisioning, he needed minions.

Various Troll nations surrounded him to the north, but Trolls were large and dangerous, and he preferred workers who were a bit less intimidating to begin with—at least until he had fully tested the magic the Ildatch had granted him. He was still learning his craft, still finding new ways to become as strong and intimidating as he knew he must. No, Gnomes were more suitable for his purposes here. Though smaller than Trolls, they were nevertheless industrious and resilient. Strong for their size and tireless in their efforts, they should be able to accomplish all the tasks he had in mind.

Thus decided, he set out for the Eastland to secure the help he needed. Two hundred workers, he figured, should be enough to begin the endeavor. He knew this would never be enough to finish, but it would be a start.

He soon discovered, however, that he had been wildly optimistic, for it proved difficult to subject the Gnomes to his will, requiring a strength of purpose he had not anticipated. Who knew that such feral little people could be so tough-minded and recalcitrant? Who knew that such empty-headed fools would often die before submitting to him?

The Ildatch had taught him to bend and control the minds of others, but these tribal rats were more stubborn than expected. They resisted him at every turn, refusing to accept or acknowledge his command. They died instead—sometimes by the handfuls—so he was forced to move from tribe to tribe to fulfill his quotas, leaving behind the impression that he was a dark spirit come among them.

They began to call him the Dark Lord.

It took him the better part of two months to acquire the number of workers he required, and by the time a year had passed, his workers had just finished honing and shaping what he decided to call Skull Mountain until it fully resembled its namesake. By then, half the workers who had started the task were dead and the others exhausted. He annihilated the survivors and spent no time lamenting their passing. He was used to killing by now. His magic made it easy.

Then he went to gather up more workers.

A second year passed, then a third, then a fourth. By now, a fortress had risen in and around the mountains. The mountains themselves formed a partial protective barrier around the fortress as well as a natural setting for its forbidding look. Its walls and towers, its overlooks and ramparts all seemed just more facets of the mountain walls and crevices, giving it the appearance of being mostly a natural part of its setting. There was little to reveal it as being anything else, and if you weren't looking for it, you might only notice the mountains and not what they hid.

He had barely left this sanctuary other than to recruit and retrieve the Gnomes he had used to construct it. But as the months and years progressed, so had his powers of control, until it became almost easy for him to subvert the workers he needed. He had even expanded from Gnomes, collecting a handful of Dwarves and Trolls to aid in his efforts as well.

So now, at last, he had a fortress from which to conduct the beginnings of his reign as the foremost user of magic in all the Four Lands. He had the Ildatch and the dark magic it contained in his service. Meaning it was now time for him to move on to the next step in his plan—taking control over all of the Races and nations of the Four Lands from Eastland to Westland, and from Southland to Northland.

It was a bold, seemingly impossible ambition, but the book gave him confidence. Since his initial stumbles, he had not met a mind he could not subvert, and he was eager to test his limits further, to prove himself the dominant power in the Four Lands, as the book had promised.

Yet to do that, he needed to go forth into the wider world. He needed to test himself against any rival he might find, to prove his superiority.

But mostly, he needed an army to act as his right hand.

He debated on which people, which nation, he should use for this purpose. There were pros and cons to each. All had their abilities and their failings, their strengths and their weaknesses. But in each instance, the principal difficulty was their inherent resistance to command. Not that he couldn't take them easily; he could. He could now bend and hold two hundred to his will. But still, it took effort—a constant, low-level maintenance over the tether that bound them, which they tried to resist. For an army of more than two hundred . . . well, if he was required to spend all his time managing them like animals, making sure they did as they were commanded and never rebelling or resisting his demands, he would have little time for anything else.

His powers of control over the minds of others were considerable, but they could not overwhelm all resistance forever. And while his skills were admittedly still developing and were likely to continue doing so for decades to come, he was not sure if he would ever achieve perfect control over a creature possessed of free will. He already suspected that he wasn't aging in the way of average men, thanks to the Ildatch—four years on and he had barely aged a minute—but he was also not possessed of endless life. (Or so he suspected.) So he did not have an eternity to deal with this problem. He needed a solution.

Thus far, he had gotten everything he had wanted with the help of the Ildatch. He had managed to obtain the magic he had always coveted. He had built himself a fortress stronghold to surpass all others. But it wasn't enough without an army to back him up, and he knew it. Yet an army not fully under his control was more dangerous than no army at all.

He pondered ways to change this but could find no obvious solution. He was left at the doorstep of his advancement into the larger world—into the whole of the Four Lands—without a good way to put his foot over the threshold.

The way was there; he knew it. He just hadn't found it yet.

So he turned back to the Ildatch, trying to find the answers he needed. There were still large sections of it he had yet to decipher, let alone master. Could the answer be contained there?

He briefly considered the possibility of raising an army from infancy, devoted only to him, but not only did he have no desire to nursemaid and train a plethora of stinking brats, but it would also set him back by years. Not to mention that he'd have to maintain a constant stable of the creatures to replace any soldiers that died.

No, there had to be a better solution. A stronger control? A way to break the spirit or free will that did not leave an apathetic wreck in its wake? (He had tried the latter with less-than-perfect results. It was hard to make a completely broken person do anything.)

Then one day, after he swatted a pesky fly into oblivion while he was studying, the idea came to him.

What if I were able to bring the dead back to life?

It stopped him mid-thought. What if, indeed? If free will died with the spirit—which wisdom said fled the body after death—would a re-animated corpse be a clean slate for his desires, the perfect blank vessel for him to fill?

But . . . how was he expected to do that? No one had ever been able to bring back the dead. Not in the whole of Human history, or even before. Not in any real way. Not in any known world. It was a dream couched solely in fantasy tales and never in real life.

But then, the desire to bring back the dead had always been more about the person, the animus, than just the body. What if he only needed the body? What if he *preferred* just the body?

If he could do it—raise a body solely under his control, devoid of any personality but the one he put into it—think of the army he would be able to build. Think of the numbers he would be able to summon and maintain. Could one already dead even be slain again? And even if so, if the body was intact enough, he could simply reanimate it.

It could almost be an eternal army, with only the most damaged pieces ever needing to be replaced.

He began to page through the Ildatch again, searching for anything that might suggest a way to regift life where it no longer existed. The book purred its eagerness to him but still did not divulge its secrets. He hunted for days, then weeks, then months. Every now and then, he found something suggestive—some hint that what he sought was possible—but never anything that gave him a clue as to how to go about it.

One of his early explorations yielded results he had not foreseen, how-ever. In addition to his use of the Ildatch, he was searching through his-tories and riddles and parables that purported to conceal truths about magic lost to time. Several legends involved creatures that had served mages of old, some of which had been very powerful. One was called a Skelter, and it had disappeared centuries ago. Yet it was written that the eggs of this monster could survive a very long time if kept protected. Once he read this, the young mage could think of nothing else, and he determined to discover if an egg might still remain.

Apparently, it did not. But writings on how to conjure such a creature did. After multiple unsuccessful tries, he managed to do as the writings suggested. The result was a monstrous beast that looked to be formed of several different other creatures—dragons among them. It was six-legged and winged, with some ability to shift shape. It could be trained to carry a rider and could travel great distances fast.

He decided to keep it for himself. If nothing else, it would make it easier for him to gather up the experimental subjects he required.

But as advantageous as this was, it still did not solve the problem of raising the dead. Time passed, then dragged. He thought often about giving up, but something kept driving him on. So he persisted. And after several months, he finally stumbled across a reference that gave him a shot of hope. It talked about using magic to expand a single drop of living blood to fill the carcass of a dead thing and allow it to live again. It spoke of restoring the heart and opening the blood vessels and breathing air back into the lungs, using magic to infuse and restore these dead organs. It was complex and decidedly incomplete, but bones of the possibility were there. So he would have to experiment.

What he needed were dead bodies and living blood. And how hard was that?

With the aid of the Skelter this time, he hunted down more Gnomes, killing them one by one, then attempting to reanimate them with a drop of his own blood. The early results were not promising. It took him months alone to craft the spells that got the blood to expand to fill the body; longer to get the heart beating and the lungs pumping. And yet still he was often left with an immobile statue of the body that could breathe but not move—under its own control or anyone else's.

It took him many more months and Gnome recruits to figure out how to insert tiny shards of himself—his own magic or will—into the body. Still, the most he could achieve was an automaton that copied his every movement but could not be ordered into independent action.

But he was close; he could feel it.

By now, he was deep into his fifth year of studying the Ildatch, and his entire personality had evolved in a way he had never imagined—or intended. The power of his magic was everything to him, but still he wanted more.

It was, he decided, time to take a name for himself. He had come to know the Gnome tongue well by now, and so decided to name himself the Spectre Telle. In Gnomish, *spectran telle* roughly translated to "bestower of life," but with his current obsession for bringing life out of death, he rather liked the whimsical twist of substituting in the Human word for "ghost."

After all, in his mind, he was to become a dealer in death.

When he first said it aloud, the book hummed at him—almost in pleasure—and he found himself stroking it like a cat.

So the Spectre Telle he would be.

And before long, the world would be his.

SEVENTEEN

Once again, Galaphile woke up in a different land—though not, he sensed, the magical world of the Gardens of Life.

No, he was back in the real world once more.

Still, as in his initial waking, all indications of the Mist Marsh had disappeared. There were no signs of the Rainbow Lake or the Silver River. He was lying in a patch of thick grasses, buried into their warmth and softness. The sun was a broad span of brightness from horizon to horizon. He could hear birdsong in the air—a bevy of different cries and calls—all of them as vibrant as the feel of the morning air sweeping his face.

He rose to a sitting position and glanced about. Though he was lying in the grass, a slope fell off before him, and a forested rise rose steeply up behind—a mass of bare rocks, cliffs, and deep crevices. It was a massive and forbidding barrier that looked impossible to ascend. Yet he somehow knew that this was where he was meant to go.

Reassurance surged through him as he remembered the King of the Silver River saying that he must go to the site of his future citadel, that his future would start there. And that his instincts would guide him.

And he knew what his instincts were telling him to do.

He took a deep, steadying breath, knowing it began here. His new life lay before him. He must find the site that his citadel would be constructed upon and face whatever awaited him there. Then he must go down into the lowlands and return to Whip's End to find Ratcher and Nirianne.

Was he meant to summon them to join him? Were they meant to be the first of those who would stand with him in his efforts to bring peace and order to the Four Lands? He did not recall seeing their faces in the group of followers the King had shown him, but now that he thought back on it, he could not recall many of the faces he had seen, so perhaps he was mistaken?

He didn't know, and this time his instincts told him nothing. In any case, the visions had shown him only a subset of his would-be followers, so perhaps his options still remained open. *Choices will be revealed,* he had been warned. *Be open to the possibilities.*

He scanned the lower slopes of the hillside on which he sat. They stretched down to distant expanses of forests and fields, cloaked in over-laying swaths of green and yellow canopies shaded by an early-morning mist. He could see nothing of the city of Whip's End, to which he must go when he was done here, and nothing of life beyond various birds darting and swooping as they went about their business. No cities, no villages, no people. A farm or two lay far down toward the floor of the lowlands, with a few crop fields, and some pastured animals. That was it.

He tried to recall all that he had heard and seen while in the dream-land of the King of the Silver River, but it was a difficult task. Little of what he had encountered he now remembered. There was a woman, he recalled, who had stood next to him at the site on which the citadel was being constructed, but he had little memory of her face. And there was another woman who stood back from all the others, her face like chalk. But all other details had faded. Even the details of the solitary man wrapped in black—the man that the King had said would haunt him most in the years ahead—were fading. How was something this tenuous supposed to guide and warn him? How valuable was the information the King revealed if he forgot it all again after?

But then, the King did tell him to trust in his instincts, so perhaps he would recall the details as needed.

Or so he hoped.

Reluctantly, he brushed the matter aside, knowing he must turn his efforts to more immediate matters. It was time to go to the place he knew was waiting. It was time to start his journey home.

He was, he noticed, still dressed in the clothes he had been wearing in the marsh, and they still seemed partly damp. When he checked his pack, he was startled to find within it the same remains of food and water he had possessed just before he got separated from the others—though with the addition of some paper and writing implements that he knew had not been there earlier, and the glorious knife he had been wearing in the Gardens of Life.

Though he had been reluctant to touch it then, he now drew it out and admired it. The weapon was about a foot in length, the blade straight and true, embellished with engraved emblems he did not recognize. The handle was spun copper infused with iron rings—Elven work perhaps. He turned it several times in his hands, then reverently tucked it away again.

It felt to him like an eon had passed, but his gear indicated otherwise.

Had days, weeks, or months passed, or only hours? It was impossible to tell.

And what was he supposed to be writing?

The midday sun was already high in the sky, but how long that would last, he did not know—what season was it in this world he had returned to? Regardless, the climb that lay ahead would be wearying.

With the briskness of the cool mountain air on his face, he set out. He did not know if he could make this climb; in fact, he thought it possible that he couldn't. He might have to find another path, a more manageable route, to succeed. But there was only one way to find out.

He climbed steadily throughout the afternoon, traversing rocky slopes and sparse patches of grass and weeds, taking care to choose his approach carefully. The slopes were tricky and frequently deceptive.

But he worked his way upward at a steady pace, knowing that if he could get high enough, he would have a clear view toward the surrounding cliffs and escarpments. The cliffside he was ascending was a huge, jagged monster damaged by splits, slides, and crevices. He felt he was going in the right direction, however, and he was not deterred by the demands of the climb.

The afternoon faded away and night began to descend. He was a good distance up the slope by now, though still not far enough to scout the route ahead. He could not risk a fall, so he needed to bed down before it got too dark to see clearly. He found a broad ledge just as the darkness started to set in and made his bed in a patch of grasses, then took a few moments to view the incredible swath of stars that dotted the skies in all directions. Before long, exhausted from the rigors of the climb, he fell asleep.

At some point during the night, however, he woke to the sensation of something being out of place. From where he lay, he could look out over the edge of his resting place and down the darkened cliff face to where he had come from. There was nothing to see, but when he rolled over to look behind him, he found himself face-to-face with a sizable mountain cat. Rough, shaggy-furred, and inscrutable, it was not as big as a moor cat but plenty big enough, nonetheless.

He held the beast's gaze because to look away would have indicated fear, and he did not care to chance revealing that. The cat's huge eyes were a deep blue in color as they regarded him, glimmering like pools of cold water in the moon- and starlight.

The staring match continued for a long time, neither one looking away from the other.

Then finally, the cat turned and sauntered back toward the cliff wall, found a suitable spot, and lay down. After one more glance at him, it closed its eyes and slept. Did it sense Galaphile's connection with Cogline's moor cats and find it appealing? Did it sense that he posed no threat? It was impossible to know. But whatever it was thinking or sensing, it clearly did not feel threatened.

And after a time, Galaphile, too, slept again.

When morning dawned, the sun rising from behind the cliffs on which Galaphile climbed, the mountain cat was gone.

After a small breakfast of dry cereal and an apple, then a measured drink from his remaining water supply, Galaphile began his climb anew. The food and drink helped, and he wondered again what had transpired. Still, what mattered was that both were there when he needed them, and he was grateful.

The day was again cheerful and bright as he climbed, the winds soft, the air warm and filled with the smells of wildflowers and grasses. Today, his path drifted first one way and then another as he sought the safest footing, which demanded that he move as often sideways as up- ward. He thought about the mountain cat more than once as he pro- gressed, wondering where it had come from and if it might return. He didn't think there was much chance he would see it again, but he didn't rule out the possibility. That it had somehow found him, then chosen to leave him alone, was puzzling. It was almost as if it had been sum- moned, responded, and lost interest. But that seemed highly unlikely. Cats were mercurial under the best of circumstances, and big cats were a decidedly independent breed.

It was past midday when he finally reached the top of the cliff and stood high enough to behold two entirely different vistas.

Behind him was a sweeping view over the low country that stretched away for miles both north and west. Northwest lay the seemingly end- less expanse of the Streleheim Plains, and northward from there you could just catch a shimmering glimpse of the River Lethe. Westward lay the Valley of Rhenn and Elven country, from which he had come.

Before him, he could see the vast sweep of the Dragon's Teeth. He stood on their western arm, probably about two-thirds of the way up their span, closer to the open, northern pass than the base of the bowl to the south—though his views east and south were blocked by what lay ahead: a massive, seemingly unbroken expanse of thick, overgrown for- est with some sort of rise beyond it. He might guess at what lay hidden beneath the branches, but he could not know for sure without going in.

Which he knew at once he was going to have to do.

Stretches of this valley were not unfamiliar to him, of course. Starns's doomed camp had lain within the circle of these mountains, though much farther to the south and east than he now stood. And he was sure that other, isolated camps were still dotted within it, fighting as always for dominance and resources. But the stretch of woodland ahead of him seemed empty of life and trouble, which was reassuring.

He began his descent into the valley. It was an easier path down than up, but it was still nearing sunset when he finally reached the valley floor and the beginnings of the heavy forest. Not wanting to penetrate the darkness under the trees this close to nightfall, he set up camp and slept.

———

The next morning, after he had broken his fast, the mountain cat appeared once more. It was the same cat, no question. Its markings, size, and startling blue eyes identified it clearly. Galaphile stopped where he was, expecting the cat to advance, but it stayed in place, looking back at him.

Waiting.

Then it turned and started walking, pausing to look back over its shoulder at him.

After a moment, it was easy enough to realize what it intended. The cat wanted him to follow. He could turn back, stay where he was, try going around the cat, or do what he knew the cat wanted. Not much of a choice. He started forward, and the cat turned its head back and moved into the woods.

Beneath the heavy canopy of branches, the light was dim and shadowed. At first, Galaphile thought he was going to have trouble keeping the cat in sight, but the farther in he went, the sharper his vision became, adjusting on its own to sudden shifts in the light. He walked between the giant trees with little trouble, wondering if this was one of the improvements the King of the Silver River had mentioned.

As he trailed the cat, Galaphile found himself reflecting on the strangeness of it all. Here he was, guided by a mountain cat into a forest maze, acting in accordance with the advice of a magical being. In searching for a place that would become the center of a dream he was seeking to fulfill, he was relying almost entirely on a mix of hope and expectation.

It was a long trek, and his surroundings never changed—just miles of forest trees, shadowed depths, and a deep-seated feeling of emptiness. Starns had been so concerned about other camps encroaching on his territory that Galaphile had always imagined this whole valley teeming with settlers, but the reality was quite different. There were no birds here, no animals—nothing but the cat and himself. Even the insects stayed silent and invisible—if there even were insects hiding in the shadows.

He hadn't allowed himself to admit it at first, but there was magic at work here. He could feel it now, deep and pervasive. He could not tell where it was coming from or what it was doing; only that it was present. Was this the King of the Silver River, keeping his promised haven free from squatters? With a faint smile, he began to suspect that it was.

Eventually the way ahead brightened, the trees began to thin, and the cat and Galaphile beheld a broad stretch of grasslands that sat upon an impressive rise. He'd traveled the better part of two days into this wilderness, winding his way through difficult terrain and constant natural obstacles provided by the jutting rocks and heavy forest. The plateau must have stood a thousand feet above the Streleheim and well above most of the surrounding peaks as well. The peak was massive and intimidating—so huge that it seemed to dominate most of the surrounding countryside. From here, it seemed that the lower-down stretches of forestland fully encircled the pinnacle before them—which was itself sizable and inviting: a lightly wooded plateau flooded with sunlight.

At once, Galaphile knew. This was meant to be the space on which his citadel would be constructed.

Eagerly, accompanied by the cat, he climbed its great height, then stopped on the open plateau and just gazed at it, filled with a mix of wonder and excitement. He could see the fortress rising in his mind. He knew exactly how it would look, how it would function, how it would dominate the entire clearing. He would find men and women to fill its ranks, to aid him in his quest to free the lands of violence.

With a sudden grin, he knew what the paper and writing implements were for. Spreading the paper open on a nearby rock, he feverishly began to sketch—walls and towers and gates, defensive capabilities and sight lines. How many stories above, and how many basement levels hollowed into the rise. He filled several pages with the plans, his excitement rising. It would be both a formidable fortress and a place of learning, with weapons stores as well as libraries.

And wonderfully defensible, on its isolated peak.

It would be magnificent.

When he had finished drawing, he paused for a moment to savor the triumph. Of course, he would need to find someone to convert his rough sketches to architectural drawings—to tell him what was possible and what was not. That was when the practical questions crowded in. How long would all this take? How long and how far would he have to travel to find the architects he needed, let alone the help to construct the place? He was alone, without coins or valuables. He had no helpers and no plans for finding—or funding—any. Beyond his dreams, he had almost nothing practical.

So how could he possibly make this real?

He sighed deeply and tucked the nascent plans away in his pack. A journey was taken one step at a time, and he was racing ahead of himself here. What should his next step be?

Walk the rise and look out to what lies below.

The voice of the King whispered in his mind, sharp and clear. He caught his breath in response, and a fresh rush of excitement surged through him. Their connection *wasn't* lost; it was still there.

Obediently, he rose and walked forward. He wasn't questioning anything by now; he was only responding.

This was what was meant to happen. This was what he had to do.

The mountain cat was lying in the grasses ahead of him but did not move as he passed it. He might have questioned its placid acceptance of what was happening if he had given thought to it, but there was no time. The cat was a fact of life but at that moment not a consideration.

When he reached the nearest edge, he slowed and looked back. The broad plateau stretched away for a considerable distance—almost five thousand yards at its longest. Beyond, to the west, south, and east, the forests dropped down into the rugged cradle of the Dragon's Teeth.

He began to walk the perimeter, as instructed, then stood in shock and wonder as he reached the northern side.

There, a broad gravel-laced dirt roadway wound downward through a series of twists and turns into and out of forested hills to eventually exit through the northern pass. The roadway had been there all along; he just hadn't realized it, because he had climbed the forbidding walls of the cliffsides that faced east.

Had he made a better effort at finding his way, he might have found that road. But was he ever even meant to? Had the King of the Silver River purposely positioned him so that he was forced to ascend to this place the hard way? Was it a trial that he must undergo?

He couldn't be sure. Much of his new life was like the beginnings of a mystery to him.

Then, from his perch atop the rise, a fresh surprise surfaced with a suddenness that was by now growing all too familiar.

On the roadway he had just discovered, wagons pulled by donkey trains and tended by copious numbers of Dwarves were just beginning to come into view, ascending in a long, twisting line that stretched down toward the valley until it was out of view.

EIGHTEEN

"My name is Sanitov Scallawen," the leader of the Dwarves announced after the first of the wagons had pulled up to the end of the road and Galaphile had walked down to meet them. "I am a master builder among my people, and if your name is Galaphile Joss, then I am your willing servant in undertaking whatever tasks you require of me."

Galaphile stared at him. "You've come here to build my fortress?" he asked in disbelief. "By whom were you sent?"

The Dwarf shrugged. "By the same fellow who sent you, I suppose. He said you would be waiting. He also said you would be surprised by our presence."

That was an understatement, Galaphile thought as he studied his new companion. Sanitov was big for his lineage—about a head taller than Varisol, though still far shorter than Galaphile himself—his burly form, muscular arms, and sturdy body a testament to a life spent as a workingman. His bushy beard and thick head of hair were a deep burnt orange in color, and his bright-blue eyes held a twinkle. There was no reason to question his claim, but every reason to wonder at his decision to undertake this project, because . . .

"I have no money to pay you," Galaphile confessed. "I am without coin and means. Did you come all this way with no guarantee that you would be fairly compensated for your effort?"

Sanitov laughed—a big, booming rumble. He clearly found his host amusing. "No guarantee? Shades, man! Do I seem the sort of fellow who would cross the flippin' street if he thought he might not be paid? Of course I would insist on payment—not only for myself but for all my fellow builders and the families who depend on them. For the materials and tools and transport as well. Why would I do anything else? Do I look insane?"

Galaphile shook his head at once. "Hardly. But . . . I still don't understand."

"The only thing to understand is this," the Dwarf persisted. "We have already been paid in full—me and all my fellow workers. We were hired, paid more than adequately, and dispatched with sufficient additional funds to procure any other materials and tools we might need. We are fully prepared to undertake the construction. We even have the plans for what we are expected to build."

Sanitov had pulled out a roll of plans from his pack, and he handed them over. "The ones on top are the rough sketches of your vision. The ones below are the actual building plans. We had to change a few things around—you know, for load-bearing walls and suchlike—but I feel like we captured the essence of your vision. Let me know if not, and I will be happy to modify things as needed."

Feeling bemused, Galaphile unrolled the plans, only to find the drawings he had just sketched—but now looking much more wrinkled and well used—lying on top. Below that, Sanitov's plans were revealed in intricate layers.

Were they any good? Galaphile studied them and shook his head in wonder. They were a miracle of meticulous detail, capturing everything that had been in his head and on the scratch sheets that had somehow ended up here. The work was so thorough that it left him astonished.

"These are perfect," he admitted. "Everything I had hoped for and more. This is beautiful work. I am pleased with every inch. Thank you."

Sanitov grinned. "I'm rather pleased with them myself, I admit. But then, your vision was remarkably clear. This is going to be a magnificent place once we've finished building it."

Galaphile agreed—but he could not resist surreptitiously check-ing his pack while Sanitov was occupied with rolling the plans back up again. He wasn't sure if he was delighted or alarmed to find that the drawings he had completed mere minutes ago were nowhere to be found.

Still, he had expected that he would have to find and organize the builders and have the building plans created all on his own. He had also expected that he would have to pay for everything, from materials to la-borers and beyond. That he was wrong on every count left him stunned by the magnitude of the help he was being provided.

Galaphile shook Sanitov's hand warmly, welcomed him to the con-struction site, and took the time to introduce himself to all the newly arrived workers and examine the materials that had been hauled to the site.

"It is an enormous task that you have undertaken, my friend," Sani-tov declared. "What I have here is only the first load of what will be required. This is a five-year build we are undertaking. All we do now is begin construction on the lower floors—on the basements and under-ground storage chambers. In other words, we begin with clearing the site and undertaking an excavation so we can set the foundation."

Galaphile had no trouble believing this, and he assured his build-ing chief that, however long it took, it would be worth the time and effort—and whatever support he could provide was at their disposal. Sanitov grunted and accepted the assurance, but Galaphile knew the man doubted his skills. After all, he knew nothing about what had been planned, had no means to pay for anything, and lacked any familiarity with the building process. The plateau was not heavily forested, but the roots ran deep, so clearing the necessary trees alone would be a terrific undertaking. That he was to become the leader of this endeavor was one thing. But to expect that he was useful in any practical sense was another. At best, Galaphile realized, it was a case of *wait and see*.

The remainder of the day was spent walking the building site and discussing the ways in which the construction would begin, where the walls and buildings would be placed, and how the finished citadel would eventually look. The locations of the three central towers, the six courtyards, the connecting walls, and the massive front and concealed rear gates were crucial to the invulnerability of the citadel, and as they walked the site, Galaphile again saw it rising in his mind.

Near the end of the day, Galaphile began considering something else that he hadn't even thought about before. If this was a five-year project, as Sanitov had indicated, it would eventually attract attention. Not just from the curious but from the rapacious as well. Attempts at theft were inevitable. This was a mean and lawless part of the country, with warring bands of Humans and Gnomes and no doubt some varieties of raider camps still scattered throughout this bowl.

"Thieves and cutthroats of every sort will inevitably attack us and the site, in search of materials at the very least," he advised the Dwarf commander. "So sentries, guards, and more than a few traps will be needed as we proceed."

Sanitov nodded, understanding the issue as well as he did. Would some who located them take advantage of what they had to offer? No doubt. And would others seek to pillage and burn and kill these intruders? Again, no doubt.

So was there anything Galaphile and those standing with him could do to stop it? The King of the Silver River had told him he had been transformed by his visit to the Gardens of Life. But what did that mean? How exactly had that transformation changed him? He looked the same, thought the same, felt the same—mostly. As far as he could determine, he was acting the same. What had changed? How would he be able to withstand the power that would be brought against himself and his helpers and this as-yet-unrealized fortress? How was he to survive the fury and the savagery that would one day come for him?

He didn't know. But he knew he was going to have to find out—fast. He resolved to immediately begin recruiting and building up a protective force for the day he needed one. Which he did not think would be all that far away.

As it happened, it took much less time than he had anticipated and came with a suddenness that was shocking.

Over the course of four months, the building of the citadel had begun in earnest. Already, the lands on which it would be constructed had been prepared. The trees had been cleared from the rise, and the footings where the structure's main towers and gates would lie had already been placed. Massive belowground basements and storage areas were being excavated and their walls shored up, awaiting stone blocks and mortar. Hundreds more Dwarves had arrived to carry out the heavy work required, summoned from the Dwarf cities of the east by Sanitov, who apparently had significant connections with the entire building community.

Certainly, the guarantees of up-front pay brought help more quickly than anything, but even so there was a real sense of excitement about the work that caught Galaphile by surprise. That the Dwarven people were so invested in this project spoke volumes and made Galaphile hope anew. He had never been shy about explaining the fortress's purpose— a way to help unite a fractured land—and his workers' enthusiasm for the cause made him realize that this project had value even to the more settled Races.

This was perhaps the most significant structural undertaking since the construction of Tyrsis and its massive walls, but it had even greater purpose.

Then one day, not even six months after the start of the project, the first attack came.

Galaphile had established a series of watch lines right from the start so that he would not be caught off guard. He knew that, sooner or later, his efforts would be discovered and his strength tested. So when the first of his sentries rushed in to announce that a sizable force of heavily armed raiders from one of the larger camps was coming up the road, he was quick to act. Strapping on his weapons and ordering everyone to stay back, he departed to stand alone against the intruders. Whatever was going to happen, he wanted it to happen to him first.

The first rule of engagement, he believed, was to create a false impression of vulnerability. The second was to set an example of what others could expect if they persisted in their efforts. The answer to any threat must be significant enough to discourage not only the attacking force but any future attackers as well.

He had thought about his choices ever since he had realized this day was coming. He had come up with a plan and rehearsed his role so many times that he was almost glad to finally get a chance to do it. After today, everyone would know what he could do if he was threatened.

When he sensed the raiders' arrival was imminent, he took up position on the roadway leading downhill, perhaps three hundred yards from where the foundation of the fortress was being excavated, and he waited. Already, he could hear the sounds of the approaching attackers, which were both raucous and threatening. What happened here on this day, he knew, would go a long way toward determining the future of his project, and Galaphile was not about to let anything threaten that.

When the raiders—about a hundred strong, he guessed, and men and women both—were perhaps fifty yards away, they paused, and he heard the first sharp twangs of longbows releasing their arrows. With a quick sweep of one arm and a few uttered words, he released a broad swath of magic and every last arrow—all that were being aimed at him— fell out of the air as if a wind had knocked them down. Some among those advancing cursed and looked about at their fellows. A few broke ranks and turned back. But the larger part came on. Their leaders called for shield men with spears to take the vanguard and form a phalanx that would sweep him aside.

Still, he held his ground.

When the leading ranks of the phalanx were within twenty yards, he ordered them to stop—his voice a booming explosion of sound. The phalanx didn't even slow, and when their forward movement continued unchecked, he again swept his arm before him, his fingers pointed toward the roadway as he drew an invisible line between himself and the interlopers. In response, the earth rose into a thick whirl of dirt and rocks six feet high, blocking the road entirely.

This time, everyone halted where they were. Through the swirling barrier, he could see them staring in disbelief.

"Come no farther!" Galaphile commanded, again using his volcanic voice. "If you do—if even one of you dares—I will tear up the earth you walk upon and drop all of you straight down into a hole that will become your graves!"

Harsh mutterings met his words, but still he faced them. From within the masses before him, a few voices rose in challenge, instructing those assembled to take the head off this impudent fool.

In a sudden rush, his attackers came for him. In response, he used his magic to take hold of the earth beneath them and rip it open like paper. The entire roadway split apart, widening in seconds into a crevasse ten feet wide and fifty feet deep, exposing a cavern that dropped away for hundreds of feet.

The men and women charging at him were moving too fast to stop themselves, and half the company vanished into the crevasse, screaming and howling in helpless despair.

The panicked cries of the stricken mostly died swiftly as their bodies struck the rocks at the bottom and their voices went silent. Only a few, somehow alive after their fall, began sobbing and crying out for help. Those who remained standing on the far side of the split, their faces frozen in horror, stared down into the gaping pit filled with the bodies of their dead and dying companions.

With another gesture, Galaphile drew the ruptured earth together. The ground rumbled and shook like a dragon rolling over, and the edges of the crevasse snapped shut with a muffled boom, silencing any that remained inside.

A long, eerie hush settled over the road. The opposing company stood as if frozen by magic—though he knew it was only horror that held them in place. A sluggish, ugly guilt stirred inside him. Had he gone too far? But they had refused to heed him, and an example needed to be made.

His enhanced voice exploded through the sudden silence. "Turn around! Go back to where you came from and don't come back!"

As added emphasis, he set the air in front of them and overhead on fire, until it looked as if the entire sky was burning.

The frozen army jolted back in a writhing mass of bodies, and its individual members scattered and fled back down the roadway, all plans of conquest or looting abandoned.

Word would get around about what had happened, and most aspiring looters would think twice before coming back.

But he couldn't help wondering if his quest for peace was supposed to claim quite so many victims.

NINETEEN

Work on the fortress resumed. Steady and reliable, the Dwarves went back to their jobs—although they would be discussing the incident for months to come. The word was out that the Elf raising this massive fortress inside the circle of the Dragon's Teeth was no one to be taken lightly—a magician of incredible power, a wielder of magic equal to anything the Dwarves had ever encountered. Better still, he was making a safehold for those who had none and planned to institute a regime of peacekeeping and security that would put an end to thieves and raiders and their invasive territorial claims. A new day was coming.

Times were changing, and the Four Lands had to change with them. It wasn't going to happen overnight, but it was going to happen. He had great hopes for a better future and was committed to a world of peace.

In the months following the shattering of the raider attack, no other attempts were made to interfere with the ongoing construction. Galaphile took it as a sign that word of his demonstration had spread. He couldn't depend on it to have the same impact forever, but he thought it might take a while for another group to grow brave enough to test him again.

In truth, tearing the earth open was as much the result of knowing the terrain as it was of his use of magic. He had studied the land and discovered that a fault was present beneath that particular stretch of roadway. He also knew that he possessed sufficient power to force that fault open and close it again after.

Setting fire to the air, in contrast, was merely an offshoot of the kind of illusions he had mastered under Starns, while Cogline had taught him how to magnify his voice. But they were mere parlor tricks in comparison.

With a time of comparative peace ahead, however, his mind turned to Whip's End. Winter had come, the first light snowfalls settling down across the higher elevations. It was time to make sure that Nirianne and Ratcher had indeed returned safely from the Mist Marsh to the city of Whip's End as the King of the Silver River had promised. Things were settled enough by now that he felt comfortable making the journey. He would only need a week or so to visit; then he would return.

So he left Sanitov in charge, wondering how long it would be before the heavier snows shut down the work until spring. It would happen all too soon, he imagined.

He chose to take the road downward—a bit of a safer descent in winter weather than the side slopes—his path winding down to more level ground before exiting the valley in a relatively straight line. Exiting the circle of the Dragon's Teeth took him two days, with another four needed to circle around to Whip's End, even traveling steadily the entire time. But he was young and strong, and hikes of this nature presented no particular challenge for him. In truth, his inclination to make this journey had been nagging at him for weeks. Reconnecting with his friends felt necessary. He wanted to make sure they had returned safely from the south; he wanted to verify what had happened to them since the three had parted ways. Time had passed, and he wasn't sure how much.

What had become of Nirianne and Ratcher? What of Varisol? As well, he hoped to offer them a chance to join with him in this effort. Ratcher's brawn was an obvious asset, and even Varisol would be welcome should he choose to abandon his tavern and come to the citadel, if only for a visit.

As for Nirianne, something about her implacable bravery drew him. He found himself missing her wry humor, fierce intelligence, and reckless insistence on doing things her own way. She would, he thought once again, be a force to be reckoned with once she had left her prickly teenage years behind—which, in fact, she must be on the verge of doing. How much would that impact the way they interacted with each other? He remembered how he had felt about Mayele. There was something of that here, too, with Nirianne.

As he traveled, he saw no signs of the mountain cats or any other sort of living creature save a handful of the large birds that dominated the higher skies. There was little evidence of other people, either, this far north. For someone who had spent almost all of his life alone—or in company with one or two others, aside from his six years in Starns's camp—he was puzzled to find that he was feeling lonely. In the colder weather, there were few signs of even the individual thieves and pillagers that had been known to haunt the building site. The whole of the mountains felt deserted.

So much that had happened to him during his life—and in the past few years particularly—had isolated him. But it was one thing to be alone when fate required it, and it was another to choose it voluntarily. He did not think the latter was meant for him.

On his journey, he encountered few other travelers, and those only on the plains as he neared his destination. He reached the city outskirts exactly six days after he had set out, and he found things more changed than he had expected. New buildings had sprouted up everywhere, and the borders of the city had widened. It felt busier than before and more crowded. Rougher as well. He worked his way deep into the core of Whip's End, searching for the Short Shot, and eventually found its familiar sign, which had been repainted. What else was new?

He walked up the steps of the tavern and pushed through the doors. The interior was packed with customers sitting at tables and bellied up to the service counter. The room was filled with the raucous sounds of conversation, laughter, and rough language. Here, at least, everything looked the same.

He looked around, noticing a pretty, vibrant young woman sitting at the end of the service counter talking with a few of the tavern workers. He didn't recognize her, but he had a feeling he should. Then she glanced over, her eyes fixing on him with an intensity that was startling.

She came to her feet instantly, shaking out a mane of long, reddish-tinged blond hair, not bothering to straighten out her tunic and slacks, and crossed the room in a blur of motion that brought her right up to him, her hands grappling his shoulders as she pulled him into a ferocious hug.

"I knew you would come back!" she whispered as she hugged him, failing to notice his stunned bemusement. "But what took you so long? Where have you been? What *happened* to you?"

It was the voice that did it, a voice that he knew instantly. *Nirianne!* Still, it took him a moment to recognize her—though when he pulled back to look at her, he could feel it all snapping into place: the ruffled hair, the knowing slant of her eyes, the crook of her lips on the left side of her mouth, even the roughness of her voice. Still, he could not believe what he was seeing. She looked *years* older than he remembered. She must have grown up fast in the time they had been separated.

"I came as quickly as I could, Nirianne, believe me."

She seized his arm and dragged him across the room, past dozens of staring eyes, through a doorway on the back wall, and into Varisol's office. The man himself was sitting at his desk, and he looked up, then grinned when he recognized Galaphile. "Well, I'll be. Never thought I'd see you again!"

He rose, came around his desk, and embraced his friend. "Look at you! You haven't aged a day. How can that be?"

Galaphile smiled back. "Hasn't been *that* long, my friend. How much do you expect me to age in a few months?"

"A few months? You've been missing for more than *five years*!"

Galaphile felt a shock go through him. "Five *years*? What are you talking about?"

"Just exactly what he said," Nirianne confirmed. "You've been gone for five years, Galaphile! Everyone thought you were gone for good. Well, everyone but me. After you disappeared in that swamp, Ratcher and I searched for you for days—with help!—but we couldn't find a trace of you anywhere. We finally came back here, but I was certain you would turn up sooner or later. Then after two years, I quit being quite so sure. But I never gave up. Not entirely."

Five years? How could five years have passed and he not know it? But apparently that was exactly what had happened. Something about being in the Gardens of Life had stopped time's passage for him, even though it had continued on for everyone else. Magic, of course. A magic that manufactured dreams and promises, forms of conjuring and predictions. A magic that he didn't begin to understand.

No wonder Nirianne looked so grown up. She actually was. How old would she be by now—twenty-one, twenty-two? No longer a child, but a grown woman.

He shook his head in wonder. "It seems I've lost a lot of time without even realizing it."

Nirianne threw her arms around him once more and hugged him so hard that his ribs creaked. "You have a lot of explaining to do," she declared. "I want to know everywhere you've been, everything you've done, how you've spent your time . . ." She exhaled sharply, grinning. "All of it!"

And as he stared at her like some kind of poleaxed steer, she impulsively reached up and kissed him on the cheek. "Welcome back, my world-traveling friend. Welcome home."

With greetings fully exchanged, Varisol suggested they have something to eat and drink in his office. After all, Galaphile had come a long way over the past few days and must be hungry. It wasn't exactly lunch or dinner hour, but Nirianne offered to have the cook heat up something for them and rushed off to the tavern kitchen.

As they took their seats in Varisol's office, the Dwarf stared at him like he was some sort of exotic animal.

"Can't believe it. Five years, and just look at you."

Galaphile tried a smile, but it didn't seem to fit. "Strange, isn't it?"

Varisol shook his head. "She's been waiting all this time. Never gave up on you. I thought she was crazy."

Galaphile gazed at his companion. "Not crazy. Just determined as always."

Varisol nodded. "You have no idea. But I'm glad you're back, Now I can help share whatever current burden you're struggling with. No, don't deny it. I know you too well."

Galaphile did not wish to start explaining how things stood or where he was now making his home until all three of them were back together, so he simply grunted noncommittally. He was still getting used to the idea that Nirianne had grown up so quickly. That they were all so much older than he had imagined.

Soon, Nirianne returned with both food and drink. "You can eat first," she insisted to Galaphile, a stern look on her face. "We'll talk when you're done."

And yet as he ate, she sat staring at him as if trying to get used to the idea that he was really there. Finally, when he was finished, she gave him a nod and said, "All right. Let's hear the explanation, then."

He gave his recitation as best he could, keeping his voice low and guarded. The office was fairly private, but he felt a need for caution nevertheless. Emphasizing that he had been lost in dreams and visions for most of the five years—skipping entirely what they were, even when she nudged him for details—Galaphile told his story. He stuck mostly to what the King of the Silver River had said to him: that he was expected to become a leader for those seeking peace and security. He finished with a description of the new citadel and the work currently being conducted by the Dwarf builders.

It was an odd recital, he knew, for he had left out a lot of what had happened in an effort to make it more believable. But even as he laid it out, he was aware that it still sounded less than credible.

"In any case, I came to find both of you and Ratcher as soon as I could," he finished lamely.

"Five years later," Nirianne repeated accusingly.

"I know that now, but I didn't know while it was happening. I never sensed it was that long. I had no idea."

"But you must have felt the time passing, the seasons changing—something!"

"I'm telling you I didn't! I didn't have any way to know. Everything felt the same all the time. The weather barely even changed while I was there."

"So where will you go now?" Varisol interrupted.

"Back to the construction site. But I have to find Ratcher first, if I can. Do you know where he is?"

"Same place you found him the first time," Nirianne answered. "He comes through the city every few months to top up his coffers, and he always stops by the tavern for a visit. Your luck must be holding, because he returned only last week and hasn't yet come to say goodbye. What is it that you want from him?"

"To ask him the same thing I am about to ask you," Galaphile said. "I'd very much like it if both of you would come back with me to the citadel and aid me with my work. I think you might like it there. It is beautiful and quiet, and it offers—or at least it will offer soon enough—good protection to all who live there. Are you interested?"

Nirianne pursed her lips. "Well, at least I wouldn't have to worry about losing you again. But I don't know. I'm still getting used to the idea of having you back. I have to think on it."

"I won't be coming," Varisol declared. "I'm too old for that sort of change. I belong here—in my tavern and with my friends. I have lived here long enough that I don't think I will move ever again."

"And I don't know that I can leave my father," Nirianne added.

"She's had her chances, fates know," the old man advised. "Had proposals from this man and that. But she turned them all down. Always for the same reason—she wants to stay with her father." Nirianne gave him a doubtful look. "But I can't say I'm sorry she feels that way."

"Nor would I blame either of you for staying," Galaphile said. "But the offer stays open. Always. One day you might change your mind. You can always come if you ever decide you want to."

"Might do," Varisol admitted with a shrug. "One day."

Galaphile found Ratcher easily enough, right where Nirianne said he would be—though this time he was playing cards. The big man looked up long enough to recognize Galaphile, then threw in his cards and walked up to him and clasped him by his shoulders.

"She said you'd be back eventually. I told her to stop dreaming, but she wouldn't listen. She always believed you'd show up at some point. Seems she was right."

After perfunctory hugs and backslaps, they went off to the bar for ale and conversation. Galaphile repeated his story—only this time, he revealed more fully the nature of his magical powers and the details of his confrontation with the raiders.

"So," the other observed with an amused arch of one eyebrow, "it looks like your future is set."

"My future includes you, if you'd care to come back with me. I need men like you at my side. I need friends I can trust."

"Are Nirianne and her father coming?"

Galaphile shook his head. "It doesn't seem so. At least not right away."

Ratcher pursed his lips. "Odd. That girl really likes you. Mooned over you like crazy when you were gone. Even suggested she might go looking for you more than once."

Galaphile shrugged. "I'm not so sure she likes me all that much anymore. She's grown up. She probably wants other things now than she did as a teenager."

"I couldn't say. She can be hard to read, that girl. Are you going back to your fortress straightaway? Are you sure you want me to come with you?"

"I am returning soon—and yes, I am sure I want you with me. I'll ask Nirianne and her father again before I leave, but I have to get back to the site."

Ratcher paused. "Are you looking for more like me to fill your ranks? You're going to need fighters—and not just ordinary ones at that. You'll need magic users, too."

Galaphile nodded his agreement, and they stared at each other silently for a moment.

"Tell you what," Ratcher said abruptly. "Leave me behind for now. I've traveled extensively over the years and met any number of people. I know some men and women who might be the sort you're looking for—fighters and magic users both. If you'll trust me, I'll ask around—maybe bring a few candidates up to your fortress, give you a chance to interview them. How does that sound?"

It sounded perfect, and Galaphile was quick to accept the offer. Ratcher would take a few weeks to do some looking around for the people they needed and then travel with them to his new home. Give him a map, he declared, and he could make the climb without problems. He could even use the roadway, if need be.

Galaphile assured him he could use any road or path he liked, and to come when he was ready. There wasn't any rush. The citadel would take years yet to complete, and his efforts to bring even a semblance of peace and stability to the Four Lands would take a good while longer than that.

The agreement made, they said their farewells, and Galaphile made his way back toward the Short Shot and the room that Varisol had promised him for the night.

He would wrap things up in Whip's End and leave in the morning.

TWENTY

When Galaphile reached the tavern and went upstairs to his room, he found Nirianne waiting. She was sitting on the end of his bed, staring at him with an intensity that was unsettling.

But then, Nirianne had unsettled him ever since they first met. She was bold, self-assured, and unpredictable, and all the promise he had seen in her teenage self was definitely on display in the woman before him now.

But there was something more to it than that. Something about her that tugged at a memory still keeping itself concealed.

"Stop staring and sit down," she said, patting the bedcovers beside her. "I don't want to leave things where we did, because I have too many questions that need answers. Have a seat."

He did so, amazed all over again at how much she had matured, and yet how very much she was still herself.

"The truth now," she insisted. "How much of what you have told me is real?"

"Do you really think I made it all up?"

"Some men would." Then she cocked her head and regarded him. "But admittedly you are not just any man."

He had to smile at that. "I like to think so. You saw what I could do when I stood up against Hydrach and the Ruhle. You know I am a mage—and a good one—but I also pride myself on being honest. What I told you about my time in the company of the King of the Silver River is all true. I'm not saying it's easy to believe, but that does not discount that it happened."

"So now you're building a citadel?" she scoffed. "A fortress up in the middle of nowhere, because you're the man who is going to single-handedly save the Four Lands? You don't see why I find this all a bit hard to credit?"

He had to concede the point. "It does sound a bit mad when the words are spoken out loud," he said. "But yes, such is my intent. I won't be doing it on my own, though. I've been told I will have aid."

A pause in which he expected her to answer. When she did not, he added, "I was hoping you might be one of those to give me that aid."

Another long pause, but this time she spoke. "And why me, in particular? Why should I aid you?"

He didn't know where to go from there. She sounded less than pleased that he had asked her at all. All of which caused him to wonder what sort of answer she was expecting. Or even what sort of answer he wanted to give.

His response surprised them both. "I've missed you."

She scowled. "Don't say that."

But it was true, he realized. He *had* missed her. Everything about her. All the quirks and idiosyncrasies and prickliness and smiles and sweetness. All of it. He couldn't pretend otherwise.

"We were friends," he said. "For those few weeks, we were friends and companions. We were close. I enjoyed being with you. When I say I missed you, I am telling you the truth. I may not be all that old myself, but I have already lost a lot of people in my life who mattered. I thought it was worth trying not to lose you as well."

"Because I mean something to you?"

"Yes. Because you do."

"You meant something to me, too. But then you didn't come back to find me." The anger was gone from her eyes, replaced by an odd sadness. "For five years."

Gently, he said, "To me, it wasn't . . ."

". . . five years," she finished. "Yes, I know. Intellectually. But you didn't have to live through those five years. I did. I had almost grown used to a life without you. And you've come back to me—only now you plan to leave again. Do you not realize how that makes me feel?"

Actually, he didn't—he hadn't given it any real thought. But he was beginning to suspect he should have. "Am I disappointing you again?"

She sighed. "When I first met you . . . Okay, I was still a young girl and unsure of myself. But I was sure about you. You were so . . . confident in your life and your abilities. You were out creating the kind of life you wanted instead of being bound by the expectations of others. Honestly, I don't know if at the time I wanted to be with you or just *be* you. But I convinced myself that I was in love. Following you on your quest was supposed to be the start of my own life, my own big adventure.

"And then you vanished without a trace, and I was back to being a tavern keeper's daughter in Whip's End, fending off offers of marriage that would just be a different kind of bondage. And I'm not saying it is your fault, but . . . It hurt, Galaphile. It hurt a lot."

He could understand that, though he wasn't certain what to say in return. She didn't give him the chance, forging on immediately.

"And now you're back with this wild tale of missing years, and you ask me to go off with you into the mountains to help save the world, and . . ."

She seemed to slump in on herself. "It feels just like it did before, when I chased after you. Like you are asking me to take another chance on you—asking me to make another change in my life—and then you might just disappear all over again, and I'll be right back where I was. Why should I risk that? I've had my hopes dashed once already, and I don't much want to risk it happening again. Do you understand what I'm saying?"

He did—all too clearly. Whether she had truly been in love with him or not, she had definitely seen him as an escape—as a way to change her life. Much the way he had, once upon a time, seen Starns. Only he had vanished entirely, and she was back where she had been, no longer trusting in chances.

"You don't think I am very dependable," he answered. "You think it would be better to stay where you are—a known quantity—than to risk another disappointment. And I don't blame you for thinking that way. I am very sorry I didn't come back sooner—that I *couldn't* come back sooner. And if you *were* to decide to come with me, I would stay close in a way I couldn't the last time . . . if it's possible. But I can't promise that it'll be possible, Nirianne. I don't think my life will allow for that sort of stability. I'm just not fated to have a steady, dependable existence."

"Because you are going to save the world?"

He felt oddly trapped. "Because I am *trying* to find a way to bring some sort of order to it. I don't know if I will succeed, but I do know that I have to try. And since it is a cause bigger than you and me—bigger than any of us—I fear that my life will never be entirely my own. I have to do what is needed to achieve my goals, and I can't always know in advance what that will be or what it will require of me. I can't tell you that I will always be there for you, because it could end up being a lie. I simply can't be sure."

He exhaled sharply. "Anyway, you make it sound like we are talking about a permanent relationship—a life partnership or something. I thought we were talking about being friends and companions, working together toward a joint goal. I hadn't given much thought to anything more, because even finding you again, but with everything so changed, was shocking. Maybe our visions for what this means are just too different."

She gave him the saddest smile he had ever seen—so sad that he shrank from it. "Perhaps they are. As things stand, I am staying right where I am for now. Have a good trip home."

She rose without a further word and left the room, leaving him alone to consider what had just happened.

He slept little and poorly that night. His talk with Nirianne had left him badly unsettled. It was clear she wanted more from him than he felt comfortable giving. He wanted her friendship—her company, wry humor, and keen insight. He wasn't thinking about anything more. But she, it seemed, was.

But then, perhaps he was not the only one burned by a prior experience. He wondered how much of his determination to keep her as a friend sprang from the pain he still felt at losing Mayele so brutally. Maybe, like Nirianne, he did not want to risk his heart again.

He washed, dressed, and went out into the still-unopened tavern to find some breakfast. Varisol was already sitting at a table alone, sipping from a glass of ale. The other man beckoned him over. "Sit. I'll have the cook bring some food. That must have been a difficult talk you and Nirianne had last night, because she still hasn't come out of her room."

Galaphile nodded but said nothing.

"What did you say to her?" her father pressed.

"Just what I said before—that I'd like her to come back with me to the mountain and help me in my quest. But it doesn't appear she's interested."

Varisol laughed ruefully. "The problem, as I suspect you already know, is not exactly *lack* of interest, but rather too much. I told you she received quite a few offers of marriage since her return from down south. She turned them all down—which was wise, I think, looking back. But she turned them down for a reason. She got herself quite fixated on you five years ago, even as young as she was. I think she was certain that if you came back for her, it would be because you were in love."

Galaphile began to grow irritated. "From start to finish, Varisol, your daughter and I have spent no more than a month together, and most of that was while she was a teenager. I am not responsible for whatever story she told herself about us back then. She was a child to me, and I have not known her long enough as a woman to feel much different about her now."

Varisol clapped him on the shoulder. "I understand, my boy. I am just trying to explain her mind. She gets these stubborn, fixed ideas sometimes, and you know how hard it can be to shake her out of them. Like when she tracked you and Ratcher down to the Silver River country. I know only too well that you cannot force down a feeling once it's there. She will get over it or she won't; it's nothing to do with you. It's everything to do with her. She's a strong, independent-minded woman now, and she makes her decisions for herself."

They didn't say anything more about it after that, just sat there as Galaphile finished his breakfast. When they were finished, he thanked Varisol for his hospitality, then went back to his room to pack.

As he set out, Nirianne was still nowhere in sight, so he said goodbye to her father and left alone.

He walked for four days to reach the start of the road back up to the citadel, arriving just in time to make camp for the night. He built a fire, cooked some food, and thought back to his days with Mayele. She had been his best friend, his confidante, his lover—a person he could talk to about anything. He had a different connection with Nirianne. How had she come to imagine herself in love with him? It was more the possibility of what he represented, he supposed, that she had truly fallen for—the chance for a bigger life. Yet when he offered that to her again, she refused it, which made him feel sad.

Maybe she was someone he could fall in love with over time; there was certainly much about her that he felt drawn to. Yet she had closed down that possibility simply because he had not told her what she wanted to hear in the moment, which would have been a lie.

Sometime during the fifth day, when he was halfway up the road and settled for the night, one of the big mountain cats appeared and lay down beside him. Its big body was warm and comforting, and suddenly he felt a little less alone. In the morning, the cat rose to travel with him the rest of the way up the mountain and stayed with him until they were within a few thousand feet of the fortress.

Then he was left alone once more.

What is happening? Why do I feel so adrift?

But he had no answers. All he had was speculation—and that was dangerous. It could lead you down paths you weren't supposed to travel.

Still, he was so wrapped up in his thoughts that he did not notice the silence ahead until he was nearly at the construction site. But once he became aware of it, he paused, alarmed. He couldn't hear any sounds of workmen or of the encampment preparing for dinner.

Something wasn't right.

He quested out with his magic for signs of life and found nothing. That shouldn't be. Carefully, he continued his approach, alert now for anything that seemed even marginally strange. He climbed the last of the rises leading to the site just as the sun began to slip below the horizon. Ahead of him, the night shadows were gathering across a curiously still and deserted encampment.

Nothing was moving. No one was present.

He slowed to a stop and stared around. There were dozens of stone objects he could not identify, humped things that almost looked like statues all over the place. He squinted at them, but the darkness defeated him. What was he looking at?

Summoning magic, he conjured a light, and that was when he realized what the mysterious objects were.

Statues. Hundreds of them, scattered about the entire construction site. All of stone, and all easily identifiable in the light. A few animals—dogs and cats, horses and cows—but mostly the statues were Dwarves.

They were perfectly formed and easily identifiable. Some of them he recognized immediately. He even knew their names. Yet they were all frozen in place, somehow changed to stone while working.

He turned about slowly and felt himself go cold. Everyone who had come to aid him, to help build a place of safety, had been turned to stone.

Galaphile walked through the mass of statues as if walking through a graveyard, his steps slow and careful. How had this happened? Were these really the men and women he had left behind, or were they nothing more than well-chiseled replicas?

But who sculpts hundreds of statues out of rocks in a bit more than a week?

On the other hand, who can turn hundreds of Dwarves into statues?

No answer he could provide seemed right. Even with magic, this was an amazing piece of work. Who could manage something of this nature?

And then a voice called out from the darkness.

"Magician!" The sound was deep and powerful, reverberating through Galaphile's body—much the same reverberation as what his magic provided to fuel his own volcanic voice when volume was required.

"Welcome home. I have been waiting for you."

TWENTY-ONE

Galaphile peered into the darkness but saw no sign of the speaker—though it was easy enough to conclude that this person was responsible for what had been done to his work crew. And that meant this was an enemy—one apparently powerful and confident enough to challenge him in his own house. But who?

He thought back to those he had faced over the years, but whoever was speaking to him now was obviously confident in his ability to face down Galaphile, which made him potentially more dangerous than any of his previous opponents. Was this new enemy a match for him magically? Until now, no one save the King of the Silver River or possibly Cogline could legitimately make that claim. But the thing with the statues was impressive.

He waited until the last echoes of the other's amplified voice had died away before answering. "What is it you want, other than to find ways to cause trouble for someone you don't know in a place you don't belong?"

Silence followed. After a bit, the invisible speaker said, "Oh, I know you, Galaphile Joss. Not personally, perhaps, but by reputation. Which is sufficient for now. I know you seek to make yourself into a recognizable force in a land you desire to call home."

Galaphile shook his head. "Desire? This *is* my home. I have lived here for the last fifteen years. Can you say the same?"

A strange booming sound echoed in the stillness. It might have been laughter, or it might have been some other form of remonstrance. Or something else entirely.

Galaphile had had enough. Summoning his magic, he sent a swath of brightness in the direction from which the voice had sounded and quickly illuminated the speaker.

A solitary man faced him, making no effort to hide himself. His size, bearing, and demeanor were oddly unmemorable—the kind of man who would never stand out in a crowd. He was young, Human, with dark hair grown rather long and a beard more wispy than full. But, at a closer glance, there was a cruel glint in his dark eyes and an air of leashed power about him that Galaphile had rarely experienced. He was dressed in black robes from head to foot, save for where his face was visible within the shadows of his hooded cloak.

"I am from this same country," the man declared, "but I do not make claim to any single part of it for myself. I come seeking an alliance with a fellow practitioner of the magic arts. I am an accomplished mage; I think what you've found in your camp makes that clear."

Whoever this man was, he was proud of and confident in his abilities.

Galaphile shook his head doubtfully. "Who are you, and why do you think you have the right to treat my workers—who have done nothing at all to deserve it—as if they were your playthings?"

The speaker ignored the first part of his question. "I wish to demonstrate my skills. I want you to witness how much power I possess. I want you to see why I belong at your side, helping you to exercise power of possession over the whole of these lands. Besides, no harm has been done. The transformation is momentary. I simply wanted you to see what I can do."

"You want to *join* in my efforts?" Galaphile asked in disbelief. "You turn all my workers to stone in an effort to convince me you are *useful*?"

"What, are you not impressed? Have I not demonstrated my abilities sufficiently? How can you possibly not see the advantage of having me as a partner?"

Suppressing his irritation, Galaphile forced himself to consider the situation. How much did this creature know about him? If it was his supposition that Galaphile sought to gain power over the people of these lands so that he could rule them, then the answer was likely little. But no harm in checking further.

"You want to be a part of what I am doing?" Galaphile countered. "Then tell me: What is it you think I am trying to do?"

"I think you are building a fortress. Then you will engage allies to enforce your power. I think you seek to become a dominant presence in the region. I want to be part of that. I want to help you learn how to use your power."

A glimmer of understanding settled in, and Galaphile saw a few truths that he had missed before. "So you seek to command jointly with me?" Although he had already suspected that, he still found himself surprised at the other's daring. Even were he to accept such an offer, the man would soon seek to eliminate him and take over what he had built. After all, it was far easier to appropriate than to build. "Who are you?" he asked again. "Where do you come from?"

"All in good time. Now, are you willing to offer me a place in your company, or do I need to freeze you in the same way I have frozen your people and carry on alone? Consider my offer carefully."

Here came the threat—plain and simple. By now, Galaphile was beginning to recognize what was happening. This fellow wasn't threatening—he was boasting. These supposed threats were not what they seemed. No one wielding magic could do what this man claimed to have done. No one had the ability to turn hundreds of living people into stone.

No, what he was seeing was an illusion, albeit an amazing one—a pretense formulated for the express purpose of deceiving him. Clever but false. Perhaps this mage was testing him. Perhaps he was doing something more.

"Why don't you, then," he answered, calling the stranger's bluff, "if you have the power you claim? But I must inform you that your assumption of what I am doing here is wrong. Unlike you, I seek no dominion over this land; I merely wish to bring it peace. Tell me the truth—who are you?"

"Your enemy, if you refuse my request for friendship. Do not think to challenge me, Galaphile! But . . . perhaps you need further convincing?"

His robed arms moved in a series of small gestures, and Galaphile's immediate surroundings began to shimmer. In seconds, a clutch of reptilian creatures that walked upright appeared, stalking through the darkness, eyes gleaming as they came.

Galaphile felt a moment of uncertainty but tamped it down. This was just more of the same—an illusion, a trick. Another effort to make him think he was in danger.

The reptilian beasts drew closer—huge armor-plated creatures that gave no indication of being anything other than what they seemed. But Galaphile knew to trust his instincts.

"Shall I call them off, magician?" the intruder asked. "Shall I save your life while I still can?"

Galaphile replied by summoning up the necessary dispel-and-reveal magic and sending it sweeping outward. At first, nothing happened, and he felt a frisson of doubt. What if he was underestimating this man and his magic was indeed a real threat? Then he tightened his resolve and bore down with greater effort. No, this was an illusion. However good it might be, however real it might feel, it was still nothing but pretense.

He was not giving up. He was certain he knew the truth behind what was happening. This was a test of his resolve and his abilities. This was an effort to discover how malleable he might prove to be.

He lifted his arms and washed the entirety of what had appeared before him away, his magic surrounding and engulfing the whole of it in a cleansing spell.

His efforts were rewarded instantly. The reptilian army vanished. The stone Dwarves disappeared. And all was as it should be, and his construction crew seemed to have merely fallen asleep.

It took him only seconds to break the spell. Then he brightened the light to reveal the true appearance of the stranger who had caused it all to happen.

But the stranger remained a shadow, clouded in mist. "You have given me my answer," the other declared. "You have rejected my overture of friendship and help, and you have made your choice. What follows now will rest solely on you. Know that I will not be dispensed with so easily. You will regret your impudence and your haste. You think yourself safe from me? You are not. Everything you value will be taken from you. Everything you trust in and rely on will be infected. I promise you this."

In a flash of light, the stranger was gone, disappearing as swiftly as the illusions he had fabricated.

Huh, Galaphile thought as his workers began stirring, yawning and stretching and looking about themselves with some puzzlement. *The threats feel real enough. But what does this other man intend that he is keeping to himself?*

He took long minutes to consider what had just happened. It had all been a test, he decided—a way to determine just how willing he was to form the alliance the other craved, or an attempt to measure his abilities and decide if they were a threat. To determine if it was necessary to come at Galaphile in a more deliberate and decisive fashion.

At some point, the man would likely attempt to do it. But how?

With the real world restored, Galaphile went in among his still-groggy workers, telling them what had transpired and assuring them that he was back and they were safe. Night had settled in by now, and nothing remained of the illusions the invasive stranger had created. Who he was and where he had gone were impossible to say, but that he would be back at some point seemed a very real possibility.

Galaphile went on to find all the members of the watch asleep as well. He woke them, reassured them that all was well and there was no reason for concern, and set them back on watch. Still, he was going to have to find new ways to ward his compound against further incursions like tonight's. And for that, he would need to go hunting.

As the camp surged back into motion around him, he felt his exhaustion grow, for the magic he expended had taken its toll. He found a place he could sleep, spread out his travel blanket, and closed his eyes.

He slept, but he did not sleep well. Visions of the intruder haunted him, and he was increasingly troubled that the other man had gotten away. But it was too late to change that now—and besides, he knew he hadn't heard the last of his visitor.

He woke the next morning determined to find a better way to protect the worksite. There were too many outlaw encampments and gangs around, not to mention sorcerers on the order of the one he had encountered last night, and more enemies were bound to test him in the weeks and months to come. So first he needed to enlist the help of men and women who could serve as a protective force for those engaged in the building project.

That said, leaving the construction a second time—and this soon after an attack—was far from ideal. His initial urge was to stay right where he was and make sure things remained stable. But that would merely be delaying any true solution to his problem. So what was he supposed to do if he wanted to be in two places at once?

He began by asking Sanitov to allow him to train at least fifty of his workers as guardsmen, to enable them to offer full-time protection to the other workers. Sanitov told him instead that there were plenty of Dwarf warriors, men and women both, back in the central Dwarf city of Culhaven, and he thought it might be a good idea to see about recruiting a number of them to act as full-time guardians.

For that matter, Galaphile decided, why not seek help from the Elves? They might be a separate nation, with their own ways and means of doing things, but their needs were not so different from those of all the other peoples of this currently benighted world. They had fought in and survived the Great Wars, which had brought them out of their concealment and back into the world. So why shouldn't they now be involved in his project, which aimed to stabilize the whole of the Four Lands?

After all, he still had a standing appointment to see their King.

But again, all this required him leaving the site and going elsewhere to muster a defensive force. And with the walls still barely under construction, he would be leaving a workforce undefended by even physical barriers. Which left only one option.

Magic was required—protective magic. Magic that only he could put in place. No other magicians were available—at least, no others that he felt he could trust. Cogline might be willing to assist, and he could send a request, but that, too, would take time, and there was no guarantee that the reclusive Cogline would agree.

No, this problem was his alone to solve.

{ TWENTY-TWO }

For three straight days, Nirianne was so angry she could hardly think. She had wanted Galaphile to stay. She had wanted him to indicate, in some significant way, that she was important to him. And not just "friend" important, but something deeper. That was why she had confronted him in his room that first night. That was why she had urged him to tell her why it was so important that she come with him into the mountains. That was why she had prodded him to show or tell her something of what she meant to him.

But he hadn't done what she expected. He hadn't done any of it. All he had done was talk about friendship and then leave without speaking to her again.

So yes, she was angry. And hurt. It felt like a betrayal.

But why?

That was the hardest part to explain—and not only to others, but to herself.

When Galaphile had first come wandering into Whip's End in search of her father, she had seen him as mostly a means to an end. All her life, she had felt herself destined for more than being just a tavern keeper's daughter. There was something big out there awaiting her; she was certain of it. So when a stranger wandered into her father's bar in search of adventure—handsome and charming, with an air of casual confidence that made him all the more appealing—it seemed like the answer she had been searching for.

She knew he had been annoyed when she had followed him. Knew, too, that her overly young appearance worked against her. It was hard enough to get anyone to see you as a grown-up at sixteen—and harder still when you looked only twelve. But she had worked diligently to bring him around, to make him see her as an equal partner in their adventure—and it had almost succeeded. In the days before the Mist Marsh, she was certain there was respect and caring growing between them. And in her case, if she was honest, more than a bit of a crush.

And then . . .

He had vanished. Disappeared into the Mist Marsh as thoroughly as if he had been swallowed alive.

And she had ended up a tavern keeper's daughter again, with no glory, no further adventures, no bigger life.

The trouble was, his disappearance was so sudden, so surreal, that she couldn't quite credit it. Had they found his body—or even any of his possessions, abandoned in some apparent struggle—it would have been easier to accept. Even so, as the years scrolled on, she woke every day expecting him to reappear. To carry her off again on some grand adventure. And every day that he did not, a bit more of her hope died and a bit more bitterness crept in.

She grew from a teen to an adult and turned down partnering proposal after partnering proposal, all the while waiting for the day when he would walk back into her life.

In truth, she wasn't sure why she became so fixated on him. But maybe it was the dreams, which started sometime after his disappearance. They began intruding on her sleep with a gentle but firm persistence.

He will come for you.

He is meant for you.

This was the man, the dreams told her, that was supposed to share her life. The one she was supposed to be with forever.

It was as if the dreams opened a window to the future, showing her snippets of what their life could be. There was a fortress ringed by mountains that would be their home. There were moments of quiet domesticity, but there was more, too. Adventures, a bigger purpose . . . even if she could not quite define what that purpose was.

She could not explain the persistence of these dreams or their odd refusal to be dismissed as nothing more than what they seemed— fantasies. When she had been with him, she had been attracted to him. She knew that to be true. But she'd had crushes before. What was it about him that suggested he was The One? When had he become so in her mind?

And still the dreams whispered to her:

He will come for you.

He is meant for you.

Eventually, she persuaded herself that there must have been something in his behavior that warranted it. Something that meant he was thinking and dreaming of her as much as she was thinking and dreaming of him.

If they were meant to be together, as her dreams insisted, then he *would* return for her. And he would declare his need for her as strongly as she was coming to realize she needed him.

And then . . .

Then he returned just as her dreams had promised. But . . . as a friend? With what seemed like no more than a proposition, asking her to join with him to somehow change the world?

It was so deeply opposed to everything the dreams had promised that she tried to push him into some deeper declaration of affection. And when that hadn't worked, she had fobbed him off with some face-saving excuse about her own lack of trust. Because how could she have been so wrong? How could the dreams she had been so certain were true be so false?

Just how badly had she deluded herself?

He had left the following morning, and after three days of rage—at herself, at the dreams, at him—the night visions returned, stronger than ever.

He will come for you.

He is meant for you.

It was, quite frankly, infuriating. What was she to do now? She couldn't go off chasing after him on what, in concrete terms, was little more than a whim. No, he had to come to her, she decided. That was the only way forward. Somehow, through whatever means, he had to realize that she was more to him than just a friend and companion.

Until that happened, all she could do was sit and wait. Besides, she was her father's primary helper by now in the management of the tavern, and that required a substantial amount of time and effort.

This worked—if badly—for about six months—until finally she decided she could endure it no more. This had to be resolved, and it was becoming increasingly clear that there was only one way she could make that happen.

And so she told her father she was taking two weeks off to hike and clear her mind—though it was hard to tell how much of that he believed. Still, she was now twenty-two years old, and he was no longer in a position to tell her what she could and couldn't do. When he had suggested she take someone with her, just as a precaution, she pointed to her hunting knives and longbow and smiled.

"I have all I need," she said.

Knowing better than to argue, he simply nodded, gave her a reassuring kiss on the cheek, and sent her off.

Maybe he understood her better than she thought. Maybe he knew what she intended. Maybe her efforts to conceal her feelings were not as successful as she hoped. It was difficult to know. Her father did not always voice his opinions or reveal his true feelings, but it didn't matter. She was leaving with his consent and blessing, and that would have to be enough.

What she needed in order to feel complete in her life wasn't here. What she required was a man in the mountains that she still believed in her heart was right for her. Even if he turned her down—if he refused her or dismissed her or in other ways made it plain that she was wasting her time—she would be better off than she was now. Because at least then she would know, and maybe the dreams would finally stop.

And if not . . .

She hitched up her backpack and her weapons and set out to discover if her dreams were true.

She walked all day, setting a brisk pace in an effort both to get to where she was going as quickly as she could and to quell those nagging doubts that kept resurfacing: the ones that whispered to her that she was making a mistake. She knew the whispers might be true, and she didn't need to be reminded. She knew she was being brash in a way she had promised herself she wouldn't be, but her need to find out the truth behind her dreams won out over both patience and the fear of humiliation. Sometimes, you just did what you needed to do, and the consequences be damned.

She tracked through countless fields and meadows, climbed slopes and ridges, and worked hard at finding paths and foot- and handholds up seemingly impassable cliff walls. She was young, strong, and agile, however, and though she demanded rigorous effort from herself, she could endure it. Besides, she was driven by a formidable determination.

Still, by the close of the day, she was only halfway up the lower cliffside and thoroughly exhausted. She found a suitable place to spend the night and made camp amid a glorious purple-red sunset. The air, warm all day, had begun to cool, and all across the western horizon, the colors shifted and deepened and left her feeling both comforted and oddly small. She watched until the fiery ball sank away and the darkness fell.

She had already selected the place where she would sleep—a comfortable grassy stretch of ground with a rock wall to her back. She did not think anything on two legs could come at her here without making enough noise to alert her. Four-legged animals were another matter, but she had her knives and longbow at hand and was capable of defending herself with either. Truly, she did not expect to be approached by anything on this clear, bright night. But if something did appear, she was confident she would hear it and wake in time to take whatever action was needed.

Still, she lay awake for a long while, thinking of Galaphile. Wondering what he was doing, where he might be, and if her dreams were truth or delusion. It was all speculation and wishful thinking—she knew that—but it addressed in some small way the need she felt within her.

She wanted him. She wanted him bound to her.

The dreams had promised.

She did not fall asleep for a long time, but when she eventually did, her sleep was deep and unbroken. And there the dream found her.

She walked in deep forest—possibly in a marshland, given the smells of water and plants, of rot and regrowth—and the air was filled with the scent of flowers. Now and then small creatures approached, birds and animals both, not afraid of her in the least. Their small voices whispered to her, telling her to be brave and strong, as she was destined for great things. Her blood was to be joined with the blood of a warrior lord, and a builder of dreams.

He will come for you, one voice whispered.

He is meant for you, said another.

He will be your forever partner. His blood will mix with yours in your children.

What he does, he will do for you.

What you create together will belong to everyone.

And so it went, the tiny voices speaking softly and encouragingly, over and over.

She believed everything she was told, though she had no proof that any of it was true. It was enough that it felt true to her. It was enough that it buoyed her hopes.

Then, just before it all vanished, an old man appeared—tall and powerful, with an ancient bearing. He came out of the trees amid night mists so thick, they seemed to cling to him. He was huge and intimidating, but she stood her ground before him and watched as he raised one arm, gesturing toward the distant peaks of what she realized must be the Dragon's Teeth.

They will come for you, he said. **They will befriend and guide you. When needed, they will ward you.**

Then the giant himself faded away, and she came awake almost instantly.

She blinked in the growing dawn and sat up. She tried to make sense of what she was seeing, as it took a moment for her eyes to adjust. Then her focus cleared, and her heart jumped within her breast.

Three massive mountain lions ringed close around her, as still as if they were made of stone. But in truth, they were creatures of flesh and blood, as alive as she was, though full of teeth and claws. She took a number of deep breaths as they stared at her. She could see the movements of their chests and sides as they breathed, the blinks of their eyes as they studied her. Two were gigantic beasts, and one a bit smaller, all of them colored a peculiar mix of gray and black.

Should she try to communicate with them? She didn't know how—not really. What were they doing so close to her like this? Were they here for a reason? What sort of reason could have brought them to her?

Then she remembered the words in her dream.

They will come for you. They will befriend and guide you.

The cats shifted suddenly, weaving around her, studying their surroundings. They made no sound—not even the huffing coughs that all mountain cats emitted. She watched them for a few more moments and slowly came to realize they meant her no harm.

Finally, she rose to her feet, and instantly the big cats turned.

Their eyes shifted to fix on her. She noticed they stood together, all three facing toward her, all lined up, waiting. *For what?* She didn't know at first, but after they continued to hold their positions for long minutes, she took a chance.

"Going my way, are you?" she asked, breaking the silence. "Are you waiting on me?"

No response of any kind. They just stared at her.

"You should learn to talk," she muttered.

With no other choice but to start walking if she intended to complete her quest, she moved toward the cliff walls once more. The mountain lions fell into step beside her—one leading, one to either side. They weren't herding her or trying to show her the way, she sensed; they were simply providing protection and reassurance.

She smiled as she walked into the sunrise and began to climb again.

It took her three more days to reach the outskirts of Galaphile's camp, and she was instantly impressed by what she saw. The building site was huge and busy with industry, and even the rough outlines of the fortress that were currently in place showed that it would be massive.

With the lions still all around her, she walked past the sentries, who took one look at her companions and backed away. She passed amid the builders, who mostly stopped whatever they were doing and stood star-

ing as she went by. She nodded at those who spoke to her, eyes searching for someone who would challenge her or finally ask who she was
and what she was doing.

Eventually, one Dwarf appeared. He came out of a crowd and walked
right up to her, ignoring the lions—clearly the one in charge. "Who are
you?" he asked in the Dwarfish language.

"My name is Nirianne. I'm here to see Galaphile." She knew the language as well as he did thanks to her father and those Dwarves who had
frequented the tavern for years. "Is he here?"

The other shook his head. "Galaphile is gone for the next month
or so. Off to the Westland. He left me in charge of the site. My name is
Sanitov."

"I'm pleased to meet you, Sanitov," Nirianne said, extending a hand.
"I'll wait. Can you find me a bed?"

Sanitov nodded. "Do you want to join us in our work while you wait
for the High Lord?"

High Lord? Such adulation! She thought about it a minute, but she
liked the idea of being involved. "I want to help him. What can I do?"

"There are lots of choices; we need workers of all sorts. Does Galaphile know you are here?"

"He invited me to come."

Sanitov glanced down at the mountain lions. "Your pets?"

She laughed. "No one's pets, I think. My guides and protectors." She
turned to the mountain lions and said, "You can go now. Thank you for
helping me."

The big cats appeared to understand. Without any sort of response,
they turned away and soon vanished back into the surrounding forest.

Sanitov grinned. "You seem to have some of the talents that Galaphile has. Do you have magic?"

She shook her head. "Sadly, I don't. And we are just friends. But he
invited me to come here, so I have. Can I please get something to eat? I
ran out of food this morning."

Sanitov smiled and nodded and beckoned for her to follow. She
smiled back, thinking, *Yes. This is where I am supposed to be.*

This was the first day of her new life.

TWENTY-THREE

In the weeks following the attack, Galaphile had turned his attention solely to ensuring the safety of his construction site. Thanks to Sanitov's suggestion, he had received a company of Dwarf hunters from Culhaven whom he assigned to protecting the site and scouting the surrounding countryside in an effort to head off any further incursions by raiders. More laborers arrived from other Dwarf cities as well, speeding up the pace of the citadel's construction. But still he felt more was needed.

A fully magical barrier around the site, he soon realized, would be too draining to maintain full-time. But small, passive alert spells that could be placed at strategic locations around the perimeter and triggered if disturbed were possible. So he installed them everywhere.

And there were further methods he could employ that required no magic at all. With the aid of some of his new Dwarf helpers, he had massive logs placed in areas he thought were too open and vulnerable to intrusions. He laid heavy chains meant to hinder the use of wheeled attack vehicles and transports. He had observation platforms placed high up in the trees so that surprise attacks could be spied out and averted.

Drop traps and pitfalls were constructed and mapped as well—though Galaphile was wary of using forms of protection that could prove as dangerous to his people as to intruders. He never forgot that the primary intent of his efforts was to protect rather than attack.

In places, he even strung tiny bells in lines both to warn off would-be attackers and to signal their approach.

Scouts and sentries ran regular circuits, and security guards were kept in place everywhere a potentially dangerous point of entry or attack existed.

In particular, he kept a careful watch for the mysterious mage who attacked the site before. And perhaps it was good that he maintained his vigilance, for several times over the next few weeks, the mage tested his new defenses, quickly learning to bypass each with ease. It was true that the bulk of his defenses were designed to keep off larger opposing forces or determined individuals—but not so much a determined individual who could cloak himself into invisibility with magic or levitate over traps. Meaning that Galaphile was forced to grow ever more creative in his endeavors.

He had no idea how many times his opponent had gotten into the building site, if at all, but if so, he had done no damage that Galaphile could see. Still, it unnerved him, and so he redoubled his efforts, eventually coming up with a way to erect a more passive magical bubble around the whole site that took minimal energy to maintain but would alert him should it encounter a rival magic.

And this one did seem to foil his enemy enough that, after several unsuccessful attempts to cross the warding lines, the man's incursions dropped away entirely.

Meanwhile, the fortress was growing by the day—if by growth you counted the number of basement levels cut into the pinnacle's rocky depths. As the lowest level was being excavated, Sanitov's workers broke through to an area of geothermal activity where hot steam rose. This greatly alarmed Galaphile, who wondered if the plateau could hold a fortress as solid as the one he planned. But Sanitov assured him that this was more of a boon than anything—that the narrow seam through which heat rose did not impact the structural integrity of the underlying mountain and could be used to heat his fortress in the winter. Some hasty retrofitting of ducts and vents was undertaken, which Galaphile knew he would be grateful for next winter.

The one important task Galaphile had not yet acted on was his determination to seek help from the Elves. Surely the Elves would want to put a stop to the growing chaos washing across the Four Lands, and having a company of their famed Elven Hunters working with him would be a boon. There was no reason to think they wouldn't be willing to provide such a company, but first he had to go to them and present his case. And that would mean leaving the building site once more.

Galaphile wasn't quite ready to risk that again yet—even if his rival mage had backed off.

So he delayed making the Westland trip for another four months, during which time his last conversation with Nirianne kept haunting his thoughts. He didn't know why he kept dwelling on it—or on her—but as the weeks stretched on, he found himself increasingly missing her. Missing her good humor, her wit, her blunt honesty. Missing her presence in his life. Every time a knotty problem arose with the construction project or any of his protection efforts, he found himself longing for her insights, wondering what solutions she might see that he did not. If only he could have convinced her to accompany him here, he thought, how much easier would it have been to confront his problems?

Still, he found comfort in telling himself that she was better off back in the safety of her home with her father, where the dangers were considerably less. One day, it would be time for her to come. But perhaps that time wasn't now.

In the end, he wasn't sure what it was that drove his decision to leave. Logically, there was no reason to delay any longer. There had been no attempts at further encroachments, raids, or efforts to disable the project for the last two months, so his protective efforts seemed to have proved a deterrent—particularly to the rival mage. He had a stalwart core of Dwarf defenders in place, and he had made the decision after the first attack to slow work on the fortress itself by diverting part of the workforce to begin constructing the defensive outer walls and gates, which were now about waist-high. And as a final incentive, he realized he could stop in at Whip's End along the way.

Turning once again to Sanitov for leadership in his absence, he packed his travel gear, and on a morning rife with sunlight and bird-song, he set out. He went alone, preferring to travel that way—to be responsible for himself and no one else.

He decided to take the more direct route to Whip's End over the mountains this time, feeling a sudden eagerness to see Nirianne again—no matter how awkwardly they had left things before. He and Nirianne were friends, he hoped, so they could work things out. The relationship between them was too important to be cast aside.

On the fourth day, it was nearing midafternoon by the time he reached the outskirts of Whip's End. He traced a path to the Short Shot and went inside eagerly. Busy as always, it was filled with late-afternoon or early-evening drinkers, the tables mostly taken, the barmaids working hard enough to suggest they might be wishing for a little more help. He stood at the entry, surveying the place. He spied Varisol sitting at the end of the bar and walked over to join him.

"Well, well, this is a surprise," the older man announced, his grin wide and welcoming. He was puffing on one of his favorite pipes. "Did you bring back my daughter?"

Galaphile stopped short, confused. "I thought Nirianne was here. I came to see you both."

"She left three days ago to find you. She told me she was just taking a few days for herself, but I know her well enough by now. Did you not see her?"

"No, we must have passed right by each other. I left three nights ago."

It was only now that Galaphile realized how much of his desire to recruit the Elves to his cause had actually been motivated by his desire to see Nirianne along the way. "She went alone?" he asked.

"Said that was the way she wanted it. She's familiar with the mountains and the flats alike. She doesn't need someone with her—"

He hadn't finished when Galaphile interrupted. "I think I'd better go after her. The other business can wait. I'll go back up-country and have a look. I mean, it would be rude to leave her up there alone for months, if she came specifically to find me. Besides, she's much too . . ."

Important, he thought, but he left the word unspoken.

For with that single unspoken word, he locked onto a truth he had been pushing away without even realizing it. Putting other concerns and worries before it. But there was indeed something more between

Nirianne and himself than common friendship. He had been denying this from the start, pretending that friendship was all there was to it. Realizing she might be in danger now, however, caused him to face up to what he had been conveniently ignoring.

She meant something to him. Something more than the friendship they shared—something more than he had felt for anyone since he had lost Mayele. And in that instant, he realized what it was about her that had nudged at his memories since he had last seen her, all grown up. She was the woman in the dreams shown him by the King of the Silver River! She was the woman who was standing beside him, viewing the construction of the citadel. He hadn't recognized her as the same girl he had left behind. But Nirianne was that woman; he was certain of it.

So now he needed to find her for more reasons than ever. Not only for the sake of his present, but for his future as well.

Nirianne was exhausted. She had spent the entire day hauling packs of mortar and work tools off supply wagons and up to the building site. Sanitov had suggested she serve as a water carrier for the other workers, but she had brushed the idea aside. How would it help her if she looked privileged and soft? She had never been one to back away from any sort of hard work, and she was not about to start doing so now.

Indeed, her willingness to shoulder the hard labor had earned her considerable respect. After only two days, she was on a first-name basis with most of the workers, who would not hesitate to ask for her help if they needed it. She ate with them, drank with them, joked and told stories with them at the evening campfires. They admired her spunk and her willingness to undertake any sort of assignment that she was physically able to do.

And not only that, but her days running a tavern with her father had helped her streamline certain processes to keep the work moving faster and more efficiently.

Still, the work was tiring, so on this night she had determined an early bedtime was best and had retired immediately after dinner. Just temporarily, and only in his absence, she had been given Galaphile's tent. The camp was crowded, but new quarters could be found for her when he returned, Sanitov told her.

She had found something right and comforting about being among his things, and wondered how she could convince him to let her stay when he returned.

She fell asleep now, nestled in his bedding, with traces of his scent in her nose—and later woke with a start when a voice hissed urgently in her ear.

"Missus, wake now!"

She sat up hurriedly. "What is it?" It was one of the Dwarves, his face familiar. "Is something wrong?"

"Some movements out there on the verge. Sanitov worries it might be an unfriendly intrusion. He wants you in a safer place. A short distance downhill is a wagon with guards. Come now, please!"

Had she not been still sleepy, and had she not been familiar with the face of her visitor, she might have hesitated. But there was nothing to alarm her, so she rose in response to his words, gathered up her work jacket and a few weapons, and followed her guide out into the night. She felt no need for further caution; she sensed no threat. Carrifset—that was his name—led her downhill along the back road to where the wagons were parked. It was fully dark by now, and she scanned the shadows for movement, her senses just starting to wake fully.

"Here," he said, beckoning her into a wagon parked apart from most of the others. "I have to go, but you can hide in here for now. You'll have guards all around you, and you'll be safe enough for a few hours, at least."

She climbed up obediently, using the spoked wagon wheel as a ladder. She pushed her way through the wagon covers and peered around in the darkness.

At once, a scented cloth was pressed over her face and a cloth bag came down over her head. The cords threaded around its opening were yanked shut, pulling the bag tightly around her face. Cords likewise pinned her arms to her sides, and an instant later, she was snatched up, thrown over someone's burly shoulder, and hauled away.

In seconds, the cloth scented with sleeping potion did its work, and she was unconscious.

Galaphile had no reason to think Nirianne was in any immediate danger or that she hadn't reached the mountain encampment safely. But still, something was troubling him even before he reached the edges of the camp close to noon. Maybe it was just the parallels to the past and memories of what had happened to Mayele that bothered him: He had also been gone on the day Starns's camp was attacked and everyone was killed. Or maybe it was something more, something he sensed with his magic.

But mostly, he thought later, it was his nagging memory of the threats issued by the dark stranger. So he had pushed himself hard on the journey home, completing what should have been a four-day trip in only three.

He entered the building site to find workers mostly going about their business save for a handful who were rushing about as if engaged in something much more urgent. He was seen immediately, and shouts went up. Before he knew what was happening, Sanitov was there.

"Nirianne arrived here at camp a few days ago, but she disappeared sometime last night. She was taken or at least lured away somehow. Come see."

He took his now panicked commander to his empty tent, where no signs of a forced capture were in evidence—save for a note:

I promised you would regret your refusal to partner with me. Now you understand the consequences of doing so. If you want her back, come find her.

A hunt of the entire camp had been under way since the morning, but there was no sign of Nirianne or any hint of where she had been taken. Yet for Galaphile, there was no doubt that the note was from his rival mage. He was being tested yet again.

Galaphile felt his heart drop. Nirianne had been taken right out from under the noses of her companions, which should not have been possible. Right away, he wondered if any of them had been responsible for her abduction. Whatever the truth might be, he knew what he had to do. He had to find her and bring her back. Quickly. But how would he manage that? He had no idea where to begin. In a camp of this size, it would be impossible to sort out the vast array of footprints, and tracking her with magic might prove impossible for the same reason.

Sanitov went off to make another survey of the camp, hoping that someone had seen something of what had transpired. A single body was eventually discovered, a Dwarf by the name of Carrifset. He had been stabbed repeatedly. But the only tracks that appeared around him were made by Dwarves.

Galaphile was devastated. The rival mage had somehow penetrated his wards without triggering them and seized Nirianne. This was his way of getting back at Galaphile, of forcing him to do what he wanted.

He was conscious of passersby glancing at him with guilty, worried looks before quickly passing on. But he was still standing in place, trying to decide what to do, when a mountain lion appeared. It regarded him for a few minutes, then walked away, stopped, and looked back.

Does it know something? Galaphile wondered. *Does it realize I am looking for Nirianne? Can it help me find her?*

He didn't know, but he had to find out. He had no other way of determining where she was and no other means of tracking her down. Whatever had become of her, she was getting farther away with the passing of every moment, and he was just standing there.

He knelt and waited for the lion to come back to him. The huge beast leaned in and nuzzled his face. He had been sent to help, Galaphile realized, and he would do what was required of him. The lion knew something of Nirianne's location, and this was Galaphile's best chance of finding her. He simply had to trust in this.

He grabbed the arm of a passing worker and gave him a message for Sanitov, telling him that he would be leaving to search for Nirianne alone. The decision was easily made. He could not lose her the way he had Mayele; the very thought left him twisted in knots.

He had to do something. Anything.

TWENTY-FOUR

U nder the lion's patient scrutiny, Galaphile strapped on blankets and heavy clothing and food packs. He had no idea how far he would need to travel, or where Nirianne was being held. Had he brought too much with him? Or too little? Well, nothing to do about it save set out and hope for the best.

The cat nudged him, then led him down the mountainside.

The note made it clear that Nirianne had been taken for use as a bargaining chip, which in some ways reassured him. Harming her would yield nothing—and killing her even less. He had some reason to hope that she would be kept alive until he could manage to find her.

Galaphile was well traveled, thanks to his early years with Starns, but he had never spent any serious time in the Northland, which he could tell was where the cat was leading him. That was Troll country, and no one was anxious to encounter creatures who lived such a harsh, nomadic existence. They were a rough-hewn people—though this was hardly an all-inclusive summary. Galaphile was not someone who painted whole nations in a solitary color or identified them by a single physical or behavioral characteristic. Life was complicated, and those who lived it were complex—no matter their origins. If the Trolls were tough and unpredictable, it was mostly because that was how they were able to survive in their particular part of the world.

It was forbidding terrain he crossed—barren, rocky, and mountainous. And while the Trolls could be dangerous, they were nowhere near as deadly as the feral creatures that cohabited with them—slinks, wiverns, ghouls, dragons, and the like.

No, there was no kindness to be found in the Northland. The whole broken, jumbled, rutted area was one vast, timeless graveyard in which the dust blew in violent storms across the barren earth and the north winds howled through the mountains unrelentingly.

Yet this was where the mountain lion—who had obviously been instructed by the King of the Silver River—led. Galaphile had great faith in these beasts, based largely on what they had done for him before, so he was prepared to extend that faith further than he would have otherwise. It was, he knew, all he had to rely on besides himself, as he had deliberately chosen not to risk any more lives than his own on this journey.

He was content to rely on his skills and his magic to see him through.

Even so, things went wrong almost from the first.

His first two days of travel went well, the skies open and clear, the air clean and fresh, and his determination strong. But by midday on the third day, storm clouds moved in. Soon, the constant howl of the wind became his unwelcome travel song and the rain pelted down almost as hard as hail. He was still traversing the empty flats of the Streleheim, but the stench of the swamp-laden waters of the distant River Lethe permeated the whole of the surrounding land. His pace slowed as the ground turned soggy, and his confidence flagged as the day lengthened with no sign of the rain abating.

It was still pouring by nightfall, and there was no shelter to be found, so he made camp out in the open. It rained on him all night and for the following days as well.

Close to sunset on the sixth day, as he was finally nearing the southern bank of the River Lethe amid a steady drizzle of rain that now seemed eternal, another mountain lion appeared—a huge beast with a worn, ragged coat and scars everywhere. This cat had seen some tough times and survived some difficult battles. It yawned as he approached, as if bored by him already, revealing the biggest set of teeth that Galaphile had ever seen.

The cat who had brought him this far was already turning around and starting back the way it had come, and Galaphile wished momentarily that he could have done the same. After so many days of rain, his clothing was thoroughly sodden.

But the new cat was already slouching along the river's edge, moving downstream toward some obvious shallows that would allow them to cross, and Galaphile had to hurry to catch up.

The river crossing was quick and easy, the waters never rising for more than a foot at this location. That said, they ran a mixture of swamp green and dirt gray, their noxious stink far stronger now that he was in their flow. But since Galaphile was already soaked through from the rains and grimy from sleeping on muddy ground, this newest layer of filth could not make him feel worse than he already did.

A single predator challenged their crossing, choosing to attack him over the mountain lion. It was a reptile that must have been fifteen feet in length, and it came for him in a churning rush of water and teeth, its jaws gaping wide. Galaphile summoned his magic and blew the creature out of the river with such power that it flew dozens of feet before landing back in the mire. It recovered from the blow almost immediately, barely shaken, but wisely decided to leave Galaphile alone.

On the far side of the river, the shaggy cat led him up a slope to a rise with a sheltering overhang that gave him a chance to lie down in a dry spot as night descended. After he had chased away the snakes and spiders, he was able to surround himself with a repellent magic that kept everything at bay.

He slept in his still-damp clothes, and the air never warmed. He was awake before sunrise and feeling so dismal that he was ready to set out immediately. His huge guide roused with a stretch and a yawn, then briskly set off.

Unlike his previous companion, this cat seemed to be in something of a hurry, so keeping up with it proved a challenge. The two walked steadily for most of the day, ignoring the fresh rains, the steady winds, and the silence. Oddly, there were few sounds from out of the vast wilderness through which the pair was walking. Now and then, an animal screamed, but not once did Galaphile witness the cause or the killer.

By nightfall, the formidable wall of the Knife Edge Mountains was before them, full of deep crevices and fissures and sheer rock faces. The rain was still falling, and Galaphile could not shake the feeling that almost anything might be lurking in the shadows. His cat guide led him directly toward a particularly deep opening in the rock wall and glanced back at Galaphile. By now, the sun had set and the blackness within seemed absolute. There was a decided hush in the suddenly windless air, and Galaphile could not hear even the rough sounds of his cat guide's breathing. He had never been more reluctant to enter a place than he was to step into that gaping darkness, but when the cat padded within, he had no choice but to follow.

Once inside, Galaphile used his magic to summon a light. He found himself in what looked to be a long, narrow tunnel that stretched away through the mountain, empty and deserted. He could hear nothing save for his own and the cat's breathing and could sense no other presence. Even the air smelled dry and empty.

But with the rock ceiling above him, at least the rain was no longer an issue. He debated casting a spell to remove the water from his clothing but decided not to waste the energy, which he might need once they found Nirianne. It would take longer the natural way, but time could solve this particular problem better than energy.

He glanced over at his feline companion, who seemed to be waiting for him with an expectant air. He smiled and gestured, then followed the cat deeper into the tunnels.

They slept that night under the mountain in an impenetrable dark, and upon waking, he conjured another light and they traveled on. The tunnel seemed to meander about, twisting and turning until he had lost all sense of direction. Still, he found himself unprepared when the tunnel spat them out again under an open sky in what looked to be mid-afternoon.

His clothes were now drier from a day spent under the mountain, so he was glad to see that the interminable rain had finally stopped. He was less delighted, however, to discover a mountain fortress hunched on the plains before them.

Rising within the vast emptiness before him, well away from the Razor Mountains where they loomed in the far distance north, was a small cluster of mountains that at its center point contained a singular solitary peak closely resembling the shape of a Human skull.

Sitting in its midst was a fortress with walls that climbed from the ground up into the mountain face and stretched from side to side across. The skull was vast and rugged in its worn and chiseled form, clear enough even from here that it had been shaped deliberately to take on its present look. And the entrance could be discerned between its upper and lower jaws.

He felt a shiver run down his spine. The skull had a demonic and ruinous cast to it, and he wanted nothing to do with it.

The cat headed straight for it, however, and as they drew closer, Galaphile watched as it resolved itself into a huge central building that was surrounded by and attached to a series of smaller towers.

The sun set as they were walking, and in the gathering shadows of twilight, the fortress looked more intimidating than ever.

By the time they reached its front entrance, full night had descended but no lights had come on from within the fortress. It looked deserted, but the cat seemed to feel otherwise.

Though the feline kept walking forward, Galaphile stopped and studied what he was seeing, searching for anything that might tell him what waited ahead. But there was only stone and darkness. No further movements. No signs of life.

So having no better choice, he gestured the cat onward. He had to find Nirianne. It had now been nine days since she was taken.

The creature rose and took the vanguard again, leading him through the gaping jaws of the entrance then through a series of doorways and into a large foyer that led into an even larger, circular chamber; this rose two stories and seemed to serve no particular purpose, though it was lined with balconies looking down. There were no furnishings of any kind, and the tower had the feel of a sarcophagus, stale and empty of life. Stairways led upward on either side, crisscrossing over and under their separated sections as they swept along the rounded walls.

The lion chose the stairs to the right and began to climb, while Galaphile followed with growing uncertainty. This felt like a trap. But then, he had learned to trust the lions who guided him. If the creatures had wanted him dead or incapacitated, they could have managed either on the journey. No, this was something else. Something yet to be discovered. Though admittedly, his unease was compounded by the open drop that loomed to one side, for the stairs had no outer railing and were barely wide enough for the cat to navigate comfortably.

The top of the stairs opened onto a broad balcony, and hallways ran in various directions deeper into the building. The grizzled cat moved to one of them and stopped. Galaphile walked up to it and waited for the cat to do something, but the creature just sat there, staring back. Once again, waiting. But for what?

Galaphile summoned a magic that searched the darkness ahead. Doorways lined the hallway farther on, all of them closed. Again, there were no signs of life of any sort.

Galaphile sighed and stepped past the cat. When he turned to look back, the cat stayed where he was. Apparently, his guide wasn't going any farther. But he had brought him this far, and seemed to believe that what Galaphile was searching for lay ahead.

So Galaphile hesitantly moved on, searching the darkness with pings of magic to determine what, if anything, waited. These revealed nothing more than the closed doors on either side of the hallway, with nothing behind them.

The corridor ended at a pair of huge, iron-bound doors. Galaphile walked up to them and tested the handles. They gave way easily, and the door swung open a crack. He pushed it all the way open and stepped in. Lights ignited the moment he entered, filling the chamber with a brilliant wash of illumination.

Shades!

Nirianne, looking worn and beaten down, was chained to an iron ring embedded in the farthest wall. Beside her was the man who had invaded their camp some months back—a still, dark, and solitary figure, although no longer concealed. His narrow face bore a lean and satisfied look, and his skin was so pale that it was almost ghostly.

The pair of them sat together near the rear wall of a vast circular chamber. Stretching out along the circumference of the entire wall were several dozen creatures carved of stone that looked vaguely similar to distorted Humans, weapons of all sorts clutched in their clawed hands— blades and daggers of all sizes and shapes, maces and axes, spears as long as ten feet, bows, bludgeons, garrotes, and clubs—all sorts of weapons remembered and re-created from ancient times.

Abruptly, Nirianne raised her eyes and met his from across the room. The smells of pollution and death were suddenly everywhere— the stench so pervasive that it felt like it was emanating from the stones themselves.

In that instant's time, he realized the truth.

All along the walls, the stone statues that appeared to be decorations were coming to life, and all of their eyes were turned toward him.

Galaphile swore in frustration. He'd been trapped.

TWENTY-FIVE

Galaphile was a seasoned warrior and a skilled user of magic, so he did not panic or freeze in the face of this threat. In less than three seconds, he had scanned the entirety of the room and its occupants, and he had taken the measure of his opposition. Already, the creatures had begun to drift closer to him, chittering and cackling and hissing in delight. They were an assorted bunch, once something more recognizable but now twisted versions of the creatures they used to be—members of the Races somehow poisoned or transformed into something other. There was an odd combination of dullness and avarice in their gazes, and they were clearly the product of dark magic.

Already Galaphile was summoning the magic necessary to defend himself.

Had his feline companion known of this trap beforehand and deliberately led him into it?

He had his answer almost immediately.

The vast chamber reverberated with the ferocious roar of the lion as it bounded into the room, slashing its way through the attackers who sought to block its way. Bodies went flying as the big cat barreled through them. Screams rose to shrieks, and all about the room creatures cringed and shrank away in an effort to escape. But the cat paid no attention to any of them, lantern-yellow eyes fixed only on Nirianne. The cat bounded straight for her, covering the fifty feet that separated them in what seemed like mere seconds. Galaphile had never seen anything move so fast or with such determination.

His rival mage rose instantly to meet the cat, bursts of fire flashing from the fingertips of his gloved hands. But before he could do any damage, the lion was on top of him, claws sweeping downward. Only by the barest of margins did the mage vanish into smoke as the lion's claws ripped through the air where he had been standing seconds before. Then he disappeared completely.

Galaphile was already in motion, as well, ignoring everything but his burning need to reach Nirianne. He wanted her safe more than he had wanted anything since he'd lost Mayele. He did not know where that feeling had been hiding; he only knew that it was irrefutable.

Racing the rest of the way through the opponents that remained, he closed the distance right behind the cat and, using his magic, wrenched away the chains that fastened Nirianne to the wall and tore them from her wrists.

As she slumped toward the stone floor, Galaphile caught her midair and drew her close against him. "I have you," he whispered in her ear. "Just hold on to me. Hold tight!"

He looked through the surrounding morass of charging bodies for some indication of where the mage had fled, but there was no sign of him. His minions, still shaken by the fury of the lion, were only just beginning to recover and start forward once more, intent on finishing the battle. Apparently unafraid of dying, they lurched and stumbled ahead. Galaphile could easily tell that there might be too many of them to be stopped, even using his strongest magic. Escape was the only sure way out.

But he would not depart without Nirianne.

The lion must have reached the same conclusion. It was acting more strategically now, slowly clearing a path toward the door.

Galaphile advanced behind it, one arm wrapped about Nirianne's waist. Moving as swiftly as he could manage, he used his free hand to summon a spell of mass confusion. Flashes of light burst into being, flooding the room with blinding colors and searing brightness. With his eyes squinted but his destination firmly fixed in his mind, he made a rush for the doors he had come through, employing the same spell he had used against the reptile in the river to cast back his attackers when they came for him.

All the while, the big cat continued its own battle until an arrow took it in the chest and dropped it to its knees. For a few seconds more it struggled to fight back against its attackers, catching hold of what foes it could. But then it lost its footing and went down in a heap, disappearing under a surge of bodies. Galaphile waited for the sound of the cat's furious roar, but there were only hungry wails erupting from the throats of the creatures that had finally overcame it.

The lion was gone. It had done everything it could to save them, but its life was over.

Galaphile was stricken. Without the huge cat's assistance, any chance of escape seemed to slip away. Yet somehow, with Nirianne clutched close, he managed to reach the entry doors and push through into the hallway beyond. He surged ahead with fresh determination as she suddenly squirmed free, shouting out to him that she could run well enough on her own. With both hands now freed, he wheeled back and threw up a wall of fire behind them to block their pursuers.

Along the hallways and down the stairs toward the lower levels they fled, finding their way back through a maze of corridors and tunnels. He could hear Nirianne talking to him—or perhaps just to herself; he wasn't sure. He could not manage to focus on her words sufficiently to comprehend them, concentrating instead on using his magic to keep their attackers at bay.

Then suddenly the doors were ahead of them, and they broke free of the fortress.

Their pursuers did not seem to be following. Still, Galaphile wasn't taking any chances.

The night was moonless, and there was little light to see by as they fled. But mostly the ground was free of obstacles as they put more distance between themselves and the fortress.

What was happening here?

While he didn't know the identity or background of his enemy, Galaphile was certain that it was the same man who had come to his encampment and sought to overpower him with illusions, and who had then tested his barriers so assiduously after. So who was he? And where was he now? Had the mountain lion done more damage to him than Galaphile realized? Why had he given up chasing them? For that matter, why wasn't *anyone* chasing them?

Eventually, they reached the foothills of the Knife Edge Mountains. Both were nearly exhausted. And since Galaphile had only a partial idea of where they were, he figured that high ground might be best for now. Nirianne was still keeping pace with him, but after her imprisonment and the events of the night, she was starting to stagger. So Galaphile found a crop of huge rocks where they could shelter and scrambled into their midst, hunkering down in the shadows.

"We can rest here," he told her, sitting at her side, fighting hard to regain his breath. "For a time anyway. You sleep. I'll keep watch."

They were the first words he had spoken to her since fleeing the prison. Nirianne stared at him as if seeing him for the first time ever and nodded in acknowledgment. She had tried to speak to him earlier, but he hadn't been able to understand her. Now she stared at him silently.

Then she lay down, turned her back to him, and slept.

He sat watching the landscape north, but no one came after them. Nothing appeared on the horizon. No sounds of movement arose from the darkness. The world might have forgotten them entirely for all their surroundings suggested.

He glanced down again at Nirianne's sleeping form and thought about all that had happened since he had come to find her. That he had managed to find her at all was something of a miracle. But to be able to rescue her and bring her back safe? He closed his eyes in gratitude. This new intense protectiveness he felt for her was both exhilarating and troubling. He had always felt affectionate toward her, but what he was feeling now was so much more. What was she to him: A friend? A partner? Something more? What of the dream shown to him by the King of the Silver River? Standing next to him as she had in that dream suggested she was to be important in his life—an intrinsic part of what was coming.

Yet how could he commit himself to his building project as well as to her? Both should be given his complete attention. With the possibility of a personal future suddenly arising, a part of him wanted to walk away from his other commitments. Why couldn't he just have the life of marriage and family that he had always intended instead of pursuing this questionable passion for bringing order to the peoples of the Four Lands? A passion risen out of the deaths of friends that in the moment had felt so important but now felt so distant?

He rubbed his eyes, which were burning with weariness, and continued to gaze out into the Northland, still wondering about why there was no pursuit.

Yet nothing appeared—and he was still looking out at an empty landscape when he finally fell asleep.

When he woke, dawn was breaking. In the dim early light, everything was a maze of shadows and mist. He half expected to see pursuers approaching, but there were none. The plains were empty.

Galaphile felt a shiver run down his spine.

"Galaphile, I'm done," Nirianne said from behind him.

He hadn't heard her either wake or approach, but he turned at once to face her.

"I came looking for you because you asked it of me and because I thought it important to discover what lies between us. Now I think I know."

"Nirianne—" he began.

But she cut him off. "No, let me finish. I saw the building site. I talked with Sanitov, worked with him and his people, and even came up with a few ideas on my own. Like I said, I know. I understand what you are doing, and its importance. As you say, it is bigger than both of us. And if you belong to this project, as I think you must, you cannot also belong wholly to me."

She paused. "A few days ago, I might have even been fine with that. When I was part of the building project, I thought I had found the kind of purpose that my life has been lacking. I felt that maybe my life would be good there, even if you never returned my feelings.

"But I've had some time to think about it over the past few days, and I'm honestly not even sure of what I feel for you anymore. Yes, there was a time I thought myself in love with you. You were attractive and settled; you had a life of purpose before you. That was appealing. Plus, I kept having these dreams that told me that we belonged together—dreams that were so convincing in their reality, they overrode my doubts about your feelings or how little I actually knew about you.

"But all I've managed to do since I got captured is make myself into a tool to be used against you, and that is not the kind of purpose I want for my life. To be constantly in jeopardy just because I am attached to you is unacceptable. No, thank you. I'd rather go home to my father and my friends in Whip's End, and it would probably be best if we don't see each other again."

That she was angry was to be expected, given what she had just been through. And her argument was a logical one—though, he suspected, sadly irrelevant now. The fact that he had gone after her had proved she mattered. But she was right: She would always be a target from here forward, whether in Whip's End or with him. But with him, wouldn't she at least be better protected?

"I don't question that you have a right to be upset with me," he said, "but any lack of contact between us is not the answer."

"And why not? That monster took me because of you—he told me I would be sacrificed if you did not come for me—and I am the one who suffered at his hands. I cannot begin to tell you how awful that was. How can cutting myself off from you *not* be a good thing?"

Galaphile sighed deeply. "It's not a good thing because it isn't the right answer! I did come for you, and that demonstrated that you mean something important to me. I'm sorry it had to happen, but I . . ."

"Who *is* that man?" she snapped. "That horrid creature? What sort of . . . ?" She shuddered into silence, unable to find the words to say more.

Galaphile shook his head. "I don't know. He came to the building site about six months ago, assuming I was amassing power, and wanted to join me in conquering this land. He made his intentions clear. I drove him off, but I never found out who he was. After further testing my defenses for a time, he seems to have decided now that the best way to get to me is by threatening you."

She laughed but not in a pleasant way. "As I've clearly learned. So, whether I like it or not, I am now tied to you. Is that what you're telling me?"

"Yes, but . . ." He paused. "Before we talk about that, we need to talk about your dreams. The ones you've been having. Will you tell me about them now?"

"Why? Why does it matter?"

"Just . . . please. Then I will explain."

She described the dreams and their setting, and it was as he had thought. It seemed that in her dreams, she had somehow entered the Gardens of Life—and that the King of the Silver River was still orchestrating not only Galaphile's life but also hers from afar.

And for a moment, he rather understood her anger about feeling like a pawn in his life. He was beginning to feel very much the same way.

"From what you have described," he told her, "you've met the King of the Silver River in your dreams—the very same spirit that pulled me out of the world for five years. The last time we met, I told you some of what transpired between us when he held me in his gardens. I told you what he showed me and said to me. What I did not tell you—because I did not realize it myself until just now—was that he showed me a future with a woman at my side. That woman was *you*. Not as I remember you from the past, but as you look now. I did not recognize you in the visions, but I see it now. When that man took you, I must have at least sensed it. It was why I was so desperate to come after you—"

"Because you had to?" she cut in. "Because I was a mysterious piece of your puzzle?"

She was still angry, and he was doing a very bad job of explaining.

"No," he said, then sighed again. "Nirianne, I think it is your turn to listen while I talk. Please?"

After a moment, she nodded. Then he told her everything. About Mayele and him losing her, and how that had cemented his goal to create a better future. About his years of lonely, driven, intensive study with Cogline. How the quest Cogline had sent him on led him to her. How his fears of losing her were what drove him now.

"You were very young when I met you," he finished. "I haven't had a lot of time to get to know the woman you have become, but I want to get to know her better—in part because I so admired the girl you once were. But I knew enough to invite you to join me at the new building site—even if I could not admit those reasons to myself yet."

He paused, then added, "The last thing I need to tell you is that while you were being stolen away, I was already coming back to Whip's End to find you. You can ask Varisol if you doubt me. I arrived in Whip's End a few days after you had left; we must have missed each other on the road."

She gave a spurt of laughter at that, and, reassured, he grinned back. "Even then, however," he confessed, "I might not have known everything about why I was coming back for you. But when I returned to the camp to find that man had taken you—when I thought I might have lost you forever—I began to realize just how much you meant to me.

"I care deeply about you, Nirianne. As a friend, yes, but more than that. I don't want a life without you. Without your wit, your energy, and your intelligence. I want us to have a chance to be together—a chance to know each other, apart from childhood crushes or any fear of commitment, and especially the machinations of the King of the Silver River—to see if there is something between us that really matters. Are you willing to try this with me? Will you give me that chance?"

Her anger had faded; he could tell by the glint of amusement that had come back into her eyes. "And not just because you think I'll be safer with you than if I'm out of your sight?"

He smiled back. "No, not that. Never that."

He reached out one hand, and—after a moment—she took it. He folded his other hand atop it, and they sat there for a moment, feeling the warmth of the promise between them.

Then he grinned again and said, "Now, you said you had some ideas for my building plans? Can we talk about that?"

TWENTY-SIX

S he did indeed have ideas—and good ones. They discussed them and more as they scrambled down from their high perch.

He had forgotten how much she liked to talk—and how much he enjoyed listening. He truly hadn't realized how lonely he had been during the long years with Cogline, with only himself for company. Having a companion made for a pleasant change.

And speaking of companions . . . he was not at all surprised to find a pair of mountain lions awaiting them when they finally reached flat ground. What did surprise him was how Nirianne walked right over to the great cats, knelt in front of them, and spoke a few quiet words of greeting.

"The King of the Silver River told me once that the lions would be our protectors and guides," he observed.

"I thought as much. They came to me, too, when I first climbed to meet you."

So that explained her familiarity with the beasts.

He liked seeing her so boldly unafraid, however; it was the same attitude she had embraced with such confidence when they had first journeyed together, and when they had fled the fortress. And, in fact, how she handled most of the rest of the journey back.

The only thing she avoided was discussion of her time with his rival mage. Any time he tried to raise the topic, even gently, she would shut it right back down again. He hoped that she would find a way at some point to process and discuss it. Untreated wounds—as he knew only too well—tended to fester . . . even the invisible ones.

Or maybe *especially* the invisible ones.

So even as she resumed her usual cheerful disposition and stream of random chatter, he could see the shadows behind her eyes that spoke of things barely acknowledged and far from healed.

Give it time, he told himself. *Give it time.*

There had likewise been no more discussion of any relationship between them—though at night, with the big cats guarding their slumber, they would lie close together for warmth, and come morning, he would find her snuggled comfortably against him.

He liked this more than he could say.

In fact, as she talked, he found himself often fixated on the movement of her mouth and his longing to kiss her. But her brisk, businesslike demeanor when he drew too close persuaded him to pull back.

Another thing he would likely have to give some time.

He wondered more than once about the lack of pursuit from Nirianne's captor. It bothered him more than he could say. Yes, he had successfully snatched her away, but it seemed wrong that her captor hadn't made any effort to bring her back. Or at least none that he was aware of. He didn't seem like the sort that was discouraged easily; neither did Galaphile think that he and Nirianne had somehow managed to avoid any efforts to detect them once they were out. If he had wanted to, Nirianne's captor could have regained her easily. So why hadn't he at least tried?

Because the man hadn't wanted to? Because there was no reason to? Had he accomplished what he intended just by stealing her away? It might all have been to demonstrate his dominance over Galaphile, but that didn't feel right, either.

Or had he done something to Nirianne before Galaphile had arrived? Had he damaged her in some way? Violated her? She hadn't said anything to suggest this had happened, but how could he know?

Or was all this just a way to make Galaphile feel uncertain about their relationship, to undermine it by creating doubts? All this and more crossed his mind during their travels back, but there were no easy answers, and Galaphile did not want to bring the matter up until Nirianne was in a safer place.

Fortunately, the rain that had trailed him here was gone, and their feline guides were efficient at finding food and fresh water. They navigated the tunnel back through the Knife Edge Mountains, and at the Lethe, there was again a changing of the guard. This time, three big cats appeared. And nine days after they had fled the fortress, they were back at the building site just as the morning's work was commencing. The lions walked them into the camp and then silently faded away. Their arrival was greeted with cheers and happy greetings from everyone present—for Nirianne as much as for him, he was delighted to see—and Sanitov was quick to assure them that all was well. That evening he would organize a special dinner to celebrate their safe return. But for now, work needed to continue.

Galaphile surveyed the site with pride, astonished at how much progress had been made in the days since his departure.

"Your stuff is still in the High Lord's tent, lass," Sanitov said, turning to Nirianne. "I know I said I would find you newer quarters when the High Lord returned . . ."

It was a tense moment for Galaphile, who suddenly found himself glad Sanitov's remarks were being addressed to Nirianne. He very much wanted her to stay—but also felt that he didn't have the right to make that decision for her.

Therefore, he was both shocked and delighted when she announced coolly, "I think the current quarters will be sufficient for now. Correct, High Lord?"

The mocking way she said his title made it clear how little she thought of it, and he found himself stammering his agreement.

She led the way to his tent, where she retrieved fresh clothing. Galaphile could tell from her expression and the way she carried herself how much better she was feeling. He tried to tell her that he was very pleased she was choosing to stay where he could keep watch over her, but she just laughed.

"One hopes you will have better luck this time," she declared with an arched eyebrow. "For now, I will make it a point to depend mostly on myself."

Then she stalked off to find something to do.

For Nirianne, the return to Galaphile's camp was welcome—not just for its safety and solidity, but also for the genuine delight the Dwarves showed on her return. This was not so much in recognition of her relationship with their High Lord as something she had genuinely earned through fellowship and hard work. She knew it—and she knew that Galaphile recognized it for what it was, which made her proud.

As for her relationship with their High Lord? Well, that was more of a work in progress. His confessions to her on the morning after her rescue had gone a long way toward soothing the hurts of the past five years, and he had been right about one thing: The two of them didn't really know each other yet, not as they needed to. Hers had been a childhood crush bolstered by dreams that turned out to have been less her own than the result of a manipulation by outside forces. And if there was one thing Nirianne hated—just ask her father—it was having the opinions of others forced onto herself.

So who had really decided that Galaphile was her ideal mate? She herself, or this King of the Silver River? Until she could determine that this was what she truly wanted, she was holding Galaphile firmly at arm's length. Even if the way he had come to gaze at her sometimes suggested that he had finally made up his own mind in the matter, at the end of the day the decision was still hers.

Complicating matters was the fact that she was still processing her time in the hands of her kidnapper. He had flown her to the fortress on the back of some hideous monstrosity, then she had spent eight long days chained to a wall with minimal food and water, knowing she was nothing more to her captor than bait for the important prize: Galaphile. She hadn't known why the man wanted him so badly, but clearly life as she had always thought it would become was over. She had learned that on the very first night, after her captor had told her that if Galaphile did not come for her in ten days, he would execute her.

She had tried to argue—to point out that Galaphile might not be back in camp for weeks—but her captor was insistent. Ten days, or she was dead. But Galaphile was not coming; she knew that already. Sanitov had told her. Galaphile was not due back at camp for at least a month, if not longer. Which meant she was a dead woman.

She had always seen herself as a resourceful person, able to find a way out of any bad situation. But she had no way to get out of this one. Her captor would not listen to her arguments, and the occasional minions who trailed him seemed mostly either unaware of or disinterested in her existence. She was not strong enough to break her chains, and even if she had managed to do so, she was stuck out in the middle of country she knew nothing about.

She was helpless, powerless—at the mercy of two men and their feud, a useless insignificant pawn in their game.

And she hated it.

Plus, he had done something to her head—planted something dark inside her that made her doubt all her instincts. She could feel it squirming inside her, undermining her confidence, her assurance. Making her question everything she thought she knew. And she had no clue how to remove it.

It was maddening.

She was only twenty-two. How could her life end here, chained to a wall, no more than bait for the man who was supposed to be offering her the start of a new existence?

And what of the dreams that had promised her a life of greatness at Galaphile's side? Those dreams were her last glimmer of hope, and she clung to the memory of them, even if she no longer expected them to come true.

When Galaphile did finally come, she wasn't sure whether to be relieved or infuriated. She would live, yes. But only because someone had saved her. Someone whom an outside force had decided was right for her.

And she hated that, too.

So, while she technically shared Galaphile's tent, it wasn't in the way most of the camp likely assumed. She continued to sleep in his cot, while he bedded on the ground in a pile of furs. And although a part of her missed waking up snuggled into his embrace, as she had on the road, such intimacy felt more perilous here, now that it would be part of real life instead of the oddly liminal space of a journey.

If she was ever to be more deeply connected to him, she had to do it on her own terms, establishing a space within their shared world that was hers alone.

If she even wanted to consider that sort of a bond between them, which she was still trying to figure out. The darkness she harbored inside ate at her, made her question their bond. Sometimes, she found herself irrationally angry at him for no apparent reason. She contemplated leaving him, even if it hurt. She sometimes wished he felt more of the pain that haunted her.

But this wasn't who she was; she knew that. Rationally. This was something the man in black had placed inside her. She tried at every turn to battle it, squash it down, lock it away. She could not bring herself to tell Galaphile, however; it felt too much like admitting defeat. Her choice, at least for the present, was to stay silent, keep the secret to herself, and try to get on with her life.

First, she set about carving out a more productive space in the camp, attaching herself to the few Healers who had traveled here in the company of the Dwarf workers. She helped with administering the basic nursing services required for the workers and their families—as more than a few had brought their families with them—and engaged in whatever additional tasks the Healers asked of her. And after what she had been through, it made a difference to help others who were suffering. It might not be healing herself, but it was healing.

Also, this time around, she stayed off the building lines and out of the way of real builders, and she made a point of leaving Galaphile alone to carry out whatever duties were best suited to him. But old habits still died hard, and her tendency to listen to and engage with everyone around her brought much of the camp gossip to her ears. That—and her logical mind from years of running a tavern—had her suggesting needed improvements in workflow and addressing small personnel problems before they became serious ones. She genuinely enjoyed carrying out these efforts and knew Galaphile was grateful for her help with such matters.

The trio of lions that had accompanied them up the mountainside on their return had vanished, gone back to wherever it was they had come from. But she suspected others of their kind were still around. Whatever else the King of the Silver River had arranged in his efforts to help his young acolytes, protection by the mountain lions was at the top of the list. Now and again, she actually sensed eyes watching from afar and knew it was no coincidence. They were there for a reason.

Matters stood as they were for the next few weeks. She had sent word back to her father in Whip's End that she was residing with Galaphile for now and had received his blessings in return. She had been deliberately unclear about what *residing* meant, but she knew that Varisol would support her whichever way things went.

Because, as she was coming to realize—whatever magic or twisted thinking the King of the Silver River and the man who had taken her had put into her head—she did love Galaphile. His deep commitment to his cause, his ability to give her the space she needed, his kindness to those he employed and tendency to put their welfare over faster progress had allowed her to further know the real man. And her infatuation soon gave way to deeper feelings.

So yes, she loved him. She was certain of it—and increasingly certain that he was worthy of that love. She loved him enough that she eventually decided that this was the man she wanted, now and forever.

One night, about three weeks after their return, she asked him to have dinner with her apart from the others. She selected the site and prepared the dinner and drink. Together, they talked about the ongoing construction. The walls were slowly creeping up, and almost all of the excavation and tunneling work for the basements and storage rooms was done. Tower locations were mapped out fully, and placements and foundations were staked off for assembly. By now, Nirianne felt she was a significant part of what was happening—enough that she was confident in her position as his closest adviser and confidante.

"Tell me of your plans for the actual citadel," she urged as dinner was winding down. "And what you hope to see happen over the next few months."

He did so in detail and with obvious excitement. Midway through his recitation—which she knew many others would have found boring, but that set her mind alight with possibilities—she impulsively leaned over and kissed him.

He stared at her in surprise—and growing hope. His face was glowing as she pulled back. "Does this mean . . ."

"I don't know, Galaphile," she confessed, a crooked smile twisting her lips. "What do you want it to mean?"

He was silent for so long that her heart quailed, certain he was going to shatter it. Then he said, low and almost hesitant, "I want it to mean that you will stay here. Stay with me." A pause. "Forever."

"Do you think that is a reasonable request?" she asked almost plaintively. "Forever is a long time."

"I know." A deep breath. "But not long enough for how I feel about you. We have come to know each other better, haven't we, in these past few weeks? Already, I cannot imagine this place without you as part of it—listening, hearing, guiding, helping. Nothing would work as well without you here. Maybe it couldn't work at all. And it isn't just about the project. It never was. Knowing you are here to share your life with me makes me feel so much more worthwhile. You are the first one I want to share my happiness with; you are the only one I want to tell my sorrows and fears to. I cannot imagine a life without you, so I don't want you anywhere else but with me. I want you with me forever."

He reached over to take her hand, and she gave it to him, her heart pounding. "I want you to stay with me, to be my life partner for as long as it is possible for us to do so. For whatever time we are given. I know we belong together, and I think you know it, too."

Abruptly, the darkness rose up to swamp her, but she crushed it down firmly. This was her moment. Hers. Not anyone else's. Still, she hesitated.

He noticed her pause, and his stricken expression stabbed at her.

"It isn't that I doubt you," she assured him softly, raising a hand to his cheek. He covered it with his own. "I know you are right; we belong together. But I worry about how much of what is happening has been orchestrated by the King of the Silver River. I feel like we are pawns in a plan I don't think either of us understands. Do you feel that way as well?"

She did not mention the memories of her kidnapper that were still lodged inside her head. She could not do that.

He nodded slowly. "I do. But I have to hope that, in the end, I can control my own life when and where it matters. I have needed his help now and then, but I like to think the direction I take is one of my own choosing."

She stared at him a moment and gave him a dark frown. "Very well. But if I ever meet with the King of the Silver River"—she burst out laughing—"I am going to wring his stupid neck for all his meddling!"

He laughed back in response, then shifted closer, framing her face with both his hands. "Can I please kiss you?"

She lifted her face, and his lips met hers in a long and passionate kiss that told him everything she needed to know about the depths of his feelings.

"Forever," she whispered when they parted, "suddenly doesn't seem nearly long enough."

TWENTY-SEVEN

Everything changed after that.

With their commitment made, the pair wasted no time in arranging a formal ceremony in which vows were exchanged and commitments to their union expressed—which occurred as soon as Varisol could be notified and escorted into the mountains to not only witness the event but also formally give his daughter away to her new life partner. Such had been the common procedure since the Old World, and Nirianne was not about to cast aside a tradition of such long-standing importance for the sake of expediency.

The marriage was attended by everyone in the camp; it was a day of celebration without work. And it came as no surprise to Galaphile, as the expectant couple stood before the designated Giver of Vows, that a gathering of mountain lions stood in the distance to witness the proceedings.

The couple had written their own vows on the same night they had first kissed and come together as lovers in the aftermath. The words were straightforward and simple:

> I pledge myself to you, now and forever.
> I promise to love and honor you always.

I vow to never betray our partnership.
Whatever I ask of you, you may ask of me.
I will stand beside you first and foremost.
I will never forsake you.

They kissed when they finished speaking those words before the gathered witnesses—and all agreed later that the kiss went on for far too long for those in attendance but apparently not nearly long enough for those who were just joined.

The celebration went on until late, and it was well after midnight when the music ceased and the last of the celebrants went off to bed. Galaphile and Nirianne remained until the very end, and when the last of the guests trundled off to sleep, Nirianne took Galaphile's arm and hugged him to her. "It's our wedding night," she whispered.

"Every night will be our wedding night," he promised, grinning.

"But this will be our first. I want you to remember it."

He kissed her lightly. "I hardly think that will be a problem."

She nodded, but her expression was intense. "I just want to make sure."

Which she did. Very sure.

Summer passed and with it the warmer weather. It had been more than a year since construction of the citadel had begun. Progress was good, and attempted obstructions were rare. A sense of satisfaction and hope had settled in, and most of those involved in the work were feeling good about seeing the completion of their efforts perhaps even before the predicted five years.

Ratcher returned after a longer-than-expected absence with the agreed-upon gathering of fighters and magicians he had unearthed to help with defending the citadel.

The fighters were a promising lot—resolute Human men and women about a hundred strong. Only one had the potential to be a bully, and that one Galaphile dismissed, with his thanks.

As for the magic users, that was a less promising crop. This group contained only about two dozen men and women for Galaphile to consider, but most of them were poorly trained and minorly skilled. By the end of Galaphile's personal interviews and testing, only three remained.

"I will be honest with you," Galaphile told Ratcher in the aftermath. "This is not exactly what I was hoping for."

His friend seemed uneasy. "It was the best I could do. Most of those I asked to come turned me down. Too many seem more interested in financial stability than altruism, and many were simply not qualified or interested. Some didn't think the pay you were authorizing was enough for the risk expected. When it comes to a choice between earning coin and saving the world, the coin usually wins. Do we have extra money to spend?"

Galaphile sighed. Thus far, the King of the Silver River was funding almost the entirety of the construction. What coin they had to cover the cost of their fighters was being scrimped from that.

"I'll have to see what I can manage. Meanwhile, beggars can't be choosers. And if the interest isn't there, we don't want to waste our time. We'll have to rely on what we've got."

"Hasn't been enough so far," the other man muttered.

Galaphile knew he was referring to Nirianne's kidnapping and imprisonment, which he had learned about upon returning with his recruits. But he was quick to back away from his comment, which Galaphile was glad for. He knew Nirianne was still troubled by her time with his rival mage; it remained the one topic he could not discuss with her.

"You've been through enough without me letting you down. I'll go out again, look about some more. But I have to tell you—some promise of more coin would help most."

After Ratcher had departed, Galaphile took time to consider the three magicians he had felt were valuable enough to keep.

Ursule Raken he recognized right away. She was the strangely pale, very thin Human woman that he had seen in one of the King of the Silver River's dreams—the same dream that showed him a grown-up Nirianne and the man who would trouble him most, who may or may not be the man he had already encountered. He remembered the chilly feeling she generated when he first saw her in the flesh, toward the back of Ratcher's pack, her gaze directed away from him and her eyes fixed on something perhaps only she could see. Even without knowing if she possessed magic, she projected a commanding presence. And her gift was a powerful one, for she had the ability to see into the future.

Parkinch Alicorn was Human as well—a tall, spare man who wore a long gray cloak hanging loose about his shoulders and open down the front. With the cloak folded tight, he disappeared. Something about the nature of the cloth enabled this, or perhaps something about whatever magic he possessed. But one moment he would be standing there, and the next he would be gone completely. It was uncanny how swiftly and smoothly he employed this trick. He could exercise his talent faster than Galaphile could track it. Parkinch was quiet and withdrawn but clearly capable.

Chelm (bearing one name only), on the other hand, was a complete mystery. Galaphile could not even determine the exact nature of his species, as he appeared to be an unsettling conglomeration of several. He seemed to be a mix of Dwarf and Gnome, but he might have been something more. He was both lumpy and muscular, his body bent at odd angles in several places, yet his gaze was so razor-sharp and knowing, it alone gave him a formidable presence. He also didn't speak—ever. Not even a word. Maybe he could but simply chose not to, or maybe he was unable. Whatever the case, when Galaphile asked about the nature of his magic, Chelm simply gestured quickly in response, and Galaphile's mind went completely blank. He forgot what he was trying to do and found himself staring mindlessly into space. It took several minutes for his mind to clear and his memory of the incident to return.

However, the presence of three new magicians—useful as their talents might be—was hardly enough to defend the rapidly growing fortress when the need to do so arose once more. Yes, they would help, but they were far from enough. They were what he had to supplement his own magic, though, so unless he could find a way to obtain other magicians with his insubstantial funds, his hopes for a significant defensive force of magic users seemed doomed. And for the moment, he was forced to pay his new recruits less than he would have liked, promising them he would do better when he could.

He would have to pose the question of salary to Nirianne. She was always good at finding solutions to things that troubled him. But on this one, even she came up blank.

Nirianne, meanwhile, was undergoing a crisis of her own. It was her own personal nightmare, and she couldn't tell any of it to Galaphile.

For a time, she believed she had put her kidnapping and imprisonment behind her. She was happy in her new married life, both with her partner and with her involvement in the construction of the citadel. Her life held the purpose she had always desired, and thoughts of her nemesis and the shard of darkness he had left in her head had drifted far enough away that they were mostly memories she could push aside.

But then came the night all that changed. One minute she was drifting off to sleep beside Galaphile, and the next she was back inside the prison she thought she had escaped. She was secured by chains to an all-too-familiar wall, watching as her former captor approached. And without being able to stop it from happening, she felt him take her hands and hold them in his own. She cringed at his touch and fought to break away, yet found herself firmly held in place. Her enemy spoke no words; there were no sounds at all. But she knew at once what he was thinking:

That she belonged now to him. That she would never again belong to Galaphile. That she must excise Galaphile from her heart.

She wanted to deny him, to scream at him in furious anger, to make him realize that he was wrong. But she could not manage any of that, so she simply lay there silently, listening to him in horror as he bent close and kissed her cheek.

His thoughts were clear. He had infected her with dark magic and she could never escape its hold on her. Forever after, he would be present inside her, and she would be his slave from here forward. His voice would always be present, demanding that she listen. She would be told to do things, and she would be compelled to do them. She would serve as his eyes and ears. She would reveal everything she saw or learned should he demand it. Worse, she would keep all of what was happening to herself. She could never reveal his presence to anyone—especially Galaphile. Her husband must know nothing of what was happening.

No, she thought. *No one can do this to me. No one can control me as you think you can. I will never be your slave!*

Perhaps, if she wished for it, she could make herself strong enough to banish him. But she wasn't sure. She could not seem to do so now, even though she was trying. She kept remembering what it had been like as his prisoner: How he controlled her even when she resisted, how she felt his magic overpower and possess her on countless occasions. A part of her knew it could be that way again, whether she wished it or not. That it would always be that way.

No wonder he had let them leave his fortress—which she now knew he called Skull Mountain—so easily. The goal had never been to keep her. It had been to infect her, then send her back as his spy. And she and Galaphile had fulfilled their parts perfectly.

Another surge of rage went through her. All she had ever wanted was a life under her own control, and now that was denied to her—perhaps eternally.

She lashed out against his power once more, but he slapped her down quickly. Again, his thoughts were clear. All attempts at resistance or refusal would result in punishment. Try to subvert his will, to resist his demands, or to reveal his presence to a single person and she would experience this:

For the first time, an inexorable wash of pain surged through her body, sudden and unbearable. She felt herself trying to thrash back against it, but she could not even manage to move. She felt herself try to scream and couldn't. She lacked any ability to control her body or use her voice. Everything was happening solely in her mind, and her physical self, while racked with excruciating pain, was frozen in place. Wave upon wave of agony ripped through her helpless body until all she wanted to do was die.

When she was just short of lapsing into mindless nonexistence, the attack on her body ended and she was left shuddering and gasping—in her mind anyway—and fighting to banish the memory of what had been done to her.

His thoughts intruded anew. This would be her only warning. This was what she would experience if she defied him. Her life was completely under his control. She would do as she was told. She would provide him with the information he asked for when it was requested. She would pay attention to Galaphile's words and actions and reveal them all. She would look and listen and report everything to him.

Or more pain would follow.

After a brief pause, he made her aware of a name. He was the Spectre Telle, and he was her new master.

And then he was gone, and she was in her bed with Galaphile once more, shocked and appalled. Her first impulse was to tell her husband everything, but then she remembered how this creature had made her feel a pain so agonizing that she longed for death and paused. Somehow, she would have to find another way around this problem. But where was she to find the help she needed if she could not speak of what had been done to her? Nor did she think she could disobey this Spectre Telle's demands; she could not tolerate that sort of pain a second time, even if it meant betraying Galaphile. But she also could not stand the thought of betraying Galaphile. So she must find another way. She must use her wits to find a way out of this horrendous situation.

But how?

She wished more than anything that she had told Galaphile about this earlier, before they wed, when she might have had the chance—but the Spectre Telle probably would have found some way to prevent that then, too.

She lay in agony, the physical pain gone, but the mental torture just beginning.

A few more months passed, and the new year dawned. Trips out of the valley slowed and then ceased altogether with the coming of the second year of snows. And with the halt in building materials coming in, construction shut down for a time. When spring arrived and the roads cleared, the construction resumed. The basement sections had been completed, and the outer walls and gates were nearly at their full height.

Then a band of Gnome hunters, whose supplies must have been running low, attempted a series of raids on their stores and work animals, and while little was actually taken or damaged, Galaphile was again reminded of how vulnerable his position on the high bluff continued to be. This wasn't the first or even the tenth time such attempts had been made, but it did reinforce the need for a larger, stronger guard force to protect the supplies and weapons.

This meant that he needed to attempt another journey into the Westland to speak with the Elven King and seek support for his efforts, as his last one had been derailed by Nirianne's capture. He hadn't given a return trip much thought after that, but now it was time. Even if the site was now safer, he still needed trained fighters. And the best of the best came from the Elven nation.

After all, as the man in black had shown him, any future attacks might be less about petty supplies and more about a bid for power. The higher the fortress rose, the more tempting a target it would be for those assuming he sought dominion—and who desired it in turn.

He advised Sanitov of where he was going and what he intended, and again left him in charge. As for Nirianne . . .

Since that first nighttime intrusion, the Spectre Telle had left Nirianne completely alone—long enough that she began to wonder if he would come back at all. The nagging suspicion that he would kept her on edge, fighting to maintain a semblance of normal behavior. Thoughts of how to rid herself of him, or at least how to subvert the demands and expectations he had heaped upon her, consumed her—though she tried to keep her preoccupation from her husband and those around her. She would not betray Galaphile, she told herself, yet at the same time she wondered how she could stop it from happening when and if it was demanded of her. So far, her captor had not reappeared, but why not? Why had this monster not exploited his power over her since that first terrible night?

For the moment, she had to tolerate the uncertainty of her situation while at the same time searching for a way out of it. She struggled with doing so for several weeks, all the while anticipating the other's unwelcome return. She longed to tell Galaphile the truth, to admit what had been done to her and how she was now compelled to serve the Spectre Telle—how she was expected to give him any information he desired and divulge all Galaphile's secrets if he demanded. But Telle's warnings had been clear on that. She could tell no one. And if she tried to subvert that . . . pain.

In the meantime, she had to continue pretending that everything was just fine.

The fact that it wasn't became apparent about a month after her enemy's first appearance. He came to her again one night as she drifted toward sleep, a presence emerging from the darkness to snatch her away. Once more, she found herself back in her dungeonlike imprisonment with the Spectre Telle looming over her—close enough that she could feel his breath and see the burning intensity in his eyes.

She could again hear his thoughts, although his voice remained silent.

Bring me the plans for this fortress so that I can copy them down. Indicate all entries and exits, visible or hidden. Reveal all of the fortress's secrets. Get me those plans. I will come to you tomorrow night.

A part of her had hoped that, in the daylight, she might be able to delay, but she woke filled with a sort of compulsion that edged over into pain the longer the plans were out of her possession. She knew where they resided, of course, as Galaphile consulted them frequently. Once she had them in hand, she could breathe freely again. She hid them away in a private place for the day, and later that evening, when Galaphile was asleep, delivered them to her tormentor in a dark corner of the construction site. She allowed him to copy the plans in silence, then took the drawings back again and began learning how to live with the guilt.

Still, that act broke something in her, and she wondered if she would ever be the same. Her guilt, remorse, and sadness were overwhelming, but she hid it all.

More weeks passed without another demand, and she continued to agonize over her impossible situation, but no solution presented itself.

Then one day she overheard Galaphile and Sanitov discussing a planned trip to the Elven homeland. She also heard her beloved suggest that it might be better if she remained at home, and would Sanitov please look out for her?

She almost wished she could remain behind, but that evening, as she fell into sleep, the monster came for her once more. She would accompany Galaphile on that trip, no matter what. If she failed to do so, there would be consequences.

And indeed, no sooner had she woken than the compulsion to speak to Galaphile about it reared up. Forcing a bright smile, she confronted him as he was dressing for the day.

"So, *life partner*," she teased, searching for a way to get what she wanted. "Remember those words? *Life partner?* They mean we share everything, isn't that so? Both good times and bad?"

She felt the sting of her own hypocrisy but carried on anyway. "What is this I hear about an upcoming journey? You weren't thinking of not telling me about it, were you? You weren't considering just slipping away without me?"

"I . . . well . . ."

"No, of course you weren't." She forced a grin, feeling nothing of the cleverness she pretended to exhibit. Instead, an aching hollowness filled her. "That would be a violation of our agreement, wouldn't it? Good thing we have a chance now to discuss it. Here is what I think should happen. *We* will travel west together. *We* will demonstrate by doing so the depth of our commitment to each other. *We* will reaffirm that we have entered into a committed relationship with each other. Isn't that right?"

He grinned happily back at her, which made her feel worse than ever. "Of course we will. I don't know how I could consider anything else."

"Good. Then how soon can we leave?"

Because maybe there were other ways she could free herself from the destructive hold the Spectre Telle had over her life. The Elves had magic; perhaps there might be some solution there.

TWENTY-EIGHT

They set out two mornings later with a solitary lion escort. They walked until sundown, the mountain lion traveling with them—sometimes leading the way, sometimes following after, and sometimes disappearing altogether before circling back. That night, after they made their camp, they sat together after eating under what seemed to be an endlessly star-filled sky. Galaphile put his arm around her, pulling her close, and for a while Nirianne tried to lose herself in the moment, just being with the man she loved. But the knowledge that the Spectre Telle was in her head and would force her to betray Galaphile over and over made her feel itchy and restless. She soon squirmed free, covering her anxiety with talk.

"Do you have any hopes for those three mages you kept in camp?" she asked.

Galaphile sighed. "I can't be sure about Chelm; I have only just begun testing his limitations. I am still uncertain about the strength of his abilities. As he does not speak, I cannot ask him much, so I must instead run tests. It seems he can only impact the memory of those standing within his view, and even now I can't be sure how many of those he could affect if faced with, say, an army. Also, the effects are transient, lasting only about a minute at most—less than that if he is trying to control more people. Parkinch has real skill, but he is limited. He can make himself vanish but no one and nothing else. Ursule, however, is a true talent. She gave me a reading this morning." He glanced over. "She told me that I should beware my pride when we get to the Elves. She said my Elven heritage would provide us with an entry but could also prove our greatest undoing."

"How?"

"That's the problem: I have no idea. Visions aren't like a series of instructions, telling you what to do and what not to do. This was all she was granted."

"And you believe it?"

"Completely. I saw the truth in her eyes and heard it in her voice."

Nirianne tried not to flinch. How could he see the truth in Ursule's eyes and yet be so oblivious to the torment in her own? "So what is your plan once we reach the Elves?"

"Meet with their King, if he will see me. Many years back, he wanted to thank me for a favor I did, but I had other places to be and didn't accept. I don't know if he even remembers me now, but he might, so maybe he will agree to an audience. I am hoping that he will send us a company of his Elven Hunters to serve as our first line of defense."

If it's not already too late for that, she thought bitterly, remembering her coerced alliance with the Spectre Telle. *I'll probably be made to betray you again.*

How could she avoid doing so? She had to find a way.

She forced herself to smile at him, hating herself all the while. "You have never told me much about your Elven heritage. Can you tell me about it now?"

Galaphile shrugged. "There isn't much to say. My parents died when I was young. I had no relatives, so my choice was between a home for the unclaimed inside the Elven borders or making my way on my own. I grew up on farmland outside the traditional Elven homeland, so I had no practical Elven heritage, meaning it was easy enough to leave behind. I hitched a ride with a wagon train going east when I was eight, and wound up in a village called Parrish Rahn. I stayed there for a while, albeit with a brief stint in Kern, then Starns found me there at fourteen. The rest you know."

She nodded, feeling a despair fill her. She had been hoping he had a deeper connection with the Elves, something that she could maybe exploit to get the Elves to help her with the Spectre Telle, but it seemed that was not the case. And she was as alone in this as she had always been.

She kissed him gently then turned away, feeling all sorts of lost.

The lion abandoned them the following morning, and it took them three more days to reach Whip's End. They visited with Varisol, which nearly broke Nirianne's heart given the dark place she was in—still trying to pretend that everything was normal, still playing at being the same young woman she had been before she was made a slave to Telle.

Throughout their journey, she struggled over and over again to say or write the words and tell Galaphile what troubled her, but she could never manage to do so. What was she supposed to do once they reached their destination? How was she to turn matters to her advantage when the Spectre Telle controlled her every move?

From Varisol, they secured horses, supplies, and a wagon for the journey and started out again. The remainder of their trip was uneventful. For the next fortnight, they encountered no slavers or gangs, no rogue thieves or raiders. The weather stayed mild and clear. Telle remained absent, but her uneasiness and fear continued to grow.

When they entered the Valley of Rhenn, Elven Hunters surrounded them, took up positions about their wagon, and guided them into the city. When they reached the city of Arborlon, they were taken to private chambers inside the King's palace. A councilor to the King met them there, insisting they must rest before being given an audience.

And still the Spectre Telle did not appear.

Two days passed, no audience materialized, and Galaphile stewed. How could he seek aid from the Elven King when the man wouldn't even grant him an audience? How could he accomplish anything if no one would see him?

It was an impossible dilemma.

When Galaphile finally decided he had waited long enough, he stormed through the doors of their appointed quarters and strode down the hallways in search of the Elven King's Council Chambers. Nirianne trailed him, looking miserable.

Together, they located the Elven official who orchestrated the Elven King's appointments and confronted him.

"We cannot continue to wait indefinitely for an audience," Galaphile ground out. "Our mission is critical to the lives of many people, and this sort of delay is discourteous."

His tone, he knew, was verging on imperious, but he made no effort to tamp it down.

The official just stared at him, then shook his head slowly. "Be that as it may," he began, "no audience is possible without first meeting the King's advisers to determine the necessity, and they have been busy with . . ."

He stopped talking mid-sentence as Nirianne raised her head, confronting him with such determination in her eyes that the official took a step back in spite of himself.

Galaphile found himself both bemused and relieved to see the spark back in his wife's eyes. She had been behaving so oddly of late—so withdrawn and disengaged—that he had not expected her to involve herself in this matter at all. He had, in fact, been wondering if she felt this entire journey had been a waste of their time. Or maybe she was still trying to process her time with his nameless rival; he knew there were wounds that were not yet fully healed, though he was trying to be gentle and not push and give her the time and space she needed to work through it.

So he welcomed her interest. And he resolved to speak to her later, to again see if he could determine what was amiss—though he did not hold out a lot of hope. He had asked several times on their journey only to be informed curtly—without her even looking at him—that she was fine and there was nothing wrong in the slightest.

Except clearly there was. And he wished he could figure out what. Though a large part of him did suspect that it all arose from his rival's treatment of her—what *had* happened to her while his prisoner? She had yet to really speak of it—a smaller and more private part of him feared that *he* might be the cause, and that she was coming to regret their reunion. He had warned her in advance that his attention would be split between her and his mission, and she had seemed fine with that in theory. But hearing about it was one thing, and experiencing it another.

Was she feeling that she mattered less to him than his mission, than his growing fortress?

It troubled him, but to voice it gave it a reality he was not quite prepared to deal with yet, so on this subject, at least, he had remained silent.

"Please listen to me," she now said, with some of her old force and fire. "You are speaking to the High Lord of the Midlands Peacekeepers"—Galaphile masked a smile; trust her to find a name for his nascent force—"so you should show him a little respect. We have been traveling for weeks to reach your land, leaving behind people who have need of our protection. We have come to speak to the Elven King not only on their behalf but also on behalf of all those in the Midlands who seek peace. That alone should give us the right to be heard."

The man sputtered and shook his head. "The Elves can refuse any—"

"Tell me," Nirianne interrupted, "when was the last time the Elven King and his people refused the King of the Silver River?"

The adviser stared at her in disbelief. "The King of the—" he stammered.

Nirianne cut him off. "Indeed. The King of the Silver River himself has sanctioned our mission. Now please tell your King that we are here and waiting."

Still smiling inwardly, Galaphile wondered why he hadn't thought to invoke that particular being himself. But this was what made Nirianne his perfect partner: She saw the things he couldn't.

He could only hope that she still felt the same about him.

"Well done," he whispered in her ear, and she gave him a grateful smile.

A few more minutes passed. And then they were standing in the presence of the Elven King and his Queen.

Nirianne had not been intimidated by much in her life, but coming face-to-face with the Elven rulers was daunting.

King Gendronane was a short, slight man with a thick mane of blond hair and a coolly detached look that bordered on irritation. But it was his eyes more than anything that intimidated her. There was in their clear blue depths a weight of years that made her feel like a mere spark before a roaring blaze: small and easily extinguished.

Intellectually, she knew the Elves lived for hundreds of years, but confronting it was another thing entirely.

Briefly, she found herself wondering what would happen to her and Galaphile as she aged and Galaphile did not, though perhaps that was all academic. Right now, the odds of either of them living to a ripe old age seemed slim at best.

Queen Rishannon stood just a step behind her husband. She was a tall, blond woman, clearly much younger than her husband; that same weight of years was not present in her gaze. Yet the way she stared at Nirianne was more than a little unnerving, as if she saw something no others did.

Though . . . what if she did?

A surge of hope ran through Nirianne. She knew Galaphile had been pleased by her initiative at getting them in to see the Elves; he had practically been glowing beside her. But that had made her feel even more of a fraud. Because the Spectre Telle had come to her on the first night they arrived, informing her that she must do everything in her power to undermine this alliance. Galaphile could not walk out of Arborlon with a company of Elven Hunters in his possession—and if he did, she would pay the price.

But it seemed Telle was not the most patient of monsters, because after two days with no audience, he told her to force the confrontation by whatever means necessary. Thus she woke with another compulsion bordering on pain that did not dissipate until she got them into this chamber.

Yet even now she could sense that compulsion lurking. If the audience went badly, all she had to do was nothing. But if it went well, how could she undermine the proceedings without giving herself away? Although . . . maybe this was her opportunity? Wouldn't publicly speaking against Galaphile hint to him exactly what was going wrong?

He was a passionate speaker, and she knew he would make a compelling argument. So if things looked to be going his way, as they no doubt would, could she use this to her advantage?

She knew her husband was not unaware that something was troubling her; he had been asking her repeatedly what was wrong. At first, she had tried to answer while looking him directly in the eyes in the hope that he would see the dichotomy between her words and her look—but she had immediately received a spike of pain in response to this potential strategy that had her dropping her head. Since then, she had been unable to lift her gaze to his at such moments.

Likewise, as she realized now that fulfilling one of the Spectre Telle's demands could be used to her advantage . . . another small spike of pain flared, and she knew this particular route was closed to her as well.

Frowning slightly, she waited to see how this audience would unfold.

"You've come a long way for this meeting," the King began. "Galaphile. I remember how you saved the lives of my people who were seized by Gnome raiders some years back. I never got to thank you for that act."

"If you would thank me, Your Majesty, it could be by returning the favor. The people of the Midlands are now under daily assault—and have been for some time."

He went on to outline the plight of the Midlands—eloquently, Nirianne thought—and his desire to become a force for peace and justice in the region. He told of his growing fortress, and his goals, and the aid that the King of the Silver River had given him. And how Elven help would benefit the cause.

It all seemed compelling to Nirianne, but the only question the King asked, when the recitation had drawn to an end, was: "And why do you think I should involve myself in the affairs of the Midlands and their people?"

"It is my home, Your Majesty. They are my people," Galaphile answered truthfully.

But it was nonetheless a misstep.

Based on the King's expression, Nirianne could instantly tell that Galaphile had offended him. Under normal circumstances, she might have put a hand on his arm, intervened in some fashion to caution him. But now she was locked in, unable to move, while a smug, monstrous joy radiated through her from her unwanted mental passenger.

"From the looks of you, you are an Elf," Gendronane said, eyes suddenly cold as shards of blue ice. "Or am I mistaken?"

"I am, Your Majesty, but . . ."

"Full-blooded?"

"Yes, Your Majesty."

"Who are your parents and where did they reside?"

"Parsoner and Afron Joss. They lived in the farmlands east of the Rhenn until they died of sage fever. After that, it was either enter a home for the unwanted or strike out on my own . . ."

"A home for the unwanted?" the King thundered. "Do you think that Elf children are ever unwanted? That we would ever take less than the most proper care of one of our own?"

From his expression, Galaphile clearly realized he had overstepped. "No, Your Majesty, I . . . that was not what I was suggesting at all."

"Were you suggesting that you did not think you could find the parental care you required here when your parents died? That the Elves as a nation were not sufficient to provide that care? Yet now they are?"

Though Galaphile valiantly continued to plead his case, Nirianne could tell the argument was lost.

"Your sufferings and those of your . . . people are deserving of our sympathies," the King pressed on. "Had you come to me Elf-to-Elf, this conversation might have gone differently. But you have made it very clear to me that you believe the problems of Elves and the problems of Midlanders are treated differently. And as you have chosen your own people, so I, indeed, must choose mine. While regrettable, your personal misfortunes are not the business of the Elves. We are our own people and our own nation. We have stood alone and apart as a nation for countless centuries and have been the better for it. We did so long before your situation arose—long before the world is as you find it now. It was your people who tore the world asunder in the days of old; we survived by remaining separate. And so we shall here as well. No, once again, you will have to manage as best you can without us."

Through all of this, however, Nirianne was very aware of the Elf Queen's unwavering gaze upon her. Why was she suddenly the sole focus of the Queen's attention?

Did more trouble lie ahead, or was this somehow the start of her salvation?

———

Just as the King was dismissing them, the audience drawn to a close, the Queen placed a hand on her husband's arm, a slight frown pinching her brows.

Not a good time for it, Galaphile thought.

But to his surprise, the Queen turned away from the King and walked over to him, taking hold of his arm. Nirianne was already at the chamber exit, and she paused to look but did not return to his side.

"A moment," the Queen requested. "One question for you. What ails your wife?"

Galaphile had been berating himself for his clear misstep with the King—which Ursule had even warned him about—but the Queen's words brought him up short.

"I don't understand the question, Your Majesty," he admitted.

The Queen smiled. "I think you do. I am, in some ways, able to sense the emotions of others; it is why I am so valuable to my husband in such audiences," she told him. "Your wife . . . She is troubled; I sense something of a shadow over her. And there is, on occasion, pain. I would very much like for our Healers to have a look at her—with your permission, of course."

Pain? Galaphile had not known of any pain, though the Queen's reference to troubled shadows did seem to confirm that much of this sprang from Nirianne's as-yet-unprocessed time with his rival mage.

Gratitude surged through him, and he was on the verge of accepting when Nirianne strode back over and interrupted.

"I am fine," she declared. "I have no need of any Healers. Particularly not Elven ones, who will muck around with my thinking."

The Queen nodded wordlessly and turned away.

Nirianne looked to Galaphile, a strange desperation in her eyes. "This audience is at an end. We will clearly find no help here. Let's recollect our wagon and head back home, where our people still need us."

And with that, she turned away quickly and stomped from the hall.

Galaphile followed her, feeling despondent. If there had been any hope for an alliance with the Elves after his blunder, he feared that Nirianne's words had driven the last nail in that coffin.

He tried to reason with her, but she was having none of it—she was near tears in her frustration—and within the hour she had them packed and the wagon hitched up, prepared to move out.

But even as Galaphile and Nirianne were settling the last items into the wagon's bed, Galaphile was astonished to find that the Queen had summoned a cohort of her personal guard, all of whom were bearing supplies.

The Queen gave Nirianne a quick look of warning and motioned for her to remain where she was. Nirianne was seldom inclined to heed such commands, but surprisingly in this case she did.

"We would be poor hosts to let you leave insufficiently provisioned," the Queen whispered so softly that even Galaphile, who was standing close, could barely hear her. She glanced over her shoulder as the guards tucked their newly gifted bounty into the wagon. And while they were occupied, she bent closer still.

"I can sense some of what's in a person's heart," she said softly, "and I can feel the genuine goodness in yours. Please know that I believe in your cause, and I will do what I can with my husband to change his mind. Though you wounded his pride, such wounds are superficial at best and will heal. So be patient and trust in me."

"Your Majesty." He bowed slightly in acknowledgment. "I am grateful. Perhaps it is also time for me to reevaluate just what my Elven heritage means to me—especially given the grace you have just displayed. I wish more than anything that Nirianne could respond to your kind offer, but she has suffered greatly and continues to struggle with what was done to her. Though she is free and safe with me, there is a darkness within her that I do not fully understand. She won't speak of it."

"Or perhaps cannot."

He stared at her anew, surprised at her perseverance. "Some things you cannot force a person to discuss or even face before they are ready."

She laid a hand on his shoulder briefly. "Indeed you cannot. Not until they are ready. But you must find a way to fix what ails your wife. Also know this: Whether you feel it or not, I know you will succeed."

TWENTY-NINE

Nirianne was having a hard time fighting off tears as they left Arborlon. She had been so close—so heartbreakingly close—to getting the help she needed. The Queen had—somehow—recognized her troubles.

If only she could have seen the Healers, they surely would have sensed the darkness inside her, and even if they didn't discover its cause, they at least could have informed Galaphile.

But thanks to the Spectre Telle and his compulsions, she had been forced to deny the offer and race from Arborlon as if an army of the damned were after her.

Worse, that night, when she was on the edge of sleep, a smug Telle came calling. His voice was a hiss in her mind, soundless and private. She had done well, he whispered. No help would come to Galaphile—particularly after how vehemently she had rejected the Healers.

After *you* rejected the Healers, she wanted to say—but of course she couldn't.

They were well out into the western edges of the Streleheim by noon of the following day, when Galaphile finally spoke of next steps.

"We can't allow things to stay as they are," he said. "So I think we have to forget about the Elves for now and look elsewhere."

She didn't respond at first, but then exhaled in disgust. "Elsewhere? Humans are in chaos throughout the Four Lands. Gnomes are less manageable than a pack of wild dogs, and Dwarves are already doing as much for us as we can reasonably expect. Where else is there to . . ."

She trailed off, suddenly realizing what it was he was considering. She gave him a sharp look. "No. We can't even think about talking to them!"

Galaphile arched an eyebrow. "We can, and we will. They are all that's left."

"But that is much too dangerous."

"Maybe not. And who else is there?" His headshake conveyed dismay and stubborn insistence both. "If you want to bow out of this . . ."

How she wished she could, but the Spectre Telle, as always, had the upper hand. "I said we were partners in all things, and I meant it. If one goes, we both go. That was the bargain we made." She took a deep breath and exhaled hard. "How soon do we have to go? I could use a few days free from travel."

"Then this is what we will do. We will ride back to Whip's End, rest with your father, then supply ourselves and set out again. We can ride up into the far stretches of the Northland to make an appeal to those we know are strong enough to stand with us: the Rock Trolls."

"The *Rock Trolls*?" She spit out the words as if they carried a bad taste. "You think we should go to the *Rock Trolls*?"

"They are the most powerful and the most intimidating. If we can convince them to support us, all the other Races might fall into line."

She gave him a hard look, then shook her head doubtfully. "I know I promised to stand beside you and never forsake you and be your equal in all things, but I never thought I was pledging myself to a madman. I hope you are certain that this is our best and only course of action, because it seems an all-too-obvious mistake to me!"

"Then perhaps it will be necessary for me to go on alone. I don't think it as dangerous as you do. But given what you have been through already, I understand why you don't want to go anywhere in the Northland."

Her scowl was formidable. "I said we were partners in all things, and I meant it. If one goes, we both go. That was the bargain we made."

Luck came in unexpected places, after all. Was there any hope that the Trolls could solve her problem?

Unlikely, but what other hope did she have?

Four days later, they arrived back at the Short Shot.

Galaphile seemed perfectly content to keep Varisol ignorant of their next moves, but Nirianne was having none of that and told her father straightaway.

Predictably, Varisol was openly and defiantly appalled. "You are not thinking about this clearly enough!" he stormed at Galaphile, his alarm apparent. "Do you have any real idea of what you'll be risking? Trolls are not easily persuaded to do anything—and certainly nothing quite so wild as serving as companions to Humans! They will eat you alive."

"Not when they hear what I have to say," Galaphile declared. "Not after they realize what's at stake for all of us."

As the argument raged on, however—there were only a few men and women present at this hour, and most of them were in service to the tavern and its owner and used to Varisol's short temper—Nirianne became aware that there might be ears listening far too intently. So she took hold of the arms of her life partner and her father and quickly moved them out of the main room and into the office, where spying ears were less likely to overhear.

Which was ironic, she thought, considering she was very likely the biggest spy in the room. But still . . .

The argument between Galaphile and Varisol continued for a time, but not even her father could change Galaphile's mind. Varisol did agree, nevertheless, to supply them with fresh horses, warm clothing for cold northern weather, food and drink aplenty, weapons for protection, and a hand-drawn map that would guide them where they needed to go.

However, Nirianne couldn't help wishing they had some means of hiding their intentions—or at least their destination—from the Spectre Telle.

The Trolls were practically in his backyard, and this worried her.

As Galaphile had promised, they spent a few days more at the tavern, resting from their time already spent on the road, and Nirianne found herself thankful for an actual mattress after the better part of weeks of sleeping on the ground. When the fortress was finished, she promised herself, she would make certain that a sizable sleeping chamber was set aside for herself and Galaphile.

Every night, she expected the Spectre Telle to come to her again in her dreams, but he did not.

The night before they were to leave, Varisol arranged for delivery of all the necessary supplies, and together they loaded them onto the wagon. Varisol pointed out which of several heavy-footed draft horses from the stables out back would be their new team. In truth, Nirianne was proud of her father. He was doing his best to be more supportive of the decision Galaphile had reached—though clearly he took some comfort in knowing that the latter was a skilled magician who had survived more than one attempt on his life.

The following morning, after hitching up the fresh horses to the wagon, the travelers set out for the Northland.

Galaphile again drove the wagon, using his persuasive voice and steady hands to guide the horses. The day was overcast and cold, and without even having crossed the broad expanse of the Streleheim, both Nirianne and he were chilled, for the blustery, harsh wind cut to the bone. In the north, it seemed late spring was not much different from winter farther south, but neither spoke of the discomfort they were feeling.

The way forward was yet smooth and straight, but it wouldn't stay that way once they had passed Dark Swallow Lake and circled the western edge of the Knife Edge range into the Kierlak Wastelands. If they made it that far, they would be in the homeland of the Rock Trolls.

It was the reception they would encounter after their arrival that remained the biggest unknown. They knew no one in that part of the Four Lands. Galaphile spoke the Troll language fluently—a skill he had mastered while still a student of Cogline's—which was a necessity if you were to travel the north country.

Still, Galaphile knew better than to expect much more than tolerance from the Trolls. Trolls did not interact well with Humans, and Humans did not care much for Trolls. Although they could communicate when required, it was done mostly from a distance. He did not mistake the difficulties; there were hard times ahead.

To add to everything else, he was deeply worried about Nirianne. She seemed more on edge than ever, especially after that debacle with the Elven Healers. He could sense it in her behavior—in the way she talked, the way she constantly looked about, the way she seemed so nervous, and the way she held herself apart from him.

At least for now, he was no longer worried that she regretted their union. There was passion still between them—maybe even with a bit of a desperate edge, as if she was trying to prove with her body and actions how much she still needed him. For the past few nights, in the privacy of their shared chamber at Varisol's, she had made love to him with a ferocity, as if she was trying to atone for something—though he had no idea what. Every time he tried to talk to her about it, he was met with a stony silence that he could not breach. And she showed no signs of pain, despite the Elven Queen's claims, though he searched her face for it repeatedly. Was this all down to trauma, and if so, what had his rival done to her? It was a mystery he could not crack.

But perhaps it was just that they were reentering her captor's territory, bringing up memories she was still clearly processing. He wished she would talk to him, but he also knew he could not force her to confront this until she was ready. The best he could do was be patient and open and hope that she would come to him in time with her troubles.

He wondered if they would encounter the man as they skirted his territory. It seemed odd that he had vanished so completely in the wake of their escape. Galaphile would have expected some attack before now, and the fact that there had been none troubled him. But perhaps the man had been waiting until they were closer to his territory.

Still, should his rival try anything, Galaphile had the use of his considerable magic, his broadsword, and the knives he always carried on his belt—one of which came from the King of the Silver River. And Nirianne had her wits and her determination, which were formidable even in her current condition. Better still, both of them had their survival skills and their mutual support and love. That would have to be enough.

For most of that first morning, they progressed north through the Streleheim, skirting the western edge of the Dragon's Teeth. That evening, they discussed small matters for a time; then the conversation drifted to what lay ahead. Without really thinking about it, forgetting her promise to herself, Nirianne asked, "Do you have a plan for what you will do once we reach our destination?" and then knew instantly she shouldn't have. She was asking for Galaphile to reveal plans that were better kept hidden from both herself and the Spectre Telle.

"I hope to arrange an audience with the Maturen and tribal council, who might heed a request for support," Galaphile answered before she could think of a way to stop him. "If I am lucky, they will at least listen and consider my request. They are neither stupid nor ignorant, and they are not unaware of how the world works. There is a good chance they will choose to help us. After all, it could benefit them as much as it will us."

The conversation drifted, but Nirianne could have kicked herself. She just had to hope that her ever-present listener was otherwise occupied.

They spent the first night in the shadow of the Dragon's Teeth, nestled down within their wagon's bed, wrapped in heavy blankets and sheltered within a protective nest of their supplies and equipment. As an added precaution, Galaphile ringed their small shelter with a magic that would alert him if anything came within fifty feet. But nothing disturbed their rest.

Once again, Nirianne slept without a visit from Telle. Her luck was holding.

By the end of the third day, they were approaching the shores of the Dark Swallow—a massive expanse of water so deep, it seemed to have no bottom. At dusk, they camped along its shores, letting the horses drink and refilling their water stores before they settled down for the night. Galaphile again set up his magical perimeter, but this time his own instincts proved the stronger, for he heard the people approaching even before they crossed the warning line—a mix of clanks and scuffs from hunters poorly trained in mounting a sneak attack. They were out there in the darkness to the south, clearly having seen and followed the wagon's tracks, no doubt out for whatever plunder they could find.

He lifted himself up, detaching from Nirianne, and she woke at once, rising with him. No words were spoken. She knew as well as he did what was happening. She reached for a longbow, tucking extra arrows into her belt before nocking the first, while he gathered his magic, wondering how many were approaching. It sounded like a large party, meaning they might be outnumbered.

He heard the perimeter warnings sound, audible only to himself and Nirianne. He gave it another few seconds, then launched a swath of light. The beam lit up the whole area and revealed the approaching enemy.

There were ten, and they were all heavily armed. They were men—their faces masked, their bodies big and strong but otherwise ordinary. Not creatures in service to their enemy, as he had at first assumed, but ordinary men, neither misshapen nor oversized.

Even so, Nirianne looked more uneasy than usual as the attack began, but to Galaphile's relief, she held her ground. She lifted her longbow to firing position when the raiders came within thirty feet and released the drawstring the moment they were revealed. She killed three of them in quick succession, her composure steady and her aim true. Galaphile used a quick swath of magic to tumble the remaining seven men from their feet, then leapt from the wagon.

Those attackers recovered and came at him with a fury so swift, he had no time to use his magic again. He slashed at them with his broadsword instead, dodging their attempts to trap him. Nirianne picked off another two, further reducing the odds. But the remaining attackers seemed to have little concern for their own safety. They came at him as if death meant nothing to them—desperate men in desperate times.

One broke past him and attempted to wrench the sword from his grasp. But the twang of Nirianne's bowstring and a sudden gasp of pain sent him tumbling away. Now there were only four. His attackers spread out, looking for a way to get inside the sweep of his blade. He feinted and repelled, holding them back.

Another managed to reach him, then another. They were too close now. Releasing his sword, Galaphile let the first man close in on him, brought out one of his long knives, and put an end to him. Two more were on top of him at once, bearing him to the ground—though Nirianne's quick bow work took care of the fourth.

For a moment, Galaphile feared for his life, for the two of them were strong enough to pin him fast. He thrashed to free himself; he tried again to summon magic and failed.

Then a flash of movement whipped past him, and one of his opponents tumbled backward, his throat cut by Nirianne's blade. With only one attacker remaining, Galaphile was able to put an end to the fight quickly.

In the aftermath of the attack, Galaphile and Nirianne stood looking around to make certain they were in no further danger. Galaphile's warning spell still illuminated the area, but death had claimed all of their attackers. Bodies lay strewn from the perimeter of the wards to the wheeled carriage of the wagon. Galaphile moved over to Nirianne and held her close.

"Are you well?" he whispered.

She nodded, but she was shaking and he felt a rush of empathy. He remembered what it had felt like, killing his first person. And she had just dispatched eight.

He held her close and wished again that she had agreed to stay behind.

THIRTY

They didn't wait for dawn but hitched the horses to the wagon anew while it was still dark and set out once more, leaving the killing field behind.

Three more days saw them around the edge of the lake and into the Kierlak Desert—though perhaps, Galaphile speculated, *desert* was a misnomer. He had not been sure what to expect; for him, deserts conjured images of heat and sand and dryness. Here, heat was clearly not the problem. Extreme cold and bitter winds felt like the prevailing conditions, and indeed they did seem to suck all moisture out of the environment. The rocky ground was cracked and parched, with dust storms swirling and falling with the winds. He was very glad they had topped up their water supplies before they left the lake.

Two more days passed—two miserable days under intermittently rainy skies and frigid winds that left them both feeling as if they would never be warm again. Nirianne was so tough with such a big personality that he sometimes forgot she was still so slight physically. The cold got into her faster, it seemed, and lingered longer, leaving her shivering uncontrollably for hours at a stretch. Though, being Nirianne, she soldiered through uncomplaining.

On their second night in the Kierlak and their tenth night of travel, the croyts came for them. These animals were a form of what had once been called hyenas in the Old World. Once plains-bred beasts, they had evolved over the years into their present form. Like wolves, they were pack animals and hunted as such. And though smaller than wolves, they were wirier and tougher, with massive jaws and dense, barrel-like bodies, making them hard to turn aside and harder still to stop.

They attacked in a swarm—at least a dozen of them, with possibly more still hanging back in the shadows—again tripping his magical perimeter, which Galaphile had moved out to a hundred feet after the last attack. He woke quickly, sitting up and casting the same broad swath of magical brightness into the dark. It revealed the suddenly hesitant forms of the croyts, which momentarily drew back.

Then he was leaping out of the wagon, aware of Nirianne behind him, also awake, grabbing her longbow and firing. As he had with the previous attackers, he sent out a hard wave of repelling magic that sent most of them tumbling or rushing away.

But a few persisted—a few that were too maddened to quit—and they were extremely fast. Before he could so much as muster his next magic, they had slammed into him with tremendous force, taking him right off his feet. He grabbed for the knives instead—almost an automatic gesture after all his years spent training with Starns—and killed two of them so quickly, it was as if someone else had done the work for him.

Meanwhile, another of Nirianne's arrows whipped past him, and one more croyt was taken out of the fight.

By then he was rolling away from the last three, regaining his feet and turning to face them. One went down with another arrow through the neck, one barreled right into him and went for his throat, and the third fastened on his ankle. He screamed in pain but at least managed to get his arm in front of his neck, barring the creature's access to his throat. Another arrow sped to the rescue, killing the croyt that had hold of his ankle but not the one savaging his arm. Wildly, he slashed at it, scoring it across the side. Angered, the beast released his arm and went for his head. He covered up as best he could manage but was thrown backward anew.

With both arms engaged in protecting his face, he had no way to catch himself. His head struck the ground hard, and everything went black.

For a time, he was lost in dreams and nightmares both, cast adrift in his mind with no sense of place or time. He found himself searching madly for Nirianne, but she was nowhere to be found. It was as if she had simply ceased to be. He jerked in response and . . .

"Slow down!" she hissed, stopping his struggles. "Easy now. It's all right . . . Sit still, please!"

His eyes opened to find her face only inches away from his own, her familiar smile fighting through the concern mirrored in her expression. Her hands held him fast, fought to steady him as he struggled.

"I thought . . . you were . . ." He struggled to say more but trailed off as words failed him. He took a deep breath. "What happened?"

"We killed most of them," she said, "but the last one knocked you down, and you weren't moving. It went for you; I had no clear shot—no shot that did not risk hitting you—and I thought I had lost you for sure!"

Tears sparkled in her eyes, and she leaned down and kissed him. He kissed her back, a wave of relief washing through him.

"Someone really big and strong raced up and tore that last creature off you," she continued. "I have never been so grateful for anyone's help."

He was aware suddenly that he was no longer outside but somewhere else entirely. He looked around, trying to determine where he was. Bare walls, rough-hewn furniture, a fireplace with logs burning in the hearth, table and chairs, some cupboards and closets—someone's home, clearly. They were alone, Nirianne and he, but someone had brought them here.

Galaphile peered about in confusion at their surroundings. "Where are we?" he asked her.

She smiled. "You wanted us to find the Rock Trolls, didn't you? Well, they found us first. A patrol, scouting the outskirts of their village. That was who saved us. Some of them overheard the sounds of the attack and came to our rescue. They brought us back here. That's all I know. They tried to talk to me, but I don't understand their language. So that's another reason I needed you awake." She leaned close. "Are you ready for this?"

He smiled and sat up. His head ached a bit, but that was it. No dizziness or blurred vision. "I think I'm more than ready."

And indeed, likely drawn by their voices, the Trolls opened the cabin door and poured in. They were physically imposing—eight feet tall and muscular, men and women alike. And there were a lot of them. There were so many of them crowding in that they forced Galaphile and Nirianne up against the rear wall. Their rough-featured faces completely masked their feelings, and if they had already made any decisions about what to do with these Southland intruders, it did not show.

"*Falx useccer quant wis-wis ruut,*" the Troll at the forefront of the gathering declared. Which Galaphile knew to mean: "Who are you?"

"Galaphile," he answered, pointing to himself. Then he gestured at his partner. "Nirianne." In the Troll language, he added, "Thank you for your help."

"Why are you here?"

"To speak to the Maturen and the tribal council."

Nirianne was looking blankly back and forth between him and the speaker, clearly understanding nothing of what the two were saying, so Galaphile smiled at her to let her know everything was all right.

"For what reason would you speak to them?" the Troll demanded, scowling.

"I have a proposition that I think will interest them. It would be of great help to your people and mine if we can reach an agreement."

A dismissive sound issued from a twisted mouth. "Since when do Humans care about the welfare of Trolls?"

"Many Humans do not care, I'll admit, but some do. Also, as you can see, I am not Human."

The Troll grunted at that. "Humans, Elves, makes no matter. It's all the same to us. Your Races banished us to this place and forced us to make it our home. Why should we care what happens to you?"

"Because what happens to us today can affect what happens to you tomorrow. What is your name, friend?"

"I am not your friend, stranger. I don't know you well enough." A long pause. "My name is Krunce Torsh."

"And the meeting? Can it be arranged?"

"Perhaps, but the Maturen will decide. For now, you can sleep. But do not attempt to leave this cabin; that is forbidden for both of you. Do not attempt to go outside. Not a step."

Galaphile smiled. "Not a step, until you send for me."

Krunce Torsh walked out the door and locked it behind him.

After what felt like an eternity of waiting, but was probably less than an hour, the lock on the door released and Krunce Torsh shoved his burly head through the doorway.

"The Maturen and the tribal council will see you. Better come quickly. They are impatient."

Galaphile nodded, hoping this went better than it had with the Elven King. He glanced briefly over at Nirianne, but it was hard to interpret her expression. She looked tense and worried, but also too tightly wound, like she might fly apart at any moment.

After they had donned their coats against the weather, he took her hand and walked with her through the open doorway and outside, and she clutched at him like a drowning woman clutched a lifeline.

It was not entirely surprising to find that it was daytime again—and a cold one at that. Galaphile wondered how long he had been unconscious. The sky was gray and wintry, the wind blowing so hard, it was scattering everything that wasn't nailed down.

Krunce led the way through the Troll village to the meeting hall, and while the walk wasn't far, it was long enough to give Galaphile a few needed moments to review what he intended to say to the Maturen and the tribal council. Just as with the Elven King, he would probably have only this one chance, and there was likely to be resistance to any plan that included recruiting Rock Trolls as fighters for what would essentially be viewed as a non-Troll problem.

But Galaphile had carried his dream of taming the Four Lands long enough that his understanding of what was needed and why it was necessary outweighed any concerns about what resistance he might expect.

And at least this time, he did not have any Troll heritage to insult them with.

The meeting hall was a cavernous, blocky building that consisted of a single large room. It was constructed from heavy stone facings and huge timbers, sealed with cement against the Northland chill. Each corner of the chamber must house a fireplace, for four chimneys belched smoke into the air. The roof was a carpet of grassy earth a foot deep that sealed the building better than any timber or manufactured covering could manage.

Four sentries stood watch at the doors that opened into the hall, all dressed in protective gear and armed with spears and swords. He gave them a glance and a nod and looked away.

Nirianne paid no attention to them at all.

The doors were opened by other sentries who were already waiting inside, allowing the escorting Trolls to enter with their guests. Within, the warmth increased substantially. The four fireplaces were indeed blazing, one in each corner of the square-shaped room, and their combined heat made the interior almost balmy.

The chamber was already occupied by the members of the tribal council and the Maturen. All of them sat in a row behind a long table, studying him as he approached. There was a distinct air of tension radiating from the council; Galaphile could already tell that his argument would have to be perfect to persuade them to his cause.

When the little group was standing squarely before the council, separated by less than a dozen feet, Krunce held up a hand to stop his companions and then bowed briefly.

"Respectfully, Elders," he said, "these are the individuals we spoke about. They requested an audience."

The Maturen nodded wordlessly. He was extraordinarily large and hard-faced, his look dour and his eyes cold. It was easy enough to tell by the way he held himself that he was used to relying on his looks to intimidate others. Yet his voice was surprisingly gentle. "Let them speak their names."

Galaphile stepped forward. "I'm Galaphile Joss, and this is my life partner, Nirianne. We would address the council, with your permission."

"Permission granted." The dark visage turned away from Krunce and toward the two guests, staring at them with an intensity that was disturbing. "Speak. Say what you will."

So Galaphile again launched into an explanation of the dangers facing the Four Lands and their citizens. If the ever-growing swarms of outlaws and raiders were not somehow brought to order, the whole of the Four Lands would eventually be engulfed in war. As he had with Gendronane, he revealed his own commitment to the cause, explaining in detail why he believed the growing tide of chaos was threatening them all. He touched on the details of the fortress he was building and to what uses he hoped to put it. He told them how the King of the Silver River had come to him in his dreams and of the time he had spent in the King's realm, where the King had chosen him to lead these efforts. He was engaged even now in trying to carry out the spirit lord's wishes, to persuade the peoples of the Four Lands to work together as one people . . .

"You have spoken with the Ancient One?" interrupted one of the tribal council members in shock. But the Maturen scowled at him and gestured for silence.

"I have," Galaphile assured them. "I am here *because* of his insistence that I act. My purpose in coming to you is to recruit warriors from among those who see the problem as the menace that it clearly is, and are willing to do what must be done to put an end to the threat—not only to help protect the peacekeeper fortress I am constructing but also to aid in its eventual work."

"So you seek our Troll warriors to support you?" the council member continued, disregarding the Maturen's warning.

Galaphile nodded. The tension in the room had grown stronger, but he forced himself to concentrate on his efforts to persuade the Maturen to his side.

"It must be you who agree to do so. Humankind are plentiful but argumentative, and those who seek control benefit from the chaos. Also, many do not believe in magic or its worth—or danger—to the population. Neither do they believe in the King of the Silver River. The Dwarves believe in magic and the danger it can bring, but they alone are not numerous enough to successfully engage any of the larger populations. The Gnomes want the dissension to continue, for they thrive on chaos. The Elves have isolated themselves and disengaged from the rest of the Four Lands. They do not see the problem as affecting them in any measurable way."

He paused. "That leaves the Trolls, and who better to begin with than the Rock Trolls? The stories of your strength and courage are well known. If you were to join with us and those who support our efforts . . ."

"Enough!" the Maturen shouted, leaping to his feet in an unexpected surge that very nearly toppled the table he sat behind. "Do you think us fools? You seek to risk the lives of Rock Trolls to put down an uprising you yourselves have fostered? You would waste our lives to save your own!"

The leader was shaking and waving his arms about as if he were possessed. His anger was so unexpected that even the remaining council members looked shocked.

Galaphile held up his hands in a gesture of pleading. "I am not seeking to waste any lives. I am trying to bring order to a chaotic land so that no more lives will be lost in the struggle . . ."

To his surprise, Krunce Torsh stepped forward, a look of alarm on his craggy face. "My lord . . ." he began, addressing the Maturen.

Galaphile paused. If Krunce was concerned, then clearly this was *not* normal behavior for their leader. "Is something wrong, my lord?" he asked.

"Shut your foul mouth!" the big man howled. He continued shaking with rage, the anger that drove him radiating from his muscular form as if it were an inner fire that was burning him alive. "We will do nothing to help you! The Troll people will never aid the weak, helpless Races that banished us here! Enemies forever, all of you!"

"Respectfully . . ." Galaphile began, but he got no further, as—with a mighty roar—the Maturen actually launched himself across the council table, screaming.

Galaphile threw up a hasty shield against this obvious display of fury. What was wrong with this Troll? From the expressions on the faces of the other council members, none of them had expected anything like this, either.

Krunce Torsh was already striding forward, facing down the Maturen as the latter advanced.

"Chieftain!" he shouted in clear dismay. "This is not our way . . ."

"No! More! Words!" The lord of the Trolls reached out, seized Krunce by his shoulders, and threw him aside. "I proclaim this council ended, and I sentence this petitioner to death! No further words shall he be allowed to speak! Silence him!"

Then his body shivered and he paused, head lowering, hands coming up to grasp his face. Some sort of struggle was clearly taking place within him. A desperate moan escaped his lips. He covered his face with his huge hands and spoke two poignant words in an almost unrecognizable voice. "Help me . . ."

Immediately, Galaphile realized what must be happening. Summoning his magic, he encased the Maturen in an iron grip and brought him down, pinning him fast against the chamber floor. Chaos ensued as the possessed Rock Troll fought to regain his footing and his counselors leapt to their feet in shock, still not sure what was happening but responding to the obvious attack on their leader.

"Hold fast!" Galaphile shouted, the strength of his voice overpowering the room. "The Maturen has been infected with a form of dark magic! Stand back and let me find a way to help him!"

Without waiting for a response, he thrust his magic into the Maturen's body, seeking out the invader he suspected was there.

He believed he could do this. He believed he could find a way. If he was quick and strong enough. If the other Trolls did not assault him before he could succeed.

He drove his magic deeper into the Maturen's body.

Something was there—he could sense it clearly—but it was moving about rapidly, evading his efforts to trap it. It was a slippery presence that wormed and slithered evasively, making it hard for him to use his magic to get a grasp on it.

This was something new for the Troll—something not yet familiar enough with its host to know all of the deep places where it could hide.

A time or two, Galaphile was able to connect to it directly, but it was swift and elusive and always just a hair's breadth from capture. Still, he pursued it relentlessly. He had to get whatever it was out of the Maturen before it burrowed into a more permanent home—someplace he could not reach it without an intimate invasion of the Maturen's consciousness, which he did not feel he had the right to make.

Finally, he anticipated the intruder's movements before it actually made them and caught hold of it. The feel of it squirming in his grip was loathsome, and he felt its sickness sweep through him in retaliation.

He held on nevertheless, refusing to let go.

It was clearly a creature formed of dark magic, and one that seemed constructed for a single purpose—to instill its recipient with suspicion and hatred against one person: Galaphile Joss.

And the longer he held it, the more he seemed to distrust and loathe *himself.*

If he was going to destroy it, he knew, he would have to do so quickly, before it undermined his faith in his own abilities.

He exerted his impressive will against it, and when it was sufficiently subdued, he yanked it free from the Maturen's body, immediately encasing it in shackling magic.

He turned at once to the Rock Trolls who were hovering uncertainly behind him and held up the thing he had imprisoned.

"Here!" he shouted, displaying the invasive creature he had snared. "Come look! This is what was infecting your leader."

They approached cautiously—some more intrigued than others. But soon the entire council was blinking at the sight of the dark, squirming presence. Galaphile gave them all a good look, then used his power to crush the thing to dust.

The Maturen struggled back to his feet, gasping for air, then startled Galaphile by grasping him into a massive, almost debilitating hug.

"Thank you, young man, thank you so much! I don't know how that beast got into me, but it was too strong for me to fight off by myself. I am only relieved that you saw the threat as quickly as you did and acted so fast." He turned to the council. "All honors to this Elf, who is to be treated as a friend to our tribe!"

Galaphile found himself jostled about as Troll after Troll thumped him heartily on the shoulder, but his mind was spinning even more violently. The fact that this invasive magic had been specifically targeting him meant that it could only have originated from one source: his rival mage.

And if his enemy had the ability to plant a dark magic into a relative stranger, then what must he have done to someone who had been in his clutches for *eight long days*?

It was less a revelation than a wave of putrid horror washing through him. How had he not known what his enemy was capable of? How had he not realized?

"Stop!" he commanded in his volcanic voice. All the Trolls halted in confusion.

He turned to Nirianne, hovering at the edge of the room, with a look of utter devastation; he recognized for the first time the truth about her condition.

"He's inside you, isn't he?" he demanded.

She didn't move, didn't speak, but he saw a flare of . . . something in her gaze before he dropped it, and a single tear trickled down her cheek.

That was enough.

"The mage who put that dark magic inside your leader has done the same to my wife," he announced to the room. "Please, give us space and privacy. I need to treat her as I did the Maturen."

Swiftly, he moved to Nirianne, drawing her to the center of the room. He was dimly aware of the other Trolls exiting the chamber, hustled away by Krunce and the Maturen.

"We will give you the space you need," Krunce told him as the last of the Trolls filed out and he lowered Nirianne to the floor. "There will be guards at the door, ensuring your privacy. Please summon them if you need anything."

Galaphile registered the words, but his attention was focused on Nirianne, who was sweating profusely.

The enemy knew he had been discovered, and now they were both in a race for Nirianne's life.

THIRTY-ONE

The minute Galaphile threaded his magic into Nirianne, he knew the situation was much worse than he had ever imagined. Unlike with the Maturen, where the dark magic still existed as a relatively discrete entity, here it had settled in, taken root, spread wide. It had been close to a year since Nirianne had been taken, and in that time it had spread across her like fungus on a log, dark tendrils reaching deeply into every part of her body and being.

How had he not seen this for all these months? The woman he loved had been breaking down right in front of him. And though he had sensed something wrong, he still had not realized the extent of the damage that his enemy had inflicted.

"I have to get this monstrous thing out of you, and I need you to stay with me. Please, my love. I need you."

Linked as he was with her, he could feel a kind of resolve in her pushing back against the invasion, and he almost smiled.

"That's my girl. There has never been anyone stronger or braver than you," he told her.

Then he went to work.

The first thing was to find the conduit through which the enemy accessed her and cut it off. Once the mage was actively out of the picture, Galaphile could start burning the rot from her, strand by toxic strand.

Knowing he was in a race against time, against the enemy, Galaphile went searching.

It was not an easy quest. The network of dark magic within her was vast and endlessly branching, but he persisted and soon found the heart of the infection. It seemed to pulse and twitch under his inspection, and he could sense the malignant presence of his enemy lurking on the other side.

He poured all his righteous fury through the link—a tsunami of rage, fueled by his love for Nirianne—and felt his enemy reel and falter under the attack. Molding his anger into a bright, sharp blade, Galaphile sliced through the conduit that linked Nirianne to his rival mage.

Then before his enemy could rebuild the link, he slammed himself and Nirianne inside a bubble of protective magic that none could penetrate.

Nirianne seemed to relax fractionally in response, but the dark magic that filled her was far from gone and still deadly. Though no longer under the mage's active control, it still pulsed and twisted sickly within her, and Galaphile knew that unless he cleared every bit of this infection from her, his rival would eventually be able to reestablish control.

Slowly, systematically—while still not letting his magical barrier falter—he began to burn the black tendrils out of her one by one, starting with those infecting her brain. With each strand that shriveled to ash, the pain that infused her grew less, her body started to relax, and he began to believe that he could and would win this race.

Still the invader fought him like a wild creature, writhing, biting and twisting, pummeling at his barriers. Like the thing inside the Maturen, this was no passive spell but an active entity, intent on self-preservation. But bit by bit, fiber by fiber, he diminished it. And with each small victory, its power grew less.

He was sweating and shaking by the time he had it out of her brain and consciousness; then it was just a matter of scorching it from the rest of her body: arms, legs, heart, lungs, torso . . .

He could not risk tearing it from her body as he had the Maturen's, for fear some fragment of it would remain that could then regrow to fill the spaces it had once occupied. So fiber by fiber he killed it, and Nirianne grew stronger.

He had almost entirely cleared the infection, his attention shifting from area to area to area, when he made a startling discovery: a bright spark of life inside her, still quite new—something not her, not him, but both.

Nirianne was . . . pregnant.

He paused, considering this. It seemed he had inadvertently brushed up against a truth she might not yet know herself—a truth with ramifications that reached well beyond the present moment.

Resolutely, he cleared the last of the infection from her, then considered again that bright spark of life. He could not see any infection in it; it seemed as clean and bright as she now did. Then again, he had not seen the infection in her, either, until he went looking.

But this new spark was so small and fragile, he knew the act of searching would destroy it, and he could not bring himself to do that.

If any traces of his enemy lurked there, they were too small to be perceived. So perhaps it was best to just wait and see.

He could always monitor the pregnancy, see if anything developed.

But for now, his wife, at least, was free of her invader.

He pulled his magic from her body and dropped his shield, feeling weak as a kitten after his battle.

Nirianne lay on the floor, looking almost as exhausted as he was.

He gathered her in his arms. "My love, I am so sorry. How I could have missed it for all this time . . ."

"But you found it. You realized. Thank you. Is it . . . gone?" She sounded almost tentative. "For good?"

He nodded. "From you? It is."

He did not tell her about the child; now was not the time. Perhaps she already knew and had been keeping it from him, but he could determine that later. For now, she was safe. "I love you so much," he added. "And I am awed by your ability to survive such an invasion. Was the pain a constant?"

She shivered. "No. Only when I disobeyed. Or tried to tell you. I found out about it shortly after our wedding; it was the reason he had let us go so easily."

Galaphile winced. He had reached the same conclusion the minute he saw the depth of the invasion. "Tell me everything," he said, gently.

"I was so afraid! I felt so helpless, knowing that he was in me, making me do whatever he wanted and being unable to stop it or let anyone know. When the Elven Queen offered me the Healers . . ."

"That was him, driving you away."

She nodded.

There was a moment of silence, then she said, "I did other things, too, Galaphile. Your fortress? He has all the plans. I am so sorry . . ."

"Nonsense," he said stoutly. "What else could you have done? We will just have to modify a few things on the fly when we get back, add in a few secrets not on those plans, alter a few others. Sanitov will understand, I am sure."

"He also wanted me to ensure there was no treaty with the Elves."

He gave a rueful laugh. "I'm afraid I did a good job of that all on my own. And the Maturen?"

"He learned of our destination from me, yes," she confessed. "Anything you've shared with me or told me since he took me, he knows that as well."

"Did you get any sense about him? What he's after, what his powers derive from?"

She shook her head. "All I know is that he is a monster, and that he calls himself the Spectre Telle."

"The Spectre Telle," he repeated. "Well, he is gone now."

"Are you certain?"

He kissed her lips and hugged her close once more. "You are free of it, I promise," he repeated.

The child, however—*their* child—was another matter. He wished he felt more certain. All seemed fine, but the child had been conceived in a body tainted by dark magic, so who knew what effects that might cause down the line?

But again, a problem for another day.

She hugged him back with every ounce of strength she could manage. "I never want to feel anything like that again."

He found he had tears in his own eyes. "I won't ever let that happen. Not ever."

He said it because she needed to hear it. He said it because he wanted it to be true—intended to make it come true. But at the same time, he knew it was a promise he might not be able to keep.

In the wake of the healing, Krunce led Galaphile and Nirianne to a different, more pleasantly furnished cabin.

"Tell me what you know about this man who calls himself the Spectre Telle," Galaphile asked Krunce in private after he and Nirianne were settled into their assigned quarters. "He lives just east of here, in a fortress crafted to look like a skull, which he calls Skull Mountain. Have you or any of the other Troll tribes had any dealings with him?"

"Is this the one who hunts you and your lady?" Krunce asked. And at Galaphile's nod, he continued, "Not in a serious way; not yet. But there have been rumors of Trolls seized from their tribes and taken away, forced to construct some fortress for a master who controls their every move. We will be looking at him more closely now, believe me, because men like that are not content with limited power. Eventually, he will come at us with something much stronger. Rumors also hold that he is building an army of the undead. An exaggeration, I am sure, but he is dangerous enough as he is."

He paused. "You haven't been informed yet, but the Maturen was impressed enough by what you did to save him from this Spectre Telle's dark magic that he has ordered a company of four hundred Rock Trolls to march south and aid you. I will be commander of those men and women, and I can promise you they will offer you the sort of strength you have been badly lacking."

Galaphile thanked him, asking him to express their gratitude to the Maturen as well. It was clear that their efforts in coming north had rewarded them with much more than they had expected.

They departed for home the following day. It was not the most conducive day for travel—windy, cold, and suggestive of worse weather to come—but then, so were many days in the north. They had gained the help they needed. A company of four hundred Rock Trolls was more than sufficient to not only protect the rising fortress but also begin to clean up the areas of the Four Lands that had fallen deepest into chaos, where rival gangs fought for dominion and preyed on everyone—but especially on those who desired a more settled, peaceful existence.

They left alone in their wagon, pulled by their sturdy, dependable horses and equipped with sufficient supplies and weapons to weather anything that might come after them. The Troll forces would follow shortly.

It was always risky to travel slow and alone, but both felt reasonably comfortable relying on Galaphile's magic, and neither wanted to linger in lands this near the Spectre Telle. They did not go back the same way they had come, either, thinking it best to choose a new path—one that would take them farther away from Skull Mountain. They left in the early-morning darkness, swinging west and choosing a path that took them straight down toward the Streleheim, where safety was more likely to be found.

They traveled for the better part of two weeks to reach Whip's End. It was slow going, but it was also freeing. Alone with each other, with fewer secrets between them and Nirianne freed of her dark magic, they found a new closeness and intimacy. It reminded Galaphile of the famed honeymoons of the Old World that married couples had once enjoyed, and he found himself more deeply in love with Nirianne than ever. In fact, he was almost regretful when Whip's End finally came back into sight.

Varisol, at least, was delighted to see them. He gave them a room with a blazing fireplace and a comfortable bed. They knew the Rock Troll company would be on its way within a week, and they were triumphant about what they had accomplished. All that remained was to travel once again to the mountain retreat that had become their home.

"I look at you two, and I am so pleased," Varisol told them during dinner on their first night back. "I see that you have found a truly happy life together, and that delights me more than I can say."

"I do love her," Galaphile confirmed with a smile. "She is always my steady light."

"And I love him even more than I thought possible," she countered.

Some things they kept to themselves. They told him nothing of Nirianne's invasion. And if she had figured out her pregnancy, she did not mention that, either.

"Come back with us," Galaphile begged her father. "Come see where we live and what we are building. Just for a few days. It will surprise you."

"Please, Father. Won't you come?"

To their surprise and pleasure, he said he would. But he could not leave his tavern untended and unsupplied, so he would take care of matters that required his presence first, then journey to the mountains in a few days. A delay of a week or perhaps two, at most, he added.

Galaphile and Nirianne exchanged a knowing look. It would no doubt be more like a month, but they would take what they could get.

The following morning, they said their goodbyes, returned the wagon to Varisol's stables, and set out on foot. Varisol promised to loan them both wagon and horses again at any time—even if they needed to travel somewhere he didn't much want them to go. He said this with a wink, but it was telling that he understood his daughter and her partner so well. The possibility of travel into dangerous country and among unpredictable people would always be a part of their lives.

The young partners traveled afoot. It felt comforting and familiar to make the journey. Birds were everywhere, their colors and their songs as familiar as the smells and tastes of the country air. So they took their time, frequently meandering off track to peer at whatever caught their interest, and they made no effort to reach any particular nighttime landmarks.

Three days later, they neared the construction site for the newly planned peacekeeper citadel. But to cool down their overheated bodies after their all-day hike, they took a familiar path by unspoken agreement. A short hour later they were confronting the beckoning expanse of Layby Lake, and not long after that they had stripped off their clothing and were neck-deep in its waters, kissing as if the warmth they found in doing so was enough to counter the water's bracing chill.

Later, filled with new energy and the aftermath of loving, they put their clothes back on and settled down to make dinner. After eating, they sat together in the growing dark. Galaphile thought about telling her what he had discovered about her pregnancy—a truth he was still keeping from her.

But was this something he was meant to tell her, or something he should wait for her to tell him? She was bearing this child, but was she even aware yet? And what if that small spark did not make it? Would she even want to know, if it never came to fruition? Should he at least wait until her body informed her of it first?

She bundled up against him as he thought it through. Then he felt her nodding and sensed she might be falling asleep. "Do you ever think about us having a child?" he asked impulsively.

She smiled up at him. "Do you think we are ready for one? Once we have it, we cannot change our minds or regret our decision. These are hard times for us, and they might prove to be hard times for our child, too."

"I will never regret having a child with you," he replied at once.

She looked at him and nodded. "I knew that's what you would tell me, and I love you for doing so. So yes, I am ready for a child. No matter the risks."

He sobered a bit at that, thinking about what those risks could be. Apparently, she was not yet aware of her pregnancy. But she would be soon enough. He would keep a close eye on her, he promised himself. And should a problem arise, they could discuss it together.

When morning dawned and they woke, neither was surprised to see a mountain lion lounging nearby. They began walking back toward the construction site, and within an hour their honor guard had swollen to seven big cats and a pair of young ones. The tribe formed a loose circle about them, keeping close watch but making no effort to hinder their passing.

When the outer walls of the citadel rose before them, the cats peeled off and disappeared back into the rocks and trees. Again, it was astonishing to see how much progress had been made in their absence. The basement structures had been enclosed, and now the first floor was starting to rise. Builders and sentries crowded forward to joyfully greet their master and mistress.

Galaphile spent long moments thinking about what it would mean to have a child of his own inhabiting this site, but it was difficult to come to terms with the impact. He had little experience with children, being an only child who had lost his parents young. What would that mean in the face of the dangers he was facing? How would he and Nirianne manage? Would he even be capable of being a father?

One question persisted and refused to be banished, however: What might the dark magic inhabiting Nirianne have done to this unborn child? Had it sensed the child as well? Had it taken any action against it? Invaded it in some small way? Or was it too new to affect?

He supposed only time would tell.

THIRTY-TWO

Nirianne was pleased to be pregnant.

She had known she was with child for the better part of two weeks after arriving back at the citadel, but she had kept it to herself. When she had first become certain of her condition, her initial instinct had been to tell Galaphile. She had been halfway there when she stopped herself, suddenly unsure. He was her partner in life, her sole lover, the one man to whom she had given herself.

And yet . . .

Everything depended on timing. Had the child been conceived in the heady days after she had been cured of the Spectre Telle's infection, or in the days before, when his dark magic had twined through her like rot?

It was hard to tell. Her courses were always subject to a certain whimsy.

It was true that Galaphile had not mentioned a pregnancy to her when he had removed the last traces of the Spectre Telle's magic from her body, and he had assured her that the infection was entirely gone. But then, Galaphile could be closemouthed on certain subjects—

especially when he felt he was protecting others—and there had been that odd discussion of children on the day before they arrived back at the camp. Had that been some obscure hint that he knew? Or had their frolic in the lake been the moment of conception, and his magic somehow sensed it? Then again, perhaps his comment was just a ridiculous coincidence.

With her husband, anything was possible.

Which again brought her back to the issue of timing. Before or after. Before or after.

And if the former, had whatever corruption the Spectre Telle infused through her also been imparted to the child? Could dark magic infect a child only days into its existence? Could he co-opt a nascent life as firmly as an established one?

Then an even grimmer possibility occurred to her. What had happened to her while she was in captivity with the Spectre Telle was still not entirely clear, but it was apparent that he'd used their time together to sink his dark magic deep inside her. So what if he was the one who had put this child inside her—not in the usual way, but in some darker way that relied on his magic to seed her? It had been a year since she had been in his clutches, but what if he had placed something more into her than just a compulsion? What if he had placed . . . insurance? Something that lay dormant until his other presence was ejected, and which then took over?

After all, she and Galaphile had been together for a year. If they could bear a child together, surely it would have happened sooner? That such a thing would happen just as the Spectre Telle's hold on her was broken seemed too coincidental.

It was a terrible thought, so dark and vile that she wanted to dismiss it immediately, but she could not. The Spectre Telle was capable of so much darkness, and he had told her over and over again how she was his slave now and would be so forever. She would never be free of him—so he had warned her. Could he have fulfilled that threat without her realizing it? What better way was there than to give her a child that was his? How more thorough would her subjugation be if she was forced to bear the spawn of a monster?

But she would know, wouldn't she? Her body would sense if there was something inside her that wasn't right, that didn't belong. She did not think Telle was Human; even if he'd begun that way, he wasn't any longer. Somehow, he had gained access to dark magic, and dark magic could subvert and alter anything it touched. But then, if this child was subverted, wouldn't she know? Wouldn't she feel that taint of corruption inside her?

She was intimately familiar with the feel of Telle's dark magic inside her—had lived with it for close to a year—but sensed none of that now. She herself was free of his presence.

But what of the child?

She needed answers, but where was she to find them?

Then she smiled as she realized who she needed to speak to.

She found Ursule Raken sitting in an exterior alcove on the west high wall, as far from the noise of construction as she could get. The sun was inching west toward sunset, and she had placed herself on a blanket-covered bench and was sitting with her legs folded before her and her head tilted to catch the last of the late-afternoon rays. She was clearly in a state of meditation, her eyes closed and her lips curved into a smile.

Nirianne hesitated to disturb this moment of personal peace and was on the verge of turning back when Ursule, eyes still closed, beckoned her forward.

"How can I help, Nirianne?" she asked softly.

Her voice was always so amazingly kind and inviting, as if she were speaking to a kitten or a baby. She was always at peace with herself and her surroundings, always in control of what she was doing. Nirianne wished she could be more like Ursule.

"I would like your advice," Nirianne admitted. "I am in a difficult situation—one to which I have no ready answers. I was hoping you might help me find my way."

Ursule opened her eyes, still smiling. "I will try my best. Does this have to do with the child you now carry?"

Nirianne blew out a breath. If Ursule knew about the child, had she already seen some vision of its future? And was that future dark or light?

"Congratulations, by the way," Ursule added.

Nirianne gave a strangled laugh. "Thanks? But part of the problem is that I am not sure if congratulations are even in order."

She laid out the issues—the dark magic that had infected her, and how she worried that it might have been severe enough to infect her baby, or even—in the worst of all possible worlds—created it.

"If it will set your mind somewhat at ease, I know enough about how magic works to know that magic alone—and particularly dark magic—cannot create life where there is none. A semblance of life, perhaps, but true life?" Ursule shook her head.

"That said," she continued, "can dark magic, combined with conception, create something other than what was intended? That, I am not sure. I regret to tell you that, in this, your fears have validity. Have you asked Galaphile about this yet? If there was no life inside you when he cleansed you of this Spectre Telle's dark magic, then felicitations are in order. You and the High Lord are becoming parents. If a child was there, however . . ." She gave a graceful shrug. "Well, you and the High Lord are becoming parents, but to what I cannot say."

Nirianne felt a shiver go through her. Ursule had dismissed the worst of the possibilities, true. But knowing that she was troubled as well—that this was not just Nirianne's fearful imagination at work, inventing problems where none existed—made everything feel a bit more real. And scary.

"You knew I was pregnant," Nirianne said. "Have you seen any visions of my child? Do you know what future it holds, and if that future is dark or light?"

"There are no easy answers to your question," the older woman said, almost regretfully. "I can see something of the future, but never all of it—and never as much as I would like to see. And as yet, I have seen no visions of your specific child or your child's future. All I saw was you, a few months hence, with a swollen belly. So I cannot speak to what this child will be once you have given birth—male or female, dark or light. It is as much a mystery to me as it is to you."

She paused as Nirianne sighed yet again, and reached out to take her hands. "But I can say this much. A body reacts to the love it receives. This child is yours to cherish, yours to raise, yours to nurture—you and Galaphile both. If there is any darkness in it, perhaps your combined love can banish it. Darkness cannot endure in the presence of great light, and both of you belong to the light."

And if not, Nirianne thought, perhaps Galaphile could find and root out any darkness in their child the way he had with her.

"I hope you are right," Nirianne murmured. "I want nothing more to do with the Spectre Telle and his foul magic."

"I can understand that. Go to Galaphile, child. The two of you must discuss this and whatever implications it may have. Perhaps you will be lucky. Perhaps the dark magic prevented conception, and it is only after it was gone that you were able to increase. But if not . . . Galaphile will help you. For better or for worse, he will stand by you, and he will stand by his child. He will give you the support you need if you trust him enough to let him do so."

Nirianne closed her eyes in relief. It was what she wanted to hear. Galaphile's support was what she most needed, and Ursule was right. He would be in this with her no matter what happened.

Impulsively, she reached out and hugged the seer. "Thank you, Ursule. Your words have been an enormous help. I am so very grateful that you came to join us here."

"The cause is a worthy one, my dear, and I am glad to be part of it in whatever small way I can. Also, to the extent I can find anything in my sightings of the future that might help you, I will share them. I will be looking. I do sense in my inner self that there is something important about this child—though this comes from a place beyond what I can see with my mind or my eyes or my magic. I see it from my heart perhaps. One thing I know for certain, though. Your baby will need your love."

They sat together until sunset, talking of lesser things, watching the sun turn red against a darkening sky, and Nirianne felt almost at peace.

Later that night, after a communal dinner with the workers, Nirianne confronted Galaphile in their tent.

"My love, there is something I need to ask you."

At her serious tone, he froze, suddenly knowing exactly what she wanted to ask him.

"That day by the lake," she said, "before we returned to the citadel, you asked if I'd ever considered us having a child. Why did you ask that? Was it because you already knew I was pregnant?"

He was glad, in a way, to finally have this out in the open; keeping his fears to himself had led to some sleepless nights over the past few weeks. Every night, as Nirianne slept, he had longed to slip a tendril of magic back inside her to see if any shadow had begun to cloud the growing spark of their child. But to do so would have been a huge violation of Nirianne's trust, so he had resisted temptation. Yet the need to know still consumed him. "I did, yes. I was not sure if you knew yourself yet, so I did not want to mention it directly, because . . . Well, I worried it seemed invasive. How long have you known?"

"I figured it out a few days after we got back. But, Galaphile, you know the next question I need to ask, because you must be as greatly aware of the implications as I am. So . . ."

Yes, of course his clever wife would have figured this out as quickly as he had. How lucky he was to have her. "I am sorry, Nirianne, but it is as you fear. You were already with child when I was burning the Spectre Telle's infection from your body."

"Did it . . . Was it . . ."

He knew what she was trying to ask yet feared to voice, so he gave her the unvarnished truth that she deserved.

"It was, I sensed, a very new life," he told her, "likely from our time at Varisol's after the Elves, but before we went up north for the Trolls. And it was bright, Nirianne—a bright, lovely spark. I sensed no darkness in it. But . . . it was also so new, so small, that I might not have seen anything. All I can say is that you were empty of dark magic, and there was nothing extending from it to you. But if that tiny spark harbored a darkness inside, digging through it to find out would have extinguished it for sure, and that was not a choice I could make for you."

She nodded and moved to embrace him, laying her head on his chest. He pulled her against him with one hand, laying the other on her hair.

"But I feared, Nirianne," he said. "Every day since then, it has plagued my thoughts. Did Telle's dark magic somehow creep into the child while they coexisted inside you? Is a shadow growing inside it even now? I can think of little else."

She nodded her head, her breath warm against his skin when she spoke. "It has been much on my mind as well. Galaphile . . ." She raised her head and looked up at him. "Can you look inside me again? Now? Please?"

There was a palpable fear in her voice. But truth be told, there was nothing he wanted in the world more than this.

At his instruction, she lay down on their cot. He sank his magic under her skin, sweeping it everywhere through her body first, save the child, just to be certain he had left no thread of dark magic behind that had again begun to swell. But no, there was nothing there save Nirianne: clean and bold and beautiful.

Then he turned his attention to the growing life inside her, and he nearly wept. It was bigger now—a tiny, almost formless bean, tethered to her by a thread—but there was a flutter of a heartbeat. And it was bright. Bright, bright, bright.

His child. *Their* child.

A surge of love and joy filled him. Perhaps it had been too new, too small for the magic to infect.

But then . . . perhaps it was still too small to perceive any darkness it might harbor. Or perhaps the darkness had a different effect on it, one that would only manifest as it continued to grow. That might be apparent only after it was born.

They would have to be vigilant, continue to monitor the child as it grew, both within her and without. But . . .

For now, all was good.

Their child thrived.

Their child of light.

He withdrew his magic and saw her looking up at him anxiously.

A tear slipped down his cheek. "It is beautiful. And there is no darkness there, Nirianne."

She brushed the tear from his cheek, smiling—but he could see the worry still lurking in her eyes. Her awareness of the one word he had not spoken but was thinking: yet.

No darkness *yet*.

But then, didn't every other new parent fear for their child, hope that everything would develop as it should? How did this make them different from any other new parents?

Whatever happened, they would get through this together.

And no matter what, they would love this bright life they had created.

Thirty-Three

The Spectre Telle had known instantly when his connection with Nirianne was severed, for suddenly the tether that stretched between them was gone, as cleanly as if sliced away by a knife. Someone—likely that upstart husband of hers—had discovered his intrusion and not only excised the bond between them but also rooted out and burned away that part of himself he had placed within her to gain control over her body. He experienced no physical pain at its destruction, but the loss of control produced hurt of a different kind.

The deprivation was keen but not debilitating. He would have another chance, he knew, to bring her back into line and under his thumb. He had the patience to wait for his opportunity. But it was inconvenient to lose the control he had enjoyed, and disappointing to be left without a source that close to his enemy.

Of course, he did have a few vessels among the Dwarf workers, placed there in secret during his early forays into Galaphile's camp. This was what had enabled him to seize Galaphile's putative mate in the first place—for he had already been alerted to Galaphile's affection for the girl. And no wonder he liked her: She was as pesky a do-gooder as her infernal husband.

Truly, it had been a joy to rein in a will that strong and stubborn. It proved to him how much he had learned, how much he had grown.

Perhaps he should reactivate his sleepers, have them acquire the girl once more.

But no, he had a more urgent need at hand. His enemy was growing too powerful. In addition to his Dwarf builders and defenders, he had close to a hundred Human guards, and now a force of four hundred Rock Trolls. And despite his obvious blunder with the Elven King, which had delighted Telle no end . . . the Elven Queen was a worry. She had seemed entirely too sympathetic to the cause, so how long would it be before Elven Hunters might be added to the force?

The time to act was now. A peacekeeping force in the Midlands was the exact opposite of what he wanted to achieve. His supreme reign would be cemented only through chaos and strife.

Plus, while his isolated northern fortress had been perfect during the years while he experimented with his powers, it now put him too far from the lands and peoples he sought to subjugate. It was time to move on, and his enemy's stronghold was much more conveniently located.

He would put an end to Galaphile Joss and claim the man's citadel.

After all, thanks to Nirianne, he had already gotten most of what he wanted—the defensive plans for the citadel, knowledge of its defenders, insights into Galaphile Joss's thinking, and a sense of the strengths and weaknesses of those he sought to destroy.

What was needed most now was no longer subterfuge and deceit, but an exercise of outright force that would crush any resistance and enable him to establish a stronghold in the Midlands—after which, the whole world could be his!

Deep in his mind, the Ildatch hummed in quiet satisfaction at his resolve.

By now, he knew, he was fully under the sway of the book and its dark desires to rule the world. He was its vessel, he realized, its tool, the thing it used to carry out its wishes. But in turn, the Ildatch was his weapon. And while he was, in a sense, subjugated to the whims of his newfound magic, he was also its master. The book was powerful, but it was also hindered by the fact that it could achieve nothing on its own. To be effective, it needed the mind and hands of a living creature to evoke and exploit its magic. Otherwise, it was nothing more than a collection of words and ideas. And power required more than words on a page. It required an actor, an interpreter.

A partner.

For that, the Ildatch needed him.

The Spectre Telle did not deceive himself entirely; he knew he had been subverted. He knew, as well, that he was the weaker and frailer of the pair. He was the one who could be replaced—although it would likely take time and effort to find a new purveyor of the craft with the right mindset and the proper cravings, and he sensed the impatience that underlay the intense needs of the book. It was meant to be used, after all. It had no other function, no other purpose, no other desire.

No other outlet for the intense cravings that infused its existence and made it what it was.

So for now this marriage of word and deed functioned. It was an alliance born of raw desire, each making use of the other as private needs and inner hungers demanded. And Telle longed for the day when the two would become one—when the last of the book's secrets were unlocked and he would bestride the world like a colossus, his name forever known and feared.

But that moment would only be achieved one slow step at a time, and the next step was pulling Galaphile Joss and his followers off the board.

In the year since the Spectre Telle had taken Nirianne, he had not been idle. Controlling her had been far from his only focus, for he was still striving to crack the problem of creating—or at least reanimating—an army that would be fully under his control. But, perhaps ironically, controlling her had given him some of the tools he needed.

Maintaining a constant link to her had proved too draining and distracting, so he had worked on modifying the fragment of his magic he had left inside of her, crafting it into a more independent entity that could not only more actively gather information—all of which he could then access when linking back to it—but also monitor Nirianne for signs of rebellion and report back when his active intervention was needed.

It had proved invaluable—and the key to everything that came after.

He hadn't been able to do much about Galaphile and Nirianne's visit to the Elves—that damnable woman had realized too quickly that any deliberate act of sabotage she made against her husband could be a clue to Telle's presence—so he had been effectively neutralized there, which he hated. But when he learned they would be confronting the Maturen of the Rock Trolls next . . .

Well, that was a chance too good to pass up. The Rock Troll leader was practically in his backyard, and it was ridiculously easy to intercept him one night and slip another controlling bit of dark magic into his head, sowing distrust of Galaphile Joss.

The problem was that placing these entities, giving them some degree of autonomy, took something out of him. He supposed it was a bit like birthing a baby—some energy was required for its formation and early care, but once it became its own thing, growing to a child as it were, it ceased to drain him and just became a thing under his control, no longer feeding off him.

Annoyingly, the bit of dark magic he placed within the Maturen was new enough that Galaphile was able to discover it—and then discover the much more powerful one inside his wife. Which, again, was a huge loss.

But also a gain, in that it had at last enabled him to crack the problem of his army. A more autonomous spark of dark magic infused with a shard of his consciousness, and placed within a newly living shell, could in time become a being with enough rough cunning to be forged into a weapon eager to fight. And as these undead had been forged of himself and the Ildatch's dark magic, they wanted what he wanted.

Even before he'd lost Nirianne, he had begun to experiment with this, creating ten, then twenty, then a hundred of these beings. Though initially draining to create, he soon learned that each shard of himself he gave away replenished inside him until he was whole once more while also continuing to grow inside each new entity gifted with it, until it filled them as well. And once filled, they were his to use with no further expenditure of energy. Instead, he had only to issue orders.

Once he had resolved to take the fight to Galaphile, he began production in earnest. Raw materials were not a problem. Dug up, exhumed, retrieved, or created, he found what he needed and used it as fodder. He also began mixing and matching. Could he combine bits of different creatures into a single entity, with elements of both? He could.

It was a slow beginning, but with Nirianne out of the picture and the Ildatch driving him on, his productivity soared. An army of a hundred quickly grew to two hundred and soon to a thousand. It was slow going in the beginning, but like a muscle, his abilities grew stronger with use and practice.

Spectre Telle had provided life to his beings, and he demonstrated to them regularly that he could take it away again should one of them prove a problem. They were nothing but weapons, and he treated them as such. They lacked thought and reason and the ability to question what they were directed to do. They were work animals without the ability to resist, and he made sure they understood this from the beginning. He created obedience based on a mix of fear, worship, and mutual desire.

Months passed, and the size of his army grew larger until he had two thousand of them at hand—more than enough to stand up to the four hundred Rock Trolls and hundred-odd Humans that Galaphile Joss had to defend him.

By now, he was convinced of his own invincibility. With the power of the Ildatch to guide him and the might of his army of the dead to support him, he would gain control over all Galaphile Joss had built and sow chaos across the Midlands.

In the end, he would control everything.

He made preparations to turn his army south, toward the Dragon's Teeth Mountains.

THIRTY-FOUR

For the next two months, Galaphile and Nirianne lived and worked at the construction site, watching as the citadel continued to take shape. It grew in increments, as such complicated structures must, expanding at a steady but unhurried pace. The number of workers swelled as more Dwarves traveled north from their Eastland cities—lured by friends and relatives already engaged—to become a part of the effort. And Galaphile was pleased to see how each took a pride of ownership in the place and felt a sense of engagement in his or her work. The project was the result of their combined efforts, and watching it come closer and closer to completion was immensely satisfying for all.

And as the fortress grew, so too did Nirianne. Galaphile checked on the child's progress weekly and saw no encroaching darkness, so all he could hope was that, by following Ursule's advice and loving this child as deeply and completely as they could, they could somehow avert any darker path.

Before long, Nirianne's condition became obvious to all but the most oblivious of workers, and knowledge that there was now an heir to this small kingdom seemed to infuse everyone with a fresh energy.

At this point, all construction on the fortress was being conducted inside the massive outer walls, which were substantially complete. Aside from the main enclosure, a separate building was being erected dedicated to housing the four hundred Rock Trolls now in residence. Krunce Torsh was their commander and served as a welcome link between the Trolls and their new companions.

As well, Galaphile's rank of Human defenders swelled as word got out about the citadel and its purpose. Especially since some additional financial help in the form of gold coins had been provided quite unexpectedly by the Elven King.

To begin with, Galaphile had the Trolls aiding the builders, putting their enormous strength to work lifting and hauling loads that otherwise would have required a complement of eight or ten Dwarves per load to manage. This aid was deeply appreciated by the already beleaguered companies of Dwarves, and before a week was out, new friendships between members of the two Races were forming at every turn as each mastered the other's tongue.

It was strange, Galaphile thought, to see such creatures as the huge Trolls and much smaller Dwarves banding together, working side by side, sharing food and stories. It indeed showed precisely how things could be once the fortress was assembled and the peacekeeping force was fully operational. It offered a measure of hope for the future.

Once the bonds formed, as Galaphile had hoped they would—a peacekeeping force would work more effectively if it saw and believed in its goals—Galaphile began to pull the Rock Trolls out of construction and merge them with some of his Human defenders so that they could engage directly in peacekeeping efforts. The sooner he sorted out the various rogue camps and put an end to their efforts to control entire sections of the Four Lands, the better. In less than a month, Galaphile devised a plan for putting his newest soldiers to work in the capacity for which they had been initially engaged, and the newly assigned effort was under way and thriving as again bonds formed between Humans and Trolls.

Separating the four hundred into sets of fifty men, each with a few Humans and Dwarves assigned to every troop, he dispatched them toward a series of rogue encampments with orders to break down each one, giving his soldiers full permission to send the leaders of these camps packing and to scatter their followers to the four winds.

Results were swiftly realized. Within three weeks, five major encampments had been broken apart, their leaders eliminated, and their members chased off. A few of the major Midland cities where controlling factions had settled in were also targeted, and in-city enclaves were destroyed.

The peacekeeping efforts were so effective that, after the first few camps went down, various other enclaves simply fell apart or disbanded all on their own. And so began a new era of peace and cooperation among the various camps, communities, and towns.

Galaphile also instituted programs for the remaining citizens to engage in, many of which included education for the children and job training for the adults. And with Nirianne's help, he tried to ensure a more equitable distribution of food and resources. Galaphile wanted to instill a sense of real community throughout the Midlands. He wanted to offer people a sense of purpose beyond simple survival—a sense of what it meant to form communities and work alongside their neighbors for the greater good.

But then a fresh threat arose.

The earliest warning came from one of the many scouts that Galaphile employed to survey the countryside north of the Midlands, bordering on the lands where the Spectre Telle held sway.

"An army is coming!" he reported, breathless, for he had been riding hard all day. "Directly toward us, from out of the north!"

Galaphile wrapped an arm about the man's shoulders and walked him toward the common washroom and then into the kitchen tent. It appeared he hadn't eaten or rested since he set out for his scouting duties. Amid efforts to refresh himself, the man revealed what he knew.

"There are so many of them—ragged, filthy creatures. The army doesn't look right—the men are all battered and decrepit, as if they were not even entirely alive, or something more dead than living. I've never seen anything like it!"

Galaphile, remembering Krunce's words about the Spectre Telle potentially raising an army of the undead, wondered if this was indeed the case. Was this monster possessed of sufficient magic to form the minions he required or to subvert other creatures to become what he needed? And if so, how?

"They've crossed the Knife Edge and even now they're fording the River Lethe. I thought for a time they were going into the Westland to engage with the Elves, but they turned this way instead. High Lord, there are too many for us to stop!"

Galaphile reassured him that all would be well and sent him off to rest. Then he dispatched a new complement of scouts to monitor the progress of the invaders, already fairly certain of their origin, destination, and leadership. Nothing else made sense. Finally, he sent out messengers to recall all of the Rock Trolls still scattered across the Midlands back to the citadel.

Then he went to his tent, found Nirianne already asleep, and sat down next to her for long moments, just looking at her in the near darkness.

As the minutes slipped by, he found himself wondering what lay ahead and how he could stop it. He had expected an attack of a sort from his enemy . . . eventually. But if the scout's report was accurate, this one was much more serious than he had imagined. If there were as many of the dark creatures as the man reported, there were far too many—even with the additional help of the Rock Trolls and Humans—for his limited defense force to withstand. As well, given what he knew about his opponent, the man would have magic to employ against him, and would undoubtedly do so.

What steps must he take, then?

He sat in the darkness, considering. He needed to choose a place to stand and fight the creatures, and he needed a plan to damage them so badly that they would be forced to turn back. Fighting outside the citadel was too dangerous, and he knew the walls were ready to withstand such an attack, so here was the better place to make a stand. But if the fight dragged on, they could easily find themselves trapped. Mobility and the freedom to choose his own tactics also seemed crucial.

At least he and Sanitov had worked to alter those of the fortress's secrets that they could, drawing up new plans and altering as many of the hidden tunnels and disguised alcoves and special entrances and exits as possible, given what had already been constructed. So any secrets the

Spectre Telle thought he knew, thanks to the stolen plans, were now largely irrelevant. The fortress was secure once more.

Nevertheless, Galaphile would need further support from other places and peoples if he could find it.

Maybe he could find aid from some of the cities and provinces where he was actively restoring a measure of peace and order—especially given the increased funds from the Elves.

Maybe the Elves would quit stalling on committing to engage in his peacekeeping efforts and send actual soldiers.

Maybe help would come from a source he hadn't considered.

Maybe . . .

Maybe . . .

He lay down next to Nirianne, one arm reaching across her pregnant belly to pull her close. Most important of all, he had to make certain these two precious lives were safe from whatever conflict lay ahead.

He fell asleep shortly afterward, but he still had no answers to his questions.

THIRTY-FIVE

When Galaphile woke the following morning, Nirianne was already up and gone. For a moment, he panicked, remembering the last time she had disappeared, but he quickly calmed himself.

And indeed, when he washed and dressed and went over to the dining quarters, Nirianne was already there, smiling cheerfully and visiting with members of the cooking staff. Galaphile gathered her up along with Sanitov, Ursule Raken, Parkinch, Ratcher, and Krunce and sat them down for a quick conference about the approaching army. In a few sentences, he revealed what he knew about it, the Spectre Telle, and the threat they were facing from both.

"If the number of invaders is anything close to what our scout has reported," he told them, "then we are vastly outnumbered and should not consider facing them on the open expanse of the Streleheim Plains. Better we make them come to us and be faced with having to break down our gates or ascend our walls. No small task, either one. Not only are the barriers significant, but all the while they will be exposed to our weapons."

"But they will have us trapped," Ratcher reminded him, glancing about at the others. "Trapped inside these walls for who knows how long."

Galaphile nodded. "Trapped, but not helpless. We have food enough to last us for months. We have our Healers and our nurses. We have a solid command structure. The slopes will be the more difficult choice for them to make because they are so much easier for us to defend and so much harder for them to assail while we have the aid of the lions. We also have stronger positions from which to counterattack."

He paused, surveying them. "Our enemies will have two ways of coming at us—from the slopes that face south and west, and by the roadway that winds up from the valley to our door. We must defend both. The slopes will be the more difficult choice because they are much easier for us to defend and much harder for them to assail, meaning there will be few places from which they can successfully launch a sustained attack.

"The road provides the only reasonable approach for a larger force, but the road can be blocked and mined with traps. And once again we will be on the uphill side, giving us an added advantage. Any questions so far?"

No one said anything. "We need to assign our Trolls and Dwarves to the places they are best suited to defend," he continued. "Sanitov, I regret having to take our workers from their construction tasks, which is what we brought them here for, but our attackers leave us no choice. It is possible we will receive help from other quarters of the Four Lands, but we cannot be certain of that and therefore cannot depend upon it. We must expect to stand alone and make the best use of what bodies and weapons we already possess. So I am making this offer now, which you can spread among all your workers—and the same applies to your Trolls, Krunce. If anyone wants to leave at this point, they can do so with my blessing. You are not required to stay, any of you—workers or soldiers or whoever else might have joined us. I want people who are here because they willingly chose to stand with us in our efforts to save the Four Lands, and I will not change that by forcing anyone to stay."

He looked around at each of them, taking their measure, pausing to look into each pair of eyes, grateful that none of them showed signs of departure. "Let's take time to help the others prepare. Krunce, you need to decide where best to use your soldiers. I thought we had enough, though now I wish we had more. But we will just have to make do."

The meeting broke up, leaving Nirianne alone with Galaphile. "I didn't want to say this in front of the others, because I am never sure how much we should reveal about his intervention, but the King of the Silver River came to me in a dream last night and told me the cats would stand with us in this fight. So what if we let them help? They can ward the slopes better than we can, leaving us better able to concentrate our efforts on the road. As you said, any forces ascending the mountainside from anything but the north will have to be small, so the cats alone should be enough."

Galaphile stared at her, not sure whether to be pleased or dismayed to discover that the Spirit King had swept Nirianne into his confidences once again. But given the dreams she'd had while he was in the Gardens of Life, he suspected she'd been under his influence for a while. "I don't want them getting killed or feeling like they have to sacrifice themselves for us," he said.

She smiled. "Think of it this way. Those lions are bigger, stronger, and more battle-ready than we are. They can come and go without us knowing. Their senses are far sharper than our own. More to the point, this mountain is their home—more so than it is ours. They have a right to fight for it, too."

"No argument there. And that does give us a few more options."

She kissed him and left, and after a few moments, he went out to help organize the others. He asked Krunce to bring a few of his more dependable Trolls and walk down the road with him to examine possible defenses. He led them to the place where he had divided the roadway nearly a year earlier to turn back the first attack on the site. While the road was whole once again, the means for opening it anew were still available.

"I think we should put other defenses farther down the road as well," he advised those accompanying him.

They continued along the roadway for perhaps half a mile, talking over various options.

"Use your Trolls sparingly. We will need their strength more to help hold the walls of the keep. Just a few would be enough here, to provide points of added strength to the other defenders."

It was nearing dusk by the time they returned to the construction site. Galaphile was surprised to find Parkinch waiting, asking if they could talk in private. At the latter's suggestion, they moved away from the camp and stood on a precipice that faced north, overlooking the partially mist-covered roadway—now, thankfully, deserted. They stood silently together for long moments, staring out over treetops of the surrounding slopes and the valleys beyond. Parkinch was clearly reluctant to speak, and Galaphile waited on him patiently.

"I want to try something," the other mage declared finally, "but it is dangerous."

Galaphile gave a weary sigh. "Everything is dangerous at this point. What do you have in mind?"

"The attackers are perhaps twenty miles from here by now and will be in sight by morning. I want to go out to meet them and see what I can learn. I am the only one among us who has the ability to disappear entirely, so perhaps I can get close enough to this Spectre Telle to hear something of use—something that might be important to us."

Galaphile frowned. "You know I have the same ability to disappear as you do. And I have stronger protective magic. Perhaps I should be the one to go."

Parkinch shook his head. "You lead this effort. You know we can't afford to lose you."

"We can't afford to lose anyone. The Spectre Telle has command of powerful magic. He could detect and subvert you. It seems risky."

"Agreed." Parkinch's pinched, solemn face did not change expression. "But I think it's a risk worth taking. Let me try."

Galaphile nodded. "What you are offering is generous. Will you take someone to stand with you? Ratcher, perhaps? Or Chelm?"

Parkinch shook his head. "I will do better alone."

Galaphile looked back to the mist-clouded Streleheim. "Please be careful. A man like the Spectre Telle—if he even is a man—is no one to underestimate. If you sense that he has detected you, get out of there at once."

Parkinch nodded. "I'll leave now and ride hard enough to reach the front lines of his army by nightfall, when it makes camp. I'll see what I can find out and be back here by midday tomorrow."

Galaphile gave his permission but watched him go with an uneasy feeling. He couldn't help wondering if he had just made a bad mistake.

The day passed quickly. There was still much to be done in the way of preparing the camp for what was coming. Various defenses were established, and assignments for where everyone would be stationed were passed out. Galaphile spent the rest of his time looking for Nirianne, but she had effectively disappeared. Inquiries to various camp members revealed nothing. No one had seen anything of her.

By nightfall, Galaphile was beginning to panic. Perhaps his enemy had already mounted some sort of secret attack, snatching her up once again to use as a bargaining chip. Or worse.

He was sitting by one of the watch fires, trying to figure out his next move, when she abruptly appeared out of the darkness and sat down beside him. "Miss me?"

He exhaled gustily. "Sometimes you scare the life out of me. Where have you been?"

Moonlight reflected off her reddish-blond hair, lending her a softness and a glow that her pregnancy only emphasized. But the toughness he found in her eyes contradicted this. She wasn't entirely what she seemed, and he needed to remember that.

"With the lions, out on the slopes. One of them came to fetch me. And guess what?" She was suddenly excited. "We found at least six places where we can trigger avalanches that will clear out whole sections of the hillside. That will provide whoever tries to come up here with a very hard path."

"The lions showed you all this?"

"Some of it. Some I found on my own. I know what I'm doing."

He was certain she did. But he also knew that she was sometimes willing to take risks she should not, and he feared for her safety and that of their child.

By midday on the morrow, Parkinch had still not returned. Galaphile wanted to go look for him, but his companions convinced him not to.

It was too dangerous for anyone to go down onto the Streleheim at this point. Already there were signs of dust clouds where the approaching army was steadily making its way closer. If Parkinch were able, he would come back to them. So Galaphile would have to be patient and wait.

The day passed with continued efforts to prepare for the expected invasion. Vulnerable areas on both the road and the slopes were further fortified. The walls and gates of the fortress were strengthened with additional safeholds, and traps of all sorts were constructed and armed. It was a wearing, tedious sort of business, but it was necessary if the inhabitants of the fortress were to survive.

It was nearing sunset when Parkinch finally returned.

Or, more accurately, what was left of him.

He came staggering up the mountainside like something out of the old stories—the ones about the walking dead. He was ragged and worn, and he was talking absently to someone who clearly wasn't there. The watch saw him coming, realized how bad it was, collected him, and carried him to the medical complex.

Then they fetched Galaphile, who rushed to be with him. What he found was devastating. Parkinch was ruined.

"I went north . . . maybe twenty miles, but far enough to find the invaders," he managed to reveal in fits and coughs that shook his entire body. "I went into their camp . . . invisible. I found the man—or devil, more the like . . . that I said . . . I would deceive. But he was the one . . . who deceived me."

He was gasping by now, and Galaphile already knew how this would end. That the man had made it this far was a miracle. "Slowly, brave one. Do not try so hard to talk. Deep breaths, careful words. I will wait on you."

The other's shocked eyes fixed on him. "He . . . he found me out . . . never saw me . . . yet knew I was there." His voice tightened, and he forced his sentences to steady. "His creatures came for me. I slipped their grasp, but I couldn't escape him. His mind! So swift and cruel! He was inside me in moments, tearing with such . . . such rage! He put something in me that . . . began to eat. I could feel it gnawing on me . . . my body, my mind, my courage and resolve. Everything! It fed on me . . . like I was something *meant* to be eaten!"

Galaphile's hand tightened. "But you escaped. You're safe now."

A vigorous shake of his companion's head suggested otherwise. "You don't . . . understand! He wanted to make me his creature! He wanted me to reveal everything I knew and then come back to betray you! I can still feel him *invading* me! Twisting all about inside me . . . but I didn't let him . . ."

He broke off again, his gaze distant, but his eyes leaking tears. "I . . . could not . . . let . . ."

He was shaking with whatever had happened to him, racked with heavy, choking sobs of despair. He was falling apart before Galaphile's eyes. Galaphile couldn't help it; he found himself picturing anew what had been done to Nirianne and, to a lesser degree, the Maturen. He reached down and placed his hands on either side of Parkinch's face, preparing to excise whatever dark magic the Spectre Telle had placed inside him.

Suddenly, Parkinch's hands clamped down hard on Galaphile's arms, drawing him close. "You have to run! That . . . creature wants you dead! I saw it! He hates you! He will destroy you! You can't fight what he can do, what he is! He just . . . breaks you down!"

"Peace, my friend," Galaphile said. Then, summoning his magic, he did the only thing he knew to do—the one thing that had saved the Maturen and Nirianne. He reached within Parkinch to try to eliminate the dark magic.

The first things he grew aware of were parts of Parkinch that were just . . . missing. Not flesh and bone, of course; nothing so mundane. But the things that made Parkinch himself were shredded and full of holes, like moth-eaten cloth.

Parkinch had spoken of the magic eating away at him, and indeed that seemed to be the case.

Galaphile felt sick.

As he looked closer, he could see the areas where the magic clung most heavily to Parkinch, chewing away at his essence.

To Galaphile's dismay, it seemed that the Spectre Telle had learned a thing or two in the time since he had infected the Maturen. Though Parkinch had possessed the dark magic for less than a day, it was already deeply rooted, tangled inexorably into his being. Yanking it free would not work, for it would take too much of Parkinch with it when it went. But neither did he have time to tease it painstakingly free, as he had with Nirianne, because this magic seemed to have an additional, ugly purpose—to invade *him*.

It was a trap he had no choice but to spring if he wanted to save Parkinch. But even as he fought to free his companion, the magic chewed and gnawed at his own being, trying to break through, until he was defending himself on multiple fronts even as he endeavored to untangle it from Parkinch.

Though he fought valiantly, it was a losing battle from the start as more and more pieces of Parkinch vanished under the magic's assault. Finally, Parkinch screamed one last time, jerked as if possessed, and died.

Leaving Galaphile free at last to annihilate the magic without fear of annihilating Parkinch, since there was no more left of Parkinch to concern him.

Galaphile sat with the body for a long time afterward, consumed by a mix of guilt and regret. He had fought to save this man as he had fought to save Nirianne and the Maturen, but this time, his efforts had failed.

He could only hope this wasn't an omen for his upcoming battle.

In less than two days, the Spectre Telle's army would arrive.

THIRTY-SIX

Galaphile slept poorly after he returned to their tent in the wake of Parkinch's death, and Nirianne had to admit she did not sleep much better. She had not known Parkinch well, but she, too, had fallen victim to the Spectre Telle's mental incursions, and she could only imagine how greatly Parkinch had suffered at his hands.

When dawn broke, Nirianne roused Galaphile, and together they walked to the valley rim to look down on the Streleheim. She wanted to know more about what it was that threatened them before she encountered it, and Galaphile, she knew, would be even more anxious. He would be facing the army from the front, whereas she and the cats would be combatting it only on the back slopes.

What they found, however, was worse than a nightmare.

The central plain of the Streleheim, for several miles, was flooded with creatures—a veritable army of monsters. Lopsided, twisted, and bent, they shuffled onward, brought to life by means that suggested the darkest evil imaginable. It was impossible for Nirianne to imagine how a deeply overwhelmed force of Trolls, Humans, and Dwarves could possibly survive an attack of this nature. They might stand for a time, but eventually they would be overwhelmed and swept away.

The ending was there before her, and she could not convince herself that any other resolution was possible.

Yet she said nothing of this to Galaphile. It would not be difficult for him to have discerned this truth on his own, so it was not necessary for her to voice it.

After a moment of silence, he turned to Nirianne. "Are you ready?"

"I am," she affirmed.

And, oddly, she was. Doom lurked before them, yet she felt resolved, settled, ready to face what was coming, no matter how dire. Maybe it was the child nestled inside her who gave more purpose to her life. She would fight harder than ever to give that child a better future than this tumultuous present.

But maybe it was just that, after all the Spectre Telle had taken from her—after all the ways he had tried to break her—she remained unbroken. Maybe she had finally begun to understand her own strength.

"Stand firm for as long as you can," Galaphile told her. "When you sense a collapse is imminent, retreat to the fortress. We will make our stand from there. Do not hesitate when you feel things breaking down. Will you promise me?"

"I promise. Do you promise the same for yourself when you are defending the road? A retreat when a retreat is all that's left to you?"

"I will." He kissed her deeply, passionately, then moved away.

And just for an instant, she wondered if she would ever see him again.

Nirianne went down the mountainside like the cats she was planning to join. The plan was to advance to where the cliffs were steepest and the footing most difficult. Below that space, the mountain lions would be waiting. If any of the attackers got past them, there was a rear guard of Rock Trolls to engage them and prevent them from advancing any farther.

She scampered down to where she could stand hidden in the rocks but still look out over the plains below. She was already aware of several lions crouched within the boulder-strewn cliffs, lying in wait for their attackers. Wordlessly, she joined them.

That was when she noticed that something odd was happening below, and she lifted herself just high enough to watch.

An odd stillness had settled over the whole of the attacking force, from front to back and side to side. Every last predator had gone perfectly still and was looking north, into the mist.

Long minutes passed and nothing happened. Then, abruptly, the Spectre Telle appeared from out of a northern bank of mists. He rode the same creature that he had used to carry Nirianne away the last time. It was, she had learned, known as a Skelter—a reptilian monster and a winged horror. It slithered, crawled, galloped, and flew—all four means of mobility at its command—so that it could effortlessly switch forms and change shapes as need dictated.

Nirianne went cold all over. She knew she was imagining it—after all, her enemy was too far away to be seen clearly—but it felt as if the monster was looking straight at her during the entirety of its advance.

She dropped back down into the rocks and closed her eyes. Her mind spun. *Shades!*

Still . . . *I am stronger than I know, I am stronger than I know,* she reminded herself again.

It took a long time for the Spectre Telle to come all the way through his hordes of obedient subjects. But slowly, slowly, the silence and the immobility of those creatures began to give way to a low, barely audible murmur that soon rose to a shout.

Before long, the front ranks swarmed toward the main road and Galaphile, while others cut for the slopes where Nirianne and her feline allies were waiting. Up onto the embankments and slopes they ascended, screaming as if they had gone mad.

And on the plains below, their master urged them on, arms rising and falling in motions that propelled them ahead, in what was clearly the beginning of an attack intended to eradicate all who thought to resist.

But the lions were predators, born to hunt. They waited, all of them crouched down and hidden as the scrambling swarms of attackers fought their way up the uncertain terrain. Some of the attackers were ripped off their feet and hurled away, thrown hundreds of feet to their death. Others were swept in waves off the rock face as avalanche after avalanche was triggered.

But this wasn't any kind of enemy Nirianne was used to fighting. They seemed to have no fear, no sense of self-preservation. All they desired was to advance, to attack, no matter how badly wounded or maimed.

The giant cats were intimidating in the extreme, but how did you fight a foe who refused to be intimidated or driven off?

She was still battling when the bolt hit her in the shoulder. It was not a deadly strike—no more than a deep flesh wound—but it was enough to cause her to lose her balance, and she tumbled hard, striking her head on a rock. She was back on her feet quickly enough, but she was dazed, and the blood from her wound flowed freely, soaking her clothes. She stumbled again and fell. Something about the wound seemed to have sapped the energy from her body. Screaming in fury, she scrambled up and drew out her short sword. There was something huge coming toward her—a ragged monster, raising his massive ax to put an end to her.

There was no time or chance for her to escape. She blinked rapidly against what she knew was coming.

Galaphile, she whispered, knowing he would never be there in time to save her.

Galaphile knew nothing of what was happening on the mountain slopes. All of his attention was given over to the hordes of demonkind that were ascending the road like a dark tide. He remembered the vision the King of the Silver River had shown him—the battlefield strewn with destruction and carnage. If he lost this fight now, was that the future he would unleash?

He had placed some strategic fighters—Rock Trolls, Dwarves, and Humans—in key positions all along both sides of the twisting roadway. Krunce Torsh commanded the Trolls, leaving Galaphile in charge of the rest.

The defensive plan was simple enough: Hold each key position as long as possible, then fall back to the next until all were lost. Then retreat into the citadel for the final stand.

Everyone had seen the number of invaders crossing the Streleheim to attack and destroy them. Every last man and woman defending the heights knew what they were up against. Galaphile had told them he would stand fast even if he had to fight alone, and these people who had come to help him believed in his abilities and courage. If anyone could stop this creature, it was him.

But he had never commanded a fighting force beyond perhaps two dozen. He knew the theory of battle, but his practical experience was limited.

Still, he believed that they could win. He believed that numbers alone did not guarantee victory. He believed courage and determination could play as much a part as anything. He did not try to fool himself about his own chances, however. Leaders were often the first ones targeted. But all he could do was his best; that would have to be enough. Whatever happened, he told himself, he must try to stay alive at least until he could tell that the tide was turning in the favor of the defenders.

As he was thinking this through, he was walking down the empty roadway to the farthest of his defensive positions. Dwarf, Troll, and Human guards warded him as he proceeded, casting glances everywhere, spinning off in ones and twos to be certain nothing was hiding on either side, lying in wait to catch him unawares.

He was almost to his target when he heard the sounds of the enemy approaching. It was unsettling—a cacophony of shrieks, howls, screams, and snarls that made him slow despite himself. The road ahead bent, so what was making these sounds was still not visible, but he could guess what was coming easily enough from his view off the ramparts earlier.

Then, as if by some devilish form of magic, Ursule Raken was beside him, her tall form appearing seemingly out of nowhere. She was breathing hard—an indication of her haste. She took his arm and pulled him aside. "I've had a vision," she managed between gasps. "You need to go to Nirianne. At once!"

He stared at her. "What sort of vision?"

"It hasn't come to pass yet, and there is a chance it won't, but my visions seldom deceive me. The enemy will reach her on the slopes." She took a deep breath and released it slowly. "She will die."

Panic filled him. "But it hasn't happened yet?"

"Nor will it if you go to her—but go now! Try to save her!"

But he couldn't. The enemy was seconds away from attacking this first of his defensive positions. If he left, he would be abandoning his own fighters. "I can't do that. I am needed here!"

With that, a rush of bodies filled the roadway—monsters and terrors of all sorts, barely even pausing as they were assaulted by bowmen and slingers from both sides of the road.

"Wait here!" he shouted over his shoulder as he dashed away to join the struggle. "Wait for me."

His intention was to summon enough magic to give them an advantage; then he could slip back to join Ursule and rush to Nirianne's side. He only needed a few minutes.

But when he glanced back to reassure himself that she was listening and had heard his command, she was gone.

Frantically, he cast about for a solution and was relieved to see Ratcher. He summoned the man over.

"Nirianne is on the back slope with the lions," he told Ratcher, "and Ursule just told me that if I don't go to aid her, she will die. But I can't leave my post here. Can you go after her, try to save her for me? Please, my friend?"

Ratcher clapped him on one shoulder. "Of course. Consider it done."

Then, hoping that would be enough, Galaphile turned back to the battle.

The main battle raged on the road for hours. It was fought with no quarter given and none asked for. The defenses were strong, and the vastly outnumbered men holding their positions were tenacious in their determination to hold back the enemy rush. Galaphile did everything he could to aid them. He used his magic to tumble the foremost attackers back down the roadway and into the arms of their companions—many of whom, in their mix of madness and wild desperation, mistook them for defenders and attacked. Three times during the next hour Galaphile swept the roadway clear to resecure the best of his defensive positions, and three times he was successful.

But all the while, a part of his mind was fixed on Nirianne. Perhaps he would not be able to alter what Ursule had seen. This, he reminded himself, was why he had held back from her at first. He had a duty to the whole of this complex he was building, and to all the people who helped him build and defend it. He could not put the fate of one person over the fate of hundreds—even if that person was the one he loved best in all the world. But this knowledge did nothing to soothe his sadness or ease his despair.

He knew that if something happened to her—if she was killed—he would never recover from the loss.

He had time to glance back more than once as he retreated and could not believe what he was seeing. Hundreds of new creatures were surging into view. With the other defenders about him, he hurried on to reach the next place in the road where he and his comrades could make a new stand.

The next barrier was a cemented stone block wall four layers deep that bridged the entire road from tree line to tree line on either side, thick enough and strong enough to withstand battering rams and tall enough to prevent easy ascension. At the tree lines, debris had been dumped and piled among the trunks to discourage passage around the wall.

Yet none of this did anything to slow the creatures urged on by the Spectre Telle. The attack came from every conceivable direction, and it did not diminish.

Eventually, the wall gave way, driving back Galaphile's forces once more.

Twice, the dark creatures almost caught up to and finished him. The first time was when a unit of climbers finally managed to scale the wall and found the mage standing squarely in front of them. They came at him, howling in glee, but a sweep of one hand released a corrosive mist that reduced them to dust. The second time, he was rushed by such a number of attackers that he was knocked over. They swarmed atop him, attempting to haul him away, but Krunce was there with his Troll warriors and threw back those who threatened their commander and hauled him to safety once more.

All day the battle raged, and Galaphile kept hoping that the attack would falter and fail, that the attackers would tire, that the numbers of able bodies would diminish, but none of this came to pass. As nightfall began to creep toward them, he knew it was time to abandon the road. Within the citadel walls, their chances would be better. Out in the open, exposed and vulnerable to the hordes who came for them, it was a losing battle. There were too many of the enemy and too few of them.

As the sun sank, Galaphile made a final stand—alone—while ordering his troops back to the citadel. As they made their retreat, he walked forward into the opposing army. Arrows, darts, and spears rained down on him, and swords flew at him, but he had erected a protective shield and nothing touched him. The choice of location was deliberate, for he had stood here once before.

So, standing alone against the gathering rush of enemies, he summoned the strongest part of his magic. Then he raised his hands in the way that the old tales said the gods had done in ancient times, fire burning from his fingers and up his arms with an incandescent shimmer. And then he flung the fires down onto the road.

A wall of white-hot flames blazed up, and under its cover he once more wrenched the roadway open.

With a thunderous rumble, huge chunks of rock and earth split apart, rising into a massive wall of broken stone that spanned the entire roadway. And as had happened before, the attackers were caught by surprise. They were rushing too fast even to slow themselves, and those behind saw little of what was happening until it was too late and they jammed up against those in the forefront, their combined weights carrying a large portion of the attackers right into the face of the wall.

As hundreds of enemies were crushed in the rush of bodies, dying with heart-wrenching screams and howls, those who escaped the fate of their fellows quickly fell back. To either side, the cliffs and the ravines locked them away. To the front, the defenders stood looking back at them from the heights of the citadel walls as they stood trapped behind a wall of rubble with a gaping chasm beyond.

For now, the battle was over.

Nirianne waited to die, but the blow did not fall. As she squinted to see what had happened, the huge creature attacking her was drawing back, looking at something standing behind her. Then the sound of metal striking metal reverberated as a new combatant blocked the raised ax with an iron bar and held it at bay. A shadow inserted itself between her and her attacker, tearing the ax free from the assailant's hands.

It was Ratcher!

The combatants closed on each other, clearly in a fight to the death.

Nirianne used the last of her fading energy to roll away, her eyes opening wide to take in what was happening. The creature and the big man were locked in battle, pressed close together, each struggling to put an end to the other. There was blood—though she could not tell whose it was.

Ratcher was the smaller of the two, but he was solid and heavyset, and his center of gravity was working to give him an advantage. Almost as soon as she realized this, Nirianne saw the bigger man stumble backward off his feet. Ratcher was on top of him in an instant, following him down, a dagger flashing up and down in one hand.

In seconds, the attacker was dead, and Ratcher was rising. He stood there for a minute, recovering, then reached down and snatched up Nirianne as if she weighed nothing, throwing her over his shoulder like a sack of grain. Up the hill he charged, trailed by attackers—dozens flinging all sorts of weapons as they screamed and howled in dismay.

But Ratcher was strong and resilient, and in moments he was among his own kind, safely placed behind a defensive line that held back the attackers, cradling a still dazed and wounded Nirianne in his arms.

The number of attackers swarming up the slopes was beginning to taper off, and between the defensive line and the snarling cats, more were falling than were arriving. Ratcher wanted to use the break to take Nirianne to the Healers, but she refused. This was her command, and she could not abandon her post.

Not until the battle looked to be lost.

And then, at some unknown signal and as dusk was falling, the remaining attackers suddenly turned and melted away.

The rear battle had ended almost as suddenly as it had begun.

THIRTY-SEVEN

L ater that night, in the quiet comfort and familiar surroundings of their tent, Nirianne fell quickly asleep. Her shoulder wound had finally been stitched up by the Healers and smeared with healing salves not an hour ago, and the ache in her head had faded, so she was declared fit for duty. But the day must have taken a toll on her, because she drifted into slumber the minute she laid her head on her pillow.

But sleep would not come for Galaphile, and eventually, restless and unsettled, he rose and slipped away.

He tried to find Ursule Raken to see if her visions might provide him with an idea of what was going to happen, but she had disappeared. He wondered who else might be able to help him and thought finally of the King of the Silver River.

Can he use his magic to figure out what is coming?

Galaphile had never been able to summon visions on his own, and he had no idea if he could determine the future by employing some form of magic. After some hard thinking on the matter, he decided to give it a try. What did he have to lose?

He went up to the top of the wall to sit alone in the early hours of the rapidly approaching dawn. There, in a time between wakefulness and sleep, he found a peaceful space. He had no idea about what he could do to summon the ancient being, so he just sat there, helplessly. After a time, he began considering defensive strategies to take his mind off his turmoil, but without knowing what they would be defending against, it all felt a bit too theoretical and pointless.

Time passed, and the world began to brighten marginally along the eastern horizon. Then, at last, the King of the Silver River appeared.

And not just in his mind, as expected. The Ancient One materialized right in front of him, emerging from a misty background to take on his familiar form and shape.

The King took a close look at Galaphile's surprised face and permitted himself a brief smile.

It is to me you must always come, should you seek answers. There are some things I cannot speak about, but when I can, I will.

"Then can you tell me what is coming in the days ahead?" Galaphile asked.

A bit—but most remains unsettled. I can tell you that the being that now calls himself the Spectre Telle will attack you again. Yet he is not the worst of what you will have to face.

"Is there no help for this? How can I do battle with things that are so much more powerful if I am alone?"

You underestimate yourself. Also, no one told you any of this would be simple. No one promised you an uncomplicated path. You wish to lead the peacekeepers you have assembled? You desire to be High Lord of this citadel you have constructed? You think yourself well suited to act on my behalf? Well and good. You are right on all counts. But you must do what is needed to earn your victory.

"Which is to defeat my enemies and scatter any who would cause strife to the four winds?"

It is.

Galaphile considered. "So this, then, is merely the first enemy I must rout? There will be more?"

There will be. But remember, not all enemies are without. Sometimes, the biggest threats can come from within.

"That I might doubt myself, you mean?" Galaphile asked.

That, yes—always. Do not believe the words of the enemy. Do not fall victim to your fears and suspicions. Believe in yourself. Know that truths will speak to you from your heart. You are the one. But . . .

That was not solely my meaning. I also speak of the future, of the child you and Nirianne will bear. It will not be an easy path you tread, my friend. You must be vigilant and strong—and prepared to make some difficult choices. From what looks like a victory can come a different sort of defeat. Much will depend on the outcome of the days ahead. I see many paths before me, and none of them certain, but all contain within them a shadow. Where that shadow falls, however . . . That is what your current fight will determine.

In the next instant, the King of the Silver River was gone—disappearing so quickly there was no time to ask him anything more. And Galaphile was left with the spirit's final words and his still-incomplete understanding of what they had revealed.

In the aftermath, he walked the parapets of the citadel walls for several hours, considering what the King of the Silver River had told him, breathing the cold night air to keep himself awake.

Questions plagued him. He knew he was going to be a father. He knew Nirianne was carrying his child. He knew there was a danger from a child conceived in a stew of dark magic. But he had been checking vigilantly, and the child remained untainted. So where would the shadow appear from? Could his child—his grown-up child—be the one to cause him the biggest trouble, and not the Spectre Telle, as he had assumed? Who was the man he had seen in the visions the King of the Silver River had shared with him in the Gardens of Life?

He had not yet been able to definitively tell if his child was male or female. If it was a girl, then perhaps the vision had shown him the Spectre Telle, after all.

But if not . . .

What was this shadow on the future that the King of the Silver River had predicted?

He finally gave up on asking and went down to be with Nirianne, still without any answers.

They woke together before sunrise and decided to look out over the walls. The whole of the peacekeeping force was inside the citadel. It was early, and most of the defenders were still sleeping, save for a few sentries. Quietly, they climbed to the top of the walls and looked out.

There were no enemies in sight. The plains were empty; the road was empty. Even the forests surrounding the road seemed empty. All the land was shadowed and still.

More chillingly, the bodies of the dead—which should have been strewn across the ground before them—were gone as well.

It was as if the whole attack had been a fever dream, an illusion. As if it had never occurred at all.

"Where did they go?" Nirianne asked, shading her eyes against the first glimpses of the rising sun. The land looked deserted, empty of any signs of yesterday's battle, save for the gaping rift Galaphile had left in the roadway and the rubble piled behind it.

"Nothing's out there," Nirianne whispered. "Nothing at all."

"I don't understand," Galaphile said. "How could they have disappeared so completely in a single night? Where could they have gone, that many of them, to leave no sign of their passage? And why take the bodies with them?"

They searched for a bit longer, partially in disbelief and partially in the hope that something might show itself. But the minutes passed and nothing appeared. The Streleheim Plains remained disturbingly empty.

"We have to send out scouts for a closer look," he muttered, half to her and half to himself. "Back down the road, or even out onto the Streleheim proper. Anywhere they might have managed to find a place to hide."

Once the sun was fully risen, Galaphile went in search of the scouts he wanted. He found four of them eating in the kitchen, and another two sorting equipment. He sent the first to find a path to cross the split or make their way around it so they could check the lower slopes. He sent the other two down the steeper back slopes to patrol the foothills, cautioning them to be wary.

When they had all departed, he helped himself to breakfast.

The remainder of the day passed slowly.

Nothing happened. The enemy did not reappear; nor did the scouts return. The surrounding countryside remained empty of life, save for birds. The weather stayed warm and clear. And Galaphile remained suspicious.

As the hours ticked by, the tension grew.

He had been so certain that yesterday's assault had been only the beginning of a larger attack. And yet . . . this. It felt like all those locked within the keep were simply marking time, waiting for the other shoe to drop.

Nirianne suggested sending out a new batch of scouts, but Galaphile rejected it. Nothing could be accomplished by risking new lives to determine the fate of old ones. Better to wait at least the remainder of that day, then he would go out himself.

Patience, after all, was a weapon, too.

The day passed slowly, the garrison's frustration growing stronger.

"I keep thinking we should be *doing* something," Nirianne said at one point, her own frustration obvious. "But I can't think what it should be. Going out of the citadel seems too dangerous, but just waiting inside seems pointless."

Galaphile nodded. He understood. Nothing useful was being accomplished right now. He discussed defensive strategies with his commanders, but without knowing what they would be defending against, it all felt a bit too theoretical and pointless.

Around sundown, Nirianne approached with Ursule Raken beside her. "Ursule has had a vision," she informed him. "She says the Spectre Telle is definitely still out there."

"But I can't tell when or from what direction he comes," Ursule added. "I do know that he brings you something, however, High Lord. He brings you great danger."

"Of what sort?" Galaphile asked.

But the seer merely shrugged and shook her head. Her skills had not provided an answer.

He asked some further questions, but it quickly appeared that what she had revealed was all she knew. Galaphile thanked her and sent her off. Nirianne remained behind. "If something is coming, I wish it would happen soon. But I'm also frightened about what that something might be."

Her hand curved protectively and instinctively over her swelling belly, and Galaphile masked a shudder. The King of the Silver River's words still hung over him like a pall. What shadow shrouded this child's future?

The only thing he knew was that he would not yet tell Nirianne of the King's predictions. The Ancient One had said there were many paths; perhaps the darkest would not come to fruition. If they prevailed today, perhaps the threat would be ended. He would wait and see; Nirianne had enough to worry about already.

Still, "I'm as frightened as you are," Galaphile admitted. "I feel so helpless just standing around like this. I would rather be in a battle, fighting for something real—not simply imagining what's going to happen."

But the sun set without any further appearance from the Spectre Telle or his forces.

Another day passed. Then two. No sign of the enemy appeared by day, but deep in the forests to one side of the road that led out of the mountains, watchfires flickered through the trees once dark had fallen. And all the while, tensions mounted inside the fortress, until everyone was jumping at shadows, wondering what was coming next.

By the third day, Galaphile decided he had to do something about it, so he took Nirianne aside to discuss the matter.

"I'm going over the gap and toward where the watchfires burn for a look around."

She was, as expected, not happy about his decision.

"Think this through," she said. "Remember who you are going up against. This creature is a monster, and excels at infiltrating people's minds. You might be walking right into a trap."

He drew her close and held her fast. He could feel her heart beating against his chest. He could feel her shaking, remembering the mental tortures she had endured.

"I promise you, I will not let him do anything of the sort to me. But I also can't just sit here unprepared, waiting for an attack that might come today or might come in a few months. Ursule said he was returning, but when? The uncertainty is affecting us all. If I can get close enough for a quick look around to see what is, we will all be much better prepared for what's to come."

"And how can you help save us if you are captured? You remain our best hope for surviving this mess. So why risk yourself on a scouting mission that someone else could do in your place?"

"No one else can do what I can. If Parkinch couldn't do it, with his ability to vanish, what makes you think a Dwarf or a Troll without any magic could succeed better? My first scouts never returned, after all. No, I can't risk anyone else when I am best suited. I can hide or defend myself better than the others. I will go quickly and return safely, I promise."

She pushed herself out of his arms and glared back at him. "You can't promise that. This is a mistake, Galaphile—a bad one."

But what other choice did he have?

As it happened, however, it was Ursule Raken who came to him with a solution later that evening. "I understand what it is that you want to do and why you think you must do it, but there is another, better way to gain the information you need other than leaving the citadel in person. If you come with me to the ramparts, I will show you."

Together, they climbed to the best point on the outer walls to overlook the roadway, and Ursule pointed down to where the distant fires flickered.

"It is there that you need to explore?" she asked.

He nodded. "For a short time only."

"Then I can help. A seer's skills are more than just prescient. Sometimes the visions come to us, but at other times we must go in search of what is hidden."

She sat herself down with her back to the ramparts and motioned for him to take a similar position facing her.

"Close your eyes and do not open them again until you are finished finding what you seek. I will ward you and try to protect you from discovery as best I can. But you must do nothing to risk yourself. You must promise you will only look around. Go where you wish; you will not be moving, but it will feel that way. Do not speak. Do not make a sound. Take my hands and do not release them until I tell you it is safe to do so. Your connection to me is what keeps you safe within the vision. Do not loosen your grip under any circumstances—and squeeze tightly if you feel you might be in danger. Do you understand me?"

He closed his eyes, squeezed her hands to indicate that he was ready, and waited on her. It took a few long minutes for anything to happen, but then the darkness behind his closed eyelids brightened marginally to become a vision of the nighttime that waited without.

He was all alone. The darkness was still eerily quiet, with no sounds of an enemy force anywhere nearby, and no signs save those flickering fires under the trees. Which was where he now needed to go.

Under Ursule's guidance and protection, he drifted down toward where the watchfires burned, descending through the heavy canopy of trees. Indeed, fires were scattered about, but this was no ordinary camp filled with activity and the camaraderie of soldiers about to enter a battle.

Instead, it was silent and still. Barely animate figures huddled wordlessly around fires as if insensible to their surroundings.

When he drifted closer, he could see that they were breathing, but there was little other sign of life. Their eyes seemed dull and empty.

The only sounds at all came from under a huge, impromptu tent— vast swaths of opaque wrappings tightly secured to tree limbs, trunks, tentpoles, and rocky outcroppings. Everything beneath it was shadowed and concealed, though from the shifting shadows that writhed and danced against its surface, it seemed a hive for the activity so lacking in the rest of the camp.

Steeling himself against the twinges of fear and trepidation already tugging at his courage, Galaphile slipped through the darkness until he found a gap in the folds of the coverings and witnessed the horror of what was happening within.

It was a nightmare of unimaginable proportions. The Spectre Telle stood in the midst of what must be an already much-diminished pile of his dead, restoring them one by one to life while minions shuttled bodies to him and away. And in one corner, more seemed to be industriously sewing severed parts together into mostly complete wholes.

But worse, Galaphile quickly realized, was that it wasn't just his own dead he was restoring. There were defenders in there he recognized— Dwarves, Humans, and Trolls. His own defenders would be co-opted and turned against him.

As the limp and lifeless bodies reached him, the Spectre Telle seemed to sink into some kind of a trance, touching each for a time with bloodied fingers. When it began to move independently, he released it then moved along to the next, seeming to grow a bit weaker with every body he restored.

Here was the proof Galaphile had sought. His enemy was restoring life to the dead. But how?

No sooner had he thought the question than the answer revealed itself. Partly shrouded in Telle's black robes was an ancient, massive book. The mage cradled it within his arms as if it were the most precious of treasures—as if he sought to make it a part of himself. And why not? Power emanated from its covers, a deep-reddish glow that permeated the near darkness of the covered space as if it were the reflection of a beating heart.

Somehow, he had located an object of immense dark power.

Power that sustained him. Power that consumed him.

And he was using this book of darkest magic—or perhaps it was using him—to seize control over the Four Lands.

Galaphile was repulsed. He had to destroy this book if he ever intended to bring any form of peace back to the land.

But he was also admittedly afraid. What a terrible power this was! However was he to defeat it?

He backed away, already thinking of how he could destroy it. Of how he must.

Either way, however, he had found what he was searching for, and there was no reason to linger here any further. The Spectre Telle was clearly delaying the second attack until he had restored all his forces. Then he would come at them again with an army entirely undiminished in numbers—in fact, one swelled with Galaphile's dead. Whereas with each attack, his own contingent of defenders would slowly drop away.

It was an impossible, unwinnable situation as things currently stood. And if it stretched on long enough, Telle would not even need to fight them; he could just trap them in the citadel and starve them to death.

Dejected, Galaphile was sliding back into the deeper shadows when he felt a *presence*. At first, it was nothing more than a finger's brush, a faint twitch of something passing by him as softly as a breeze, but he froze instantly. It was just the smallest of contacts, yet he could feel a decided weight behind it.

He knew what it was that sensed him—*who* it was—but he did not sense that the questor yet understood what he had discovered, if anything. But once he was trapped and identified, that would be the end of him.

If he could stay still and quiet, maybe his rival would think he was just a part of the background. Nothing to worry about, nothing to see . . .

The presence butted up against him more firmly this time, as if first trying to make a determination of what it was up against and then to test the strength of its resistance to intrusion. It took everything Galaphile had not to panic. He found it almost impossible to remain calm, to not try to bolt for safety, but to remain still and firm. He could sense what he was up against—its identity, its power, its darkness—but he tamped down his feelings and waited patiently for the pressure to ease. What he did in an attempt to protect himself was to slowly tighten his grip on Ursule's hands, trusting in her abilities to extract him. One wrong move, a single unfortunate twitch in response to what he was feeling, the slightest hint of panic, and he would be lost. He had put himself in this situation willingly, and he had only himself to blame for whatever happened next. The shadow continued to press up against him, nudging at the edges of his consciousness, ready to enfold and devour him . . .

Then abruptly he was back inside the tower of his citadel, sitting across from Ursule, his hands clasped in hers, staring into her startlingly pale eyes.

"Welcome home," she whispered and gave him a smile.

He left her then and walked back into the keep, still steadying himself as he sought out Sanitov and Krunce. On doing so, he drew them away privately to describe what he had discovered—all but the unknown book of magic. That was a secret he kept to himself. That was an evil he suspected only he was going to be able to overcome.

He wasn't at all sure what he would do about it, but at least he now had a better sense of what he was facing.

THIRTY-EIGHT

Two days later, Spectre Telle launched his next attack on the citadel.

First, his minions poured in from the woods—both survivors of the first battle and those he had reanimated in the days that followed. They mounted the roadway en masse, stopping only when they came to the pile of rubble and the chasm that split the route asunder. And there they stood, regarding their target with a passive blankness.

It was horrible. Though Galaphile had warned the citadel's defenders about what would come, hearing that you might encounter a former comrade among the foe was very different from seeing it. Especially when those faces were soulless and mindless and primed to kill, with no recognition of the person they used to be.

It was, Galaphile thought, even worse than losing them to death, and he could see defender after defender reeling back in shock at the sight.

Worse, the Spectre Telle must have retained enough of his humanity to realize this, for they were all lined up at the front of the army—first to attack, and the first for the defenders to cut down.

As for Telle himself, Galaphile was pleased to see that he still looked a bit pale and drained when he flew into view on the back of the creature that Nirianne had said he called a Skelter. Knowing that something had been spying on him—even if he did not know the nature of that spy—he must have decided it was better to attack sooner rather than later, before the attack could be brought to him.

Galaphile wondered if he could use this to his advantage.

Still, Telle clearly had enough of his power back to fix the main obstacle before him. He waved a hand almost casually, and the rubble that blocked the road fell back into the pit from whence it came. The roadbed snapped back together with a boom.

The army surged forward—led by what had once been comrades and allies.

Galaphile shouted out instructions, and archers raked the attackers from above—though most, Galaphile noticed, fired instinctually at the rows behind their former comrades. This could be a problem, but the fortress was well armed, and although the defenders were outnumbered two to one by their attackers, the walls of the keep made up for the difference.

Still it was a grueling attack, with each side working hard to gain the upper hand. For the next hour or more, Galaphile was everywhere, it seemed—finding cracks in the defensive lines and sealing them up, using his magic to damage the attackers. But his efforts were insufficient at every turn, for more attackers kept coming.

Then the first of them reached the wall top and fought to break past the defenders. Krunce sent a handful of his Trolls to aid in their defense, and they cast off the attackers successfully. But more came, then still more—an endless rush of bodies that seemed impervious to fear and uncaring of death. Eventually, a handful took a section of the main wall and began to advance along the rim as others quickly joined them.

Using a form of magic that twisted and turned like a snake, Galaphile lashed the attackers away, casting them back to the ground, and soon the wall was retaken and secured anew.

But he was beginning to see how this would end. There were too many of the enemy and not nearly enough defenders. If the attacks continued, spreading from one wall to the next, the enemies would eventually break through.

And indeed, within another hour, the wall had been taken in at least three places. While the Trolls were doughty fighters, their numbers were down and many were fighting with injuries already incurred. The same applied to his Human defenders. Save for his defensive force of Dwarves, Sanitov's main crew were construction workers, not soldiers. And though most joined the battle willingly, they were not trained and thus prone to mistakes.

Which was why Galaphile almost missed the next threat when it materialized. At first, all he was aware of was an extra flurry of activity along a spot of wall where Dwarf defenders outnumbered the rest, which he figured was due simply to inexperience or battle nerves. But then he heard his name being shouted urgently from that sector and hurried over, only to find one contingent of Dwarves brutally attacking another, trying to clear the way for a fourth incursion of Telle's forces up the wall.

These were, Galaphile swiftly noticed, many of the original workers— the ones who had first arrived at the site. How many of his workers had the Spectre Telle co-opted before he had seized Nirianne? (Though, now that Galaphile thought of it, undoubtedly this was *how* he had seized Nirianne.) And how long had he been waiting to play this hand?

Feeling a rush of fury, Galaphile roared for aid from the nearest Trolls, who rounded them all up. He ordered them to be locked into one of the basement chambers; he would deal with them later.

But with some of the Trolls pulled off the walls to attend to this duty, it left a hole in the defenses where another group of attackers soon broke through.

Slowly but surely, their defenses were being overwhelmed.

Yet Galaphile still had a few tricks up his sleeve. Or, rather, he had one magic user whose skills he had yet to put into play.

Ursule Raken's seer skills were useless in a pitched battle. But Chelm was a different matter entirely.

Galaphile grabbed his last remaining magic user and made a hasty circuit of the walls, pausing at each place where their defenses had been overwhelmed to let Chelm activate his powers.

Indeed, it was here, as Galaphile had always suspected, that Chelm's abilities became invaluable. His talent for creating confusion might not operate over a long distance, as some earlier experimentation had proved, and the effects would fade after minutes unless Chelm was actively enforcing them. Yet still he was able to disrupt the bonds between the Spectre Telle and his creatures. And so in waves, he scrambled the minds of the attacking minions, cutting them off from all the directions being issued by their master.

Instantly, the attackers either stopped dead or flailed about in confusion, their sense of purpose shattered. The defenders were quick to regain control over a situation that only moments before had seemed lost, and soon all parts of the citadel walls were retaken.

And here, finally, the Spectre Telle's exhaustion was beginning to show, for he seemed to have trouble regaining control over his troops once a group had been cut away. He would gather up one group, Galaphile noticed, only to have another fall into mindlessness some distance away.

Until this moment, the Spectre Telle had held himself aloof from the battle. But now, as if needing to get closer to his troops to reestablish control, he stormed onto the battlefield on his Skelter, the dark book held close to his body as he screamed at his army in fury, urging them to advance—unaware as yet why they had fallen from his control. Even from atop the walls of the citadel, Galaphile could see that Telle did not fully understand what was happening.

If ever there was a time to strike back, this was it.

Discarding caution and giving way to sheer rage, Galaphile charged down the stairway toward the lower levels of the fortress, determined to make up for lost time and opportunities. Determined to avenge what had been done to Nirianne and so many others. If he could reach the battlefield and cross it to where the Spectre Telle pranced about on his creature, he had a chance of retrieving that monstrous book and putting an end to this forever. He knew he was being impulsive, impetuous, and probably foolish. He knew the danger that he risked by trying to take possession of the dangerous tome. But, thanks to Cogline's training, he believed himself strong enough to resist its lure.

He had barely reached the side gates when everything abruptly changed. With a series of deep, heavy thuds, drums began to mark a steady cadence.

Boom! Boom! Boom!

The reverberations echoed like thunder in the silence of the moment. They broke the stillness with shocking force, arising not from the battle site but from a place out of view of the fighters.

The Spectre Telle looked off in the direction of the drums, and there was a quality to his movements that suggested further uncertainty.

Galaphile pushed his way through guards and a set of lesser side doors set in the forward walls of the keep and turned to look as well.

Boom! Boom! Boom!

What was happening?

Then new sounds rose to match the beating. Wails, high and shrill, rose and fell in a pitch that matched the deep hammering of the drums—a strange sort of symphony that spoke of something even more powerful than the forces arrayed against them.

The Spectre Telle was staring fixedly now in the direction of the sounds, unaware that Galaphile was bolting across the battlefield in his direction.

Quite abruptly, the wails turned into roars, and thousands of bodies appeared over the rim of the forward cliffs—bodies dressed the same, in woodland garb, and bearing blades of all shapes and sizes. Flags flying from the standards designated various divisions of fighters, each marching in step to the beat of the drums, in close lines of attack as if all were one.

The Elves had arrived!

And there were hundreds of them! Nearly a thousand, all formed into organized companies, banners flying before them, spears and blades raised as they marched into battle against Galaphile's enemies.

The Spectre Telle held his ground a moment longer then wheeled his carrier about, yanking back on its reins. The monster spread its wings and prepared to lift skyward, away from the attacking Elves.

But an enraged Galaphile was already there, leaping up to seize the creature's reins and its rider.

For a moment, he had firm hold of both. Then the animal screamed and tore at his leg in an effort to dislodge him, and his enemy held the book before him as if it were a shield and summoned its magic. Galaphile—his leg bloodied, his strength weakened, and his hold loosening—had only a moment to cast his own magic. He lifted a hand and rained blue fire onto the book.

He knew instantly it was a mistake. His power was significant, but it was nothing compared with the vast, ancient reserves that this book brooded upon, like a dragon over its hoard. He might as well have lit a candle in a hurricane.

No, worse. It was like trying to fill a bottomless well with a bucket. He would drain himself dry before he even began to touch its power.

Also, that magic was now . . . regarding him. There was no other way to describe it. It was weighing him, measuring him. Getting to know the one who sought to destroy it.

Instantly, he cut the contact, shifting his attack from book to bearer, his blue flames lashing across Telle's exposed face.

He had only an instant before the book noticed and wrapped its bearer in its power, shielding him. But perhaps that instant was enough. He might not hold a power close to what the book contained, but his flames still had teeth. Telle was shrieking—a high agonized pitch—and instinctively jerked his hands up to cover his face, almost losing his grip on the book. But Galaphile could not see what, if any, damage he had caused, for the beast heaved upward in response to a guttural command, and Galaphile lost his grip.

He fell heavily to the ground as the Skelter launched upward and flew away without slowing.

After that, it was just cleanup. Deprived of their master's control, his soldiers went either passive or mindlessly feral, and it was relatively easy to dispatch them.

Learning from his previous mistakes, Galaphile ordered all the bodies—friend and foe alike—to be transported to an open area of the plains, where he then had them burned. That way, Telle could never reanimate them again.

None were willing participants in his enemy's schemes, so he afforded them all the honor of a noble release.

As Galaphile stood, watching the flames, Nirianne approached, seizing hold of him and almost shaking him in her fury. "Are you insane? Are you trying to kill yourself? What were you thinking attacking Telle like that?"

"I wasn't thinking anything," he managed.

"Well, start thinking! When I saw you leap up on the Skelter and grab the Spectre Telle . . . Well, I thought I'd lost you for sure! I thought *we* had lost you," she emphasized, curling a hand around her belly. "Don't forget there are two of us who need you now."

"I know. I'm sorry. And I love you—both of you—far more than I can say."

She kissed him, long and deep. "Just know you are my one true love, Galaphile Joss. My one reason for doing everything."

He shook his head and kissed her some more. "You are a miracle!"

"*We* are a miracle," she corrected, her voice gone gentle again. "You and I, together."

In the aftermath of the battle, Galaphile met with Elven point commander Aelia Jovesin, who headed up the Elven troops.

"Thank you so much for coming," Galaphile said to her. "We owe you so much—though I must admit, I didn't think the Elves would ever aid me after my last blunder."

The commander nodded, smiling. "I will say this only once and never admit to having done so, but it was the Queen who saved you. The King was irritated by both you and your request, but the Queen saw the virtue of your cause. I have it on good advice that she ordered him to send the army. Either he would do so, or she would bring it herself. She is the sort who might, so the King listened."

Galaphile smiled, remembering Rishannon's last words to him. For all men's posturing, it was women, he suspected, that held the real power in the world.

"Then please convey our thanks, and tell her we stand ready to return the favor at such time as it might be needed. Our love and admiration are hers."

Aelia Jovesin nodded and extended a salute. There was a warmth in her deep-green eyes that was unmistakable. "Not all Elves are as insular as our King. Like Queen Rishannon, many of us realize that the problems of the wider world are Elven problems as well—or will be soon enough. So I am charged by the Queen to suggest to you that we formalize our alliance—Elves and peacekeepers. Will you consider?"

"I will do more than consider. I will accept, Commander," Galaphile assured her. "I pledge my alliance to your Queen. And to your King. I have been away from the Elves for a time, but I suspect I am more Elven than I know, and I will be pleased to learn more of my heritage." He took her hand once more and held it fast.

Aelia pressed his hand warmly; then her face turned sober. "One more thing, however," she told him. "We Elves are not strangers to magic, and that tome Spectre Telle carried . . ." She shuddered. "There was a dark power there—an ancient power. One that predates even our time in the world, I suspect. Having such power currently active . . . troubles me—and I suspect it will trouble my King and Queen as well. Power like that should be guarded, to save it from falling into evil hands."

"I could not agree more," Galaphile said. Perhaps, as part of his peacekeeping efforts, he would make a point of finding and guarding what magical artifacts he could locate, to save them from falling into the hands of creatures like the Spectre Telle. If he could create a legacy of guardians for such objects going forward, using their powers only for good and locking those of pure evil away—then the world would indeed be made a better, safer place.

"You seem to have injured its bearer, at least," Aelia said. "If there is a chance of finding where he might have gone to ground and wrestling it free of his clutches, then that is a course we must pursue, if your future of peace is to have any hope. Do you know where this man makes his lair?"

"I do," Galaphile said, "but whether he will still be there is anyone's guess. For myself, I doubt it, but we will check. I can lead you and a force of Elves to his fortress. But if I may ask you a question in turn: What do you and the Elves know of this book?"

"Me personally? Not much, I'm afraid. But given what I sensed of its age, I'm sure there will be records of its existence in our libraries. I will tell the Queen when I get back, and we will put some of our best scholars to the task of finding out just what it might be. Unless, of course, we find it ourselves. How soon can we leave?"

Galaphile kept to his promise and set off two days later—after he had spent a day burning the remains of the Spectre Telle's dark magic from his compromised Dwarves—leading Aelia and a smaller Elven force to Skull Mountain, but it was as he'd predicted. The skull-like fortress was deserted, with no trace of the Spectre Telle or his book.

His enemy had vanished entirely, and the book with him.

Still, Galaphile had a feeling he had not seen the last of either.

THIRTY-NINE

Huddled in the deserted farmhouse he had once abandoned for grander locales, the Spectre Telle cursed Galaphile's name. His enemy hadn't possessed the power to destroy the Ildatch but had possessed enough to destroy *him*.

He had only been exposed to Galaphile's flames for a heartbeat, but it had been enough to mark him—perhaps forever. The pain had been excruciating, like nothing he had ever experienced. Worse, perhaps, than what he had done to Galaphile's wife. His face felt like it was both melting and on fire. And his eyes . . .

All he knew—at least at first—was that his vision had gone black. Yet even blinded and in pain, he realized he could not return to his fortress home. Thanks to his seizure of Nirianne, Galaphile knew where he lived, so that refuge was barred to him—at least until he could build up an army large enough to defend it.

The only other place he could think to retreat to was the farmhouse. But how would he even get there? How could he guide his creature, if he could no longer see?

It was the Ildatch who gave him the solution. The Ildatch recalled the place, so it guided him while he guided the Skelter.

He had been worried someone might have discovered it after he departed, but it seemed not. The place smelled stale and deserted, and there were no sounds of life.

But it was hard to tell completely, without his eyes. Plus, the flight here had inflamed his wounded face, and he was running a fever. He barely made it inside the door of the house before he collapsed.

He did not know how many days he drifted in fever dreams. But when he woke, the pain was . . . gone.

But so, still, was his sight.

Tentatively, he ran his fingers over his head, his face.

His hair was gone, his scalp lumpy with scars.

Ditto his cheeks, what felt like a stub of a nose.

He didn't want to know what he looked like—not that he was likely to have a chance to discover it. For when he ran his hands across his eyes, he was repelled to find only empty pits.

"Why couldn't you heal me?" he howled at the Ildatch. With all the power it contained, surely it could restore him as he had once been.

It chuckled at him, smugly. It *had* healed him, fast and efficiently. Without it, he might have died.

"You call this healing?" he wailed. "My eyes, my . . ."

It pulsed at him, hunched and resentful, annoyed by his ingratitude. Didn't he know that you could not replace what was gone completely?

"So will you find a new set of hands now that I am useless?" he accused it.

But it did not consider him useless. This was a setback, no more—minor, in the grand scheme of things. It had magic, so he had magic. And with magic, anything was possible. He might not see in the ways he had previously, but see again he would.

Perhaps he could still fulfill his dream of bestriding the world—if it was even his dream anymore instead of the book's. But he'd need a new army—a better army. He had created the last one too quickly, too imperfectly. It was too vulnerable, too incompletely under his control. When Galaphile had severed his connection with his minions—however his enemy had done it—that connection was too hard to regain. Plus, it had still required too much of his active intervention just to make that army do what he wanted.

During the first attack, he had felt himself stretched to his limits with only two thousand fighters. Swelling the ranks with the citadel's dead—as clever a trick as that was—had proved even more of a challenge, like trying to balance a few too many items at once. So he had been forced to abandon any attack on the back slopes—not that those damnable cats would have let up anyway.

Then there was the exhaustion of reanimating so many of the deceased after the battle. Wasn't the whole point of raising the dead that they *couldn't* then die again? So why had his? Even if he grew stronger in his powers, even if he could come to channel more of the Ildatch's power, he could not spend time between battles reanimating his troops. It was a waste of energy. Once resurrected, they needed to stay resurrected. They needed to be unstoppable. Unkillable.

He would have to start all over again. Find the flaws in his former plan, rethink his whole approach. Restart his experiments.

It could take years.

Maybe even decades.

So what if that upstart brought peace to the Four Lands in the meantime? It would only be a greater pleasure tearing down what he had so carefully built.

Hatred surged through him, but he tamped it down. Time for hatred later. Time for *revenge* later.

For now, he must think.

First, his sight. He was nothing until he found a way to restore that—or at least learned a new way to perceive the world. But then . . .

The same concerns that had first driven him from this farmhouse applied. He needed more space. More privacy. A ready supply of bodies on which to experiment.

Where to find that?

The Ildatch revealed through his thoughts what it had already decided. It knew—then so, of course, he knew, too. A previously assembled fortress in an isolated valley. Robed acolytes already trained to protect him—or, more accurately, to protect it.

He would heal first, then he would go there. Make it his new base.

No one had found the Ildatch there for centuries. For millennia, maybe.

They would not find him there, either.

At least, not until he was ready to be found.

In the weeks after Galaphile returned from Skull Mountain, life settled back into a routine. Aelia Jovesin returned to Arborlon with the majority of her army and a promise to discover what she could about the mysterious book and send word, but she left behind a contingent of Elven Hunters. So Galaphile again created mixed companies—this time of Humans, Trolls, and Elves—and sent them out on peacekeeping missions.

He had liked the term *peacekeepers* when Nirianne had first coined it for the Elves, but the more he thought about what this fortress could be in the wake of Telle's attack—especially knowing that Telle carried an artifact of dark magic—the less the term seemed to apply. Certainly peacekeeping would be an aspect of their wider mission, but there should be other valuable components as well. The finding and guarding of magical objects, for one. And also becoming a repository of knowledge.

This latter impulse had been growing on him over the past few weeks. Perhaps knowing the nature of the Spectre Telle's book might not have changed the outcome of this battle, but . . . what if it had? So much knowledge had been lost with the destruction of the Old World, and someone should be in charge of gathering up what was left and preserving it, forming a repository available to all Races, not just the Elves.

So his order needed a new name to reflect its wider mission—and he likely needed a new title for himself, as well, if he was to nip this annoying High Lord business in the bud. He was no lord. He was an orphaned Elf living in the Human world who had decided to take on a seemingly impossible mission. What title could possibly embrace both the nobility and the potential foolishness of all that?

He had no idea, but he would give it a think. Something was bound to occur to him soon.

Beyond that, he was also a husband and a father—positions he was coming to relish even more as the days went on, free for now of the Spectre Telle and his shadow.

He and Nirianne had taken to visiting the walls every night near sunset to gaze out over the valley and road—not just to make sure no monstrous army was approaching but also to enjoy a peaceful moment surveying this community they were building. Seeing Elves, Humans, and Trolls in easy fellowship behind his walls, beholding the beautiful, tranquil land on which the citadel sat stretching out before him, all filled him with a quiet pride.

It was a wonderful thing indeed that they were adding to the world.

He said as much to Nirianne one night as they stood surveying their domain. He had another secret to share with her as well—one he had discovered only this afternoon during one of his routine checks on their child, whose light remained undimmed by darkness. But this came first.

"It needs a name," she said, tucking herself under his arm and gazing out over the landscape before them. "We can't just keep calling it the citadel, or the building site, or whatever else takes our fancy."

He laughed aloud and squeezed her shoulders. "As always, my love, you are one step ahead of me. That was precisely one of the things I wanted to tell you tonight. I've been thinking over that problem for days, and I think I might finally have a solution."

She looked up at him, grinning. "So? What have you come up with?"

"Well, as the Dwarves are the builders of this fortress, I wanted to give it a Dwarven name. There is an old and fabled Dwarfish term— one that Cogline taught me, but I had almost forgotten about it until I overheard Sanitov mentioning it to one of his fellows the other day. It refers not to a place or a person or an event, but to a condition. If a thing is stable, well settled, and enduring—in the manner of mountains and rivers and stones—it is said to be imbued with *paranor*. So what do you say, Nirianne? Shall we call this place of ours Paranor? Because those are the qualities I most want it to possess."

"It's perfect; I love it," she said, and he could see her blinking tears from her eyes. "Yes, Paranor it shall be."

She brushed her hand softly, almost reverently, against the stones of the outer wall, warm under the light of the setting sun. "Hello, Paranor. Welcome to the world."

They stood together for a moment in silence. But being Nirianne, she was never one to let a silence stretch on. "So if that was one of the things you wanted to tell me, what are the others?"

He grinned. "Just one other."

"And?"

He gazed down at her. The golden light of the sunset washed over her, sparking copper lights from her hair and making her skin glow. Her belly was rounding more by the day, and she had never looked more beautiful to him.

The mother of his child.

The mother of his *son*.

He laid a hand over the curve where the boy lay growing. He could swear he felt a faint flutter of acknowledgment.

"Just to say that we are creating the perfect home for our child to be born into. I know that he will love it here."

It took her a moment to realize what he was saying—but only a moment. It was one of the many things he loved about her.

"Of course we are, but . . . *he?*"

He nodded, feeling happiness swell through him. "A little secret he revealed today, when I was checking on him."

Her smile seemed almost brighter than the sunset. She laid her hand atop his. "A son," she said. "*Our* son."

He laughed. "Indeed."

"Well, he'll need a name, too," she said practically. "And since we seem to be naming things tonight . . ." Her eyes twinkled up at him.

"Do you have any suggestions?"

She nodded decisively. "I do. And since you named Paranor, I feel like this one should be mine."

"I couldn't agree more. So tell me, what name will we give him?"

"Abronja," she said. "But I think I prefer the diminutive. I shall call him Brona."